Preying Mantis

The Story of Tarissa

Lyn Thomas

ISBN: 0692467602
ISBN 13: 9780692467602

Dedication

This book is dedicated to Margaret, whose goodness saw me through all my adult peccadilloes and crises for almost half a century, and who inspired and enabled all my personal successes. Some debts cannot be fully repaid in one lifetime.

Quotation Page

"Only he who is smitten with the arrows of love knows its power."
(Mohandas K. "Mahatma" Gandhi)

Acknowledgment Page

THE AUTHOR, A retired engineer and scientist, has two prior published books. He has had a long fascination with English language and literature and currently runs a blog, CutTheBabble.com, a commentary on the nuances of the American dialect of English in written communication.

1
Memories

And now the purple dusk of twilight time
Steals across the meadows of my heart
High up in the clouds the little stars climb
Always reminding me that we're apart.
You wandered down the lane and far away....

THE DARK CLOUDS of reminiscence that nearly carried Lennox Obi to Elysium gathered one sad evening as he sat in a rocking chair looking out of the rear window of his study. He was too tired to rock the chair; he just leaned back, motionless, mentally surveying the wreckage of his life. His heart was broken and, it seemed to him, his life spent. The final nail in his coffin was the realization that Tarissa Adoja, his long-beloved Trish, was just an opportunist who admitted to "messing around" for fifteen years while professing to love him.

He had just finished reading again the plaintive email he had sent to Trish two days earlier, baring his soul to ease the hurt that was gnawing relentlessly at his heart. The best way he knew how to do that was with the haunting lyrics of his favorite singers. The email opened with a quote of the lament of Nat 'King' Cole, that doyen of jazz singers:

Answer me, oh my love!
Just what sin have I been guilty of?
Tell me how I came to lose your love
Please answer me, sweetheart.
You were mine yesterday
I believed that love was here to stay
Won't you tell me where I've astray
Please answer me my love.

The message was a hysterical, incoherent, and groveling missive penned in the dead of night when he woke up at 4:00 am after an all-night vigil of reminiscence and weeping for his lost love. The email was incoherent because his mind was scrambled by torrents of conflicting thoughts, hysterical because his feelings had been pickled raw for months now by deep grief. Snot oozed from his nose. The waste basket under his desk had filled up again with discarded tissue; he had to empty it soon and flush away the contents before his wife came in and saw the mess.

Len's message recounted the numerous efforts he had made in recent months to elicit from Trish just a word of encouragement saying all was not lost, or an explanation of what had gone suddenly and horribly wrong in his universe — a universe which in the past fifteen years had devolved entirely around Trish. He knew, the message continued, that because of pusillanimous hesitation through the years he had forfeited all claims to her affection even as every fiber of his heart told him Trish was the only woman that really mattered in his life.

Yes, he admitted, he had hung on to his long marriage out of habit, albeit a habit born of dutiful concern for the welfare of his family. His wife, Magdalene, was a decent woman to whom he owed support and honor; but every moment of every day in the last fifteen years his heart beat only for Trish. Why had Trish not pushed him into the decision for which his heart yearned even as his head urged restraint on account of Magda, on account of his three splendid sons with his wife, and on account of the dozen adorable grandchildren that now graced his life? No matter, Len's message continued, he was now ready to be shoved; indeed he needed no shoving. "Just say when and where, dear Trish, and Len will be there, on his knees, ready to bind himself to you with any kind of bond you desire."

He was aware, he reminded Trish, that love was an inexplicable sort of madness. Didn't they both marvel together so often at the impelling illogic of love? And hadn't he told her innumerable times she was the great love of his life, the one and only woman who could fill the aching void in his heart? Hadn't he told her he believed the majority of humans never really got to experience the full depth of true love? That those who received that gift got it but once in their lives? Or that the emotional experiences of most people were mere hillocks and foothills compared to the majestic summit on which he had lived his life since the day he met Trish? Or that nobody traveled that uplifting road of love twice in a lifetime? Or that one has not really lived until he has felt the upwelling rush of warm and soft love beneath his wings as he soared to celestial heights?

If she had tired of waiting for him he would understand. If she now felt like kicking him off that pinnacle, as Lucifer was sent plummeting from heaven, he would not blame her after all she had gone through in the past fifteen years. If another man now had a claim to her affection, he would understand that too. All he requested in that case was that she should level with him. "Tell your suffering Len it is all over between us. Then I won't pester you anymore. Remember: I love you for a hundred thousand reasons, reasons too many to recount here. So please answer me, my love!"

He counted, he said, over a hundred voice messages and text messages and emails and postal letters he sent to her since the middle of March, each of them singing the same refrain: Have mercy, my princess; come dry my tears or, at least end my misery with a message of finality. He suspected that his ceaseless importunity was now irritating her. Why else would she clam up so tightly? He loved her too much to want to continue annoying her with his importunity. So, couldn't she relent and send a message of explanation or of severance? What he needed was a candid reply; without candor there could be no closure between them, and without closure there would be no healing for him. Any kind of response from her would do, even a definite dismissal, so that he could lick his wounds, and then allow time, the great healer, to close the jagged sore in his heart.

But not a word had come back from Trish, so that Len concluded she was not reading his entreaties. Still, he had to implore her one more time, from the edge of the abyss of despair. He had signed off on that email with a postscript quoting the valedictory wail of Jim Reeves:

> I've been accused, convicted, and condemned.
> The trial is over and now I face the end.
> Is this your way of telling me we're through?
> When all I'm guilty of, is loving you.

But the echoing silence and the tightening knot in his guts told him it was over. He realized it ended on that dolorous afternoon of Saturday, March 15, his *Ides of March* as he came to call it, when Trish sent him a puzzling text message stating: "I'm totally confused." That message was in reply to his own text which wondered why, uncharacteristically, Trish had not responded to his offer to come down the following week, on Saint Patrick's Day, to discuss issues affecting them both, issues mooted and delayed for so long now. Knowing Trish as well as he did, Len realized that her "I'm totally confused" meant one thing: there was now another man in her life. He had expected that Trish would level with him if and when that ever came to pass; hers was an open character and they had loved each other so deeply and for fifteen long years now!

Because he was not a possessive person, Len never thought to set limits on Trish any more than he had set limits on his wife. Love, he and Trish used to say with resignation, had a mind and a logic of its own, and you couldn't channel it at will, no matter how hard you tried. It was their accustomed saying to reassure themselves whenever Trish recounted snide remarks sometimes cast at her by friends or relatives who thought she was too good to waste herself on a married man (the same friends who had been pressing to introduce Trish to this or that other, worthier man).

Anyway, Len knew that he could not control Trish's behavior even if he wanted to. She had a free spirit, was very confident of her qualities and abilities, and was so actively engaged in her community and beyond that she could easily get any man she desired. Every time Len went to visit her there were relays of groups of people, men and women, single or in couples, who came and spent long hours at her house. They were friends, relatives, colleagues, compatriots from her home town, or associates in the various social groups in which Trish served as a member or an official, classmates in high school or college. She was very popular among them. They came to talk, to gossip, to hold meetings, and to debate issues. Above all they came to relax and eat, for she was a good hostess and an inspired cook. There was always finger food arrayed on her kitchen table and replenished as proceedings wore on. Len remembered few weekends when her house was not humming with guests at all hours. Some men brought cases of beer; Len always stocked her kitchen with wines. Sometimes Len joined their conversation, but more often his reclusive nature made him sit and read in her bedroom as the hubbub raged on, mostly around Trish's kitchen table or in good weather on her back porch.

Though she engaged in all that socializing, Len felt secure enough in Trish's affection not to be jealous, except of the time her visitors took away from their mutual attention. Sometimes the topic of fidelity came up between them, and Trish would enfold Len in her arms and declare as always "You are my one and only love. I will always love you and nobody else." He knew she was sincere, and he knew also that she felt secure in his affection. They both were surprised how much of the time they thought of each other: *Every moment of every day*, Trish would mutter without antecedent or preamble, looking deeply into Len's eyes. And Len understood what she meant because he felt the same way. Once or twice he broached the topic more directly: Did she never feel attracted to another man? Trish would look wounded and tell him that if that ever happened she would tell him.

Yet, these days not only was Trish not informing him, but she was actually dodging the topic each time he brought it up. How the times had changed! But, he reflected, fifteen years was a lifetime and, as the song says, time changes everything. What a fool he was to have left such a gem of a woman exposed to gossip and insecurity and temptation for so long.

When he received her cryptic message about being totally confused, Len was taken aback, and pique got the better of him and he replied:

"Well, stay confused then. I shall not bother you anymore."

How he regretted that outburst now! What an idiotic thing to say to the woman who ruled his heart, who had waited for him fifteen years to make up his mind. He reflected on the matter miserably. The next day, a Sunday, he called her but got only her greeting which prompted him to leave a message; he did. The same thing happened everyday, through the week. Evidently, she was screening his calls.

The voice messages he left her were all conciliatory, even fawning, but none elicited a response. Finally, the following Saturday, one week after his *Ides of March*, he left her a message threatening to come down and park at her workplace or at her house for as long as it took for her to grant him audience. That did the trick. When he called the next day to repeat the threat she took the call. She lit into him right away with the ferocity of a tigress.

The Trish who answered that call was not the woman he loved; this was some avenging dark angel. She recounted how long she had waited for Len while she weathered many a storm swirling with malice and gossip about her affair with him. She disclosed that all was not tranquility in her house all those years: Her family had asked her repeatedly how long she would wait for Len; even her daughters had wondered whether Len had misled her. Len could understand that her relatives would be impatient; they came up frequently from Nigeria for respite, vacation, or to shop, and in the last three years her mother, her sister, niece, and brother had come and taken up what appeared to be permanent residence with Trish. When that happened Len had throttled back on his visits both because there wasn't enough room in her house for a resident crowd, and because he suspected that his presence could create tension. They liked him but, damn it, he was married and they knew it! At least, Trish said they knew (but Len had only Trish's word for it).

What Len found hard to swallow was the notion that Trish's daughters also wondered how long Len would stay half in, half out of their lives. That saddened him because it implied a strain in the abundant filial love established between him and Trish's daughters, Vivica and Geraldine. Affectionately, Len called them "Viv" and "Jara." His term of endearment for Jara was "My Little Shrimp," because she was so lithe and petite. Not having daughters of his own, Len regarded them as his proxy daughters waiting for full induction into his life "soon." But upon reflection now he was no longer sure of anything about

Trish or her family, how much of his memory of them was based on fact and how much on wishful thinking.

All along, there had been more than just a tacit understanding between Len and Trish that they would end up man and wife. The depth and breadth and duration of their love were too big for just a side affair. In the second half of their relationship, especially during the four years before Len's "Ides of March," the topic of marriage had come up twice. He was distressed as much as Trish by the untenable situation in which their relationship placed her. The most extensive discussion they had about "when" was in their twelfth year, when Len went down to celebrate Trish's birthday and they had spent an afternoon on a park bench. And it was Len, not Trish, who broached the topic.

There was light at the end of the tunnel, he told Trish. While she was gone to Nigeria on a visit, Len interviewed for a Dean's position in a regional campus of Kent State University, a location about an hour from Columbus. All indications were that Len would get the job. He had solid experiences both as head of a department and dean of a school in the universities where he had taught; his research and publication portfolios were ample. His former bosses at the NASA Glenn Research Center backed his candidacy with strong recommendations as did the heads of the departments of engineering in Cleveland-area universities where he taught several courses as adjunct professor during and following his NASA sojourn. Above all, he was actually stooping to seek that job at KSU: the salary offered for the position was about half what he had earned at NASA.

During the interview Len had been asked about being overqualified in terms of teaching, research, and university administration experiences —whether he didn't think it a step-down to accept the much lower pay. He had replied that, it being a rural campus, he presumed that cost of living was commensurately lower than in Cleveland. But low pay or not Len had decided to take that job and adjust to the hefty pay cut in return for the chance to be closer to Trish, and away from his Cleveland friends and her Columbus associates. It was a perfect opportunity. And he heard through the grapevine that there were not many takers for that position on the sleepy, remote KSU campus.

Sitting on that park bench and discussing their future, Len promised Trish that when he started the new job and once again had independent income, he would file for divorce from Magda. He explained to Trish again that he could not just sneak away in the night and abscond from Magda, who had been an honorable wife and deserved to have his exit arranged in a proper way. Magda had a soft heart and was vulnerable as jellyfish, he told Trish for the umpteenth time. Magda would rather weep softly for the loss of something she held dear than blame anyone else for the loss. He would ask Magda for the divorce when the time was right, and the right moment was not far away.

But it was not to be. Three weeks after that discussion with Trish he received a letter from the faculty search committee informing him that the expected subvention to support the new dean had failed in the Ohio Congress and the position would no longer be filled. Len thought there was more to it than that. It was an all-white campus in rural, southern-Ohio where a prominent, black boss would be troubling to most. That was not a notion he could prove but in the United States race was always a factor. Well, Len was back to the drawing board. One month after he raised Trish's hope with news of his expected new job he had to relate the bad news that he was back to depending on Magda's goodwill not to scuttle his source of income —their family business— if he filed for divorce. Len felt sure that Magda would do that just to spite him.

On that occasion and some others Len was the one who mooted the question of how long they had to wait to tie the knot and belong to each other exclusively and officially. Trish brought it up only twice: once when her brother sent her greetings from Nigeria and accompanied the greeting with a hint that they were waiting for the wedding day to be announced; the second time was one year later when Trish told Len about nosey people who made it their business to bug her about Len. On the first of those two occasions Len replied, rather flippantly, that it was understandable for her relatives to nudge her towards marriage; that union was how they viewed man-woman relationship. Len should have used that occasion to discuss their future but, fatuously, he let the chance slip away. On the second occasion when Trish hinted at her discomfort he responded with a proverb of his people:

"If you reflect too much on the contents of stream water you'll never drink it."

And Trish cut in to ask impatiently, "But how long shall we just sip this water?" Her meaning was clear and so Len reviewed his plans for their future. Since Len would have to relocate, he had to retire from the family business he ran jointly with Magda in order to carry out the plan. He had notified the company's board of directors of his intention to retire the next year and the board had approved it and also agreed his pension. Thereafter, Magda could not freeze him out of a living when he asked her for divorce. Len said all he needed was one more year, which seemed to satisfy Trish; or at least she seemed resigned to that plan. Anyway, she was still reluctant to move from Columbus where she had set down a complex network of deep roots.

On those two occasions when Trish broached that specific topic, she presented it casually as a "by the way" matter. There was no doubt that, if Trish had even once faced Len with a do-or-die, "now or never" choice, he would have dropped everything without hesitation to run to her side. But Trish was a tactful person and that tact made it easy for Len to procrastinate and plan a perfect transition that caused the least amount of discomfort for all concerned. He did not pick up on the urgency behind Trish's subtle hints. An overconfident man not given to easy jealousy, Len had lulled himself into a false sense of security, even going so far as to hint to Trish now and then that it was OK for her to explore the company of other men if she wanted, because he was foolishly certain she wouldn't find another man who loved her like he did.

Subconsciously Len had regarded union with Trish as a done deal just waiting to fall into place at the right moment. But if Len was foolish in that regard, so was Trish who left that matter entirely up to him. The tiniest nudge from her would have tipped Len her way, but she was too cautious to push. Unaware of the volcanic pressures welling up inside Trish, Len went on living in a fool's paradise, thinking Trish was safely his for all time. Now, that volcano had blown his dreams to pieces. The Trish who had now retreated behind a wall of hostility and silence, spurning all overtures from Len, was not the Trish he thought he knew. This new Trish was heartless, truculent, inaccessible. Clearly, she hated Len now.

What hurt Len most was that it was all unraveling now, when his moment of deliverance was near. The time frame for retirement from his family business and severance from his marriage was firmly set, and he was ready to turn to that important new chapter and make Trish the exclusive focus of his attention. But Trish apparently had reached the end of her tether and would not respond anymore to his messages. He kept trying to regain the attention of that precious woman who had, until now, made his life a succession of happy days. But she had clammed up on him firmly and implacably. Three times after his *Ides of March* he drove to Columbus crying all the way, hoping to see her and talk to her, or just hear her voice and feel alive again. Trish would not come to the door.

That third time he went to beg for audience with her, Len was met at the door by Trish's daughter Viv. The young lady told him her mother did not want to see him again. He handed her an envelope with a note and a CD and asked her to give it to her mother. The CD was a compilation of songs, "My Songs of Pain" as he labeled it. The note was written in advance (just in case Trish was not home) to alert her to watch the sky over her house the next day for a messenger aircraft that would trail a personal message. But Viv brought the envelope back saying her mom declined it. Len was crushed. It was as if he and Trish no longer lived in the same world, as if Len's remembrance of their days of bliss was mere illusion. The gate of paradise had been slammed resolutely in his face. He turned and stumbled to his car.

Like a boat with a broken rudder Len drifted aimlessly, listlessly, during these last seven months since his Ides of March, wondering how he was going to survive his misery and negotiate a life suddenly plunged into darkness by the loss of its sole source of light. The thought overwhelmed him and he sank to his knees to weep bitterly once again. These daily bouts of weeping took Len by surprise. He knew he had a soft heart; Trish told him that many times, once suggesting that Len had the gentle sensibilities of a woman. But he never knew, until now, that he could be so weepy, not even like a woman but rather like a baby separated from its mother. Each time his mind turned to Trish his dam burst and spilled rivers of tears.

Len's epic fifteen-year affair with Trish had lifted him into orbit so many times, brought him untold joy, and opened his heart to the sublime experience of true, deep, pure love. But his exhilaration was now turning to despair as information began to emerge about the real character of Trish, the suddenly enigmatic woman he thought he had gotten to know over so many years. Trish's defection was by far the biggest loss in Len's life, but what made it an unbearable tragedy was the callous manner of it. The way she kicked him off her trail smacked of crass ingratitude. In addition to the emotional hurt, Len began to smart from her ingratitude over the substantial financial splurges she had inveigled out of him.

One perplexing matter concerned Trish's use of $20,000 that Len entrusted to her. He knew she used $15,000 as hospital deposit for her sister's cancer treatment. She never explained what happened to the balance; but $5,000 was a small matter. The elephant in the room was the failure of her entire family to even mention Len's generosity in their moment of need. That failure cast shadows on the matter of candor between Trish and her family, especially over her relationship with Len. Any family in the world that received such a donation would show its gratitude. But not even one word of acknowledgment came from Trish's family: Not on the many occasions when he visited them after they arrived in Columbus from Nigeria —not even at the funeral of their daughter who finally succumbed to cancer. At that funeral Len gave another large sum of cash to the family through Trish, to help pay for the catered funerary repast for mourners. That new donation was never acknowledged, either.

The seeming ingratitude of that family was bizarre. What kind of family was it? Len could only conclude that Trish didn't tell her family where all that money came from. Perhaps she didn't want them to know the extent of his support for her. Trish, who was now coming across as a consummate pretender, must have made her family believe that the money came from her savings. And she did not level with her family even after she decided that Len was played out and used up; instead she proceeded to kick him to the curb and move on to her new lover. Trish Adoja was a class act! She had elevated pretence and ingratitude to the level of a fine art.

But that did not exculpate her family from their connivance with her vice —not by a long shot. It was scandalous for a sanctimonious family like theirs to overlook the fact that Trish, a single mom, supported herself and her children as well as her extended family, on her lower middle-class income while maintaining a four-bedroom suburban home where she entertained often. She also owned a Lexus SUV that proudly sported her maiden name on a vanity license plate, —as well as a Toyota Camry. Her family must be afflicted with a case of willful blindness. While Len had supported Trish quite generously over the years, his support and her moderate salary could not account for her profligate lifestyle. In any case, Trish had bought her suburban house from her own resources soon after Len met her, before his generosity towards her began.

Len pondered the following poignant facts about Tarissa Adoja:

- Her moral turpitude in living for years, more or less openly, as a courtesan with a lifestyle that was way beyond her means;
- The venality of her family (daughters, siblings, mother): living with her and thereby to all appearances conniving at her conduct, knowingly benefitting from the proceeds of her essential prostitution and opportunism (a condonation that was tantamount to pimping);
- His large and unacknowledged donations to her family when none of Trish's relatives or friends could help: a sacrifice that made possible her sister's coming for treatment;
- Len's ultimate realization that Trish was not only a home wrecker, perhaps a serial home wrecker, but quite a methodical one who selectively preyed on Igbo men that lived too far away to notice she was "messing around" (in her own words);
- Trish's eagerness to file spurious legal charges against Len for "stalking" and "harassment" just to get him off her back and clear the way for her new lover;
- Trish's insinuation that her friends and family considered her to have been reckless in exposing her daughters to Len, who might easily have preyed on the girls in her absence.

Human nature was appalling, he concluded. Finally in his depression that Sunday morning he gathered his reeling wits about him and wrote a farewell letter to his sons. He signed it and sealed it in a smaller envelope which he inserted into the larger envelope bearing his Last Will and Testament. It read:

My dear sons:

I love you all very much; don't ever forget that, no matter what. I am proud of you too, for your development and accomplishments. Above all, your mother and I have been immensely gratified by the fact that you are all phenomenally good and attentive fathers to your children, even more so than we were to you. We always take delight in watching each of you interact with your children.

I now take my leave with the full assurance that you will nurture my beloved grandchildren as well as is humanly possible. You are the custodians of the Obi legacy, and that legacy is in good hands.

I never got around to talking with you about the other kind of love, the sort between man and woman, so you have had to grapple with it at your own time, in your own way. I tell you now belatedly that, after filial love, perhaps even more than filial love, it is the strongest force of interaction between humans. Nothing is more powerful or more sublime than that kind of love. So perhaps you will understand and forgive me my exit at this point. Though I have honored and protected your mother all these four decades plus, because she is a good, good woman, I only realized starting a decade ago that her union with me was based on factors different from the kind of love that ambushed me and held me captive for the past fifteen years. You are witnesses to the recent events caused by my fifteen years of deep affection for another woman, and the severe ruptures that it has now caused in all our lives. For those traumatic disruptions I apologize to you. Learn from it that your father was human, a fallible man. Let that lesson serve you well.

Once more I embrace you. Please pass that embrace to each of my grandchildren and, along with it, give them the blessings of all our ancestors, which I now pass on to you. And please take care of your mother: she is a noble and honorable woman betrayed by forces beyond her control, beyond our control.

I love you all.
Your Dad

In the evening Len tidied his apartment and prepared for his final act. He went to his bathroom cabinet and took out the pillbox to which his tortured mind kept wandering with increasing frequency. Tenderly he counted out those little white discs onto the saucer on his bedroom night stand. The end of his misery. Twelve tablets, one for each year he spent in paradise as a resident in Trish's heart, before she began to cool on him. It was time to let go, time to follow his memories into the ethereal universe. He got a glass of water and set it beside the saucer with the tablets. Then he took down two framed photographs that sat on the headboard of his bed. One was a picture of Magda as a nursing student before she and Len met. From that black-and-white photograph a lovely girl at the cusp of womanhood stared at him accusingly. Len flipped it over, face-down on the mantelpiece. The second was a picture of Trish —his favorite photograph of her. Old but not faded, it captured her first and radiant blush of womanhood at college. Len slid it out of its frame, kissed it, turned it over and wrote on its back:

Forgive me, my princess, but I can't take any more. Wherever you are, whatever you do for the rest of your life, do not forget that I have loved you all these years more deeply than any man ever loved a woman. I have had a productive and satisfying life. The productive part may have been of my own doing, with Magda's untiring assistance, but the satisfying part was largely wrought by your presence in my life these past fifteen years. Think kindly of me. Goodbye, my darling.

Remembering Marty Robbins' "I'm Sending You A Big Bouquet of Roses," Len would have loved to close out the Len-and-Trish chapter of his life by sending her a truckload of roses, one for every time she thrilled his heart. But lately Trish had disdained his flowers, in contrast to their early days when each bouquet he sent her drove her to call him and fill his ears with sharp squeals of delight.

Len's troubled mind went back to the last time he had taken a bouquet to Trish, on the Mothers' Day following his *Ides of March*, when reproof was stamped all over her attitude. First, she had let Len stand there on her porch for five full minutes while she finished a phone conversation. Then she opened her door but did not let him in: She came out to her porch and talked to him there. Len was put off by her unwelcoming mien. He had not seen Trish for so long. That Mothers' Day visit was only the second time he had seen Trish in a couple of years. One year before that Len was in Columbus for a workshop and Trish came to see him in his hotel room. That he now stayed in a hotel rather than with Trish when he went to Columbus underscored their estrangement, which neither of them talked about.

On the prior occasion they were intimate in his hotel room, but neither of them got satisfaction because Len's libido had not recovered from the decline caused by his recent spate of health problems. Len's doctors had all assured him his appetite for sex would be restored in time and with medication, but this insipid performance which left him and Trish embarrassed just took the stuffing out of him. Trish tried to put a positive spin on it with "It is not important," but Len felt otherwise. It was the first time he had been intimate with any woman in the years, since his heart problem escalated, leading to the implantation of a regulating device in his chest.

As Len stood on Trish's porch on that last, Mothers' Day, a disregarded bouquet of roses in his hand, she surveyed him with deliberate coolness. He realized a new and hostile phase had dawned between him and Trish, his very own dear Trish as he had come to think of her. When he held out the flowers she jerked a thumb to indicate he should set it down on the bench at her porch, and then she stared at him with joyless eyes. There wasn't even a Thank You, only a "Yes?" Something was eating her. Just the week before, he had sent her another long string of cultured pearls for her birthday and she had sent it back to him by return of post. Standing at her porch, he started with: "Honey, I'm so worried about you, about us. Why did you return the pearls I sent you?"

She brushed the question aside with a wave of her right hand as she replied, "Because they would wonder why she is still accepting jewelry from him."

She actually referred to herself and Len in the third person. That hinted that she was just a medium relaying that message to Len. She didn't explain who "they" were and Len did not press the point. He assumed Trish's friends were in on the conspiracy. Some of them had been urging her for so long to cut her ties with this married man. One of them persisted, offering to find Trish a fine man, a white man if that was what she preferred. Apparently, they had finally succeeded in swaying her while, foolishly, Len dragged his feet waiting for the elusive "correct moment" to leave Magda and cleave to Trish.

"What has happened to you?" Len asked, and a tirade spewed out of Trish.

"Lennox, you know your way to my front door because you have been here countless times. You have been here, in fact lived here, and met all my relatives each time they came up from Nigeria, met all my friends and neighbors. You are on intimate terms with my children, my family, my closest friends. I let you into their lives and they welcomed you. But tell me, Lennox, how many of your relatives or family or friends have I ever met? Not one! Not ever! You call that a relationship?"

Len thought she had a point there. She looked ready to kick him in the stomach; her dander was up. This was a side to Trish he had never seen before or expected ever to see in his life. What could he say now? That he shielded her from his people to spare her their resentment? That he did not live alone and so could not bring her to his house? That he was now ready —nay, eager— to make amends and change all that? That he had never lost an opportunity in the past to let her know she was the queen of his heart, or that he had tried to let her know his timeline for making that final move? All that seemed trite now.

When his catastrophic heart failure had confronted Len with his mortality four years earlier, during the doldrums in his affair with Trish, he took his youngest son into his confidence and told him all about his feelings and goings-on with Trish. He had chosen that son because he was most similar to Len in temperament, prone to wearing his fragile sentiments on his sleeve. Len instructed that if he passed away his son was to notify Trish and spare her the agony of silent uncertainty. And Len told Trish about that instruction to his son. But today as she railed at him Len could not cite that charge to counter her accusation. Cite it as proof of what? Trish was right: A "living will" kind of instruction like that did not constitute a proper introduction of Trish into Len's intimate circles the way Trish had introduced Len to everyone of importance to her.

Len was confounded. All that pent-up aggression now erupting from the heaving chest of Trish, where was it during all those years when she had waited for him to make his move? When a simple "Honey, let's get married" kind of nudge might have got Len off his lazy, comfortable ass? And if Trish was content to play along all that time, biding her time till a more available man came along, why not say so now to Len, instead of taking refuge behind this you-were-never-serious-with-me accusation? Len had coasted along for fifteen years on a path of least resistance, true, but at no time was it pointed out to him that his course of action or inaction was entirely unacceptable. And so now he, too, felt betrayed, no less than Trish. He too had been led down the garden path of illusion.

But Len admitted to himself that the ball had really been in his court for so long. He and Trish had had a private joke about procrastination: "Why put off till tomorrow what you can put off for a month?" However, in as much as a joke was not funny when you were the butt of it, this joke was on Len. He had failed to "shit or get off the pot," as the saying goes.

But Trish had more to say, and what came out of her mouth next blew Len entirely away. She said her family and her friends had been saying she was such a fool to have let Len so deeply into her life, into her home. They shuddered to think, and they wondered as they shuddered, that Len could have been a pedophile who molested Trish's daughters when she left them with him. Len was really dumbfounded. Molest Viv and Jara, his proxy daughters?

Why! On weekend nights Jara used to stay up very late, watching TV because she could sleep-in the next day. When she got tired she sometimes crept into Trish's bed and went to sleep lying at the edge of the bed. But if Trish went to work the next morning, Jara, a restless sleeper like all children, would slide and roll until she snuggled to Len. Len would notice her when he woke, smile, kiss her hair, and cradle her affectionately as she slept on innocently. What diabolical minds would impute a corruption in that filial bond between Len and Jara, his "Little Shrimp"? Was there no limit to the depraved imaginations of people? Len wondered. His wounds opened up and bled anew.

And it was not only Trish's hostility that put him off on that lamentable occasion, but also her physical appearance. She looked matronly in her Mothers' Day outfit, a three-piece costume from Nigeria which accentuated her spreading girth. She was adorned in *Igala* attire, with a loud but coordinated string of large jade beads and earrings to accentuate a towering head tie. Len did not like the outfit, which only seemed to announce that Trish had coarsened in the past year or so and now had a thick neck and barreling chest. It turned him off. When a woman not so tall puts on extra weight and bulks up in the neck and bosom, the effect is unpleasant. His elegant Trish had let go. Now she was puffed up, her short and stiff neck bulging as her dander came up. She looked like a bullfrog.

But Len did not feel he was in any position to comment even tactfully on Trish's need to regain her trim profile. Anyone might let go under the buffeting episodes of hard times which Trish had seen lately, but Trish used to have more spunk than that. She was the one who motivated Len in their early days more regularly to work-out with a more effective regimen of exercise. In fact, ever since his early days with her Len kept himself shipshape, notwithstanding that he was a full dozen years older than she.

2
Tandem Workout

Heaven, I'm in Heaven
And my heart beats so that I can hardly speak
And I seem to find the happiness I seek
When we're out together dancing cheek to cheek

TRISH AND LEN used to work on mutual reinforcement to encourage each other to keep fat at bay. Starting with walks around Trish's block they strayed farther each day: first to a nearby elementary school that had a convenient playground around which to walk. There, out of earshot of other people they would march or skip along like children to the tune of a song or rhythm of a poem, like:

The Noble Duke of York,
He had ten thousand men.
He marched them up to the top of the hill,
And marched them down again.

And when they were up, they were up,
And when they were down, they were down.
But when they were only halfway up,
They were neither up nor down.

One day they ranged a bit far, to the neighborhood middle school and onto a wooded public park behind it. Next day they mounted a pedestrian bridge spanning Interstate 71, an 8-lane highway. There was a sub-division on the other side of that highway and Len suggested that they explore it. But half-way across the bridge Trish swooned and freaked out as vehicles whistling noisily past some twenty feet below generated a fearsome wind and whoosh. She closed her eyes and began to sway. Len ran his arm as a brace across her waist and led her gently back the way they came because Trish refused to go any farther. She was in no physical danger, because pedestrians on the bridge were protected by a sturdy steel wire mesh welded to the fat rails and arching far overhead. But Len recognized that she was in psychological distress.

He was to encounter her sudden attack of motion or height phobia a few more times in the future. One such time was when he took Trish and her children to an Ohio county fairground in session. They let the children loose on the more ambitious rides with enough money for a couple of rounds, while Len took Trish onto an innocuous looking Ferris wheel. The wheel started with Trish and Len in the lowest position. As it started to rotate and rise, Trish gripped Len in fright, and when the wheel arm on which they sat passed horizontal position, Trish closed her eyes and grew rigid. She began to claw his shoulder and her breathing became sharp and irregular, in gasps. She was in such distress that Len waved frantically until the operator stopped the wheel.

As soon as he got Trish down she retched and threw up. The experience taught him not to take her on such rides again. However, when he took her and her children to Disney World one year later he once again coaxed her to try a high swing. He pushed Trish to and fro on the swing while the children went to whoop and scream with glee on the more breath-taking roller-coaster rides. Again Trish freaked out and nearly fell off the swing when it was high. Again Len stopped the ride and took her down.

Len himself was also afraid of heights, but really only at considerably greater elevation. He had experienced vertigo on occasions, such as when he rode a helicopter between the Heathrow and Gatwick airports of London. To spare Trish any more scares, Len wanted to buy bicycles so they could range farther afield and see sights while getting some exercise. But Trish's eyes grew round with fear. She said she had never learned to ride a bicycle, and Len was astonished: Here was a person who learned to drive motorized vehicles with supreme confidence bordering on recklessness, and she did not know how to propel a slow, two-wheeler craft? He told her there was nothing to it, he would teach her. Magda had been exactly the same when he met her, but when they moved back to Cleveland Len taught her to ride a bike, and now his entire family liked to go biking together on weekends. But he could not make Trish budge. She was simply not going to ride any wobbly, two-wheeled thing. Len gave up but took to teasing and scaring her with threats to just go out one day and bring her a bicycle. Each time he did so her eyes shot daggers at him. He never did buy Trish a bicycle; they just kept walking.

She and Len were opposed to the idea of surrendering to the spreading girth or bulging belly of middle age. It was a surrender that revealed lack of discipline, a certain weakness of character. There are essentially two ways to keep one's body trim and firm. One is to eat only as much food as necessary to replenish energy used in daily activity and to restore needed nourishment. The other was by constant exercise. In middle age a person must have recourse to one method or the other.

And now on this Mothers' Day occasion, here was Trish, his gold standard for everything he thought a woman should be; here she was looking a bit like a dwarf python after a meal, confronting him on her porch with an insolent air. Trish's new girth and thickening neck made it easier to realize she was only of average height, whereas Len used to think of her as being above average in everything. This new stocky frame reinforced her new stiff attitude that signaled to Len that his beloved old Trish was gone; this person standing in front of him with a disdainful mien was an alien.

But still Len wanted Trish back, with all his heart. If not the slim-trim Trish he remembered, then this matron would do. Who knows but that he might coax her back into fitness once again? In any case, slimness was not everything; what he valued most in Trish was her spirit of irrepressible playfulness, her feisty readiness with mischief, the never-a-dull-moment way she kept him entertained. Yes, he was physically attracted to her before, but it was her mind that attracted him the most and he would take whatever he could get of Trish now, if only she would relent and take him back. Trish in any shape was infinitely better than no Trish at all.

Over the years she had become Len's main confidante. Whenever a new idea or news came to Len, his first instinct was to share it with Trish. He might call her several times in one day to ask, "Have you heard about...?" She often was ahead of Len on the news, and she always had an interesting take on events. Her views were seldom at odds with his: She really was his soul mate. He knew that he would be lost without her. But now she totally rebuffed him. She would rather see him dead first. And Len so wanted to die rather than stay in this new hell to which she had consigned him. She finally showed Len out of her house and jerked her head to indicate dismissal, and Len slunk away, backwards, to his car. She shut her door and a new era of total loneliness engulfed Len.

But a heart desperate in love is not easily persuaded to give up. As his birthday came up he sent an email imploring her to "give me the birthday present of my life: Please say yes to me and, if I don't drop dead with joy I shall fly down to Columbus to do your bidding, whatever it is." But she didn't reply, and so one week later he commissioned a Sky Message outfit to display an aerial message over Trish's home on the next Saturday, and on the day after that to repeat the display over the church where Trish attended Mass. That was the occasion when her daughter Viv came to the door and told Len that Trish did not wish to see him or accept the envelope containing his messages. Trish had decided to cut Len's throat and that was that. That was the end of the road for him.

He could not reach Trish with flowers anymore. So Len reluctantly decided to end their chapter to the strains of those "Songs of Pain," which she had spurned on his latest visit to her, just like she spurned his Mothers' Day flowers. He was ready. The kitchen radio-clock was set to alarm mode to go off in twelve hours; the volume was turned up to loudest level. The kitchen window was open a crack. Somebody was bound to hear the racket of the alarm when it went off, and then notify the apartment manager. But since he had no idea how soon it would be before he was discovered or what might happen in the mean time, Len also attached his farewell letter to an email addressed to his sons. The text of the email contained just one sentence: "Goodbye, my dear sons."

He sent the email, walked into his bedroom, turned on his bedside *Bose* player and popped in the CD, setting the unit at a low play-back volume on an indefinite repeat loop as he always did when he went to bed. Then he dialed Trish's number and hoped her answering machine would record at least some of his valedictory. Twelve songs: twelve ways to say adieu to Trish Abba Adoja, the one and only woman he really loved and for whom he was now giving up his life. Pouring the twelve tablets into his mouth and chasing them down with a quick gulp of water, Len lay down on his back and clamped Trish's photo to his chest, fingers interlaced firmly to prevent slippage, her image facing his heart.

He pushed the play button and the CD player opened up with *Stardust*. As Len embarked on his epic journey down memory lane, the purple dusk of twilight time stole across the meadows of his heart, and tears came oozing down again. Soon the other songs would follow in their sequence: *Love is A Many-Splendored Thing; Fly Me to The Moon; Take These Chains from My Heart; My One And Only Love; Sometimes When We Touch; I'll Never Smile Again; When I Need You; Somewhere My Love; You Taught My Heart to Sing; There'll Never Be Another You; I Won't Forget You.*

Len closed his eyes, and a smile settled on his lips as he let his mind drift into play-back mode, to review how it all started and where the wheels came off. Ah, the beginning: How sweet and simple it was! A Saturday night party among acquaintances, in the home of a friend: Could there be a more unlikely setting for a seismic experience?

3
Serendipity

Walking backwards down the road
Looking all around
Never thought I'd find love....

TWO WEEKS TO Christmas. It was going to be a fun night, Len thought as he drove round and round to find a place to park, somewhere within two or three blocks of the home of "Dr. and Dr. Mrs. Ojemba" as they were known to the title-conscious immigrant community of Nigerians living in Columbus. Cars were parked bumper-to-bumper and not a few straggled with higgledy-piggledy abandon onto tree lawns. In front of the Ojemba residence were cars parked right on the lawn, causing Len to mumble that many of the revelers gathered tonight must be strangers to suburbia, oblivious to the niceties of maintaining decorum in residential suburbs. No doubt, cops would be arriving later, summoned by miffed neighbors to come and ask people "politely" to move their cars. "And please ask them to tone down the racket. This not Africa and we need our sleep."

Len left his car in the middle of the street in front of the driveway, went to Ojemba's house, rang the bell, and got help to offload the drinks he brought, and the food Magda made —dishes requisitioned by Tina from among Magda's culinary specialties. Then they drove off to continue the search for a parking place. Magda insisted on going with Len because she said by the look of things it might be a long and lonely walk back. Not finding an open spot, Len moved to the next block, and then extended his search to the block after that. He was not in the mood for a long walk back to Ojemba's residence. What if the snow came down? It was winter, after all.

Such a party, he grumbled to his wife sitting beside him, should be held in a hired hall. But he was aware that his compatriots were money-grubbers saving up for house-building projects back in the home country. That was a time-honored indicator of accomplishment among his people. Nothing a man did or achieved at home or abroad was regarded with approval as much as building a house of his own in his father's homestead. Indeed among traditional Igbos a man could not get up and address a gathering until he had built his own dwelling, preparatory to taking a wife. And with the new breed and large crop of Len's peers, the baby-boomers, now holding impressive positions at home and abroad, the building craze in Nigerian villages and hamlets had become an obscene competition to outdo the other fellow. So Nigerians in the diaspora saved their money for house building back in Nigeria, even if that meant holding their parties right in their living spaces.

Everyone knew that such parties were always crowded. It was not that people were drawn by the prospect of free food and drink, excellent though the ethnic foods were on such occasions. It was just that in this community people strove to show off, resplendent in their robes and caps, the ladies in their party costumes and ceiling-scraping head pieces. It was not unusual for couples to send out engraved invitation cards for the first birthday of their child, and end up providing repast for three times the number of guests invited, with hordes of those guests' children scampering underfoot, in spite of the clear message on the invitation: "Adults Only, Please!" Parties were popular in this community. If you forgot to invite an acquaintance they would crash the party anyway, and then never let you forget you had slighted them. "Is it because I am not a Doctor?" they would inquire. And to mollify them you would coo, "Oh no, the printing company omitted some names. You know you are always welcome!" And if an invitee failed to show up, you took offense as well at the "slight." Painfully aware that, as new immigrants they were not fully integrated into America's melting pot, they clubbed together clannishly and, within their intimate little club, jockeyed fiercely for preeminence.

Len always arrived late to Nigerian functions. It was assumed to be a case of the "African Time" mentality that all Africans shared, and which Africans themselves commented upon in self-mockery. (An apocryphal joke Len heard, said that African diplomats made sure to print two different invitations to official functions: one for Africans, in which starting times were set down at, say, 4:00 pm; and a different set for Westerners, in which the corresponding time was stated as 6:00 pm.) Still, he explained each of his late arrivals at African functions with a specific apology, saying that he overslept, started out later than he wished due to unforeseen events, or was delayed by traffic. He did not want to seem a snob by telling his friends the truth: That his late arrival was an ingrained habit formed during the ten years he sojourned in Nigeria before returning to the U.S.

The truth of the matter was that, by arriving late, Len was trying to avoid the silly preliminaries with which every Nigerian occasion started: Distribution of an agenda, Calling "dignitaries" to get up from where they sat in pretended modesty and proceed in triumph to The High Table, then prayers, and the chairman's opening remarks. Not a single one of those particulars was ever omitted. Even a party to celebrate a baby's first birthday might have a designated Master of Ceremonies, a printed agenda, and a High Table at which the designated chairperson (who was always the chief ranking invitee) was centrally seated and flanked by the lesser dignitaries. Those proceedings were kicked off with a prayer, carefully worded to avoid offending partisans of different faiths by naming specific gods. Envelopes were then distributed and, at some point during the proceedings, a basket was usually passed around for attendees to pitch in their donation, with the chairperson expected to make a particularly handsome donation. Len was relieved to note that in recent years, among Nigerians in the U.S., the most ostentatious steps, such as a High Table were being omitted at parties given in a person's home.

This, though, was no ordinary party. Everyone knew the hosting couple: an affable man and his pretty wife both of whom taught at a local university, he taught horticulture and she education. He was turning 50 (so they said, but that was a different matter, Len chuckled) and his wife was hosting for him a party to mark that landmark birthday. The man recently took a traditional title, bestowed on him by the people of his hometown back in Nigeria, and he had thereby earned the right to be addressed as "Chief Doctor Ojemba." Proliferation of the title "Chief" among Nigerians is an amazing phenomenon, Len often reflected. Nigeria is perhaps the only society where chiefs outnumber their subjects. The propensity to self-aggrandizement is also reflected in the fact that Nigerians wear their occupations as titles: One is addressed as "Architect X," or "Pharmacist Y," or "Engineer Z." Few Nigerians want to be called "mister" and the now rampant proliferation of online Ph.Ds., some of which can be earned after only a few weeks of "study" and "research," is a boon to that ingrained yearning for titles.

The Nigerian will cling to his title once he gets it, and if no one ever bestowed a title on him he would award it to himself anyway. And he does not replace an earlier title with a new one; he wears them all together, strung up like beads on a necklace. Thus he may be addressed as "Chief, Professor, Alhaji So-and-So." Len liked to tell the story of a worker at his university who took a chieftaincy title in his village soon after being promoted to Chief Engineer on campus. He liked to be address as "Chief Kuru, Chief Engineer." Finally, aping the military tradition then entrenched in the country, everyone called him "Chief-in-Chief"; and behind his back his subordinates referred to him, tongue-in-cheek, as "Chief-Squared."

The craze for self promotion may have started with chieftaincy titles, Len reflected, but now it had exploded among the "religious" righteous (which in Nigeria meant nearly everyone). Those who disdained chieftaincy titles, such as academics, became enamored of the title of "Sir," which was attained through knighthood. After Nigeria became independent the rare honor of being knighted by "His (or Her) Britannic Majesty" became unavailable. The Pope filled the gap for a while, conferring knighthoods to those recommended by their bishops. And finally the explosive growth in demand of knighthood caused Rome to delegate the minting of knights to the bishop of each Diocese.

A knight is called "Sir" Such-and-Such, and his wife as "Lady" So-and-So. Thus, a prolific mill of knighthood began to spin furiously all over the country. These latter-day knights like to don ostentatious uniforms to public functions. In some chapters (or "Commanderies" in their local jargon) the uniform consists of a heavy, dark tunic with shiny brass buttons, topped with the sort of two-pointed military hat made famous by Napoleon Bonaparte —now worn in the front-to-back style of Marcus Garvey. Since these modern knights fancied themselves as "Warriors for Christ," they were encumbered with swords swinging from their hips: In most cases they were imitation swords hewn from wood and stained a dark color. Nothing looks more quixotic than a Nigerian knight in armor (well, *dashiki*)—except perhaps Jean Bedel Bokassa on the day he crowned himself "Emperor of the Central African Republic" after failing to convince the Pope to come down and do the honors.

Referring to the title craze among Nigerians as he tucked his compact car into a tight space, Len asked his wife: "Well, now that

Cyril is "Chief Doctor," is his wife to become known as "Lady Doctor Augustina"? Magda laughed. It was common knowledge that a Nigerian wife coveted those titles even more than her husband. The wife of a titled man would let it be known that she no longer wanted to be called "Madam" So-and-So; now it would be "Lady" So-and-so. Then some years down the line she would up the ante to "Dame" So-and-So to stay ahead of the competition. And of course her wardrobe would bulge a little further.

Lennox expected to see quite an array of flowing robes and red caps among the crowd tonight: The necks slung with large coral beads, wrists adorned with cowrie shells, and hands busied with waving fans of bird feathers or tapping the floor with ivory-tipped walking sticks. It was going to be fun, which was good as he had had quite a trying time in the laboratory all week long.

He and Magda walked quickly because snow flurries were starting to fall. He spread a broad handkerchief over her head to keep the flakes from settling into the folds of her *gele*, which was ridiculously tall as an Episcopal hat and ornate in the manner favored by Nigerian ladies of fashion. It was made of stiff brocade, and a lady had a different *gele* to match her outfit for each occasion. They typically spent hours tying and retying it at leisure, and then hanging it up, ready to don like a hat when needed. To have to remove it, shake off snow flakes and retie it would annoy Magda, so Len protected it with his handkerchief. They got to the porch, shook off specks of snow from their clothes, and stepped into the house.

Len had no way of knowing that the outcome of this night would rock his life.

The host and hostess greeted them with bear hugs. They were almost family. Len and Tina came from the same village in Nigeria; indeed, the eaves of the houses of their respective parents almost touched. They frequently exchanged visits, notwithstanding the two-hour drive between Cleveland where Len and Magda lived, and Columbus where Cyril and Augustina ("Tina") Ojemba lived. Magda and the ladies ran, giggling, up the stairs to adjust their outfits and preen in front of mirrors. Len began his usual rounds of greetings. Walking past the dining room and into the living room, he literally collided with his destiny. Out of the corner of his eye Len saw someone familiar, wheeled towards him, and bumped into a lady coming around the corner. They exchanged a surprised "Excuse me!" and he caught a whiff of her mild and pleasant perfume just as she slipped away.

After renewed pleasantries with Cyril, Len began to look around for the lady with whom he collided. When he saw her again, or rather heard her, her back was to him. In the far corner of the long living room a lively debate was in progress, prompted by "breaking" news scrolling over and over on the TV. A man raised his voice to ask the question:

"Does anyone still think Iraq has weapons of mass destruction? Are those weapons now so minute that intrusive UN inspectors must search every room of Saddam's presidential palace to please the U.S. contingent?"

Someone else interjected:

"After all these years of embargoes, bombings, no-fly zones, and prying with satellite cameras that can distinguish occupants in a parked car, hasn't the poor country had enough?"

There was a hush. It wasn't the sort of topic one jumped into while America was in the grip of war fever. But then a lady's voice broke in, soft and clear:

"It is all about the oil. They want to attack Iraq again, this time for oil. Everything else is an excuse to justify an invasion."

Len recognized the voice and sidled closer. There were three men and two women engaged in that conversation. The other lady was quiet, draping herself all over the man beside her; they were obviously man and wife. The woman who just spoke was standing off to a side, all by herself, one elbow leaning against a wall. The third man turned on her with some heat and challenged her:

"But are you not a U.S. citizen? Isn't it your patriotic duty to support this country in times of war?"

The lady with the golden braids, Len's collision lady and his main quarry now, answered:

"The USA has been at war with one country or another since before our time, yours and mine. It always cites one cause or another. America fights too much. My children are US citizens and I tell them they have a duty to fight for their country tooth-and-nail, even to death, but only in defense of this country. And I mean real defense. Going thousands of miles to someone else's country to attack them in their homes in the name of self defense defies common sense. You don't come into my home with a gun to defend yourself."

Everyone around her sat still and looked at the floor, so she continued:

"Can anyone here name a date, any one day, when the US has not been fighting in some distant country or another? I can't."

The woman who was leaning on her man like the Tower of Pisa asked languidly: "Are you saying the USA is always wrong in every war?"

Golden braids regarded the other lady with a half smile and replied:

"No. But we shouldn't forget the many instances when the U.S. has been wrong. America is adept at giving easy apologies many decades and centuries after the fact, when the damage can no longer be undone. America now apologizes for 400 years of slavery and for one full century of discrimination against blacks following emancipation, for wiping out whole populations of native Indians, which continued until the last century, and for the slaughter of innocent civilians during the Vietnam War. Right now Americans are beating their chests in sorrow about those injustices and others committed against so-called enemies in the past. But while the atrocities were in progress, Americans were cheering their government and their soldiers to inflict more. American people seem to need enemies all the time. That need becomes a prophecy that fulfils itself. You can be sure that one hundred years from now Americans will be apologizing for Iraq, for Somalia, and for more atrocities that will happen in our time. Apology is cheap when it is for injustice that can no longer be redressed."

The man who was supporting the Tower of Pisa countered, "But the U.S. is in a crusade to spread democracy and human rights...."

But Golden Braids cut back in: "You used the right word: 'Crusade.' History books tell us the European powers used similar justification two centuries ago as an excuse to colonize and plunder the world: "Bringing civilization and Christianity to savages." Today the buzzwords are "democracy" and "human rights" but it is the same game. America won the Second World War in 1945 and the Cold War too in 1989. Yet we go on fighting. The U.S. is the only country that is still fighting on a global scale today. War has become a bad American habit. I don't mind myself or my kids fighting and dying for a just cause, but not to advance the naked greed of someone else."

Len stood riveted. Here was a kindred spirit, his alter ego. It was as if she had heard him make those same points ever since the drums of war began to roll in the Middle East. Who was this indomitable lady that sounded so calm and self-assured, who was so brave in a setting where others were biting their tongues for fear of who might be listening or taking notes? She got up and began to circulate among the guests, stopping here and there to exchange greetings and crack a few jokes. Fascinated, Len followed her with his eyes, and then with his feet. Here was another thing she seems to have taken straight out of Len's very book: The habit of circulating freely in a party, going here and there and everywhere instead of planting herself on a chair in a remote corner just to observe, or to keep out of action altogether.

Len was known for that habit of circling at parties. In fact it was a habit that always evoked Magda's disapproval on their way home from every party: "Must you flirt with every woman you see?" she would hiss at him after a pointed silence and Len would deny he was flirting.

"That woman in the sequined blue dress: You should have seen the sidelong looks her husband gave to you as you smiled into her eyes. What's the matter with you?"

"No, my dear, I was not flirting; I was making conversation, just as you were doing."

He had indeed encouraged Magda long ago to find her own feet at parties and mix freely, not hanging all over him as if she were afraid. As soon as they got in the door at a party he left her to her own devices and went methodically around, getting acquainted. Len did that because he liked to engage people one-on-one, rather than in the group dialogue favored by his friends. Thus reassured by his denials on their way home from the party, Magda would relent and say, "Well, you seem to do it to everyone, the men and women alike, even the children. But it always seems you are the only man engaging the ladies in one-to-one conversations that go on and on and on. Sometimes it makes me uneasy."

Len would become subdued and pensive at that point. That was the point, he thought. The fellow Nigerian men he met at parties, seemed to make an exaggerated effort not to be seen chatting up the ladies. (Magda joked that the ones who were illicit lovers used to exchange messages with hooded eyes, blinks and nods, while a fake Don Juan like Len fluttered visibly from one lady to another.) The men at Nigerian parties habitually clustered around a loud TV set, watching a game in progress or some news bulletin, interjecting comments now and then. Occasionally news from or about Nigeria came up and they became animated. Fancy coming to a party to watch TV, Len mused.

The ladies would gather around the kitchen table, assisting the hostess who busily fussed over dishes; they chattered about celebrities in the news, or about issues concerning their school-age children. After dinner was announced and everyone helped themselves to the food that was inevitably served buffet style, the women gathered again into an exclusive colony of ladies, or the married ones each went to sit next to her husband. When spouses were present together at a function it was obvious who was whose husband or wife: they stood together, sat together, and ate together, as if neither husband nor wife had an independent existence. It must be a security or modesty thing, Len used to think. Perhaps they did not think they could trust their spouse's fidelity out of earshot or out of sight.

One incident stood out in Len's memory. He and Magda had come separately to a party hosted by one of the wives in their Cleveland community. It was a small reception for close friends to celebrate her husband's birthday. Since their circle consisted of couples made up of busy professionals in their individual rights, spouses could not always coordinate their calendars, so it was not unusual for husband and wife to arrive or depart separately. Len and Magda were known for that, due in part to their conscious effort to forge independent identities, at Len's constant urging. The hostess this night was a younger woman who was quite fond of Len but not necessarily in an amorous way. Her husband had a reputation for beating the crap out of her if he took a notion that she was paying too much attention to another man. Cops had been called to their home a few times, sometimes by neighbors.

When Len arrived at that party, late as usual, Magda was already there, seated beside a man whose wife had traveled out of town. Len did his usual circuit of shaking hands and greeting everyone, then dropped onto a couch seat beside the hostess. But the moment he sat down the hostess shot up and out of her perch with such sudden agitation that everyone noticed. It was like a trampoline effect: Len's impact on the couch catapulted the hostess right off. It was clear she feared the reaction of her husband. Len was nonplussed but he put a brave face on the incident.

When they got home Magda used the incident to illustrate the point she often made, and which he just as often refuted, that Len's insouciance towards ladies at parties sometimes offended husbands. But, Len countered, what was the point of going to a party only to stay glued to the company of the person one saw all the time at home? In any case, he told Magda, he was pleased that she had stopped being clingy towards him at parties.

When they had met in Nigeria and embarked jointly on the road to adulthood, both barely out of adolescence, Magda was naïve and vulnerable. In truth she was clingy: She hung tight about him each time they ventured out. A young lady on the threshold of adulthood, without much accomplishment under her belt, could not be expected to possess much self-confidence. He was no more accomplished or older than she, but then he was a man and men were supposed to brave the rough world with more ease, or at least more bravado, than women. Regardless, Magda resisted the idea of striking out on her own at parties. It took a lot of argument before she bought the idea. Eventually she got the drill down pat. These days, as soon as they got into a party and hung up their coats, she left him to make her own circuit of introductions, always starting with the hostess who invariably hovered near the kitchen or the area where ladies were busy setting out food for dinner.

Len himself hardly ate at parties, only pecking at the dishes enough to avoid offending the hostess. He preferred to socialize, and that was hard while stuffing one's mouth with food. Also he preferred his wife's irresistible dishes. Besides, experience had taught him that party food was an invitation to a belly ache. It did not matter whether or not the menu was catered. African food always turned out to be a disaster when mass-produced for scores of people the way a caterer profitably might do. So, people hosting big African parties usually got their friends and other volunteers to bring along their specialty dishes. A Nigerian party was not complete unless the familiar native dishes were laid out, often in a needless superabundance that Len found unreasonably wasteful.

The affair became a potluck smorgasbord, with emphasis on the "luck." Each donated dish had to be hurriedly reheated (or the red palm oil used in cooking it would "go to sleep"). Of course, reheating cooked food always leads to unsatisfactory and uneven results when done in a microwave oven, and therein lies the danger! Since Len was hypertensive and diabetic, with a palate that rejected excessive grease, salt or sugar, he often could not stomach the foods at big parties. Magda, ever the thoughtful wife, often brought along her own dishes for Len if she thought they would not get back home in time for supper.

The bottom line was that his wife had spoiled him with her superb cooking. After decades of marriage to Magda, Len had not found a single person to rival her culinary skills. If he were a ravenous eater he would be wide as a house after all those years! Magda was from a part of Nigeria whose women were proverbial for "luring a man with their cooking." But, of course, Len did not know about that when they met so many decades earlier, both of them barely out of their teens and groping their way into adulthood amidst the devastation and tumult of the three-year Nigeria-Biafra civil war.

Magda soon became known, wherever she and Len lived, for her endearing qualities, not the least of which was her cooking and her generosity. She was in the habit of cooking for friendly families, most often unsolicited. If someone was ill, had a baby, was displaced to a hotel while their home was under repair, or was unable to cook for any reason, Magda took dishes to them. No month passed in which some Nigerian or other, even men with families of their own, did not call to request one of her treats, food such as *Ekpan-kwukwuo* (an itsy-bitsy dish as fantastically mouth watering as a true Hungarian *goulash*) or *Edikang Ekong* (literally, "food fit for a king"). She was widely appreciated for specialties like that.

And although Len's own family's preference ran to Nigerian foods, it was not only African dishes that Magda prepared with uncommon expertise. She made dishes from anywhere come alive: Chinese, European, American, Caribbean. She knew what to bake, what to broil, what to sauté, what to marinate or baste, and the best spices to use with which cuisine. She had an unerring instinct for what works in the kitchen and what does not. If she didn't know, she experimented, often with excellent results. Her weekend pastime was cooking dishes to stow in the freezer for her family or to give away.

She was especially adept at what one of her friends aptly called "import substitution." If a key African ingredient for one of her delicacies was not immediately available, Magda determined what off-the-shelf substitute from the local grocery store to use as a good substitute and whip out a lip-smacking facsimile of the original dish. If Len thought that culinary art was the chief criterion for marital satisfaction, he would never for a moment contemplate leaving Magda; but he craved romance and excitement, in addition to a happy meal now and then.

The children became spoiled on it as well. Not to miss out on the experience, Len and Magda took the boys out to dinner now and then, but each time they dined out the boys picked at their food, gave up, and asked her sheepishly: "Mom, can we go home now and eat?" It was the same whether they lived in Egypt, in Europe, or in the U.S. Restaurant outings were just a chore, and a wasteful one at that. Being married to a woman of such culinary distinction, Len was reluctant to dine away from home, much less at a large party.

After dinner was ended at a party Len would get up and embark on another round of *tet-a-tet* while general conversation began to bubble and swell from scattered comments to a torrent of shouting. The shouting was gross! Guests shouted for the childish reason that no one wanted to yield to another. Nobody would let a speaker finish before jumping in with contradictions or concurrence. It didn't matter that a person planned to say the same thing the current speaker was saying; a person cut in anyway with his or her own observations. The usurped speaker was likely to cut back in impatiently, while others plunged in. Soon everyone was shouting to be heard. It was a prescription for a headache, and Len would slip out at that point to go engage the children of the household in a more pleasant, albeit rather timid and halting dialogue.

But tonight he did not think of the children; instead he scanned the throng of people for that enchanting lady. Again he saw her in a corner chatting briefly with this person and that, as her honey colored braids, gathered into a loose bun atop the white satin band around her head, bobbed up and down. Then she moved along, a set smile on her lips, grace in her gestures, and a twinkle in her eye. The dimple on her right cheek deepened as she pursed her lips to listen intently to what the other person had to say.

Len made a beeline for her, saying "Excuse me— again! I don't believe we have met before. Well, except for our collision around the corner. My name is Lennox Obi. My friends call me Len, and some make it Lenny."

He watched her eyes light up as she recognized him from the collision.

"You're not going to bump into me again, are you?" she challenged, looking squarely into his face. They both laughed. She did not back off, or feign shyness or disinterest the way other ladies often did. She studied his face as he spoke to her and Len found her manner refreshingly direct.

"I am Tarissa. My friends call me 'Trish' —sometimes 'Tess,' but I prefer 'Trish.'" She shook his hand firmly and warmly, just as a man would.

"Then I will call you Trish. It has a short and sharp ring to it."

Len told her he couldn't help overhearing her oration earlier in the living room, about the looming war in Iraq; and that he had taken a notion she was a teacher or a librarian. "Which is it?" She smiled while he spoke, not interrupting him until he stopped talking.

"It wasn't an oration. Just something that came from the heart. And the accuracy of your guesses is amazing! Or have you been asking about me? How did you manage to hit on my two professions so very precisely?"

Oh no, he hastened to assure her. He didn't mean oration in a negative way. Just that she was eloquent and passionate, and it showed she was sincere.

"Teacher and librarian: What a combination for an educator! Well, I happen to feel exactly same as you do about the war hysteria. Listening to you, I heard myself talking. Belligerent U.S. foreign policy happens to be my pet peeve these days. A country with so much potential for good in the world is resorting to constantly bullying smaller nations. Did you study political science as a minor?"

"No, just education and library science. Right now I work in a prison library, the Marion Correctional Institution. But I maintain my teacher's license because I would like to return to teaching sooner or later," Trish explained.

She still held his gaze as she talked to him. He looked at her hands, noticing that her left thumb was hooked into the waist band of the gold-and-green *Hollandis Wax* fabric she wore as ankle-length "wrapper," Nigerian style, below a pale-blue satin blouse. Her right hand clutched her car keys. He recovered his manners and offered her a drink.

"I'm going to get a drink. May I bring you some? Wine perhaps? White or red?"

"Yes, thank you, white."

He hurried off, wriggling through the crush of bodies with "Excuse me! Excuse me!" and made his way back with two glasses of chardonnay, half expecting her to have disappeared. But he found Trish right where he left her, talking to another man, who drifted away as soon as he noticed that Len was itching to get back the lady's full attention.

"I hope you will like this. The only other white wine they have is White Zinfandel, and that saccharine-sweet stuff is poison to me."

Running his eyes over her as she reached for the drink he noticed that her entire outfit beautifully set off the caramel color of her light and smooth skin. He extended the taller glass of chardonnay to her, holding back the smaller one. She gently reached past the larger glass and took the smaller one, all the while holding Len's gaze and smiling at him. "Thank you, er..., Lennox?" Her voice was reedy, like an alto saxophone, Len's favorite wind instrument. What a lady!

"Yes, but please call me Len."

Len noticed a vacant spot in a couch and motioned her to it. She sat down and he squatted right on the floor in front of her, looking straight into her eyes like a puppy to its mistress. Len was too far gone in wondering contemplation of this lady to realize that it was an awkward situation for her. Trish squirmed with an evident embarrassment and the man sitting next to her vacated his seat; Len grabbed it gratefully. The rest of the world faded away as far as he was concerned. Right then, there were just the two of them in his consciousness, in that room, in his whole universe. The questions came cascading out of him in a torrent. He asked and she answered without hesitation.

Where in Nigeria was she from, the North? Was she *Fula*?

"North of where? If you mean north of the Niger-Benue river confluence, yes, I'm from the North. Your last name tells me you are Igbo, right? So you are from the South, then."

But no, she was not Fulani; she was from Kogi state.

How long had she lived in the USA?

"Since 1982."

Had she been back to Nigeria since then? Yes, every couple of years. She returned to Nigeria at the end of her undergraduate education at Ohio University in Athens, intent on putting her education degree to good use at home. Her father, however, urged her to return to the U.S. to pursue a Master's degree while she had momentum and a Nigerian government scholarship that she could extend to graduate studies. She quickly returned to the U.S. and completed a Master's in Library Science.

Finally she turned to him and asked: "Do you always query strangers like this?"

"I'm sorry to pester you," he declared. "It's just that I find you quite fascinating."

And he reflected on how much their lives ran n parallel. Like her he had rushed back to Nigeria not long after getting his Ph.D. Well, not immediately —he had landed a promising position as a tenure-track assistant professor in a U.S. university, only to abandon it two years later when Nigeria finally embarked on an interlude of civilian political rule after two decades of military juntas. The clarion call from President Shagari had gone out, urging all émigrés to come home and help rebuild the country. What a short and rotten interlude it turned out to be! No sooner had they left their U.S. academic jobs and landed in Nigeria than incumbents on the ground made it clear that they were interlopers unwelcome and unappreciated. Strenuous efforts were made to oppose any and all attempts made by the new returnees to effect changes that would tidy things up. The returnees began to see that there was a method to the madness that ruled in Nigeria: It was chaos contrived to cloak and aide the rampant corruption and nepotism. "Dis no be America-o!" ("This is not the USA!") was a frequent response to their initiatives.

One by one, his generation of aspirants, who had cut their professional teeth at meaningful professional jobs in the U.S. and Europe, had slunk back abroad in disappointment and with the forlorn hope of regaining the jobs they had relinquished in their eagerness to go home. Len was among the last to leave Nigeria in that "second exodus," after spending a decade of frustration-stagnation. He could not stand the stifling mediocrity and squalor amidst oil wealth and an abundance of educated manpower. Len was reluctant to leave Nigeria a second time —because he knew that if he left he would most likely never return. But his wife had left first, going to the UK to resume her career as a nurse-midwife. After one year she moved over to the U.S. and sent for their three sons. She told Len he could stay and rot in the country that cared nothing for patriotism or merit, where jobs and favors were doled out strictly on the bases of ethnicity, and any indication of honest industry earned a person resentment. Would he, though, please send up the boys to resume their education in the States? He complied, and then prepared his mind to follow them.

So yes, he and Trish had that in common: Self-imposed exile in an alien land, a land that removed through emotional barrenness what it offered in terms of material opportunity. He looked at Trish again, seeing in her his alter ego. He did not realize he had fallen silent for quite a while, until she glanced at her watch and said,

"Goodness! I must be going. It is almost midnight, and my children must be restless by now."

"Children?" Did she have children?

"Oh, yes, she answered. I am a woman, in case you haven't noticed!"

Len recovered from the faux-pas gallantly:

"And a beautiful specimen of womanhood if I may say so! What I mean is, I haven't seen any man hovering around you. What manner of husband would leave such a splendid woman unattended? Or is he watching us from some corner and plotting how best to ambush and murder me tonight?"

Trish shook with laughter.

"Yes. Watch your back as you walk to your car," she joked. Speaking seriously she added, "My husband is in Nigeria. Now I must be leaving. It has been a pleasure meeting you, Lennox."

Before Len could pry more deeply, she got up to leave. He realized in panic that he had not even asked for her phone number. He followed her to the door and at he landing she turned and said to him.

"What about you? Are you not married?"

"Oh yes, I am," he sighed, "and she's probably wondering what has become of me!"

"You mean your wife is right here?" she queried with eyes wide open.

"Oh yes. Somewhere chatting with Tina's sister; they are such good friends. Tell me about your husband. When is he coming back, or are you going to join him in Nigeria soon?"

"Not likely," she answered, "he has been gone four years now. It is a long story. Perhaps another time."

As she turned to go down to the basement to get her children, he tugged at her sleeve. "May I have your phone number?" at which Trish opened her handbag, dug into her purse, and gave him a card. He read it and carefully inserted it into his wallet while she went down and came back up with her three children. Her son, a boy perhaps on the cusp of teenage, was carrying his baby sister, a girl about 8 years old, who was asleep. Len took the girl from him and carried her to their car, set her down, buckled her seat belt, shut the rear door and went over to the driver's side.

"Trish...may I call you Trish? You are a fascinating woman. It really is my pleasure to have met you tonight. I shall be in touch. Drive safely. Good Night!"

She patted his hand resting on the window sill and he felt something of an electric thrill. "Good Night, Len" she said, and drove off.

Lennox was in turmoil. What a woman! And to think she was unaccompanied and unafraid in the company of men. Len had almost come to the conclusion that the Nigerian woman with an independent mind was a myth. Well, was he wrong! He ambled in a leisurely manner through the thickening flurry of snowflakes and back to the house, into the party, and back to his reality: his wife. Magda was looking for him and he explained that he had escorted a woman and her children out of the party because a baby girl needed to be carried to the car. He had no need to lie to her — yet!

On their way back to Cleveland Len was uncharacteristically quiet. Mercifully, Magda was garrulous, brimming with tales from her friend, Lovina ("Vina"), Tina's older sister. Between sorties to keep the buffet tables stocked and the coolers on the mantelpiece supplied with drinks, Magda and Vina had huddled to chat about their children, plans for joint business ventures, and in general just catching up on news from home. Magda was so much a-twitter she did not notice that Len was unusually subdued and pensive, only now and then interjecting a "Yes?" "Really?" and a "Wow!" His own thoughts ran riot. Like a magnet they pointed in only one direction and he was powerless to rein them in, try as he might. They clung stubbornly to a certain remarkable lady back in Columbus: The lady with a caramel complexion, a quick and open smile, and strong opinions —like himself.

4
Is This Love?

I'm on the top of the world lookin' down on creation
And the only explanation I can find
Is the love that I've found ever since
you've been around
Your love's put me at the top of the world

ONE P.M., SUNDAY. Len had awoken a half hour earlier. Magda was off to church and would not be back for hours. Eighteen hours had passed since he met Trish, fourteen hours since he bade her Good Night, and Len was jumping out of his skin. He fished her card out of his wallet to read it again. It offered only her workplace number and other basics: Marion Correctional Institution, Tarissa A. Adoja, Librarian. But it was Sunday, so Len surmised that she must be home or at church, not in a library. On the other hand, libraries were open on Sundays, so she might be at work after all. He should try his luck. He dialed, asked for her extension, and was put on to her voice mail:

"You have reached Tarissa Adoja at the Marion Correctional Institution. Please leave a message. If your quest is urgent, dial zero to return to the operator. Thank you."

It was her voice, and it put him off! What was he to say? He hesitated and hung up. A half hour later he screwed up his courage and tried again, this time with a message prepared:

"My name is Len Obi. I am calling for Trish Adoja. Ms Adoja, we met at Dr. Ojemba's house on Saturday night. I am calling to say Hello. I hope your day is going well."

It was lame, but what else could he say in a voice message on his first call? He settled in the rocking chair by his bed and read his magazines, with Sonny Rollins' CD, *The Bridge,* playing in the background. He set the coffeepot perking and returned to his latest issue of *The Economist,* but his mind would not focus on the stories and analyses. It kept straying to the lady Trish. How ridiculous, he thought. Magda might come right in and find him moping in a stupor of total abstraction. He went down to the basement and put in some exercise on the treadmill, on which he tried to work out a couple of times each week at least, to get his money's worth before he gave it away. His doctor had advised him to get a stationary bike for indoor exercise in winter to spare his knees and ankles the pounding action of running. After a half hour he had a warm and wet feel and he showered and changed. Why didn't he think to ask Trish for her house phone number last night, he asked himself. Just then Magda came in the front door, with a crowd in tow. It was going to be a chatty afternoon with her friends. He greeted them and retired to his study. It was one long Sunday.

By the time Len woke up Monday morning he was all alone in the house. Their youngest son was off to school and their second son was away in college. Their oldest son was spending time with friends in Europe, having just graduated from engineering school in the summer of that year. Magda always left Len to his sleep every weekday morning. She worked constant day shifts now, having moved onto a managerial position in the University Hospitals of Cleveland, so that she no longer had to work the night shift she and Len hated.

Len was not a morning person. By the time he went to bed between 1 and 2 am others were half-way through their forty winks and would soon be stirring to start their new day. His favorite time for deep sleep was between 5 and 9 am; that was when he luxuriated in dream-laden slumber. His breakfast was a cup of coffee or two, and Magda always packed his lunch in a brown paper bag which she propped against the coffee pot; anywhere else and he would miss it, then leave for work without lunch. Even if it was left in plain view she still might find the packed lunch untouched, when she returned in the evening. Her sons did the same thing. She had concluded long ago that men simply did not grow up; a woman might wipe their noses today, and still have to do it for them again tomorrow.

But this morning was different from Len's usual routine. He was agog as he started the coffee pot, brushed his teeth and took a shower. Still in his bathrobe he poured a cup of coffee, and sipped it while he dialed MCI. The call was forwarded to Trish, and he began: "May I speak to Ms Trish Adoja." A lady quickly cut in with "Ms Adoja does not take personal calls while at work!" She did not hang up, but Len almost panicked. That was Trish. Surely they wouldn't fire her for saying hello? So he tried again. "My name is Lennox Obi and...."

The voice at the other end spat out: "I know who you are, Mr Obi. You left a message here yesterday, a Sunday for Chrissakes!"

Len almost jumped with a start, just like Dorothy did when, from behind a screen belching puffs of smoke and flashes of lightning, The Wizard of Oz barked at the hapless girl: "I know who you are and why you are here!"

Len hesitated, unsure how to proceed, but then a giggle came down the line. It was Trish. Len breathed again as he said to her:

"You mean so-and-so! I ought to come down and wring your neck. You nearly gave me a heart attack. And to think I spent the last day and night thinking about you!"

"Serves you right for bumping into me the other night," she cut in. They chatted briefly. He asked for her home phone number and she gave it. He committed it to memory and also wrote it down. He wasn't going to take a chance on losing it. She said she liked her job but was on the lookout for a suitable teaching position in Columbus or its vicinity because teachers enjoyed more security than did librarians, though perhaps not as much respect or peace of mind. And what did he do? Len told her he was a scientist.

"What does that mean? That you sit at a desk and just think?" Len chuckled. She really was feisty.

"Yeah. Quite a bit of that too, but most of the time I toil away in the laboratory to generate data to think about. You know what they say: Genius is one percent inspiration and ninety-nine percent perspiration."

But in whose lab did he work? Trish asked, to which Len replied that he worked at the Research Center of NASA, the National Aeronautics and Space Administration. So then, she added, he was a rocket scientist?

"Well," he cut in, "that is a misleading expression. Yes, my work is about rocket engines, but it is not as esoteric as the phrase suggests. I'm not engaged in calculating trajectories for missions to Jupiter."

Trish said she had to get back to work, and Len made a spur-of-the-moment request. "I have to come to Columbus next Saturday for a meeting of our professional society at OSU. May I stop by and see you?" Trish said she might be working that Saturday but he could call her during the week to see if her schedule changed. Len did not have any meeting coming up in Columbus or anywhere else, but he would really like to go and see Trish again even if he had to make a special trip.

"Trish, I really, really enjoy talking to you," he said and quickly ended the call to spare her having to make a response to that. His coffee was cold, and he never liked to sip coffee or tea that was not quite hot, to the point where he often re-heated his cup of coffee in the microwave oven. Right now, though, he needed no chemical stimulus. His adrenaline was gushing like a geyser. Trish was heady hormone in a woman's skin. What a feisty woman, and full of mischief too. He dressed and went off to work.

The week went by in a blur and Len resigned himself to thinking about Trish all the time. He recalled a professor in grad school, a rotund man much liked by his students, especially for his off-color jokes with which he livened up his lectures. The professor used to tell his students: "Either you get it or you don't; there are no half measures. A girl cannot be half pregnant, can she?" One day he came to class with a copy of *Readers Digest*. When he saw a student looking dopey after a half hour, he opened a page of the magazine and read a joke. It was about a man who taught a high school civics class and was concerned that too many of his students looked distracted while he taught them. To see who was alert, he asked the class, "Is it true the typical high school junior spent half of his time in class thinking of the opposite sex?" A boy in the back row looked perplexed and said, "*Half* the time? What on earth can they be thinking about the rest of the time?"

Len could not remember ever feeling like this or thinking so much about someone he had just met. He remembered how it was when he met Magda. They had also met at a party, a dancing party given by the nurses in her Biafra Army Field Ambulance detachment for the benefit of the infantry soldiers deployed in nearby camps. He and Magda partnered for a dance; they danced well together, and exchanged names. It was low-key. They exchanged visits and in time she came to spend every off-duty period with him in his barracks billet where, as a ranking captain in the Army Headquarters Intelligence Corps, he had a two-room suite.

His posting there was initially for recuperation following his discharge from combat duties after injuries that got him hospitalized for two months. Deployment in rear units of an army at war was valued by all but the most ambitious officers who were hungry for promotion. For Len, who had volunteered with gung-ho enthusiasm at the outbreak of hostilities, interrupting his highly promising education to do so, surviving the war came to seem more important than ranks and promotion once incapacitation by serious injury dampened the zeal to go out and bloody the enemy's nose. And young people had to have some fun, war or no war, so a lot of partying filled up the leisure hours. That was the era of Otis Reading and Nigeria's *Hykers* and *Fractons*.

Magda was a pretty, petite and unassuming young lady, unsophisticated but intelligent, quiet and undemanding. Soon Len proposed to Magda and she accepted. They journeyed to meet her parents where they squatted in a refugee camp, and their wedding day was set. Len planned for a grand military wedding, with a ceremonial slow-march through a tunnel of crossed swords arching overhead. He requisitioned a special Captain's uniform from a lot that came in from France by way of Gabon. But the quick end of the war in January, 1970, just days ahead of their wedding day, put an end to his grand design. Len and Magda retired to his village to wait for calm normalcy to return to people's lives. Soon Magda found a job at a rural clinic and there, on her birthday, May 1st, 1970 (a day of clear blue skies and bright sunshine) they were wedded.

Len's encounter with Magda had been a sedate sequence of events from start to the present —nothing like the raging urge he now felt for Trish. Magda could be likened to a mild and fruity dessert wine that teases one along in a gentle, agreeable seduction till the drinker is suffused with a feeling of well-being. Trish, though, was a champagne that explodes as fireworks on the senses from the moment it hits the palate. There was nothing subtle about this champagne: It just shoved Len into a heady desire for more. Unfortunately, it also got him too intoxicated to remember that champagne always left him with a huge hangover the next morning.

5
Slip-Sliding

Getting to know you, getting to feel free and easy
When I am with you, getting to know what to say
Haven't you noticed, suddenly I'm bright and breezy?
Because of all the beautiful and new things
I'm learning about you day by day.

SATURDAY DAWNED OVERCAST and dreary, with a milky canopy above and white snow on the ground. It was the kind of morning when Len loved to sleep in or, if he was not sleepy, to loll and laze about in bed. But not today: He was alert at 7 am, his mind already gone ahead to Columbus. The night before he had told Magda the fib about a meeting in Columbus and she had tried to dissuade him, knowing the forecast was for poor driving conditions. But Len said he'd be okay, that he could not afford to miss the meeting and risk being saddled with some unpleasant task that his colleagues liked to assign to absentees. To cut off further protest he had told her he would stop at Tina's home and retrieve the pots and casseroles Magda left there the weekend before. This morning she did not even stir as he got out of bed and went to get ready.

He knew his car would be snow-bound and need to be dug out. Magda's two cars, a Lexus for work and a Mercedes for church, occupied all of their two-car garage, so that his tiny Toyota Prius was always out in the cold. Len always preferred small cars; he thought that big cars were a showy menace on the roads, a wasteful obsession in America. But women seemed to like big vehicles, ignoring the fact that if enough people upgraded to large vehicles any initial advantage the SUV had quickly disappeared.

Like all ladies Magda liked fancy cars, and she liked them big too. She was profligate in her use (or non-use) of her expensive cars. She got her money's worth from her first Mercedes (110,000 miles in 8 years). But her next one, a 320-S, sat in the garage with only just 31,000 miles put on it in the 8 years before it was scrapped, hardly used, as her Lexus SUV did all the heavy lifting; and her third Mercedes, a 550-S which she used just for Church outings, was driven only about 2,000 miles a year so far —while depreciating at the amortization rate of $30,000 each year due to "age." It was the ultimate white elephant! Len, though, might excuse the love of luxury cars by a person who can afford it, but he just disliked SUVs. He thought they should be banned, or taxed as trucks since they were nearly all built on truck chassis; that would reduce their appeal.

Len dug his little car out of the snow, then went in for a brief work-out and a shower. He got dressed, picked up his book bag, and got on the road. Snow had been coming down non-stop for two days, and accumulation was quite high everywhere. Shaker Heights, the suburb in which Magda and Len lived, was right in the middle of Cleveland's snow belt. With nearly the entire northern boundary of Ohio bathed by Lake Erie, from Ashtabula in the north-east to Toledo in the north-west, winter weather in northern Ohio is dominated by the south-easterly sweep of cold fronts from Canada and Alaska down over Lake Erie. The "lake effect," as it was called, caused moisture laden clouds coming down from Canada to be lofted over the warmer body of the lake and then dumped on the landmass just past, on the South side of the lake. Shaker Heights was right in the middle of that dumping ground and always got several times the average snowfall registered by most other Cleveland suburbs each winter.

Snow accumulation on the streets looked fearsome, but Len knew it would thin out when he hit the highway —or so he hoped. His Prius handled well in snow and, in any case, Len prided himself on his dexterity when driving on snow-bound roads. During his days as a graduate student Len was the go-for person that Magda's friends begged to run errands for them when the roads got laden with snow. In those days, he drove a stick-shift Toyota Corona and his trick was to shift to higher gears early to lessen traction, and roll right over the snow.

But ice was different, and it always scared Len. Snow drifts on the open planes of Ohio were another concern when he was on the highway. To get to Marion by lunchtime he decided to leave home at 9 am. Today he took his time because he had left home early. The wind was mild and soon the sky opened up, bright and blue. Ella Fitzgerald's naughty song sprang to his lips:

> "It's a lovely day today
> So whatever you've got to do
> I'd be so happy to be doing it with you...."

It was nearly noon when he pulled up at the prison. He called and Trish came out. He invited her to lunch and she consented, but reminded him she was at work and could not be gone too long. He spent another half hour reading a magazine while she went back to clear her desk before going out for lunch. He always carried his copy of the Economist, Smithsonian, or National Geographic with him in case he had to sit and wait for anything. Finally she came out with her handbag.

They got into his car. He started it, then went out to clean the windows of snow. As they rolled off, she said: "It is a major effort to come so far in this weather, and all for some meeting?" Len looked sheepish as he told her there was no meeting: He had made it up just to see her. "A major effort it is," she repeated and looked at him quizzically. "Do you play hooky from home often?" Len looked wounded. "Yeah," he replied, "I risk my life in the snow to go after every woman I meet once." Trish's delightful laughter rang out, her head tossed back and her left arm swept over her braids which were not covered this time. She directed him to a little restaurant where they could get clam chowder, which he said was just the thing to chase away chills in that kind of weather.

Over lunch Len grilled her: about her husband, her parents, her siblings, her past, and her children. Again Trish answered without hesitation. Hers was an open soul which seemed to hold nothing secret. On this score, too, she was Len's kindred spirit: He was not given to keeping secrets. He asked Trish so many questions she had no chance to put in any of her own. One hour later she asked him to take her back to work. "Next time," she said with the endearing twinkle in her eye, "next time it will be my turn to ask the questions, Len."

To make up to Magda for the fib about his meeting in Columbus, Len went to the home of Cyril Ojemba and rang the bell. Nobody was home, so he stuck his card between door and frame and set out for home. He arrived around 7 pm and he called Trish at her home. She said it had taken her an hour and a half to get home, twice the usual time because she had to creep along due to the bad roads. On a whim he asked her what she would do if she had got stranded on the road and she said she would call a friend. Did she have Triple-A coverage? She said yes, but she hadn't attended to it for a long time now and was not sure it was still current. Len decided to check that out. He called Triple-A and was told that Ms Adoja's coverage had lapsed and needed to be renewed. It was rash of him to contemplate giving her a gift after their first date, and an impromptu date at that. But he recoiled to think she might get stranded some cold night in the middle of nowhere. He renewed her AAA road-side coverage right then and called her to tell her that her coverage was now current. Trish was touched by the gesture and likened it to "something my dad would do." Len felt 10 feet tall!

Len got into the habit of calling Trish every day to find out how she was doing and to ask if she needed anything. He called around 6 pm each day, when Trish was at home and Magda was not yet back. (A frequent shopper, Magda always detoured to some shop or another.) "I am fine," Trish always assured him, but the calls started lasting longer and, after a week, she started calling him back. They would spend hours chattering about nothing, while his heart beat a tattoo in his chest. A typical session consisted of reciting childhood ditties and doggerels, of which they both had plenty from early childhood education. She matched him poem for poem and song for song; their repertoires were nearly the same because they were both products of the same Catholic school system back in Nigeria. Those were weekend calls made from his home. Len worried that Magda would discover the marathon calls, so he bought prepaid phone cards for his calls to Trish. He gave Trish the access codes so she could use the same cards to call him back. They talked so much that each $20.00 card often hardly lasted a week.

On weekdays she called him each evening at his NASA office around 10 pm; it was her usual bedtime and an hour when, she knew, he was settled in his office and writing up the result of the day's experiments preparatory for leaving the lab at midnight to go home. She called just to say "Good Night, Len. I'm in bed." Len would softly croon a lullaby or a nursery song to her, such as "My Bonny Is Over the Ocean" or some bowdlerized version of it. When she bought a house, moved in, and complained that large flocks of birds in a big tree behind her house woke her up too early each morning with their clamor, Len would sing her one of his two springtime songs, "Mockingbird Hill," or Percy Granger's "English Country Garden."

His voice was no better than Satchmo's but Trish never complained about that. Sometimes by the time Len finished singing she was already gone to dreamland. He knew because if he called her back soon enough he got a busy tone indicating that she had fallen asleep without replacing her bedside phone on its cradle. On days when Len worked through the night (usually preparing some papers for publication or a research proposal for funding) he called Trish at 4 am before retiring to bed. He was her alarm clock, since she always made an early start to her day.

They began to exchange their love vows daily, then several times a day. To avoid disrupting each other's work or activities with constant and long conversations they devised a simple code to stand for "I love you": Tapping "123" on the keypad. When he got impatient for her reply he prefixed the code with a zero: 0123 meant "I love you not," and that invariably elicited her immediate response. "What did I do now?" she would plead with him.

Trish told Len how wonderful it was to be partially woken in the middle of the night by a metallic 123123 clacking in the phone on the pillow beside her ear. Once, she put it this way: "The sublime caress of such a message coming in at 2 am cannot be adequately expressed. One has to experience it to appreciate it. Suddenly you know you are not alone, that you are loved —that you are in his thoughts at that moment. You roll over and plunge more deeply into slumber. Nothing beats knowing that you are loved." Len could not agree more. "Nothing Pass Love" (a pidgin English translation of that last sentence of Trish) became a motto which Len emblazoned on his personal letterhead.

Then he began writing to her, and to receive her replies he rented a post box at a nearby post office. Each letter to her started with quotes of a stanza or two from a song and ended with one. Among his favorites, besides his beloved jazz, were Jim Reeves, The Carpenters, The Everly Brothers, Simon and Garfunkel. Each time she got his letter she would ring him immediately and start singing the opening song in that letter. Len would join in, and fumble her off the song because he always sang off-key, which made Trish stop, giggle, and then resume with a note closer to his. Or they sang school songs and church hymns, in Latin, English, or Igbo (Len's childhood vernacular), or he recited for her the old nursery school rhymes and doggerels he loved, such as James Stevens' "Little Things":

> Little things that run and quail and die in silence and despair
> Little things that fight and fail and fall on sea and earth and air....

> Or Cecil Spring Rice's "I Vow to Thee, My Country":
> I vow to thee my country, all earthly things above
> Entire and whole and perfect, the service of my love....

Or perhaps their favorite song, which he had adapted to their special circumstances:

> My bonny lives down in Ohio
> My bonny is waiting for me
> My bonny lives down in Columbus
> Go bring up my bonny to me.

They mostly sang cheerful tunes of happy childhood, but much later in their relationship, when cruel fate began to deal Trish a succession of blows with cascading bereavements (her father, her son, her brother, her sister) and her mood nosed down to somber levels, she liked to hear Len sing mellow Christian songs:

Whispering Hope,
It Is No Secret What God Can Do,
How Great Thou Art,
Brighten the Corner Where You Are,
Bianu Solum.

The last one was a song in *Igbo*, sung to the accompaniment of drums during the dolorous vigil of Good Friday in rural parishes that kept such vigils. The percussion rhythm always got people to their feet, singing and clapping, or at least tapping their feet and nodding heir heads. The very idea was to wake up those children and the elderly who had dozed off during the long chronicling of the *Stations of the Cross* or the equally interminable recitation of the *Litany*. The lyrics simply called the faithful to come and join in weeping to commemo-rate the crucifixion of Jesus Christ:

Bianu solum, solum, solum ("Come, come, come with me")

Bianu solum bey akwa nwa-oge ("Come ye all and mourn with me a while")

Zukobanu ka anyi bey akwa ("Gather ye all and let us weep")

Akpogbulu Yesu Nna anyi. ("They crucified Jesus our Lord").

The dancing congregants at the vigil are, of course, not rejoicing that Jesus was crucified. They are re-enacting a time-honored Igbo funeral ritual. Igbos bury their beloved with song and dance amidst all the wailing and mourning, a bit like a New Orleans jazz funeral. Dancing on the fresh grave of the beloved serves to relieve the gloom and, especially, to compact the grave and prevent it from disquieting cavitation as the contents settle with time and rain.

Some of the songs Len and Trish sang appealed to her for religious reasons, especially the Latin songs and the solemn songs in Igbo. To Len they were just happy, moving childhood ditties, but for Trish they evoked feelings of devoutness because she was an active Catholic. She never razzed him about his apostasy and, whenever he came to spend a weekend, she learned to let him sleep while she went to Saturday choir practice and to Mass on Sunday. It was Len who brought up the topic of religion now and then, especially when Trish told him he missed his calling as a priest. Her message to him was always the same: "You should really believe in a cause that's bigger than yourself," to which Len replied that he believed in family, community, country, and so forth, all of which were causes bigger than he. What he wouldn't do anymore was believe in supernatural gobbledygook and crazy fairy tales; he had shed that whole bag of superstition right with his high school uniform upon exit from teenage.

"Why then do you keep singing all the Christian songs?" she persisted.

"For the same reason that I sing 'Follow the Yellow Brick Road,' and 'Santa Claus Is Coming to Town.' They are songs I like. Singing them does not make me a believer. And when I sing 'The Internationale' it does not mean I am a communist. A song is a song and I like good songs." They never went further than that over the matter of belief versus reason. In that regard Trish was exactly like Magda: she left Len alone in his unbelief.

Len knew no joy that surpassed the thrill of opening Trish's letters or hearing her voice on the phone. Slowly and without being conscious of it, Lennox was completely reeled in over his head. He was ordinarily a cautious man, almost old-fashioned, one might say.

Not that he was shy to talk to women; on the contrary, he naturally sought out ladies at parties and gatherings to chat up in small talk or to engage in serious discourse because he often found them more interesting than men. But when he chatted with a woman he was cautious not to incite rebuff by a poor choice of words that could convey the impression of amorous interest. However, with this wonderful woman Trish he had absolutely no inhibitions. He felt like the proverbial frog in a hot tub. If you threw a frog into hot water it would leap right out, it was said; but if you put it in lukewarm water and slowly raised the temperature the frog would relax until it got cooked. Len Obi was getting cooked.

At the end of spring thaw Len resumed his happy pastime of refereeing in the Youth Soccer program organized by the US Soccer Federation across Ohio and beyond. Starting in the early 1990s when he had just returned to Ohio with his family, Len answered the call for adults who were knowledgeable about the rules of soccer to help in building up the youth soccer program. He got his FIFA license after due examination, USSF being an affiliate of the International Federation of Football Associations, or "FIFA" as the French acronym rendered it. One year after obtaining his license Len was persuaded to become certified in the High School Soccer program of northeast Ohio as well. It was a more rigorous league, established for older boys and girls, unlike youth soccer which mostly catered to pre-teen aspirants to the game.

In terms of seriousness high school "varsity" soccer was on par with college soccer, with which he had a pleasant association back in his early professional days. The very first year he started his academic career as an assistant professor of engineering in the University of Florida, Len was pressed into service as coach of the university's female soccer team, the "Lady Gators," turning down their offer to pay him small honoraria when he realized those stipends would have to come from the dues paid by the players. The Gators played in college conferences that included Mississippi, Louisiana, and Georgia. Soon Lennox was having a great time, traveling with the Gators team all over the southern states and coaching them twice a week on the UF campus. The university had a tradition of promoting fun in the sunshine of Florida, and Len found time to audit courses in bartending, scuba diving, and sky diving, in addition to his engagement as informal soccer coach.

Now in Ohio Len had a déjà-vu feeling as he plunged eagerly into youth and high school soccer. Between those two league engagements Len had enough and more to absorb all his leisure hours from spring to fall each year. During that interval his weekends were not his own, and he would be found on the fields of soccer as early as 7 am on Saturdays and Sundays, pooped and dirty but enjoying himself. When Len worked weekday games he changed into his referee's uniform right in his office at NASA, and soon his colleagues started teasing him about it. Since many faculty members from universities in the U.S. and outside came to NASA to conduct funded research projects during summer and many of them liked to play soccer for relaxation, they soon organized soccer tournaments at NASA too, and Len found himself refereeing those as well.

Len grew up with soccer, as every Nigerian male child of his generation did, but when he got into high school he found there were many boys with better skills, so he never had a chance to play for his school. The most he did in high school was play for his House. His Catholic high school housed the students in dormitories, each "House" named for a saint. Len had played for St. Thomas House but was never called to play for the high school. This adult foray into youth soccer in Ohio gave him a precious opportunity to play "The Beautiful Game" once again, if only by proxy. Because of his experience of actually playing the game in his youth, an advantage his colleagues in the U.S. Youth Soccer program seemed to lack, Len rose in the ranks of licensed referees and was in demand to do the more challenging games, such as those of the travel leagues. He had a ball every weekend (in more ways than one), as well as Tuesdays and Wednesdays if he could find time to work a game or two in the afternoon. He called Trish on his way to or from games, every chance he got, and regaled her with tales of the contests, the tantrums of "Soccer Moms," and his clashes with *Prima Donna* coaches.

Then tournament season arrived. It began in May each year. Len used to limit himself to the really serious tournaments, particularly those that attracted teams from outside the U.S., from Canada and Europe. But this year he kept scanning the schedules for tournaments that were held in central and southern Ohio, games that would offer him the chance to divert his itinerary via Columbus. Len identified quite a few each month of the season and he signed up for all he could. Qualified referees being hard to find, he was in much demand. A certain Ramada Inn in North Columbus became his regular haunt where he got the best rooms, with ready upgrades to a suite for the price of a double. He paid for his room but Trish kept him stocked with cooked meals, as well as roasted peanuts, his favorite snacks.

Len learned that the most delightful thing about Trish was that she was down-to-earth: She did not play hard-to-get. Len grew up quite shy about chasing women because he was sensitive to the slights a man often got for his efforts. During his teenage, Len's discerning relatives were quick to notice that reserved attitude of his towards girls. His cousin, a girl two years older, tried a couple of times to "hook him up" with one classmate of hers or the other, but nothing came of it, as Len did not show enthusiasm.

Once, after his cousin tried to talk up one of her classmates and Len sat quietly listening, she asked, "Are you not interested in girls?" In his adult years later in the U.S. that would have been a loaded question, but during his teenage years, questions of sexual preference did not occur to anybody. A boy did not have sexual interest in other boys any more than he might have had in a goat or a cow! Len told his cousin it was not due to a lack of interest: He did think about girls quite a bit but he hadn't the stomach for their hard-to-get antics. If a girl liked him she should just come out with it, instead of pretending he was unworthy of her attention as most girls did.

Len was never impressed with the conventional notion that a girl was valuable or virtuous just because she played hard to get. And later, as a young adult in college in Cairo, he was perplexed by the obsession of Arab people with the chastity of their daughters as the main determinant of a family's honor. That deadly obsession, he was told by gloating American young men who had tasted the Arab girls, spawned a brisk but illicit business by foreign doctors in the repair of breached hymens. How totally gross! When Len joined the *American Atheists* organization and read attendant scholarly literature, he was saddened to learn how superstition (*aka* "religion") had utterly ruined the sex lives of a majority of women down the ages. Religious people and their gods seemed absolutely to hate the notion of humans having and kind of fun or pleasure: pain, yes! But pleasure, no! That was perhaps the main factor that made girls in his youth play hard-to-get.

Sometimes he heard his sister and cousin sigh and worry that he was so innocent regarding women that he was liable to get too close to a bad woman and get scorched. Those two young ladies were a couple of years older and perhaps a little wiser than Len, but they were of the opposite sex and Len knew nothing of the mind set of their gender. He didn't take their worries to heart. Whenever he approached a girl he feared more about being rebuffed than about her character. And Len never asked a girl more than once for a first date: If rebuffed the first time, he did not return for a second chance. His sister and cousin predicted that he would marry the first girl who gave him time of day —and that's almost exactly what occurred with Magda.

Clearly the same was going to happen with Trish. Gorgeous as Trish was of mind and body, she did not make Len have to chase her, most likely because she was as attracted to him as he was to her, which meant Len had no trouble getting Trish to spend increasing amounts of time with him in his hotel. What's more, she brought him cooked meals knowing he was not much for eating restaurant foods. The next several years were definitely the best of his life. The most difficult moments came when he had to tear himself away from Trish and incline his reluctant footsteps northwards to Cleveland. On several occasions Len broke down and cried softly at the prospect of leaving her again to return to his life in Cleveland. On one such occasion he said,

"I believe in reincarnation, and in my next life I want you to be the very first woman I will see when I open my eyes for the first time."

They both thought about that, then she said: "But that means I shall be your mother!" and they burst out laughing hilariously.

He never had a dull moment with Trish. She fulfilled his fondest desire for a woman who could meet him on the intellectual level as on the physical and emotional levels. If ever a woman was specially made for a man, Trish was made for me, Len told himself time and again. With Trish Len felt no need to pretend to be anything or anyone other than himself. There never were any miscues between them; he could guess her thought and she could figure out his. With Trish, as with Len, what you saw was what you got because it was all there was: no dark corners, no kinks, no secrets, no needless guilt.

Still, Len struggled to muster courage and tell Magda of this woman who now held a lien on his heart. But how does a man tell his good wife of three decades that he had fallen in love with another woman? How did one set about getting a divorce? People in America did it with so much apparent ease, but nobody in Len's family had ever got a divorce. How was he to explain it to his friends, to rearrange his life away from those of his friends who would not approve? More importantly, how could he inflict such hurt on Magda who was a good wife? Len dithered, and as he did so the opportunity was lost because the imperatives of duty sucked him into an emergency that required him to come full-tilt to the aid of his family.

6
Family Problem

When it's time to cry we can cry together
Know that I'll be with you,
With you through whatever
When the times get rough
Know that I will be right by your side

ONE OF LEN'S sons was in dire straits and the situation demanded all of his attention and energy. Their third son was the one born at a time when Len and Magda both had achieved the means and the status to secure the family in middle-class comfort. He had everything going for him, unlike his older brothers who were born during the years when the family struggled because Magda and Len were both students. But this son's passage through the cataracts of the typical American school system became fraught with problems that soaked up both Magda's and Len's attention.

When Len left his university in Nigeria on a sabbatical leave of absence to join his family in the U.S., Magda and the boys lived in upstate New York while he resided in Cleveland. Len used to embark on the ten-hour drive every fortnight to visit them. Some claimed it was an eight-hour drive but Len was never able to make it in less than ten hours. The same friends also insisted that Chicago was only four to five hours away, whereas Len took the better part of six hours to reach the Windy City. He didn't like driving fast, especially because he often began to nod off after a couple of hours and needed to pull over and nap a bit —at which point the sleep would vanish from his eyes. Since Magda's profession was eminently transferable anywhere in the world, and she had held an Ohio nursing license anyway, Len convinced her to move to Cleveland. Soon she joined the University Hospitals of Cleveland.

Before Magda and the boys moved to Ohio, Len searched for a good school for the boys, bearing in mind that Cleveland was reported as the second most racially polarized city in the U.S. He found out that the high school of a suburb adjoining NASA and the airport was recently rated among the top-ten schools of excellence in the U.S. And since it was in close proximity to such cosmopolitan establishments as NASA and an international airport, Len supposed the schools in that city would have a racially mixed, balanced, and tolerant school body. But that was too important to leave to supposition, so he phoned the local chapter of NAACP to ask about racial harmony in the schools of the city where he intended to settle his family. He was told there were no untoward reports in the NAACP records, so Len enrolled his two younger sons in the middle school and high school, respectively, having bought a home in that city. His eldest son was in New Jersey, continuing the college education he had started at the precocious age of fifteen years in the flagship University of Nigeria, Nsukka.

It wasn't long before Len and Magda found that the reputed placidity of their community was illusory. Their sons were trailed all over by the city police outside of school hours and constantly stopped and asked "Who are you, and what are you doing?" even when in the company of white children who lived in their neighborhood —especially during weekend school games. Knowing that the police liked to operate by intimidation as a deterrent, Len gave his sons a simple brief: Always be law-abiding and do nothing to attract the interest of the police. But if they got harassed they should stand their ground. When his middle son was shoved into a squad car and taken to the police station just for talking back to a policeman, Len wrote a pointed letter to the city's Chief of Police, and the police harassment eased considerably.

But more trouble soon reared its head inside his sons' schools. The boys were teased and taunted, and as a result they got into altercations and fights. The fallout from one fracas finally moved Magda and Len to transfer their youngest to a local parochial school. But that did not improve matters, since the parochial schools were not boarding schools and pooled their students from the same catchment area as public schools in their neighborhoods. So Magda and Len decided to move the family out to a suburb on the East side of Cleveland where the racial mix was more balanced and segregation was more by income than by race or ethnic origin. But being of big stature and having acquired a reputation for not backing down to racial intimidation, the boy was viewed by his peers as a leader, and was soon drawn into groups that were more interested in macho social dynamics than in academic pursuits. Len and Magda started having to order him not to bring this girl or that boy to their home.

But it seemed that the damage had already been done. Their son seemed to prefer rough company. Matters came to a head one day when Len was summoned to the police station and given the bad news that the boy was in custody on charges of selling illegal drugs. "Drugs?!" Len exploded. "I am not sure I could recognize an illegal drug if it hit me in the face!" They told him the boy was caught on video selling marijuana to an undercover agent. Much later, after the hubbub subsided and Magda asked her son to level with her: Did he really try to sell the weed? He admitted it and explained it was just a lark to secure his initiation into a cult of braves, but the "buyer" turned out to be really a cop. "Mom, he looked so much like a genuine *Rastaman*. I would never have guessed he was a cop!"

It was the oldest trick in covert surveillance: Using the most authentic-looking character to pose as a ragamuffin and entrap people suspected to harbor criminal intent. A seasoned veteran of shady deals might have seen through the too-perfect ruse, but Len's boy was a greenhorn and he fell right into the trap. They denied him bail and Len went home filled with rage and chagrin. He got a lawyer, who told him the cops were perhaps not after his son; in fact it was likely they would let the boy go if he just divulged the name of his supplier. But the lawyer cautioned that if it were his own son he would not encourage the boy to do as the cops urged. The boy's gang handlers must have warned him that if he disclosed the identity of his sources he would go from initiation to termination in no time at all.

At the arraignment, when Len's son was led into the court room, in handcuffs and wearing the orange jumpsuit of the County Jail, Magda burst into tears and leaned on Len's shoulder. "My baby! Just look at my baby!" she moaned. The boy looked over at Magda and hissed: "Mom, Be strong!" But everyone could see it was mere bravado, and Magda did not buy it. She collapsed totally onto Len's laps and wailed. The judge gave her a baleful glance before resuming his impassive and inscrutable expression intended to signal his unemotional involvement in the proceedings.

Judge Tim McGinty's reputation preceded him: He was known to be tough judge, due to his strict adherence to the prevailing conservative viewpoint that harsh sentences were the best deterrent to crime. When Len asked about him before the hearing, he thought all was lost. But the judge belied his reputation and surprised them. It was only a hearing and not the trial yet, so he did his best to appear fatherly. After all, the accused was still a minor. The judge asked Len where he worked, and then he posed a few pointed questions about some top NASA brass he knew, no doubt to ascertain that Len did indeed work for NASA. That seemed to let some air out of the overinflated wheels of justice.

Before the hearing, the lawyer Len and Magda hired to defend their son leveled with them. Their son was caught dead-to-rights on video and voice tape, and witnesses were credible. His best hope was to be presented as a victim of both peer pressure and dependence on the weed himself rather than a drug pusher. Since he was a juvenile chances were good that he could be remanded to the half-jail facility in a nearby city, essentially a detoxification and rehabilitation center. That ploy worked. Two days after the hearing Len and Magda were delighted that their son was being transferred to the rehab facility on an indeterminate confinement until certified fit for release. The lawyer assured them the average residence time in that center for juveniles in similar circumstances was a few months; but if there was a relapse or any other kind of bad behavior, an inmate could be returned to court and perhaps be sentenced to more draconian incarceration. That worried Magda.

A devout "Born-Again" ex-Catholic and presently a deaconess of her charismatic Pentecostal congregation, Magda practically lived on her knees throughout that anxious season. She and Len went to visit their son each weekend, mostly on Sundays, taking food to him as well as materials that, they learned later, never reached him. The possibility of his returning to court and on to a proper jail hung on Len and Magda like the *Sword of Damocles*. Night after night Len would be woken from sleep by soft singing coming from behind closed door:

"Amara Chineke agaghi ekwe k'ihere me'm," (God's compassion will not let me be shamed.)

It was a popular song of charismatic churches in Len's homeland. Magda was born into a different ethnic group than Len but, like most city-bred Nigerian children, she grew up fluent in several of Nigeria's major languages, including Igbo, because Igbos were a dominant resident group in many of Nigeria's northern cities, where Magda was born. In addition, Magda spoke four other Nigerian languages including Hausa, Efik, Umon, and Yoruba. Stealing into their master bathroom on tiptoes, Len would see his wife on her hands and knees, covered in tears and begging God to spare her son and return him to the loving fold of his family.

"Lord, how am I to tell my people that my son, Obianuju (one born at a time of prosperity) is in jail? Lord, better take my life before I live to see such humiliation. You are my Lord, God. I place all my trust in you," Magda prayed, through her tears. She was in distress.

Her supplication reminded Len of his days as an altar boy, and the *Introit* recitation of a lament from Psalm 42 at the start of Mass: "Quia tu es Deus meus, fortitudo mea; quare me repulisti et quare, tristis in cedo, dum affligit me inimicus?" *("Because you are my God, my strength....")* Even the cynical heart of atheist Lennox Obi melted before the fervor that was gushing from his distraught wife, and he found himself squatting down beside her on the bathroom floor to console her and reassure her that all would be well. That went on night after night. If only, Len thought, children knew how much pain their thoughtless deeds inflicted on their poor mothers!

Len realized that this was no time to compound his family's misery by confessing his own peccadilloes, which seemed frivolous in comparison. Trish must wait while Len tried to salvage his family and see Magda and their son back on firm ground. He told Trish so in an emotional session when he drove down to Columbus with the cryptic forewarning to Trish: "I need to talk to you, honey!"

7
Freefall

I belong to another, whose arms are grown cold
But I promised forever to have and to hold
For I mustn't want you, but darling I do
Please help me I am falling in love with you.

IF ONLY TRISH hadn't been so patient and accommodating (rather like Magda herself) Len might have taken the plunge early gone over to Trish. But she was understanding and complacent. Len was an unconventional person, an iconoclast, and if he thought about it he would see no reason why a marriage proposal must flow in only one direction, from man to woman. In fact, before Len met Magda he had nearly married a girl who proposed to him, an impulsive and vivacious medical student similar in intellect and temperament to Trish. Len met her just as the Nigerian civil war erupted and disrupted everybody's education. While on furlough from combat duties he traveled a long distance to see her. He was billeted for the weekend at a comfy Officers' Mess in the town where she resided.

She came to visit Len in his digs at the mess quarters. On impulse she said to Len, "Let's get married." Len agreed and, since his valet had not accompanied him on that tip, Len started to iron his uniform so they could go and see the chaplain for arrangements. But a silly argument came up and both of them got animated, youth being always impetuous. Her waving arm hit the ironing board, knocking the hot iron over. As she tried to grab it, it burned a welt on the back of her hand. The incident ended any thought of immediate marriage, but they did remain friends. Yes, she had proposed to Len in the 1960s, and now in the U.S. in the twenty-first century, it did not occur to Len that a progressive woman like Trish could not propose marriage to a man she loved. It's not that he insisted a lady should be the one to propose, but surely a woman, who really desired marriage to a man she loved, could broach the topic and push the agenda. Trish id not; perhaps it never occurred to her.

It was not that Len waited as a matter of principle for Trish to propose to him. He had simply become complacent between his traditional view of his marital obligations on one hand, and Trish's seeming acquiescence in his complacency on the other hand. If Trish had proposed to Len at any time he would have jumped to it; and if she had leaned on him to propose, he would have done that as well. Len needed a nudge to move him from his comfortable dead-center perch between Trish and Magda, but that pull was not coming from Trish, and Magda seemed unwilling to push him, either. In the final analysis, of course, it was Len who failed everybody through his hesitation, and he was to be the one who suffered most painfully for that failure.

After Len told Trish the full story of his son's predicament she offered nothing but warmth and affection, saying: "All in good time, honey." She shook Len out of his somber mood over his son by hugging him and rocking him until they both fell asleep in each-others arms, to the strain of Sonny Rollins' "Finest Hour" CD playing repeat loops in the bedside *Bose* unit that was his third birthday present to Trish. As Dizzie Gillespie worked his mischievous lyrics of "Sunny Side of the Street" on that CD Len sank slowly into a refreshing sleep. Afterwards, each time he heard that song he remembered that evening. Thus did he miss a good chance to do what his heart told him to do. There would be many such missed opportunities.

The next morning Len woke up feeling a sublime relief after a restful night of magical dreams about weightless flight, the like of which he used to experience as a child. One moment he was running away from an unseen menace, and in the next he raised his arms and was lofted into air, exhilarated! Trish's no-nonsense bed was conducive to deep sleep, with its firm mattress on a wooden platform. It was the exact same kind of platform bed with extra-firm mattress that Len had in his home, for himself and everybody else in his household. Nobody in his house ever woke up with any kind of ache in the back, such Len sometimes felt after sleeping on a "luxury" bed in many a hotel. This was one more thing he and Trish had in common: preference for firm support while sleeping.

When Len stirred in the morning Trish's gaze was upon him. He found her eyes; smiled back, and kissed her nice and soft on the dimple in her right cheek. She stroked his chest, pursed her lips, and softly said, "What a gentleman you are! We were both exhausted after the day's struggles and you chose to go it easy. Thank you."

Len understood what she meant: he had not tried to make love to Trish for a nightcap; he had instead dissolved happily into slumber. He now searched her face as she said that, to see if there was a hint of disappointment. Was that her way of telling him she had wanted more than he gave? He thought about it, but all he could find on her face was a happy smile and relaxed satisfaction. It was true they were both pooped after a long day that started early because her appointment at the Regional Office of the US Immigration and Naturalization said 9 am, and it was a two-hour drive from Columbus to Cincinnati. And upon arrival they had spent all morning in the crowded and tense lounge of the INS shifting on the hard bench and waiting for her turn to be called. The immigration officials, with their air of importance and condescension shut the counters for lunch without the courtesy of telling the crowd what was afoot. They reopened after 1 pm and, after another hour passed, Trish was called in for her interview. All went well with her Naturalization process, she told Len; a letter would come to notify her of the date, time, and venue for the ceremony admitting her to U.S. citizenship.

And then followed a race to beat rush-hour traffic exiting Cincinnati, make it to Columbus in two hours to get Trish home before her daughters became hungry. Half-way home they hit a big chunk of truck tire blown off a semi-trailer and lying across two lanes. Hemmed in between a car and a pick-up truck speeding along in the lanes on either side of them, they could not swerve to avoid the debris. Len braked hard but the impact hit the underside of their car with a loud thump and a sustained rumble, nearly knocking them out of their lane. But the car showed no sign of any disabling damage and they carried on, tentatively at first and then more swiftly home. He softly began to hum a tune, a Beatles' number that belted out a steady rhythm to match the pace of highway driving: "Obladi oblada."

Like Molly in that song, Trish's fingers sought Len's and interlaced through them firmly, as she joined in the refrain: "Obladi oblada life goes on bla, la-la how the life goes on…" This was bliss. Even the car seemed to hum along happily in time, and soon they arrived home. It was after dinner that Len told her the full story of his son's predicament. Neither of them had stamina left for love making; they had both crashed in each-other's arms and slept until morning.

Len had not really thought of love-making at all, so it was not that he made a special effort to spare her a hard labor of love. He only did what came naturally to him. Never considering himself a stud, his main pleasure in life came from sleeping long hours. And he would just as soon cuddle with the woman he loved and go to sleep and feel satisfied with no thought of sex. His love for Trish was not predicated on sex; it was more like a meeting of the minds. Sex is ballyhooed, but it really is cheap as food, a commodity one can get any time, and for no more money than the cost of a good dinner.

Nevertheless, Len sometimes wondered whether Trish might eventually tire of his low sex drive. Magda had resigned herself to it, but not without an occasional teasing remark about her colleagues who bragged about getting frequent action and others who listened with envy to such bragging. But when Len did make love he was satisfied with doing it just once, and slowly, rather than engaging in the kind of all-night frenzy his friends boasted about. Whenever he discussed that propensity of his with his friends, especially his buddy Henry, they thought he was nuts to prefer sleep over sex. They made Len feel inadequate because of his moderation, so he would say to them: "Look, if you're still banging away at it after one or two rounds, then you really are not getting satisfied; you are not doing it right. Good sex is the greatest release there is. Do it right, and you are spent: happy! Take it nice and slow, man. Let your mind do the work, and you don't need second helpings."

Len believed that he got more satisfaction from sex than many other men who talked about pumping away all night. Perhaps flogging it all night was what some women wanted —he could not speak for them. But as a man he knew he got better performance by engaging his mind rather than just his mechanical equipment as the primary tool of love-making. That required slow and deliberate reciprocation rather than furious piston action. Luring one's mind into participation produced a richer climax. But for that technique to work the man and his partner needed to act in tandem, letting the muscles of their loins find coordination in unison. An impatient and wriggly partner only foiled the resonance. Len was convinced that his method of slow and hypnotically deliberate reciprocation was best.

He theorized that the method he proposed would especially benefit those women who were born into conservative and traditional African societies. Most such women had their equipment cruelly truncated in infancy by the prevalent but deplorable practice of clitorectomy, most often just days after being born. Just about the time a baby girl got a name she lost her clitoris. For women in that category, piston pumping was insufficient stimulation towards a rich climax because penile friction against the clitoris was known to be a major inducement to orgasm.

Len was a scientist and, before that, had been a combat-forged army officer. Both occupations conditioned him to plan his experiments as well as their execution in advance. In consequence, he knew that the desired coordination between man and woman during sexual intercourse was best achieved after discussing the process ahead of time. He had seen dogs try to part in mid-coitus when embarrassed humans threw rocks at them to stop the action. Since dogs do not think, they tried to separate quickly with a tug-of-war, yelping in pain because the penile bone is dogs made mechanical separation difficult when in full erection. But humans do think and there is no reason why the all important process of sexual intercourse should not be discussed and agreed in advance between partners. As anthropologist Margaret Mead seminal 1928 book, *Coming of Age in Samoa*, demonstrated, our fumbling furtiveness and guilt over sex is inculcated by nurture rather than inborn in nature. In modern times our callow attitude to sex is mostly conditioned by parents who were influenced by superstition (or religion).

But most women, especially the same ones who might benefit most from such deliberation due to their guilt feelings about enjoyment of sex, were usually uncomfortable talking about the details of intercourse. They would rather do it, however ifeffiently, than talk about it. That was a sad fact of traditional African practice which, unfortunately had been greatly reinforced by the "civilization" brought into Africa by neurotic European missionaries who set out to scorch the joy of sex everywhere they went because, apparently, their god simply hated the idea of recreational sex. To them sex was only for procreation. And yet when modern science provided a means to implement their theory, to bypass joy and just achieve procreation in-vitro, the same inconsistent women and men of religion objected vociferously! Their beliefs are those of out-and-out troglodytes. There was in it also an element of misery loving company. Catholic priests and nuns are enjoined by their vows of "perpetual chastity" to abjure sex; why should they not repress it in everyone else?

So, Len wondered whether he should explain those views of his to Trish. Should he tell her that merely kissing and cuddling with her gave him nearly as much satisfaction as intercourse? Or that, once dissipated in a good orgasm, he needed a few days to recharge his system before he could put it to work again. Or should he let her go on thinking his seeming forbearance last night was due to chivalry, to his concern not to overtax her. Well, she would find out for herself as time went by, he decided. But just as he wavered, she saved him the trouble by jumping out of bed and into her domestic morning routine. In no time the hazelnut aroma of her coffee suffused the house. It was time to get up.

It was a Friday morning but Trish had arranged to take that day off work, intuiting that Len would want to spend as much time as possible with her. But when he got to her kitchen he found she had gone out to buy groceries, leaving him a note on the coffee pot saying she would be back soon. He stepped down to the basement and busied himself with a little workout on the indoor elliptical exercise bicycle he recently bought her as a present when she mentioned the difficulty of keeping fit in winter weather. It creaked and groaned as he got on it; some bolts were loose. Trish's robust son was flogging the machine to death. Len went to his car, brought down his big tool box, got out the Allen wrenches and tightened the loose joints. While he was at it he applied light, penetrating machine oil to the joints and worked in some motion till the machine no longer squeaked.

Len liked to fix household appliances, to the delight of Magda, who proudly told her friends that Len was handy about the house. But it was a skill that had not come easily to Len, or to most people who grew up in developing countries where household machines were a rare luxury. He had picked it up in graduate school after discovering that the average American teenager was not awed by machines, and each of them actually disassembled, cleaned, and then reassembled many of the table-top and even bigger equipment they used in their research —whereas Len and other foreigners in their group often needed to beg a fellow student to help them tweak performance out of their lab equipments. Being an independent minded and curious person Len began to tinker with small machines about the house, then bigger ones like his Schwinn touring bike.

Eventually he found himself going to Cleveland State University library, borrowing Chilton's Manual and using the beautifully illustrated step-by-step instructions to repair his rusty old Toyota Corona. He took to changing the brake pads and carburetors, balancing the tires, etc. So Len had several tool boxes stowed in cabinets on different levels of his house, and he kept a rather large one in his car. It was to come in handy whenever he visited Trish because the linkages, wheels and handles of her lawn mower and snow blower were always wobbly and noisy, and her dining chairs swayed too. On the first day of his usually extended visit he would spend a busy afternoon servicing those things for her.

After firming up Trish's exercise machine Len got on it and rode for a half hour. Then, drenched in sweat, he went in Trish's basement shower and scrubbed himself. Whenever Len was in a shower he sang, most often songs from his school days. The memories of his childhood always put a smile on his face. But today it was the *Nicene Creed* that sprang to his lips, the very long and solemn hymn that anchored the *Liturgy of the Word*, the business portion of *Missa Cantata* (a "Sung Mass") and set a cathedral chamber resonating when a skilled organist accompanied the choir. The *Credo* was quite an awesome literary work. In essence it was a diktat, a litany of "this we believe" affirmations cobbled together by an assembly of scholars and clergy gathered at *Nicaea* in Asia Minor (present day Turkey) early in the fourth century of the Christian era.

The Roman Emperor Constantine, lately converted to Christianity and having become a zealot, had summoned renowned bible scholars in ancient Christendom and instructed them to sculpt a uniform orthodoxy onto the fledgling and fractious Christian community. And, like the work of any large committee it rambled, wandering all over the place. Indeed, in adulthood when Len encountered and fell in love with that tremendously relaxing jazz song, *Stardust*, the only song he knew to compare it with was the *Credo*. Each was an epic journey, rising here, falling there, turning a corner and going soft, then surging, all the while unreeling its story of seductive and soporific magic. Len always started the *Credo* softly, in a low note, in slow tempo:

Credo in unum Deum, patrem omnipotentem, factorem coeli et terra, visibilium omnium et invisibilium, et in unum Dominum Jesum Christum....

On and on he droned until he came to his favorite passage, the strophe that is usually spoken softly like a Gregorian Chant rather than sung out loud to a melody:

"*...et unam sanctam Catholicam et Apostolicam Ecclesiam, confiteur unum baptisma in remissionem peccatorum...*"

Then his voice rose again when he got to:

"...et expecto resurrectionem mortuorum..."

Here Len just thrummed for three or four seconds as he always did in imitation of the organ that accompanied a choir on an occasion when he watched a fascinating High Mass celebrated on television. At "mortuorum" the choir slowly drew in its breath as the organ thrummed a single note in deep bass which must have reverberated all over the cathedral rafters for several seconds to give time to the choir to catch its breath.

And finally Len let the rest spill out in faster time, rising to a euphoric crescendo:

"...et vitam venturi saeculi, ah.a.a.a.a...ah.a.a.a.a...ah.a.a.a.a.amen!"

As Len drew in his breath after that long *'amen'* a loud cheer and clapping erupted behind him and gave him a start. "Bravo! Bravo!" he heard. He was not aware that Trish had come home and crept up to the shower stall to listen to his singing. How much did she hear? he asked.

"I came in at *'...et iterum venturus est cum Gloria....'"* She peeled off her clothes and joined him in the shower.

Sing another one, she urged Len. "Another what?" he asked her. Another Latin song, she answered. He broke into the fast-tempo Benediction hymn:

"Laudate Dominuuuum omnes gentes, omnes populi..." but she cut in and said:

"No. Not Benediction. Sing a High Mass song."

He asked Trish to tell him which particular song to sing, and she just began with:

"Gloria in excelsis Deo...."

And Len quickly joined, struggling and failing to match or even complement her higher note:

"...et in terra pax hominibus bonae voluntatis, laudamus te, benedicimus te, adoramus te, glorificamus te, gracias agimus tibi propter magnam gloriam tuam...."

Suddenly Trish, who was standing behind him in the stall, cut him short with: "Geez! What about the back?"

Len looked around, puzzled. What back? The song had no back!

"No, dummy, I mean your own back! It has not been touched by water, soap, or sponge. It looks dirty!"

Len said he was unable to reach his back, and Trish reminded him that few people could reach their backs, "which is why we have these long, ropey sponges and these brushes with long handles," and she jabbed her fingers at those implements hanging right in front of Len. He grumbled defensively that nobody else saw his back; and she countered that the same goes for much of the rest of his body, but they still needed to be scrubbed. She took a sponge, lathered it and began to give his back a soothing scrub and massage. She had him squat down and she scrubbed his arm pits, his scrotal recesses and his whole legs and feet down to the webbings between his toes. Len took the sponge and returned the favor. Then they straightened up and enfolded each other in a passionate embrace. "I love you!" they gushed in unison as if on cue.

She made breakfast and he ate well, unusual for him because he seldom ate breakfast. Indeed, Len also typically ate little at lunch but then pigged out at supper. His doctors told him that his eating habit was terrible; like a tiger that would eat half a carcass of large deer at one sitting. He needed to eat small morsels three times a day, they said; some even told him he needed five meals a day. And Len would mutter, "Yeah, like a hen." What was that? They would ask, and Len would ask them: How can one find time to eat *five* meals a day? It amused him because it lent credence to the Europeans' snide remarks that Americans were always chomping and wolfing food, in public places too. No wonder they were all overweight, the really uncharitable critics said.

8
Crossroads

In the misty moonlight
By the flickering firelight
Any place is all right
Long as you are there

TWO YEARS AND half had passed since Len met Trish, and he was as comfortable as any man could be when settled between the practical comfort and support of a good, competent wife and the emotional luxury of an engaging mistress. Because of the perilous predicament of his youngest son, Len told himself, he was not quite ready to strike camp from his family of thirty-odd years to take up residence with Trish. Nor did Trish pressure Len in any way. They sometimes discussed the issue of where to settle as man and wife so as to avoid the daily disapproval of the communities in which they currently lived. Trish, a gregarious powerhouse, was totally immersed in the affairs of her Columbus circle of friends and unwilling to uproot herself. She served as an official of this women's organization, that ethnic association, and yonder support group for sundry causes. Len was a bit of a loner, not bothered too much with peoples' opinion, but he wasn't sure whether it would be best for Trish to move to Cleveland and face the coolness of his friends who knew him as Magda's husband, or for him to move to Columbus and face Trish's clique.

Len proposed a middle ground: they could settle in mid-Ohio. They considered and rejected Mansfield and Delaware on account of Trish's children who were still of school age. And, anyway, those mid-Ohio towns were yet to emerge from their reputation for rustic racial bias. In the course of their weekend ramblings, she and Len had explored those regions and found them totally provincial and lacking in amenities. Besides, how could she tear herself away from her circle of friends and the satisfying activities she performed in her Columbus community? Forthrightness was one of the many sterling attributes which Len appreciated in Trish, and she had let her friends know she was in love with a married man and was not ashamed of that fact. Early in their affair she had surprised Len by telling him she had disclosed to the close cousin of her ex-husband that Len was married. Trish was pragmatic and her logic was unassailable: "If he's going to condemn me, let him do so now and get it over with." That was vintage Trish: Confront criticism up-front and disarm it before it festered beneath the surface.

Over time, Len had gradually revealed to Trish the story of his life, and she told him hers. The narratives began one Saturday evening as they sat on her back deck, browsing through photo albums: pictures of her school days and college days, and of her years as a young mother. His life and hers had many parallels. Like him she married in her early 20s, which was early because Nigerians tended to wait till they were materially comfortable enough to take care of spouse and resultant children. While studying in the U.S. she married a fellow student who hailed from her hometown and happened to be attending the same university as she. In her first year of graduate school her son was born. There followed a four-year hiatus before her second, a daughter, was born; and three years later her third child arrived. The intervals between her babies were similar to those between Len's sons.

Her husband proved shiftless. He was unable or unwilling to get a job and soon delved into get rich quick schemes. Credit card and banking fraud were in vogue then among some Nigerians in the U.S. Indicted for federal crimes, Trish's husband jumped bail and fled to Nigeria. Credit card fraud was a precursor to the Nigerian "419" scams that were to become sensational in the U.S. from the 1990s as many indicted practitioners of credit card fraud jumped bail (or got deported to Nigeria after serving prison terms), set up shop in the relative impunity of Lagos and Abuja and from there launched the famous "419" era. The code "4-1-9" referred to section of the Nigerian criminal code in which the Nigerian government sought, ineffectually, to proscribe such activities.

Trish had three small children to raise, one of whom needed special health care, and so she stayed back in Columbus. Rumor had it she was an accomplice in her husband's schemes and was spared indictment only by the fact that her husband escaped trial by fleeing to Nigeria before he could implicate her. Of course, rumor is rumor and any indictments for criminal complicity would not be a matter for public disclosure, so the conjectures lacked grounding. Trish maintained her innocence, but disclosed to Len that she had been under stressful surveillance after her husband's flight.

In narrating her experience to Len, she was indignant that on some occasions armed agents of government (whether they were from Immigration or the FBI she was not clear) raided her house with firearms drawn, at inconvenient times when her little children were up and watching. Agents also trailed her to work and back and around town. Slowly the surveillance and raids tapered off. Having three young children to raise all on her own probably gave Trish some advantage: The feds would not be too keen to have to consign the children to foster care unless the case against their mother was both strong and important. Since her husband could not return to the States, Trish eventually divorced him —or rather had the marriage annulled, because she was a Catholic and her father (a knight of the Church) made a strong case for her.

"So, did you go back to your maiden name?" Len asked her.

"No. My maiden name is Abba. I kept my marital name, Adoja. Otherwise I'd have to change many documents again."

The special medical needs of her youngest daughter were more reasons for Trish's strong reluctance to relocate somewhere else with Len. The girl's delicate health and her brave acceptance of her frequent hospitalizations and harsh interventions (pain medications and blood transfusions) endeared her to Len; he dubbed her "My precious little shrimp." The doctors and school authorities in Columbus were familiar with the girl's needs since her birth, thus Trish did not want to start anew somewhere else. Her reluctance to move from Columbus was an added drag on Len's already tentative and long-drawn-out resolve to leave Magda and make a life with Trish.

9
9/11

I love Paris every moment
Every moment of the year
I love Paris, why oh, why do I love Paris?
Because my love is near

ONE DAY LEN plucked up courage and opened a topic that he had longed to broach with Trish but was afraid because she might say no to him for the first time.

As an established scientist in his field, Len was often invited to scientific conferences and workshops where colleagues engaged in research similar to his own compared notes on findings. Each year he attended two or three such conferences in the U.S. and one or two abroad. NASA administrators were stingy with permission to attend conferences in foreign countries for reasons of both fiscal prudence and the need to safeguard the security of NASA work, much of which was classified as matters of national security. For this year Len had chosen to attend a workshop to be held in the second week of September that year, 2001, at Arcachon in the Bordeaux region of France. The conference was to be devoted to reviewing high-temperature processes. Len was due to present a paper at the workshop on progress made in his evaluation of special new materials for use in high-performance jet and rocket engines.

It would thrill him if Trish would come along with him. They would make a vacation of it, explore some of the famed mellow wines of the Bordeaux region, and take in Paris on their way out there or on their way home. To his huge relief Trish said yes without hesitation. He turned to her and whispered: "Darling, you have no idea how happy you make me, always!"

They planned their itinerary. They would be gone for seven days. The conference was to begin on Sunday September 8, 2001, and end Friday 14, but Len's papers were to be presented on Tuesday morning, the eleventh, and Wednesday morning, the twelfth. They wanted to leave the conference one day before it closed, spend Thursday at a Bordeaux winery, and Friday in Paris before flying home on Saturday September 15. So she needed to take a full week off work, really six workdays, to give her one full day to get her children situated starting the day before departure, as well as the full weekend upon return to step up from the relaxed tempo of a vacation and be ready for the fast-clip pace of her work day, starting Monday September 17. Since they were already into August, and Trish needed a visa for France on her Nigerian passport, they had to apply right away for that visa to allow at least two weeks for consular processing. On an impulse Len asked Trish to check her passport. They discovered, to their dismay, that it had expired and needed renewal.

They set off for the Nigerian Consulate General in New York that same night, a Sunday, and Len called Magda from the road to say he had to stay over to referee the final soccer tournament match that was postponed to Monday so that games which were tied could be resolved with replays on Sunday. Spending the night at a roadway motel in Harrisburg, Pennsylvania, Trish and Len set out early, reached New York City around 10 am, rushed into the consulate, and put in Trish's papers for processing before lunch time. By a fortuitous coincidence their schedule was favored by an unusual political situation in Nigeria. Olusegun Obasanjo had just been elected the president of Nigeria, succeeding the much detested Sanni Abacha. In the new dispensation civil servants were on tenterhooks and striving to please, so that Nigerian consular staff abroad suspended their usual sloppiness and arrogance and attended briskly to business. With any luck they could get the extension endorsement stamp on that same day. And they did: Trish's passport got extended by 3 pm, and she and Len began speeding back home.

Trish was so relieved and relaxed she took the driver's seat and ate up the highway. He realized she was bolder at the wheels than he. If he had driven, his sedate pace of 65 to 70 mph would have made it an eleven-hour trip; instead, it took just nine hours with Trish driving. She drove, he sang songs and fed her snacks. It was a routine to be repeated on the many road tours they took thereafter, often with her kids: twice each to Cocoa Beach, Chicago, and Niagara Falls. It was on the way home from a Chicago trip that she suddenly pulled up as they approached Gary, Indiana to announce that her nerves were shot. She felt nausea and dizziness and could not go faster than 50 mph. He took the wheel and got them home; Trish was never again able to drive far or fast on interstate highways. Her doctors diagnosed her with an anxiety disorder and panic attack syndrome that required calming medications, with strictures to avoid highway driving. But that was several years in the future. Today Trish sped them down from New York City to Columbus at a gallop while she and Len went through a large repertoire of songs.

Back in Columbus she called the French consulate and got information on what to include on her visa application. Above all she was to include a statement from Len saying he would be responsible for her expenses all the way, as well as a copy of Len's latest bank statement and the brochure describing the conference. Len went back to Cleveland and made reservations for their flight to France. At the weekend he emailed to Trish advance copies of the documents to include with her application after she received the forms from the French consulate, including copies of their flight tickets —even though the French consulate did not necessarily require them. He wanted to leave nothing to chance. Trish got the forms eleven days before they were to depart, completed and sent them off by overnight delivery. Then they waited with bated breaths.

With any consulate, it was usually dicey whether one got action in good time, or at all. The U.S. consulates were the only ones Len knew of that posted a large and intimidating warning that visa was issued at a consular official's discretion, and that the official did not have to offer an applicant a reason for denial: A visa was not a right or an entitlement. It had become clear to Len during his travels abroad that all consular officials were just as capricious as the U.S. ones and sometimes you needed to catch one in a good mood to get a visa.

On the Tuesday before their departure Len called the French consulate and they assured him the visa was approved and Trish's passport was being sent via certified US mail that same day. Trish got all her travel stuff ready. Then Thursday came and went and the passport had not arrived. They were to leave the next day, and their flight tickets were neither refundable nor exchangeable. Things looked grim. Friday arrived and by 11 am Len got jittery. He called every half hour and got the same reply from Trish, "Nope!" Trish said that mail to her home usually arrived before noon; if it wasn't there by noon it meant it wasn't coming that day. He gave her instructions: She was to hit the road the moment she got the package, but if she was not at the Cleveland airport by 4 pm, Len would have to board the 6:05 pm flight alone. At 1:30 pm Len got a call from Trish. Thinking she had disappointing news he answered in a muted tone. But she said, "Honey, it is here!"

Trish's sagacity and instinct were phenomenal. She had suddenly remembered that mail runners sometimes inserted sensitive mail under the front porch mat when a resident was not home to claim it. On a haunch she lifted her mat and there it was. The carrier must have come in the brief interval when Trish went to a nearby shop to buy last minute supplies for the trip. She hit the road at once. Her panic attack syndrome had not developed yet, and she hit her usual peppy stride on the highway. By 4:30 pm she was at Cleveland airport and into Len's arms, and he danced a jig in delight. It had been a close call!

The overnight flight was uneventful —if one can describe a night of breathless bliss as uneventful. At 7:45 am they landed in Paris, groggy from insufficient sleep but happy as larks. As the pilot announced their descent into Charles De Gaulle airport, Len serenaded Trish with "I love Paris" thinking nobody else heard it, but an old lady seated directly behind him broke into applause when he finished. "I love Paris too," she whispered. It was Sunday morning and the city was only coming alive as they took a train to the *Gare du Nord*, and from there connected to the TGV, *Trains au Grand Vitesse*, the bullet-nosed high-speed train system that was to take them Southwest to connect with a more conventional rail line.

Len had never before ridden a TGV but he had read much about them, the engineer in him awed by their speeds that were supposed to exceed 550 km/h (340 mph) on a good stretch — exceeding the take-off speed of some commercial airplanes! Len expected to experience the same exhilaration as he always felt when a jumbo jet surged down the runway to take to its wings. But he and Trish were so listless in the advanced time zone that they slept through the westward segment of the journey to Le Mans, where they changed to a train of more sedate speed for the final leg to Bordeaux and Arcachon. Well, he thought she was sleeping but, as they sped past green pastures she muttered to him: "I love you so much, Len." He was too happy for words and merely rubbed his cheek against hers and snuggled closer.

Arcachon turned out to be a popular beachfront on the Atlantic coast, teeming with vacationers crowding the beaches as far as the eye could see. Even more than in Paris, their first fascination was with the micro cars: automobiles so small they could almost be lifted to one's shoulders and carried to the back of one's house. They were the kind of cars Len liked; they made sense in a country where the cost of gasoline was about five times as much as in the U.S., but they looked downright comical to a person unfamiliar with them.

Trish and Len hit the beach soon after checking into their well-appointed hotel suite. People were swimming far out to sea and there were balloons and buntings and buoys and different kinds of unfamiliar craft surfing and flying around gaily, but Len and Trish stayed close to shore, in any case not venturing beyond the red-and-blue buoys. Africans did not make so much ado about aquatic recreation as did Westerners.

Along the beach they fell into conversation with an exquisitely tanned couple that looked the color of slowly-grilled hot dogs, a bronzed man of middle age and his companion, a copper-toned young lady of indeterminate age. Trish muttered mischievously that the couple must be spending too many hours in a tanning salon. Len said *Hello* and the man replied in English: "Good Afternoon." To make conversation Len asked if they lived there in Arcachon; the lady shook her head and the man said that they were from Toronto. Len introduced himself and Trish; the man replied: "I am Benson Silva. Please call me Ben. This is my wife Roxanne." Len had an uncanny acuity with names, picked up from years of travel and from his habit of talking to people he met. He would hear a person's name and right away tell them they were from Hungary or had Hungarian ancestry —that kind of thing. And their eyes would get hooded with surprise or suspicion: How did he guess that, they would ask.

"Pardon me, Ben, but your name sounds Portuguese. Or is it Brazilian?"

Ben said they were originally from Brazil but now lived in Toronto where he taught Computer Science at McGill University. He and Roxanne were on vacation; they arrived the week before. Len told him about himself and about Trish.

"Oh, you live among our hot-shot neighbors to the south," Ben teased Len, and they quickly found common ground in their views of life in the U.S. Len asked where one might get a good, affordable meal in Arcachon. Ben made a wry grimace. "Good is easy, but I don't know about affordable!" If you'd like to join us tonight we can show you a good place we discovered, OK? Len agreed to meet them in front of the convention hotel at 6:30 pm. They went to a beach-front restaurant within walking distance of Len's hotel. The food was good. Trish chose mutton and Len pork, which he preferred to some more exotic fares on the menu, like frog legs. Ben selected a *Saint-Émilion Château* red blend made from Bordeaux grapes; Len sampled it and approved with a nod and a smile. Trish and Roxanne drank half a glass each; Len and Ben polished off the rest.

Over dessert Len opened up on the comparative merits of American and European life styles, starting with the ubiquitous micro cars they saw on the streets of Arcachon. When one had the kind of public transportation system that interlaced all cities, towns and hamlets of European countries with interlocking and coordinated bus, tram, and railway schedules, why encumber the streets and highways with monstrous gas guzzlers made by Cadillac and Buick? Ben agreed: Whereas Americans preferred ostentatious living in big suburban homes with two-car garages, Europeans found merit in apartments (or "flats" as the British called them) and townhouses.

Trish interjected that comparing those two lifestyle choices was a judgment call unless one had to take note of the reasons for each choice. America had wide open spaces while Europe was congested, and European governments kept gasoline prices artificially high in order to generate revenues to support community amenities. The real difference to note, in her view, was the attitude with which one side viewed the other's lifestyle: Americans tended to be parochial and noisy in their insistence that their country was a place of supe- rior merit, "God's own country!" Roxanne softly interjected, "We are the greatest!" Trish and Len looked at her; that was the first time she had spoken all evening. Len had begun to wonder if she spoke English, which she clearly did, because she continued, adding that all through history, chauvinism was a major cause of wars. Len was startled. This was déjà-vu: Three years earlier Trish had grabbed his attention with those same sentiments when he first set eyes on her. Len felt like playing devil's advocate. He pointed out that Muhammad Ali went a long way with his "I am the greatest" boast. Trish gave Len a disapproving look and countered with: "And look how much pummeling Muhammad Ali got for his troubles. When you proclaim obnoxiously that you are the best people want to knock the chips off your shoulders."

Ben weighed in with an anecdote. You carry more conviction if you claim to be second-best, he said. They all looked at him and he added that in a certain town a barber hung up a big sign proclaiming he was the second-best barber in town. That got attention and cus- tomers started flocking to him. But when someone asked him, "But who is the best barber in this town?" he shrugged and said he did not know; every other nearby barber claimed that honor! Len agreed, and said when he was a student in Lagos a certain tailor got attention the same way. It was a time when fashion-conscious men and women had their clothes made by local tailors instead of being purchased without detailed personal pre-measurement and fitting. Every tailor posted a sign proclaiming that he was "London-trained" and people wondered how so many local men had travelled to London to get trained as tailors. So, to gain more credibility, one tailor's sign said: "London-trained-trained." Ben chuckled and muttered that that "train" could get quite long in the end. On that note they left, having exchanged contact information.

Because Len was pre-registered for the conference he needed only a brief stop at the registration desk to pick up his name badge. Then they retired for the evening, tired but happy. The next day, Monday, Len took in the morning session of presentations, leaving Trish to amuse herself. Then in the afternoon they walked all over the Arcachon beaches until they dropped from exhaustion and snoozed in each-other's arms right on the warm beach. They looked for the Silvas along the beach front but did not see them again. In the early evening Trish and Len left their beachfront hotel and walked into town to browse the shop windows and buy a few souvenirs. Back in their hotel they watched a TV movie and retired early because Len had to start early at the conference next day.

Tuesday morning was crisp and clear. Len's paper was scheduled for 9:20 am as the third paper in his morning session. He was relaxed, happy and confident. In any case, Len was always cool and collected when he addressed a scientific audience. It was a studied coolness because, as he was often the only black presenting papers to an august assembly of scientists in those meetings, he knew he could not afford to appear nervous or uncertain. Besides, he was not disconcerted when he was merely reporting results from his own work. The only *faux pas* on such occasions tended to come from uninformed staffers manning the registration booths.

One of those occurred this morning. On his way to his session he stopped at the Registration desk at 8:30 am and asked for two tickets to the conference banquet scheduled to be held the next day, Wednesday night. He wanted to take Trish to the banquet as a special treat. As Len opened his wallet a lady behind the desk brought out the receipt booklet. Len said, "Two tickets: eighty dollars?" but the lady cut in with: "It is half-price for students, so you pay only forty dollars. Is your companion a student too? Just present your tickets and your student ID cards at the door." Len smiled and told them he was not a student, and the lady with the booklet said, without bothering to apologize, "OK, eighty dollars." The older lady in the back of the room recovered quickly enough to say hurriedly that Len looked "so young!"

But Len was not fooled. He often got that sort of dubious compliment in Europe. Sometimes it arose from genuine perplexity about his age. There was the time at the 1972 Olympic Games in Munich at which he joined a vast team of student temporary workers at the many menial jobs connected with running the Olympic Village. A tall and beautiful blonde girl from Sweden who claimed to speak seven different languages became interested in Len and they dated a few times. One night, after a kiss, she astonished him with a backhanded compliment: "When I look at you I cannot tell whether you are eighteen or thirty-eight." Len smiled and told her to keep guessing. He understood her difficulty. When he was young, his fellow Nigerians used to say it was impossible to tell a white person's age just by looking at them. One needed extended interactions to become calibrated to cues for age —in other races as in other species!

But at other times he was mistaken for a student for a less flattering reason. One case Len would never forget occurred the year before he met Trish. He was at a conference in Firenze (Florence as Americans called it). At the beginning of his session the chairperson invited scheduled speakers to move up and sit together in the front row so they didn't have to wriggle up the aisle and over the knees of attendees who were seated for a paper a paper that was already in progress. As Len got up and moved to the front a gorgeous lady whose hour-glass figure looked like it had been poured into her blue pant suit followed him with her eyes. When he looked at her she smiled and nodded and he smiled back. Through the session her eyes were on him, even when she stood at the podium and delivered her paper it seemed as if she was addressing her comments to him.

After her presentation she went and sat on a vacant chair right next to Len and resumed her scrutiny of him. There were two more speakers and then it was Len's turn, just before lunch break. As Len spoke the lady beamed her eyes at him, and his accustomed aplomb began to waver. It was disconcerting. When he was done there were questions, which he answered, then applause. For most attendees present applause was just a polite formality; for that lady it was so enthusiastic Len felt embarrassed.

Len stepped down and made his way to the snack counter. He wasn't a lunch eater, so he ordered what looked like a quiche sandwich and a cup of coffee. Then he saw that lady; she had followed him. She made a beeline for his tiny table and he stood up to let her sit. Len began to entertain ideas: Surely her interest was personal, amorous perhaps. He fancied himself a Don Juan and smiled broadly from ear to ear. She fixed her stare at him and finally spoke to him, totally bursting his bubble. "I am really pleased to meet you, er...." And Len finished it for her: Lennox. "I am Gina, Gina Guardiola," she continued, extending her hand for a shake.

"I hope I have not made you uncomfortable with my attention, but I am astonished, because we are told there are no black scientists!"

Len was deflated. Aloud he said to her, "Oh, we do exist, only not in great numbers yet. Would you like to have a drink with this rare breed of scientist, or would you rather wait till there are more of us?"

She looked puzzled for a moment but then caught the joke and said, No, thanks. She had to be going soon. They made a desultory attempt at conversation and then she took her leave. Her business was over and she was done, her curiosity satisfied. So much for a cozy evening of tryst and delight, Len sighed. The plaintive Everly Brothers song came to his mind, especially Linda Ronstadt's rendition of it in a quicker tempo:

> *"I've been cheated*
> *Been mistreated*
> *When will I be loved?"*

Today Len was not deflated by the faux-pas that labeled him "student" in the consciousness of the ladies manning the reception desk at Arcachon. In any case he was in a buoyant mood, what with Trish waiting at the hotel to go rambling with him around this lovely town. He went and gave his paper, then came down to the lobby only to find everybody crowded around the big-screen TV set gasping as they watched what looked to Len to be a Hollywood movie stunt. Two lofty towers standing like twin sentries over a city were shown over and over again to burst open and collapse as an aeroplane careened into the top of one of them —or was it two planes side-by-side?

First one tower burst into flames as the top of it was sheared off or blown off; it was hard to tell which, with so much smoke pouring out. Then an airplane approached the second tower from behind and cut off its head too. Slowly the two towers seemed to slump, or just sit down. Len was reminded of the awe he used to feel whenever he saw a modern demolition team in a U.S. city bring a sky scraper gracefully down in a heap of rubble, unlike demolition teams he had seen in Lagos, Nigeria, or in Cairo, Egypt, where the process sent boulders and shards flying so violently that traffic and human activity had to be stopped or cordoned off before demolition was attempted. He had inquired about it during a visit to downtown Chicago and was told it was a scientific matter of placing suitably measured and shaped charges at the proper strategic locations in a building and detonating them in a coordinated manner. He was impressed.

When the captions over the horrific images told him what was happening, Len realized that while he was droning on and on about mundane scientific data the world had been jolted by cataclysmic events. He ran to the hotel room and found Trish glued to the TV, round-eyed and stunned. They watched together and tears came down her cheeks. "Terrorist Attacks," "New York City," "World Trade Center," the messages played over and over; thousands of lives were feared lost. Unable to watch anymore, Trish turned off the TV and collapsed into Len's arms, sobbing. When she calmed down sufficiently to sit down, Len tried to call home several times, without success. The lines were jammed. Mercifully, an exhausted Trish began to breathe rhythmically: She had fallen asleep. Len laid her down on the bed, tucked her in, and switched the TV back on.

More news bulletins came in. Four planes were said to have been involved: Airline passenger jets had been hijacked in flight and used as diabolically improvised aerial torpedoes, the fuel in them serving as the explosive. Two planes hit the twin towers of the World Trade Center almost simultaneously; a third slammed into the Pentagon; a fourth one went down in Pennsylvania after being hijacked by terrorist and turned around to head towards Washington, DC, targeted, it was speculated, at the White House. There was speculation that more attacks were coming, so President Bush had gone into hiding. It seemed like the world was ending. As far as Len knew, continental U.S. had never come under attack in his lifetime. This was indeed surreal. But was it really surprising?

Len instantly thought of the series of prescient warnings in the books of Chalmers Johnson which he had read in a sequence two-three years earlier. The main book in that whole series was Blowback: The Cost and Consequences of American Empire. Johnson had been a CIA consultant on a few of the many dirty tricks by which that agency sought to undermine and sabotage foreign countries thought to be unfriendly to the U.S. He explained that "blowback" was a term used by operatives who feared that if the U.S. kept subverting foreign countries, assassinating their leaders, and destabilizing their economies, no one should be surprised if and when reprisals came to haunt Americans in their homes too. Len had bought and read three of the man's books: *Blowback, The Sorrows of Empire*, and *Nemesis*, each of them considering from a different perspective the same problem of predatory U.S. foreign policies.

The holocaust unfolding on that fateful day, 9/11/01 was a vindication of Chalmers Johnson's prediction. It wasn't even the first: Eight years earlier, on February 26, 1993, the same twin towers of the World Trade Center had been targeted by Islamic extremists bearing the U.S. a grudge. The intention was the same as in 2001: Blow down the twin towers and kill as many people as possible. But damage from the 1993 episode was minimal because the perpetrators hadn't the knowledge of how and where properly to locate the charges or how to detonate them for full effect. They were quickly rounded up, tried, and sentenced to prison sentences so lengthy they could not be completed in one person's lifetime. The sentences, running to hundreds of years, reminded Len of when he was a child, and a villager who was rumored to have been sentenced to a dozen years of imprisonment came home after a few years. Len asked his father why the man was released early. His father, not wishing to seem ignorant, told Len that in prison night and day were counted separately, as two days. It was clear as mud, but if your dad said so....

Len lay down beside Trish, kissed her, enfolded her, and fell asleep too. The tragedy of the WTC towers had ruined their day, and indeed the rest of their trip. Len lost interest in the conference proceedings.

Starting late that afternoon and lasting through all of Wednesday, the weather turned sour at Arcachon, as if sympathizing with the U.S., and the beach was almost deserted. He and Trish browsed shop windows for souvenirs but their hearts were not in it. Thursday was more cheerful as the weather improved and the shock of the WTC attack wore off. Trish and Len got through on the phone to relatives in the U.S. and were reassured that all was well with their families. They strolled along the beach again but all thoughts of visiting a winery had disappeared. They packed their bags and got ready to board the train to Paris early the next day. Archachon and Bordeaux were forever linked, in Len's mind, with the horrors of 9/11.

Len's second paper, scheduled for the next day, fell victim to the World Trade Center calamity. Many speakers on that session could not come in. They had perhaps scheduled their arrivals for that black Tuesday only to find all flights grounded. When Len reported at 9 am he saw a notice saying his session had been scrubbed. That only deepened Len's gloom as he and Trish spent Wednesday and Thursday ghosting about a beach resort that had suddenly become eerie.

Len and Trish spent Friday afternoon and evening around the Eiffel Tower in Paris and, after a take-out dinner eaten in their hotel room, settled down to sleep that was made fitful by fretting about what the following day would bring as they tried to fly back home.

What they found at Charles De Gaulle airport bore out their fears. The place was jam-packed and chaotic. Ragged lines meandered forever in all directions. People were tense. Some said they had waited at the airport since that fateful Tuesday to board their flights, but there had been no departures to the U.S. that day or the next day. It appeared U.S.-bound flights were permitted on Thursday, but clearance to take off was granted so slowly that not many flights departed. Every bag was subjected to the minutest inspection and everyone was watched closely. A semblance of normalcy was restored on Friday, but the going was rough and slow. That meant that the airport was super-crowded with overflow passengers who missed their flights from previous days.

Security was exceedingly tight. In addition to the plainclothes US security guards one found in abundance at all terminals for U.S.-bound flights in European international airports, De Gaulle was crawling that day with lean, uniformed soldiers, wearing beret caps tilted jauntily to one side. Snub-nosed machine guns poked out from under windbreaker jackets worn over sweaters and camouflage-pattern shirts, or pistol butts stuck out from waistband holsters. It was as if the French authorities expected an army of terrorists to invade Paris. It took four hours from their arrival at the airport to the time Trish and Len boarded. They did not notice a lift as the airplane took off because the cabin resembled a college dormitory on the Sunday after a Homecoming: Everyone crashed and snoozed as soon as they hit their seats. Few woke up for lunch when it was wheeled past.

10
Space Shuttle

Fly me to the moon
Let me play among the stars
Let me see what spring is like
On Jupiter and Mars

THE TRIP TO Arcachon, which Trish and Len came to refer to privately as "our 9/11 escapade" was the start of a thrilling period of vacations spent together. Like Len's interludes of Youth Soccer refereeing getaways, scientific conferences provided opportunities for him to take Trish on trips that became as much fun as business engagements. His scientific work was going swimmingly and in the dozen years he had been working at NASA he averaged three or four papers published each year in scientific journals, bulletins and other outlets or presented to audiences at workshops, meetings and conferences. For a research scientist, publications were a self-reinforcing phenomenon: the more results a researcher reported the more he or she is noticed by colleagues and so the more invitations came in to this and that meeting; and the meetings themselves provided a forum for cross-fertilization of ideas which, in turn, boosted one's work.

The next conference to which Len was invited was scheduled to be held in Cocoa Beach, Florida. It was an annual event held each January and timed to give a pleasant respite to U.S. scientists working in the frosty northern latitudes, but of course it attracted scientists from everywhere. It actually featured two conferences held back-to-back: an unrestricted mid-January meeting for scientists and academics in general, and a later "closed" conference for the benefit of scientists working on "classified" aeronautical and space-related projects, as well as the administrators who managed those projects. The "closed" conference required an invitation to attend and Len was scheduled to give two papers at the closed sessions coming up at the end of January, 2003. He asked Trish to come along and she agreed; they planned to stay for one week in Cocoa Beach and meander to nearby areas. Florida was an irresistible attraction when snow was thick on the ground and Ohio's air chilly as in a freezer.

Actually, this was to be their second conference-cum-vacation trip to Cocoa Beach. They had gone there two years earlier, but on that occasion they took Trish's children, who had buckets of fun from two special diversions. One was a trip on Saturday, before the conference started, to the Kennedy Space Center, the largest of NASA's visitors' centers, in which a "Space Garden" featured vintage NASA and Air Force rockets exhibited outdoors, with their noses pointing straight up as at the moment of blast-off during launch, the roosts where the astronauts scrunched during flight being too high up to see from the ground. Numerous plaques and billboards chronicled the rockets and their exploits, so that school children and their parents and teachers came in droves and soaked up information, not to mention loading up on souvenirs at the gift shop that did lands-office business. The other diversion that made the trip even more exciting and memorable was a full day spent in Orlando, taking in Disney World. It was a refreshing vacation for the kids as well as for Trish and Len. This trip, like their excursion to Sea World in Sandusky, Ohio, during the summer that same year, helped forge good bond between Len and Trish's children.

Whenever Trish accompanied Len on a trip she brought along enough food, and then some, to last the whole period. She was no more enthusiastic about restaurant meals than he was. They used to joke that in their respective Nigerian languages there were no words for "restaurant." The closest word used to express "restaurant" was "hotel," which was pejorative; and in Len's native language one might say that he "ate hotel" (rather than *in* a hotel!). The first time Len took Trish out to dinner and a movie in Columbus, she complained that she had good dishes of her own in her own house. And so she did. Being the eldest child in her family, and a girl at that, she had had to learn as she grew up how to cook good meals, and she had learned well.

Among Trish's favorite preparations was meaty fresh fish (such as grouper or snapper) sautéed with peppery spices and onions, then dried slowly in her oven. She served it with lots of green vegetables, especially cucumber, broccoli, and sprouts. Like Len, she was not a big eater but she believed in eating only 'healthy' foods. Her other specialty dish, which was in demand among her friends was *akara*, a delightful Nigerian finger-food always served as snack or appetizer before the main meals at a party. *Akara* was a simple affair of very few ingredients, namely beans (black-eye peas) ground into fine puree, mixed with condiments and fried in oil. But because Nigerian dishes were not set to specific menus (at least not when Trish was a young girl), how a dish turned out was inconsistent: It depended very much on the experience, intuition, and skills of the cook, including such knowledge as in what sequence to add the ingredients, in what quantities and at what stages. Nigerians have a native saying that if a (polygamous) man gave identical ingredients to his wives, one would turn out mush and the other would come up with a finger-licking delight. Trish's finger foods were always big winners, so she carried credibility when she talked down restaurant fare.

Trish fancied herself an excellent chef. It was of course not unusual for African women to think they are better at cooking than they actually are, because that was perhaps the one domestic skill upon which might depend their appreciation a wife. If your mother-in-law came to visit and pronounced your cooking bad, you were toast! But by all standards Trish was a good cook, only not of the top shelf like Magda. On Len's scale of 0–10 Magda would score a 9 and Trish an 8. That was, of course, an opinion that Len did not betray to Trish for fear of hurting her feelings. Trish could analyze and critique cuisines and dishes with greater facility than most. Restaurant foods were just bland stuff larded up with fat and sugar, she said. That's why they first ply diners with cocktails in a Happy Hour: When one becomes too inebriated and starving to mind the taste of the food. Sometimes if you closed your eyes you could not tell whether the fare was fish or fowl, or even plastic; the only taste you got was of the condiments.

She didn't like Italian restaurants much because she stayed away from Alfredo sauce: "One spoonful of it and you gained three pounds," she once warned as Len took halting bites of his pasta served with that thick and creamy white sauce. And monosodium glutamate in Chinese dishes put her off too: "The stuff is said to cause cancer in rats." Len replied that rats were tiny and their digestive systems probably different from a human being's, but she countered that she read in some magazine that all animals shared more than 90 percent of their DNAs, and cancers were triggered at that biochemical level. Her erudition never ceased to amaze Len. In time he learned as much from her as he taught her. In fact they often to complimented each other with, "You taught me much of what I know," and each of them meant it.

So they ate a lot of sautéed game fish on their domestic trips. Being carefully dried in her oven, the fish stayed well-preserved through a vacation lasting a week or so. She brought them in large coolers packed with ice, which is why Len rented only minivans for their outings. They were packaged in lots each small enough to be completely consumed in a meal. Len always reserved only hotel rooms or suites that provided a stove and a microwave oven. As soon as they arrived at their destination Trish would scour area groceries for fruits and vegetables, including cucumbers which, to Len's surprise she ate raw —unlike Len who liked his foods cooked, whether vegetable or meat.

Trish's preference for bringing along her own cooked dishes proved especially useful in Florida. As they catered mostly to crowds of tourists from everywhere, restaurants along coastal Florida tended to feature a narrow range of cuisine which were nondescript enough to be tolerated by all comers. The previous year when Trish's children came along they had tried a beachfront Mexican restaurant that billed itself as a steakhouse, at the urging of the kids. Len ordered pork chops and it was served with apple sauce. Yikes! When the head waiter came over and asked how everything was and Trish emphatically drawled, "*Sweeeet*," the waiter beamed with smiles, thinking it a compliment.

On the present trip, however, because Len arranged so much leisure time in his schedule and they ranged farther than usual into the hinterland, he and Trish discovered that local dishes which were mostly based on sea foods were, to Trish's delight, more palatable at out-of-the-way restaurants far from the crowds, no doubt because the cooking was done in reasonably small quantities rather than on a production scale. They had more satisfaction on the couple of occasions when they drove far and took their time to look for ethnic restaurants.

This time, 2003, Len hoped to bring his association with the Space Shuttle Columbia full circle. Columbia was NASA's first space shuttle, designated STS-1 on that very first occasion twenty-two years earlier, when it blasted off from Cape Canaveral on April 12, 1981, for a maiden flight that kicked off America's 30-year love affair with human space flight aboard machines more akin to airplanes than rockets.

Len and Magda had decided to return their family back to Nigeria permanently the following year, 1981. In order to see a bit of America before saying adieu, he and Magda and their sons had embarked on extended trips all over North America, starting in 1980 with a six-day trek from Gainesville, Florida, to San Francisco by way of the southern states that bordered Mexico and the Gulf. They had so much fun they decided to take a similar safari in 1981 before leaving for Nigeria in July of that year. He learned that the maiden flight of America's vaunted shuttle craft was scheduled for April 1981.

Len and his oldest son, who was 10, were space enthusiasts and when the maiden flight of Columbia was announced Len had to take his family to observe the event. It was convenient that they lived in Gainesville, only some four hours away from Cape Canaveral, the site of the shuttle launch.

The memory of that first shuttle launch, which they watched from a mile away as the craft slowly rose on a pillar of fire and quickly zoomed skyward to disappear from view a minute later, lived with Len through his decade in Nigeria and the next decade when he was back in the U.S. In his offices at the Nigerian universities where he taught, Len displayed, to inspire his engineering students, a large poster of Columbia riding piggy-back on a huge Boeing 747 specially designed to ferry space shuttles between their assembly points in California and their launch site in Florida. And when Len began work at NASA in 1990, his main task was evaluation of materials proposed for use in the combustion chambers of the proposed next-generation space transportation vehicles, intended as successors to the Space Shuttle. So Len's association with SST Columbia was direct and indirect, general and specific.

Now, after twenty-seven space missions spread over the intervening two decades, Columbia was slated to be retired. Its twenty-eighth and final flight was scheduled for January 2003. It was to be the last huzzah for a worthy workhorse of America's space shuttle service. Following that flight, it was to be decommissioned. Len was to be at the upcoming Cocoa Beach conference about that same time, and he hoped that last launch of Columbia, scheduled for January 16, 2013, would get delayed (as happened often) until he was in Cocoa Beach. He intended to be there, up close, cheering as that veteran craft took wing for the last time.

But it was not to be. This time the weather did not intervene and Columbia took off right on schedule two weeks before Len's conference even began. But it was an extended mission, carrying seven brave and bright young men and women who went on that mission to advance the cause of science and technology. But, what goes up must come down, Len thought, and anyway, he had seen Columbia take off before, in 1981. It was perhaps more fitting that he should now see it land. So he extended his conference trip to end on Saturday, February 1, 2013, the day of Columbia's planned touch down. It was a most convenient schedule: He would share the thrill of the event with Trish. The only thing that might thwart that hope was if the weather over Florida precluded a landing at Cape Canaveral, which meant the craft would then be guided to land in California, at Edwards Air Force Base. That would be disappointing for Len.

As usual, Len spent more of the trip with Trish than he spent attending the conference sessions, though he sat through all of the sessions in which his paper was presented as well as those of others whose work interested him. When he was not attending the sessions, he and Trish drove the length of Highway A1A (US Route 1), over and over again, from Cape Canaveral down to Indian Harbor Beach. The myriad gift shops along that highway were studded with

numerous kinds of fascinating marine creatures fashioned into dec-
orative household items, lampshades being popular. Of course, it
being Florida, a land of sunshine, surf and beach, the most ubiquitous
souvenirs were swimwear, surfboards, T-shirts, sunglasses, hats and
visors.

One souvenir shop where Len and Trish rested their tired feet for
two hours after trekking for miles on the beach, was some kind of
outlet for Jimmy Buffett's delightfully eclectic music. Len and Trish
loaded up on Jimmy Buffet CDs (like *Off to See the Lizard*). One more
interesting activity they discovered was night-time gambling aboard
the many cruise boats moored at this cape and that. You arrived at
sunset, paid your entry fee, and boarded the floating casino. When it
filled up, or as darkness fell, they cast off and you spent a gorgeous
couple of hours getting drunk and not caring if you came out winner
or loser at the end. Trish and Len tried it once, and then a second
time. As long as you disciplined yourself not to take too much cash
aboard, it was great fun.

When Saturday dawned clear and crisp and the forecasts said the
weather was splendid for a shuttle landing, Len and Trish checked
out of their hotel early and headed for Cape Canaveral to watch the
shuttle touch down. They were told to expect Columbia to break
through the clouds around 9 am EST. That appointed time came and
went. Soon it was 10 am, and still there was no sign of the shuttle and
no more news came on the radio about whether or not there was a
delay. At 10:45 a disappointed Len suggested that they should set
off on their long journey home and follow the rest of the event on
the radio. They had a longer drive home because Trish wanted to go
by way of Atlanta and see that city, especially the famed Ebenezer
Baptist Church whose historic importance was given so much luster
by its father-and-son co-pastors, The Reverend Martin Luther King Sr.
and The Reverend Dr. Martin Luther King, Jr.

On their previous trip to Cocoa Beach in year 2000, they had come from Ohio riding down I-77 all the way to Columbia, South Carolina, then detoured east to Savannah, Georgia, where they picked up I-95S and rode it all the way to Cocoa Beach. Trish drove the rented Nissan Quest minivan most of the way with her customary speed and deftness, and Len spelled her at the wheel when she needed to rest. After fourteen continuous hours on the road they were in Cocoa Beach, and at the end of the one week stay there, they returned home along the same routes.

This time, in 2003, they also came down I-77S and I-95S to Cocoa Beach, but they were going back via Atlanta, Chattanooga and Nashville, Louisville, and on to Cincinnati, where they would connect to I-77N for the last leg home. So at 11 am they set out. Because they had somewhat different preferences in music, their rule was that the person at the wheel decided what kind of music CD to play, or which radio station to tune to. Len took the first shift on this journey home, but he could not play his jazz as he drove because Trish wanted to stay on the news concerning Space Shuttle Columbia. Crossing the Georgia border, approaching Valdosta in mid-afternoon, they pulled into a roadside farmers' market to buy pecans for Trish. They then resumed their northward trek, and almost immediately the news broke that NASA spokespersons were confirming that the Space Shuttle Columbia had broken up on re-entry over Texas into the Earth's atmosphere and there were no hopes for its crew.

That horrible news cast a pall on the rest of the journey back home, and neither the memorials of Ebenezer Baptist Church nor the colorful bazaars of Underground Atlanta could rekindle the joy of vacation in Len or Trish. Len was living in Nigeria in 1986 when the similar tragedy of Challenger Space Shuttle shocked Americans and nearly spelled the end of the space shuttle project. On that fateful day, January 28, 1986, space shuttle Challenger, with operational designation STS-51, broke apart one minute after launch at Cape Canaveral, sending all its crew to their watery graves. Len only felt that tragedy vicariously because he was so far away. Christa McAuliffe, an intrepid school teacher, was the first civilian to fly in a space shuttle, and she perished in that disaster along with six other astronauts. It was the most shocking tragedy since the inception of the U.S. space program.

Well, most shocking to the public, anyway. There had been some other harrowing losses of life in the course of the US space program but, until recently, such information was muted. For instance, the cabin fire mishap in which Gus Grissom, Virgil White, and Roger Chaffee got immolated on January 27, 1967, in the early days of the *Apollo* program did not attract much immediate public attention because the circumstances were murky at best. The three men were strapped down in their rocket cabin waiting for simulated take-off when a fierce and fast fire swept through the oxygen-charged cabin and roasted them as it incinerated the command module. Even when Grissom's family went public twenty years later with claims that the fire which killed Gus Grissom was no accident, the affair stayed somewhat low-key.

Perhaps the US public was more willing to accept human casualty then in the frantic race to leap-frog the Soviets — who had stung President Kennedy to the quick with their *Sputnik* satellite in 1957, galvanizing the President to announce from out of nowhere in 1961, an intention to land a man on the moon before that decade ended. Americans were confident that their technology was superior to the Soviets' and in the panic to offset the huge propaganda score of *Sputnik*, all stops were pulled. But now, twenty years and scores of space missions later, Americans were jaded on space topics and hesitant to risk human lives in the space venture, especially when it seemed intended as a mere publicity stunt, like sending a female school teacher into harm's way.

Those who died in the Challenger mishap included Ronald McNair, the first black astronaut to die in space; and Judy Resnik, who ranked with Christa as the first woman to die in space. Ellison Onizuka was similarly distinguished —as the first person of Hawaiian descent to die in the U.S. space program. However, McAuliffe's name became the one most prominently associated with that disaster because she was a civilian, while the rest of the crew aboard were military personnel who knew that lethal danger was the other side of glory and lurked behind every mission.

NASA had ballyhooed that Challenger shuttle mission as a caper to reignite public interest in a space program that was stagnating after lunar landings became all but routine. Including a female civilian on the crew was an imaginative idea that sold the plan to President Reagan. But while the US public was warm to that idea of showing that space travel by civilians was coming within reach, it was bowled over by the raw shock of the loss of a charismatic schoolteacher, and the resulting furor denouncing a cavalier "cowboy attitude" to space adventure nearly scuttled the whole space shuttle program. And now, when the U.S. public was becoming reconciled to routine space shuttle missions, the loss of Columbia threatened to kill the interest.

Len and Trish did not sing much on the way home this time. They were shaken to the core. It was like Arcachon and 9/11 all over again: You set out on a vacation singing, and came back glum and sad. The radio was switched off, not so much because of the depressing news of the Columbia disaster as the fact that the whole expanse between Nashville and Cleveland was just the Bible Belt, an infernal wasteland as Len pronounced it, where the only thing one could tune up on a radio was gospel music and fiery sermons. It made him sad. What kind of joyless people lived in those areas that would not sponsor one measly jazz or classical music station? How could the people put up with so much condemnation of earthly pleasures? In the enforced silence, Len's and Trish's arms found each other and elbows interlocked, interlaced fingers squeezing tightly to reassure each other of their love as they drove grimly home. Five years later he and Trish were to embark on another sad journey to Knoxville, Kentucky, across much of the same Bible Belt; that time Len was prepared and fortified with his throve of jazz CDs, mostly bebop and hard-bop, much to Trish's unease. His taste ran to jazz and classical music; hers was a bit more eclectic.

11
When in Rome

Oh when the saints go marching in
Oh when the saints go marching in
I wanna be in that number
When the saints go marching in

IT DID NOT take Len and Trish too long to succumb once again to the lure of a vacation trip spent together. Len was invited to give papers at a conference in Firenze, Italy; and again Trish agreed to come along. Until they took the plunge and became man and wife, the conference trips presented good chances for extended togetherness. Besides, Trish came from a family with strong Catholic affiliations, and she jumped at the chance to detour to The Vatican. Len was delighted, not only because he could no longer have a good time unless Trish was around, but also because he was not keen to travel to Rome again alone. He was once bitten and twice shy.

Six months before that fateful party at which he ran into Trish, he was attending a conference at the same venue in Firenze and, while the conference went well, his experience en-route was unpleasant. First of all, he missed his early direct flight from New York to Rome and was put on a later flight going by way of Madrid, Spain. Len was disappointed because he really wanted to be relaxed in his hotel room by early evening to watch what was for him the seminal match of the World Cup soccer tournament that was underway in France. That Saturday, June 13, 1998, Nigeria was to take on Spain in a Cinderella encounter. A loss to the much fancied Spanish team would likely knock Nigeria out of contention for the elimination rounds that were about to start. It was a do-or-die affair for both teams, and Nigeria was the underdog. The delay and re-routing of his flight meant that Len was still crossing the Atlantic when the match concluded.

When he alighted in Madrid and went up to Immigration desk he asked aloud if anyone on his flight had heard the outcome of the Spain versus Nigeria match. He hadn't contended with an English-speaking immigration clerk, but it was the clerk that announced, without enthusiasm, that Nigeria won by 3 goals to 2. And when Len handed over his U.S. passport and the clerk saw from the endorsement that he was a Nigerian, he looked balefully at Len, who felt glad to get out of that terminal without a black eye. Len was jubilant, but he kept his joy to himself.

Arriving in Rome three hours later Len disembarked and waited two hours for his luggage. He then filled complaint forms at the baggage counter and was told the bags would be brought to his hotel before he had to leave next day, Sunday, by train for Firenze. They never came. On his way home one week later he found that the compensation for his lost bags was ample, but in the mean time he had had to buy some new clothes to wear at the conference. It so happened that Len had some underclothing and toiletries squirreled away in his carry-on luggage and so did not have to go shopping at night in the disorienting Leonardo da Vinci-Fiumicino airport.

But it was not by luck that he had those undergarments and items of toiletry handy in his carry-on bag. Len had learned that precaution from a similar experience in 1982 when he went from Nigeria to New York and there connected with a flight to Bermuda for a conference.

At the La Guardia airport of New York, Len changed into a T-shirt and a pair of shorts like most people going to vacation in Bermuda and checked in all his baggage. He was tempted to check in his briefcase too, as he felt awkward carrying that attaché while in shorts; but luckily he didn't, for his luggage never arrived in Bermuda. The inconvenience of hurriedly shopping for tooth brush and such stuff in a strange place left a lasting impression on Len, so that thereafter he always carried a small cache of provisions in his cabin baggage. His prescription medicines for one thing, were always carried in his hand luggage.

When Len got back to Cleveland and narrated his lost baggage experience at the Rome airport, one of his colleagues told him he was lucky not to have lost his wallet to pick-pockets as well. The colleague told him how her husband arrived at Fiumicino airport some years earlier and as he turned a corner to go to the men's room, a pretty looking young woman came up to him, smiling. As he took a step back to avoid a collision, she threw open her cassock and bared her shapely torso to show she only had a bikini on, all the while smiling invitingly at him. She closed in and rubbed her nipples against his chest brazenly in public. For a moment he was dazed and did not realize that while she distracted him a man was going through his pockets from behind. In a flash they were both gone; the duo were pickpockets. They were Roma (Gypsies), Len's colleague said, and in Italy the Roma worked in husband-and-wife teams of thieves and pick-pockets. Len's colleague said her husband needed the help of U.S. embassy officials to continue his journey home. "When in Rome, beware," she counseled.

Hence, on this impending trip to Italy, his second, Len was glad to have Trish along for moral support. There were no visa scares this time as Trish had become a naturalized U.S. citizen a couple of months after the trip to France. He and Trish decided to carry as little as possible since they had multiple destinations within Italy and didn't want to be encumbered with too much haulage or —what was unspoken between them— to risk loss of baggage that might go astray. Trish resolved to go along with a good camera, for it was going to be a historic trip and a pilgrimage for her even more than France had been. Len got her a good Nikon camera, after telling her about the experience of his friend, who went to the Holy Land without a camera.

Len's friend Henry was returning to Nigeria from Germany after getting his Ph.D., and decided to go by way of the Holy Land. Henry's wife was a devout Catholic and Henry thought she would like to see Jerusalem and other biblical places. They flew into Tel Aviv and took a tour bus for a two-day excursion to Jerusalem, and Jericho (which was in the Israeli-occupied West bank of the Jordan). But they forgot to take their camera, which was packed with their checked luggage, anyway. Trouble was that when Henry got to his village and mentioned that he had been to Jerusalem and Jericho they doubted him. Skeptics said Jerusalem and Jericho were not of this earth: You couldn't get there unless you died first. One village "Thomas Didymus" mumbled: "Jericho? Isn't that where Joshua's horn blew down the walls of the city?" Assured that it was, his eyes grew round. Others remained skeptical. Henry had no pictures of himself in Jericho to show them. It took a lot of fast talking to convince his villagers he had not dreamed it up. Still, some of them rolled their eyes each time they referred to him as the man who went to Jericho and came back alive. "So, honey," Len said to Trish, "I will make pictures of you when you stand in Vatican Square."

Other aspects of their preparation for the trip were simple. As a US citizen like Len, Trish was not even required to take along an inoculation record to show at the airport before boarding the flight to Italy. It was as if the Italian health officials thought Americans to be free of vexing parasites carried by people from developing countries. Nor were security checks as intrusive and ostentatious going out to Europe as they were when you came in the opposite direction.

Customs checks for contaminating flora and fauna were perfunctory too. Everything went smoothly, but Trish showed a certain unease and Len asked her what was amiss. She blurted out that she hoped there would be no mishap this time. Every time they went on a trip together these days some calamity struck. Len too was thinking of Arcachon on 9/11, and of Cocoa Beach and the Columbia tragedy. He hugged Trish and whispered in her ear: "Honey, don't jinx this trip. Nothing bad will happen."

Nothing extraordinary happened —on the outward leg of their journey. They landed at Rome's Fiumicino airport as dusk was gathering and continued northwards by train to Firenze and then beyond it, to Montecatini Terme which lay another half hour to the Northwest of Firenze. The hotel at which Len had a reservation was in Montecatini, a pleasant tourist and spa resort situated a half hour by train from the heart of Firenze. But most European cities do not really have a single 'heart' or downtown area as in the U.S., and the closest thing to that designation in Firenze is area around the famous *Duomo*, a Gothic cathedral whose cupola (or dome) is the world's largest, dominating the Firenze skyline. The convention center for his conference was about equidistant between the *Duomo* and the main railway station of Firenze, *Santa Maria Novella* (SMN), a hub of tourist travel. The expanse of SMN, with its cavernous interior and special rail lines for the high-speed trains that whistle like javelins between European cities, bespoke its great importance as a gateway to Lombardy, the industrial region of northern Italy.

Len and Trish stayed four nights in Montecatini: three nights during Len's conference and a fourth afterwards because they wanted to explore the surrounding Tuscany area, home to Siena and Pisa. Len liked Montecatini; he had stayed there before and found it agreeable, affordable, and pleasant, although the first time, his experience was nearly marred by a sordid encounter. Heading back to his hotel early in the evening one day after conference sessions in Firenze, Len got confused. After riding for almost one hour Len realized he had taken the local train to Pistoia instead of another to Montecatini Terme. With a quizzical look on his face he mouthed "Montecatini" to a man who went through the train checking tickets. The man looked at Len's ticket and said one word of English: "*Wait*" and pointed at his chest. At Pistoia the man came back, took Len, and led him to station officials with instructions spoken in rapid-fire Italian. Smiling to reassure Len, the officials took him off the train and on to the platform for southbound trains. They put him on a train going back towards Firenze as a man in halting English told him to "Change in Prato."

Twilight was descending as they waited at Prato for the train to Montecatini Terme. While they stood there on the platform, Len suddenly heard a group of young women talking to each other in his own native language, Igbo. There were about four of them and they had the easygoing air of people who had no set designation but might go in whichever direction the wind took them. "Shall we stop at Montecatini tonight or are we going to Lucca?" one of them asked aloud in Igbo, and another one interjected in pidgin English, "It doesn't matter." Len got the picture: Nigerian media were often decrying the numbers of young Nigerian girls leaving the country to ply their wares in the booming sex markets of Europe, particularly Italy. He was saddened to encounter the reality of that flesh market here at twilight, in the middle of nowhere.

At Montecatini Terme he got off and two of those ladies got off also; the other two presumably continued west, perhaps to Lucca. The next morning as he waited for a train to take him back to Firenze he saw two young black women. They must be the same ones who rode in his train the previous night, he thought. They looked unkempt and haggard, squatting on the platform, hawking phlegm from their throats and spitting it out right on the tracks. Len was not sad anymore; he was disgusted and looked away.

Now, as the train carried him and Trish slowly toward Siena, Len narrated that experience to Trish, who was more forgiving, pointing out that, as James Brown sang in *Hot Pants*, "You got to use what you got to gonna get what you want."

That put Len in a mischievous mood and he told her the bawdy story of St. Catherine of Siena, the lady whose name lent prominence to an otherwise ordinary Italian town. Saint Catherine is a patron saint of Italy (a distinction she now shares with St. Francis of Assisi); she was promoted to Patron Saint of all Europe just before the dawn of the millennia —and by no less a respected pontiff than Pope John Paul II, who was Trish's favorite pope. The fame of St. Catherine rested to a large extent on her graphic accounts of intimate, some would say erotic, visionary encounters with Jesus Christ and some saints.

When Catherine was barely out of teenage and fanatically devoted to a reclusive and ascetic life, she claimed to have experienced an intense and rapturous encounter with Jesus Christ, which she actually called a "mystical marriage" to Jesus, culminating in a physical union during which Jesus came as a shaft of light and penetrated her body, infusing her with intense ecstasy. That claim was sensational in its time, and even more so in these days of skepticism. Irreverent scholars have been quick to point out that what she described was probably sexual fantasy, perhaps brought on by self-stimulation (*aka* masturbation), which she conflated in her mind with a holy experience rather than an all-too-human desire. Trish was disgusted with the story, and especially with Len's evident delight in telling it.

From Siena they went to Pisa, which was a more secular and mundane experience. They visited the famous Leaning Tower. The weather being gorgeous, the place was swarming with tourists most of whom kept making pictures of themselves and their companions stretching out their hands so that their photos gave the illusion they were supporting the leaning tower. Len and Trish enjoyed that excursion very much. Then they went back to Montecatini Terme to pack for their trip to Rome next day.

Trish liked Montecatini Terme as much as Len did. The lives of the natives and residents did not seem complicated: At least there was little evidence of tension and insecurity, such as one feels in U.S. cities, with people wary and distrustful of each other. Len and Trish felt safe walking around the town at night, observing families gathered in one square or another. Plazas were comfortably lit and featured nightly scenes of families walking around in a leisurely manner, exchanging greetings and conversation, sipping tea (or something stronger), lounging with neighbors, or dancing in the open. Perhaps it was some kind of festival time. There was usually a local band playing dancing music in each plaza, enticing old men to dance with their wives, daughters, or granddaughters.

On their first morning in the town the bustle of daily activities started early, waking Trish and Len up at 5:30 am. From their open hotel window they saw that much of the early morning bustle centered around a clearing not far away. It looked like a market. But who went to market at such an ungodly hour? They decided to go there for fresh air and perhaps good coffee. Len and Trish were both avid coffee drinkers who found much disappointment in the quality of coffee served in the U.S.

Americans drank perhaps as much coffee as anybody else, but it was all tepid stuff, watered down and so thin and pale it looked like urine. American beer was the same way: It was advertized with so much razzmatazz but in the view of foreigners it was light and mild as lukewarm water. People of the British Isles thought of American beer as nothing more than mere 'shandy,' a concoction of beer and soda pop which women favored because real beer tasted kind of bitter and left an undesirable taste and smell on the breath afterwards. Visiting friends and relatives from Europe or from Nigeria, as well as European colleagues whom Len hosted for conferences and so on, always said they would rather drink an ounce of real, intense coffee or a glass of beer with character, than the buckets of dilute stuff Americans drank. Len agreed: He liked Turkish coffee (*ahwa Turki*, as Arabs called it) or, failing that, French or Italian coffee, which were served in small cups rather than the sixteen-ounce pitchers that Americans called mugs.

At home, in his study, Len made that point by displaying, in juxta-position, two coffee cups on his shelf. One was a thin and dainty por-celain coffee cup he took home from a conference visit to Cambridge University in England; it was so small it could be held up by the handle, even when full, with just the thumb and index finger. The other was a double-walled plastic mug (really a bucket) which was thoughtfully provided with a non-slip grip pad on its wide bottom. It was proudly inscribed with "Harvard Law Library" and the crest of the school. Len had bought it at Harvard University during a stop-over after giving a seminar at the Massachusetts Institute of Technology; it was so big you could only lift it with two hands when it was full, and it took all of twenty-two fluid ounces to fill it.

Len used the dainty one to drink coffee and the jumbo mug to drink water. An assortment of the more regular ten-to-twelve-fluid-ounce American coffee mugs was also displayed on the same shelf. Each time a guest came into his study he offered them coffee or tea and asked, with a mischievous glint in his eyes, which cup they preferred. Nobody wanted the protuberant Harvard pot, so he won-dered why such a monster was made in the first place.

For as long as he could remember, Len had always bought whole-roasted coffee beans for his own consumption; he ground it only when he was ready to brew it, and he brewed just enough for two good cups each morning, and again before bed time. He could not understand the reputation coffee had as a stimulant that keeps people awake; nothing kept Len awake when he was ready to sleep, and sleep was his favorite activity —well, inactivity. Incidentally, Magda and Trish were enthusiastic drinkers of Len's type of coffee. Like Len, Magda would drink a cup or two of good coffee, then turn around and promptly go to sleep for the night.

Petite (four-cup) coffee percolators adorned the shelves in Len's home: in the kitchen, in his office, and in the bar in the basement. On their trip to France the previous year, one of the souvenirs that Len and Trish bought was a pair of French presses for brewing coffee "just right." Putting that gadget back together after washing it following each use was a trying ordeal (and for that reason Trish soon put it aside to return to her conventional percolator), but Len mastered it, for it brewed coffee with a fresh and delicate bouquet. French-press coffee is to connoisseurs of coffee what cognac is to liquor aficionados.

Trish too had been looking forward to drinking splendid Italian coffee on this trip. Arm-in-arm, she and Len went out into the cold morning air, singing, "Here we go round the mulberry bush...on a cold and frosty morning" and stepping out in time to match the tune, pretending to be unaware of the smiling faces that regarded them with friendly amusement as they went towards the clearing. Being with Trish, like being in a shower, always brought out the child in Len, with a song on his lips. The little plaza they spied from their hotel window turned out to be some sort of entry way, with a larger square behind it and cordoned off with a fat chain and lock. When they got there the area had just been opened and groups of families were ferrying fruits and vegetables and deploying them on tables neatly arranged in rows in front of stalls. But it was 6:30 am and the place was not yet open for business, and not knowing how to ask in Italian when transactions would start, Trish and Len turned the corner to go away.

As they got to a corner a girl tending a kiosk smiled at them and said "Alloh!" Len replied, "Bon Giorno!" The young lady continued in English, "Good Morning!" causing Len to smile broadly in relief and appreciation. Here was progress at last. And it was not by dumb luck that he and Trish ran into a girl here, in the middle of nowhere, who spoke English. In most European countries Len had visited, he found that students were learning English language starting in middle or even elementary school. EU countries were offering teenage students curricula that included two or more foreign languages such as French, Spanish, and German in addition to English and the local languages of their country. As with their uniform adoption of the metric measuring system decades earlier, European countries were positioning their citizens to be cosmopolitan. In contrast, in the U.S. where even such august institutions as NASA and the universities were still measuring things in the medieval units of feet and bushels and ounces, there appears to be no general desire to conform to any but American ways of doing things.

Len asked the girl the name of the place and she replied *Mercato Autofrutticolo*. Len leaned forward to indicate he didn't quite catch the phrase. The girl repeated the phrase and Len said it after her: *Mercato Autofrutticolo* (with the 'r' in 'mercato' rolled). Trish remained puzzled. Len said perhaps he could translate it by association with *Latin*. '*Mercato*' obviously stood for 'market' and '*frutticolo*' must be related to fruit cultivation, the '*colo*' being of the same root as '*agricola*,' *Latin* for farmer (hence the English word "agriculture"); "auto" was now a universal prefix in many languages for modern processes. So Len said to the girl: "A market for fresh fruits?" to which she nodded with a broader smile. Len repeated "Mercato Autofrutticolo."

However, Trish grappled with that phrase with pretended clumsiness. To all appearances she couldn't get her tongue around it. But Trish was full of pranks like that. In reality she was, of course, a remarkable linguist, like Magda. Come to think of it, Len often thought that Trish had so much in common with Magda. Did he perhaps subconsciously regard Trish as a surrogate for Magda? If the vivacity, the companionability, and the feisty playfulness of Trish were grafted onto all the other superb qualities of Magda, and religion leached out of the mix, the resulting creature would be the ultimate consort of Len's dream. But wishes were not horses…. Anyway, at *Montecatini Terme* that morning Trish stumbled hopelessly over *Mercato Autofrutticolo*. The best she could render it was '*frutticata*.' So they ended up calling it "*The Fruticato*." They went there every afternoon after returning from Firenze. It was a lively and colorful place to buy fruits and those vegetables which Trish loved to eat raw (like a goat, Len once said to her).

They were a little sad to leave *Montecatini*. By the time their express train from Firenze's Santa Maria Novella station pulled up at the Roma Termini station, it was already late. Len had made a reservation at the Hotel Barberini, an excellent but expensive place to lodge (expensive to Len because he was personally bearing the cost of that discretionary diversion to Rome as it could not be charged to his NASA conference account). Len chose that chic hotel in part to impress Trish but also because it was on the municipal train line, Metro Line A, which would take them to Vatican City the next day. He and Trish were tired but full of anticipation for the next day, an entire day to spend exploring all the sights they could cover.

Trish was agog with excitement. Rome is a living museum, a place of fascinating history going back to the beginning of time, or at least to the beginning of the Christian era —which was the beginning of time as far as Trish was concerned. She wanted to see all of it, but since they had only one day to spend, a Saturday for that matter, when the sights were crowded, they settled on seeing Vatican City, the Coliseum, and whatever other sites were conveniently located nearby. Rome was the ultimate tourist place, as touted by the bandied phrase, "See Rome and die," and throngs of people flocked to Rome, so that on any given day there were more visitors in Rome than there were residents and natives combined.

Vatican City, seat of The Holy See and powerful citadel of the Catholic empire that sprawls all over the world, has a history and aura to awe anyone. Its gateway, St Peter's Square, is a vast and open courtyard that is always a crush of lay visitors as well as pilgrims most of whom come in large tour groups from their faraway countries. On that Saturday morning as always the square started its day with a parade of the Swiss Guards who grace the square in their bold red-blue-and-yellow-striped uniforms. Each of the guards was young, spare, and tall, looking like Garibaldi in full ceremonial regalia. Clearly, in these modern times they are chosen for their looks rather than their historic role as mercenary guardians of the Vatican (as well as of other European royal courts) since medieval times. Trish and Len posed for pictures with the willing guards, replete with a background of swirling throngs of people and the commanding dome of St. Peter's Basilica.

They went into the Basilica, with its imposing interior that took their breath away with its hugeness. Multiple altars, gilded papal chair, and innumerable alcoves high off the ground, along with fluted columns and candelabras soared from floor to a ceiling forty or fifty feet above and topped with paintings on the distant ceiling. Tourists gaped and gasped at the grandeur of it all until dizzy, staring at the gorgeous baubles erected by vain men *ad maioriam gloriam Dei* (toward the greater glory of God). These grand structures were of course built in times when the Papacy had political powers rivaling and exceeding those of secular monarchs, indeed when the Pope wielded dominion over emperors and kings of earthly realms. Those were the days when temporal power was construed as divine empowerment, an attitude that was enshrined in an old English song, "The Vicar of Bray" (which was sometimes sung to the same "Handkerchief Dance" tune of Sir Percy Granger's *English Country Garden*):

In good King Charles' golden days when loyalty no harm meant
A zealous high churchman was I and so I got preferment.
To teach my flock I never missed were kings by God appointed
And damned are those that do resist or touch the Lord's anointed
And that is the law I will maintain until my dying day, Sir
That whatsoever king may reign still I will be the Vicar of Bray, Sir.

Accordingly, those basilicas reflected the majesty of the Church, and yet St. Peter's Basilica was only the second grandest of Rome's four basilicas. At the apex of the totem pole was St. John Lateran's Basilica in which resided the gilded Papal Throne from which roost, in the olden days, the Supreme Pontiff commanded obeisance from the entire Christian world in his capacity as unchallenged secular Imperator, and "Vicar of Christ" as well.

After gawking at the interior of Saint Peter's Basilica, Len and Trish followed intrepid men and women to climb all the way to the top of the Cupola, Trish being more strongly motivated and crawling ahead of Len, on hands and knees, to the vertiginous tippy top of the structure —a lofty roost where one had a bird's eye view of the gateway St. Peter's Square below. Climbing down after an hour, they went to the rear of the basilica and into a manicured courtyard with a grotto and a fountain beside which was engraved the message, "Vidi aquam egredientem de templo…" (*I saw water flowing from the Temple….*) Everybody stopped there to touch the trickling water to their face or throw a coin into the pool.

Then Trish and Len followed the crowd and filed into the crypt where the popes are buried, in a sequence all the way from St. Peter, followed by St. Linus, and on to the most recent overlord of the Catholic empire. The resting spot of each pope is marked with an engraved plaque giving a brief account or history of that pontiff. Trish ran her finger over the plaque marking the as yet unoccupied final resting spot for Pope John Paul II, far and away her favorite pope. When Pope John Paul II died of old age three years later, Trish watched over and over, with tears in her eyes, the deeply touching documentary, "Witness to Hope," which chronicled the life and mission of that humble, little man, born as *Karol Wojtyla*, who strove so hard to give a human face to the forbiddingly rigid and aloof hierarchy of Church leadership.

Leaving St Peter's Square, Trish and Len decided to undertake a walk around the Vatican. On the cobble-stone roadway that goes completely round the Vatican, they trudged, hugging the Walls of the Holy See. Along the other side of that retaining wall was an orchard of sorts, where apples and other fruits hung over the wall just out of reach, tempting pedestrians to want to scale the wall and reach up to pluck some fruit. But Len saw no one stealing the fruits; indeed, the roadway that hugged the wall around the Vatican was almost deserted. Len was instantly reminded of the trees of the Garden of Eden, and he rolled his eyes in mock fright when Trish urged him to get some of the fruit. He whispered in her ear that a crazy serpent might be lurking around the base of those trees, and she elbowed him in the ribs. An hour later they were back in St. Peter's Square, having walked completely round the Vatican.

Next, Len took Trish to see the Coliseum, another breathtaking landmark of historic Rome even in its current state of ruin, which dates from much further back than the Vatican. They were exhausted from exploring the Vatican and hiking around it; they had little strength left to check out the Coliseum in any detail, so they contented themselves with posing for pictures with re-enactors who were dressed as Roman gladiators. Playfully the gladiators charged from around some nook, taking one by surprise and eliciting gasps as their collaborators made pictures of a wide-eyed tourist at the mercy of a scary-looking gladiator. These were valuable souvenirs.

After the Vatican and the Coliseum, one place Len yearned to visit was the Basilica of St. Paul. Paul was the only gospel writer that Len thought of as a scholar, and a skilled one too. To Len, the other gospel writers were mediocre in their prosody and unconvincing with their wooden approach to their narrative. But not Paul! His oratory was vaulting and soaring. One couldn't miss the fact that he was an orator and a passionately committed preacher, a man whose erudition dated from his early days as *Saul of Tarsus,* the learned and terrible persecutor of Christians.

As Saul, he had been the scourge of the early Christians —a foolish cult, he thought, whose members followed the teachings of a man that dared to put his new-fangled doctrine above the authority of Rabbis and the sacred *Torah.* Then, Christian mythology tells us, he was struck down on the road to Damascus and emerged as a dedicated champion of and spokesman for Christianity, having taken the new name of Paul. But whether one knew his as Saul or Paul, one couldn't accuse him of tepid half measures when he took a notion to engage a cause —whether that cause was to repress or to advance an idea.

Len was intrigued with Paul's passion, which shone through in everything he wrote as he did a volte-face and began to peddle the claims of the new followers of "Christ." Paul was a scholar after Len's heart, never mind the fable he promoted with so much zeal to the bitter end of his long and eventful life. His powerful tool for promoting the fledgling Church was his Epistles. All the way from his Catholic youth, Len's favorite passage from Paul, indeed from the whole Bible, was Paul's Epistle to Timothy. Len's high school mates had loved to recite that epistle during Mass near graduation time because of what it said about having finished one's course. In written instructions to his young protégé, Timothy, who was then gathering a Christian community among the Jewish refugees in Ephesus, Paul wrote:

All scripture is given by inspiration of God, and is profitable for doctrine, for reproof, for correction, for instruction in righteousness: That the man of God may be perfect, thoroughly furnished unto all good works.

And again:

For I am now ready to be offered, and the time of my delivery is at hand. I have fought a good fight, I have finished my course, I have kept the faith: Henceforth there is laid up for me a crown of righteousness, which the Lord, the righteous judge, shall give me at that day: and not to me only, but unto all them also that love his appearing.

Such soaring prose appeals to the mind as well as the heart. In our present day and age of vanity, Len thought, a man of such conviction and rhapsodic eloquence, effortlessly and routinely wielding such turn of phrase as Paul did, might be head of a "Mega-Church" of the type whose super-wealthy adherents come to his revivals in private jets; or such a speaker might hold forth with the grandiloquence of a demagogue on the floor of the U.S. Senate. Instead, Paul was beheaded by edict of Nero (that most callous and deprave emperor of Rome) and thus joined Peter the chief Apostle in martyrdom for the nascent Church —or so Catholic tradition tells us.

Len was not disappointed in his expectation of St. Paul's basilica. It was not busy with hordes of visitors or crammed with artifacts in the manner of St. Peter's Basilica, but it was no less grand. The main thing that impressed Len was its open spaces, especially the lofty height of its interior, within which fluted colonnades swept up to far ceilings as in St. Peter's Basilica. Len dragged a visibly wilting

Trish around as he explored the immense open hall. When they got ready to leave, Len fell into a long conversation with a couple of nuns who were in attendance at the entrance. They were bemused that a lay black man had come all the way from America to see St. Paul's Basilica. Len told them that his very first school in Nigeria, where he started in the "Infant" class for five-year-olds, was named after St. Paul, thus he felt a connection to St. Paul.

12
Mid-Air Crisis

Bye-bye life
Bye-bye happiness
Hello loneliness
I think I'm gonna die

THEY WERE RETURNING to the US the next day. Len and Trish arrived at the airport in good time, boarded the flight and took off without incident. The plane was a Boeing-777-300ER wide-body jet that could seat upwards of 400 passengers. Its interior was spacious, with ten seats across from window to window: four seats abreast in the center column and three more seats abreast in the side columns between each aisle and window. Len sat in a window seat as usual because he liked to enjoy the view of a majestic blanket of clouds that looked like a cushion beneath the aircraft as it glided serenely on its way at cruising altitude.

Trish sat next to him in the middle seat, and another passenger sat in the seat between Trish and the aisle. Totally exhausted from their happy gallivanting around Rome the previous day, Trish and Len barely stayed awake as lunch was served an hour after take-off. Lunch came with small bottles of full-bodied Italian wines, of which Trish drank only half of a bottle of the white, while Len drank two bottles of the same and then finished the remaining half of her bottle. Trish did not like dry wine. What's the use of grimacing, she asked, when one should be smiling with each sip of wine? She liked to tease Len about it, but he just kept telling her that most dry wines did not interfere with the flavor of the food, and he was always glad to polish off what she left over.

After their trays were cleared Trish began to slow down. She leaned her head on Len's shoulder and her eyelids began to droop. Len drew the little window blind, gave Trish a peck on the temple, and cradled her shoulder with one arm while with the other hand he held the magazine he was reading, *The Economist*, which he bought at the airport. He too fell asleep, but an hour later he felt the urge to go to the restroom. Gently easing Trish off his shoulder, he unbuckled his seat belt, wriggled past her and the aisle-seated lady, and stepped onto the aisle. But the moment he stepped onto the aisle, Len felt dizzy and the floor beneath him seemed to collapse. Swooning, he crashed to the floor and his lights went out. The next thing he heard was the anguished voice of Trish asking him urgently, "Honey, are you OK? Honey, please answer me! Are you OK? Honey!"

Len opened his eyes and saw a beautiful lady peering into his eyes. He blinked. The lady was on her knees, astride Len. But, funny, that was not Trish. The voice he had heard was Trish's but the face was not. Was he hallucinating? Len's first thought was that he had died, and this was one of the comely maidens Muslims believed a good man should expect as a reward if he ended up in paradise. The lady's hands pinned Len's down over his chest, her thighs splayed over him, athwart his torso in a very suggestive way. Paradise was cool as long as Trish was there with him; and this lady who must be part of his paradise reward, was cool as well. But if this was a dream, right on....

Len smiled. The lady did not. Seeing the glint in Len's eye the lady quickly said: "I am a doctor. Are you OK? Can you breathe?" A stethoscope hung down from her neck as if to confirm her statement. Maybe pinning Len's arms down was the lady's common-sense precaution to forestall him from trying anything to consummate what her posture might suggest to a mischievous mind. Or maybe she had finished administering CPR on him or was about to do so. Was he resuscitated or did he wake up by himself? He could not tell.

A man peeped at Len from over the lady's shoulder and said he was a doctor too. "You passed out and fell. Help is on the way. We are taking you straight to a hospital. You'll be fine." How so down-to-earth, Len thought. He turned his head and saw Trish, and relief swept over him. Trish was here with him and OK, all was well. Life was good. Whether he was in paradise or on earth did not matter as long as she was with him. But as they slowly and cautiously helped him up, first to a sitting position on the floor and then onto his feet, a peculiar smell rose from his clothes. The back of his underpants felt warm and sticky. Len figured out right away that he had lost control of his bowels while he was out.

But Len was not embarrassed. Not only was the smell faint and mild, but the only people who were crowding him appeared to be medically trained professionals; they live with the smell of bodily efflux all the time. Of course Trish was here too, but there was never a soul more tactful than Trish; she wouldn't let on that she smelled anything offensive from his body. She regarded Len's body as an extension of her own, and vice-versa; there was never an awkward moment between them. And Len was not easily embarrassed, anyway. He had a reputation as a non-conformist, almost an iconoclast. He was never much concerned with what people thought or said about him because his personal philosophy was that what mattered most was what he thought of himself. He didn't think that spilling his guts while unconscious was something he should be ashamed of: It certainly was not something he could have prevented.

Nor was he secretive about his body, as he had often explained and exhibited to Trish. The first time Trish happened upon Len in the bathroom of her own house he was seated on the toilet, with the door ajar. Trish's daughters were about, so she reached out and shut the door, but when she noticed the same thing the next day she asked him if he never shut the door while easing himself. Len replied that he was only peeing. "You pee sitting down, like a woman?" Len recalled that he had recently discussed with a male friend the necessity for a man to stand closer to the pot or sit down when peeing, and the man objected with a frown, paternalistically saying: "That's what women do!" So he explained to Trish that women certainly had more common sense about such things than men. Men thought nothing of standing far away from the toilet bowl and spraying the rim and the whole pot as well as the floor with urine that soon turned yellow and sticky —a mess which they, the men, seldom thought to wipe off afterwards.

When he stepped out of Trish's restroom that first day, he repeated his lecture about bodily functions. It was silly to be so secretive about our bodies. If nature had wanted us to hide our bodies we would be born with clothes on. She was impressed with his guilt-free attitude about his body, but wondered aloud if he had ever been embarrassed in the presence of strangers? Len reflected on that question, smiled, and told Trish a story.

In his last job as Head of the Chemical Engineering Department at a Nigerian university before coming to the U.S. on sabbatical leave, one of his perks was a private restroom situated right behind his desk. Because a closed door separated him from his secretary and all visitors, he did not worry about being discreet whenever he needed to slip into his bathroom to pee. Usually he undid his fly as he stood up at his desk before turning to walk into his restroom. It became a habit, which, unfortunately, he took with him when he went to NASA on his sabbatical leave.

One day, as he walked to the men's room at the far corner of the hallway of his NASA building, he forgot where he was. His zipper was already down as he neared the rest room and at that moment one of his lady colleagues turned the corner, saw him with his hand fumbling at his open fly, and looked quickly away with a smile and a giggle. When Len finished his business in the men's room he hunted down that lady and explained himself, and the lady roared with laughter. Trish roared too, when Len told the story to her.

Len was scathingly dismissive of the hypocrisy of Western societies concerning the human body. Westerners were encouraged to develop a prurient interest in the human body. Their missionaries took that neurotic attitude wherever they went to "civilize" native peoples. They were also taught to be disdainful of young women in African and American Indian societies who, of necessity or out of accustomed innocence, went about with only beads or leaves to cover their private parts. But the same sanctimonious bigots think we should "ooh" and *"aah"* at photographs of vain white women wearing dresses that show half of their nude, bulging breasts hanging out, or who pose for the media wearing only postage-stamp sized bikinis with the protuberant bulge of their *mons pubis* clearly accentuated.

Len used to wonder why they did not just let it all hang out, tits and all outside their dresses, the way that men of some innocent American Indian tribes walked about with nothing but a gourd to sheath their penises and protect those vital organs from harm. But he knew the answer to that one. They let part of their breasts bulge out just to achieve the desired effect: evoke erotic thoughts in men. If you were half naked because your people had always lived that way, or because you lacked a sex-fixated consciousness, well you were primitive. But if you exposed your tits or drew attention to the bulge of your cunt in order to titillate men's fantasy, that was *tres chic!*

Len maintained that being secretive about one's own body was a sign of neurotic propensities. In time, those who associated with Len closely came to acquire the same attitude of equanimity towards the human body, his own children among them. Now in this airplane where he had passed out, he was not embarrassed that he soiled his pants when he lost consciousness.

But when the doctors told Len they wanted to help him back to his seat, he knew that Trish would be particularly affectionate towards him in the present situation and he did not want to cause her serious discomfort with a musty smell for the rest of the flight. So he told them he wanted to use the restroom. They led him gingerly down the aisle and to the nearest men's toilet. He told the flight attendants and male doctor who hovered anxiously at the door that he would take a while, but he'd be OK.

Len got into the airplane toilet and wriggled to undress from the waist down. He had no shoes on that might get in the way. It was his habit to kick off his shoes and lie back every time he sat down in an aircraft; otherwise, his expanding feet would come to feel quite tight in his shoes as the flight progressed. So he would just jettison them as he sat down. Comfortable feet were a major priority for him. For that reason he always bought his shoes one size too big and used thick woolen or cotton socks to pad the fit. He also liked to go about in his own house with no shoes or socks to cover his feet. He liked the proximate feel of the ground on the soles of his feet.

Sliding off his pants and then his underpants, he threw the latter in the hand basin and ran water over it to wash off the waste. Collecting enough water in an aircraft hand-wash basin is always a challenge: The system is designed to prevent flooding the floors in mid-flight, so one has to scrub one hand by itself while holding down the water release button with the other hand. But he got the soil entirely rinsed off. Then he wrung the wet underpants repeatedly with copious amounts of paper towel. He scrubbed his hands and face, wrapped up his underpants in layers of paper towel, and stepped out of the toilet. They led him ceremoniously back to his seat. Trish, who was always prepared for eventualities like a Boy Scout, had a plastic shower cap in her handbag, and Len threw his wrapped apparel in it. Trish inserted it in one of those air-sickness bags that were always stuffed into the pocket in front of every aircraft seat, and then put the package in her handbag.

The lady who had sat beside Trish was asked to yield her aisle seat and ushered to an empty seat elsewhere. Len was laid awkwardly across two seats, his head on the lap of Trish who now sat at the window. Trish strapped Len's seat belt from his right shoulder and across to his left hip the way one deployed the shoulder belt of a car. Len heard them tell Trish the position was not safe and if there was turbulence or if the captain required people to resume their proper positions, Len would have to be propped up on one seat. A flight attendant wrapped Len in two blankets and Trish leaned over him, squeezing his shoulder, her eyes beaming love and support. Softly she sang to him: "You are my sunshine, my only sunshine...."

Len went right to sleep and was woken up when the pilot announced that they would be at Cincinnati airport in about twenty minutes; all passengers must be seated securely and fasten their seat belts. Seeing the puzzled expression on Len's face, Trish told him the flight was being diverted to Cincinnati because of his condition. It was the nearest international airport.

When their aircraft came to a stop in late afternoon, emergency vehicles with winking and flashing lights were already waiting at the tarmac. Len was slowly ushered down the aisle to the exit while some passengers wished him good luck and others clapped gently. Red-jacketed emergency crew carried a stretcher into the aircraft cabin door. Len was laid on it, secured with straps, and lowered down the steps. Other emergency personnel received the stretcher, laid it on a gurney and strapped it down also. Many other persons with walkie-talkies fussed around Len on the gurney. Trish held tight to Len, clutching his arm firmly, reassuringly while her eyes held his and she mouthed "I love you," over and over. A voice whispered to Trish that they were taking "your friend" straight to hospital. Her accommodation had been arranged at a hotel right near the hospital. But she shot back quickly: "Oh no! I'm coming along to the hospital." She climbed into the ambulance with Len and kept stroking his hair. He winked at Trish and asked her to come closer. She did and Len whispered into her ear: "I should do this more often!"

She thumped his shoulder playfully and said, "If you pull this scary stunt again I will kill you myself."

Len stretched and yawned and mumbled to himself: "Well, they say 'See Rome and Die!'"

Trish gave him a wry smile and said: "Tell me about it! You tried to prove them right, didn't you?"

They rolled off to a cacophony of screaming sirens and about a half hour later came to a stop in front of the hospital Emergency entrance. Whispered instructions were given to Trish. They gave her a number to call when she was ready for a ride to take her from the hospital to her hotel and told her their baggage (hers and Len's) were continuing to their original destinations and would be forwarded to their home addresses. Len's gurney rolled into the hospital and other emergency personnel took over from the crew that brought him in.

They brought him admission consent forms but since they would not let Len get off that gurney yet, Trish took the forms and completed them, asking Len for the requisite information. For his Marital Status she checked "Married" and gave the name of Len's spouse as Magdalene O. Obi. Trish hesitated at the contact phone number for Magda, and Len told her to write down his home phone number, which Trish knew. Then she passed the clipboard to Len who signed the consent form. While they waited for this and that procedure, the admitting nurse told Len they had called his wife and apprised her of his situation. Apparently Magda had insisted on talking to Len to make sure he was OK, so they brought Len the phone and he reassured Magda he was in good hands and she should not worry.

Magda said she was driving down to Cincinnati the next day to take Len back to Cleveland. Len gave the news to Trish, who reflected on it and then said quietly they should avoid an awkward scene in that hospital. But it was a four-hour drive at least, she added, and since her flight was leaving around noon she would be gone by the time Magda arrived. She pulled up a stool beside Len's gurney, sat on it quietly with a faraway look on her face while she stroked Len's hand. Len guessed what was going through her mind, and he muttered to her, "Soon, honey, soon." Trish smiled at him, got up and moved over to sit in an armchair in a corner.

Len drifted in and out of sleep between checks and tests. Nurses repeatedly checked his blood pressure: while he lay on the gurney, after he stood up, and when he sat on the stool. They wheeled him into a room and ran an EKG, then wheeled him back, then into a room where a doctor examined and questioned him. They wheeled him back. Trish fussed over him like a mother hen and he enjoyed her attention immensely. Trish sat down and he dozed off. Another hour or so later a nurse came up with a phone and told Len his wife was on the line and wanted to talk to him again. Magda said she had called Vina, who promised to come and see Len within an hour.

Vina? Len's mind went blank, but then he remembered that Vina, Magda's good friend and sister of Tina Ojemba, now lived in Cincinnati where her family had moved a couple of years earlier. Vina's arrival would complicate things. Len did not feel well enough to come up with an explanation for Trish's presence, especially since Trish and Vina knew each other well from when Vina had lived in Columbus. Trish came over to Len just as he handed the phone back to the duty nurse.

Len said to her: "Honey, have you called the kids?" No, she said. She was still wondering what to tell them about when she would get home. When she got to her hotel room she would call the number she was given, confirm her arrival time in Columbus, and then call her children. Len told her that Magda had just called to inform him that Vina was on her way over. "OK," Trish said, "I guess I better go to that hotel now." She leaned over and kissed Len on the forehead, then on the lips. She sighed and turned to head towards the door. Then she stopped and sat again in the armchair by the corner. She was struggling to gather her resolve, but wasn't doing well. She sat there for a long while until Len realized she was crying softly.

Len's heart gave a twinge. Why did Trish have to go through this? He and Trish had carried on in this manner for five years now. Trish did not deserve this. They loved each other deeply. The time had come to let Magda know how things stood. As if she read his mind, Trish looked at him, shook her head, came over, and whispered: "Honey, not tonight —not in a hospital." She kissed him once more, hitched her handbag over her shoulder and headed towards the door. Again she hesitated at the door, came back and said to him: "Honey, I really hate to leave you here alone and sick. Are you sure you are OK?" Len nodded and Trish said she would return later that evening. Len looked at his watch and pointed out it was already past 8 pm. He told her to just go to her hotel room, settle down and read, but Trish said her mind would not be at rest while he was lying alone on a hospital bed.

Just then a nurse came and told Len a room was ready for him. Trish followed them, just to see which room it was, she said. While attendants transferred Len from gurney to bed, Trish sat down on a chair. She looked beaten, irresolute. Finally, with great difficulty Len persuaded her to go to her hotel. He clinched it by threatening to climb down from his bed and walk her to the door.

A few minutes after Trish left, Vina and her husband arrived. After receiving assurances that Len was feeling well they told him they had run into Trish as they came into the hospital. Was she with Len? There was no way of dodging them, so he replied that, yes, Trish was coming from Nigeria, boarded his same flight in Rome, and offered to accompany him to Cincinnati after he fainted during the flight. Vina and her husband did not press further the obvious flaws in that story; so Len knew that they already suspected the truth. After, all he and Trish had carried on for five long years, almost openly. Their kind of affair could not remain secret for long and they made no special effort to hide it; they had merely waited for the right moment to come out with it. Vina picked up Len's clothes and placed them in a plastic bag. Len also handed her the bag containing his soiled underpants, explaining to her what had happened. Vina said she would launder his underclothes and his shirt for Magda to pick up and bring to Len when she arrived the next day. Then she and her husband said Good Night and left.

Soon after they left, as if on cue, the duty nurse told Len there was a call for him. It was Trish, just as if she had watched Vina and her husband depart. She wanted to come back to the hospital, but Len tried to dissuade her. She argued that she couldn't just keep pacing the floor, wondering if he was OK. The only question, she insisted, was whether he wanted her to bring him anything: perhaps some food? Len said a good bottle of mellow *Riesling* would be fine, thank you, and Trish said, "Fat chance they'll let me bring alcohol into your hospital room!" Len did not want to argue anymore, knowing how stubborn Trish could be, so he consented; but he expected they would turn her back at the hospital reception because it was already past 10 pm.

But Len had forgotten how persuasive and persistent Trish could be, and thirty minutes later she stepped into his room and flew over to kiss him.

"Geez! They actually let you in?"

"They had to. I told them I had your reading glasses and your BP medications in my purse and you simply must have them tonight. The duty nurse at the reception desk told me they could not let me bring strange pills into the hospital for a patient; so I suggested she could walk over to the night pharmacy and have the medicine checked out. Still, that nurse would not relent. She offered to bring the pills in to you herself and I replied: 'Certainly, if you will kindly write on this diary of mine that you are taking medicines from me to give to Len.' She thought better of it and waved me in."

Trish kissed Len absent-mindedly, then sat down and stroked his arm. Each was waiting for the other to mention the earlier, unplanned and awkward encounter between Trish and Vina. Len did not want to distress her with any hint of reproach. They both knew that if Trish had not dragged her feet when they found out Vina was coming, Trish would have left in time to miss Vina and her husband. But what was done was done, and worrying about it now was of no use.

Trish's stroking of Len's arm slowly stopped and she sat still, looking at her feet as if in deep thought. Len asked if she was thinking about the earlier run-in with Vina and her husband in the hospital, and she nodded. Len told her not to let it bother her much reminding her it was no use fretting over what cannot be undone. "But I might have prevented it if I had left all the time you were urging me to go," Trish objected. Len reminded her that he had not been very keen to let her go, either, so they both were guilty, if anyone should be blamed. He told her again there was no use crying over spilt milk. In any case, he added, perhaps that was the way fate would choose for them to go public with their relationship, now that their secret was out.

To nudge Trish out of her groove of guilt, Len playfully asked her: "So, what are you going to do now, sleep here with me?" "Yes," she answered and he shot her a look of alarm until he noticed she had that mischievous twinkle in her eye. She sat on the edge of Len's bed, on the far side from the bedside pole that supported IV tubes and bag, and cables taped to Len's chest and running to a machine fixed to the wall. It was a wriggly uneven hospital bed, with joints and motor-driven adjustments, and Len had put it in a jack-knife position for ease of pecking on his laptop PC. The nurses must have forgotten about Trish for no one came in to ask how much longer it would take her to give the pills and eyeglasses to Len. She and Len chatted while she held his hand and rubbed it absently but again her erratic strokes on his arm told him she was back in thought. She wanted to say something to him but could not seem to come out with it.

"Magda is coming tomorrow," Len reminded her. There was no doubt Vina would tell Magda about finding Trish in the hospital with him. Magda would ask him about it sooner or later and that would be his opening to tell Magda everything. The only problem, Len continued, was that after he had that conversation with Magda he would have to move out of his home. Of course, he could relocate to Columbus and either live with Trish or find an apartment of his own in the interim, but it would be too tiresome to commute more than two hours in each direction to go to work daily in Cleveland. But if he moved into an apartment in Cleveland, Trish would have to do the commuting, perhaps less often but still frequently enough for it to pose a logistical problem, what with her children living and schooling in Columbus.

The logical thing was for them to look for a suitable community between the two cities, and then they both would commute daily:

he to Cleveland and she to Columbus. But the expanse of land in-between was a wasteland of provincial, farming communities. Those communities, he reminded Trish, would not have suitable schools, or friends for her children to associate with. Trish and Len had gone round and round with that quandary many times before.

The conservatism of that area of Ohio, generally known as mid-Ohio, was not confined to racial matters; the people were simple country folks, essentially rednecks. The main cities of Ohio are Cleveland, Columbus, and Cincinnati, three cities connected by I-71, with Columbus located approximately midway between the other two. The areas surrounding those three cities are designated as "Northeast Ohio," "Central Ohio," and "Southern Ohio," respectively; the area between Cleveland and Columbus is usually called mid-Ohio, with Mansfield as its nucleus. In the course of their explorations for a suitable mid-way habitat between Cleveland and Columbus, Len and Trish often drove all over mid-Ohio. The terrain was pleasantly flat, featuring a rated "Mid-Ohio Sports Car Course" that Len and Trish visited three times.

On one such safari they rode in Len's Toyota Prius. Len had always preferred small cars, unlike Magda who preferred luxury cars (Mercedes and Lexus sedans) and Trish (who longed for, and eventually got a Lexus SUV). Before the Prius, Len had owned a Nissan Sentra and then a Toyota Corolla, both compact cars; he saw no need to move about in cumbersome, gas-guzzling, big armadillos. And when the Prius made its Ohio debut, Len was among the first persons to get on the six-month waiting list for one (according to the dealer). Len was proud of his Prius, which fetched a delightful forty-two miles per gallon.

After rambling all afternoon in that Prius through mid-Ohio, they stopped at Ontario, a small satellite village near Mansfield, for a late afternoon meal. Len parked and they went into a restaurant. They emerged about an hour later and saw a group of six men or more in two Ford pick-up trucks parked beside the Prius. Sensing trouble, Len and Trish went back into the restaurant and waited for the men to leave, but they didn't. After waiting a half hour it became obvious that the men were also waiting, casting looks in the direction of the restaurant. Finally, Len and Trish decided to brave it and walked to the Prius. All at once, the men in the trucks began to heckle them: "Why don't you fucking drive your fancy car to Japan?" But the men seemed to be all talk and no action, so Len started his car and drove slowly off, with the two pick-up trucks tailing him and the men hurling abuse at his Prius. It was the season when the Prius first appeared in the U.S., and the country folk were reacting to news speculation that cars like the Prius, coming from innovative Japan, were going to put Detroit and its twelve-miles-per-gallon behemoths out of their misery.

Trish and Len had been in no physical danger, but encounters like that confirmed Trish's skittish feeling that mid-Ohio was not a fit relocation destination for a twenty-first-century black family with young children. The matter of where to live always struck Trish and Len as a silly little logistical problem, but one that defied satisfactory resolution.

Maybe it was time for him to find a new job, perhaps in Columbus, Len mumbled. But which job? There was only one place in Columbus where he might find meaningful engagement and that was the Ohio State University. But he knew that universities were notoriously reluctant to hire any person who was past their prime —that is anyone who had already arrived at middle age. Exceptions were made for luminaries like Nobel laureates and Nobel-class researchers, but scholars of ordinary merit usually got into academic positions from their youth and then grew into whatever they would become. Breaking in at the top was becoming nearly impossible. Added to that was the fact that Len really liked working at NASA: He liked what he did there and was good at it, and he liked the fact that he was not bothered with teaching obligations.

Teaching was the real grind in academia. Students were going to college less well prepared or willing to exert themselves in the process of acquiring knowledge. Indeed, increasing numbers of students just wanted the grades, never mind the knowledge! The joke among his colleagues in Len's teaching days was that when a student earned an 'A' he or she would jubilantly tell friends, "I got an 'A'," but if it was a 'C,' he or she would say, "The professor gave me a 'C.'" Teaching had become a job to avoid if one could do so. Len taught occasionally in Cleveland-area universities, but only when he chose to do so, or when approached to help in an adjunct capacity. NASA had no teaching encumbrances and, even more appealing to Len, it conferred on its researchers a good international name recognition that carried prestige.

Trish and Len remained perplexed over what would become of them when he broke with Magda, and the issue always sat heavily on their minds, sometimes killing the joy of the moment. It was a problem they must solve, he and Trish, because they ached to formalize their relationship. Naturally, Trish left it to Len to grapple with that thorny question. They didn't consider that Trish' own occupation was perhaps more portable than Len's. That was because Trish had never shown any inclination to move out of Columbus. She more or less thought herself wedded to that city. When it came to migrating from place to place Trish was definitely not an adventurer. She was enthusiastic about traveling with Len everywhere, but that was travel; settling down elsewhere did not appeal to her.

Sitting by Len's Cincinnati hospital bed, Trish was beginning to nod off and Len remembered it was past her bedtime. She always preferred to be in bed by 10 pm because, unlike Len, she had disciplined herself to wake up everyday around 5 am. Len shook her gently, kissed both her eyes, and told her it was time to go. He walked her back to the reception, where Trish called for a cab, and they both sat down to wait. She fell asleep across his laps and was out when the cab finally arrived. Trish promised she would be back in the morning with Len's cup of coffee, then got in the cab and it drove away.

Len was still sleeping at 10 am the next morning when Trish came. Her golden voice and cheerful Good Morning woke him up. Then her footsteps, always brisk and purposeful, sounded down the hallway. Was she going away? He soon heard her footsteps again as she returned. She entered his room with a fistful of sugar-alternatives to sweeten his coffee. He noticed she had placed a paper cup full of coffee by his bed before she went out for sweeteners. He also noticed that breakfast was laid out on a tray on the little corner table. The hospital staff no doubt decided against waking him up and just let it sit there. Trish beamed a smile at him that was like sunshine and he smiled back. She gave him a peck twice on the forehead and put down the sachets of sweetener, reaching into her handbag for a toothbrush and toothpaste she had bought for him. How thoughtful of her, he thought. She had remembered that he did not like to take anything by mouth in the morning until he had brushed his teeth. Len stepped into the shower cubicle of his room and brushed his teeth. Then he came back and gave Trish a prolonged kiss. "You are an angel," he said.

Opening the lid of the paper coffee cup she poured one packet of sweetener into it, stirred it in and gave it to him. She also brought out a donut for him. He ate it gratefully along with the coffee. Len really liked his coffee quite hot, same as the tea which he preferred upon waking up from the occasional afternoon nap on weekends. If his tea or coffee was piping hot he sipped it, slowly and with relish,. But if it was only warm, as it was right now, he gulped it by mouthfuls. After two gulps he set the coffee down and sang to her: "You are my sunshine...."

Len asked if she had had breakfast, and she said yes, and a good meal at her hotel too. Yes, it must have been, Len reflected. Though the *Bible Belt* from Cincinnati south to Miami was what Len considered a "dead zone," in terms of the radio programming, a person passing the night in any hotel in that zone was sure to wake up to a sumptuous breakfast. Len remembered that fact each time he saw the phrase "southern comfort." Rather like the Dutch people, whom Len observed closely during a leisurely biking excursion once upon a summer in the area around Zandvoort on the North Sea, people of southern U.S. believed in a hefty breakfast to fortify one for the day ahead.

He asked Trish if she would like to eat his breakfast too, pointing at it. She made a wry face and said, "Ha! Hospital food! No!" She sat down and Len said he hoped his crisis in the airplane had not ruined her vacation. She assured him it hadn't; his company, she said, was all the vacation she needed. Len said it was exactly how he felt about her too, so all the excursions they had were icing on the cake. Trish then reminisced about the Vatican, which was her special icing, pure "chocolate delight." Len said his icing had been the 'Frutticato.' They burst into laughter. Len lifted the little cup of orange juice among his breakfast and used it to wash down his pills which he dug out from his toiletries bag.

Trish's flight to Columbus was to leave at 12:10 pm, so it was time for her to call the airline for her ride to the airport. She promised to call Len once she arrived home and she added, with a smile, she would, as usual, be thinking of him. Picking up her handbag, she asked Len: "Did you know your heartbeat is irregular?" She explained that when she came in that morning she had stopped at reception and the duty nurse informed her the plan was to discharge Len when the doctors came on their rounds today. His own doctor would follow up on his care when he got back to Cleveland. She asked what the diagnosis was, and the nurse replied that it was for the doctors to disclose that, but from what she gathered from the EKG results Len had irregular heartbeat.

Len confirmed he knew about that diagnosis from prior physicals but it had never before caused him to faint. During one physical examination he was told his heart had a "murmur." But it was said so casually he thought it was not an alarming development. He did not know whether the "murmur" and "arrhythmia" were one and the same diagnosis, but no one had recommended treatment before, so he thought the condition or conditions were things he had to live with. Well, this time he should find out, Trish suggested, and he agreed. He got up and walked her to Reception to wait for her ride to the airport. Just as they got there a man from the airline came up and asked for Ms Adoja. Trish kissed Len, and walked out with the driver. She did not turn to look back once. Len understood: If she turned back it would be harder to take her leave the second time. Trish was a sensible woman.

After she left, Len fell into reverie: about Trish, and about the life he dreamed the two of them would live together. If Trish had any flaw as a woman Len had not seen it so far. Or, maybe there was one, a tiny one. There was the matter of her disorganized domestic style. Len was punctilious about tidiness in a home because he learned early to equate personal comfort at home with ease of moving about. So he took a long while to reconcile himself to that weakness in Trish. In the long time it took him to accept it, he had come close a few times to telling her how he felt about it. But he realized the habit was too deeply ingrained to be remedied easily. He would only make her feel guilty and inadequate.

Trish's house on Riverbirch Drive in North Columbus —a compact subdivision of colonial-style family homes— was ample in size, but overcrowded with all kinds of stuff, useful and useless. The sprawl and congestion started in the garage. It was built for two cars and that is supposed to mean that when two vehicles are parked in it side-by side there should be enough clearance beside and between the cars to enable reasonably comfortable ingress and egress for the car occupants. But Len found that if he succeeded in squeezing his little car in it beside Trish's SUV, he could barely come out of his car, and then only by shuffling sideways, with his back scraping the wall and his feet negotiating booby traps on the ground.

That garage always reminded Len of a junkyard after a storm, strewn with all sorts of household flotsam and jetsam, serviceable and unserviceable. The upshot was that the garage could hold only one car at a time, and even at that one had to move things out of the way to bring in the car, or run the risk of crushing one thing or another. Rather than complain, Len braced shelves to one side and installed hanging hooks and pegs along the walls of the garage and reorganized the stuff. But when next he came for a weekend visit it was back to chaotic sprawl.

Every room in the house was similarly choking with excess stuff. Bedrooms had sundry items sitting on the floor or stacked on top of one another; dressers were crowded with toiletries, and towels were draped all over the bed frames or hanging from the doors. Closets were so stuffed with clothes stacked on shelves or hanging from hangers that it was difficult to insert any more clothes. Spaces under the beds were stuffed with boxes and bags and cartons.

Whereas the rooms were merely overrun with stuff but otherwise clean, the kitchen was a disaster, for it is hard to keep a kitchen clean if it is not tidy, because grease and grime and soot and dust settle on every-thing. That was particularly true of Trish's kitchen because she loved to cook, and she constantly entertained groups of friends that gathered around her kitchen more readily than in her sitting and living rooms. Tidiness usually required that deployed items be kept to a minimum, or at least down to manageable quantities. Generally, teenage children of U.S. households tended to need persuasion to wash dishes and put them away. Trish's children were no different, so that her sinks were always spilling with dishes and utensils waiting to be washed, while the dishwasher was occupied by dried dishes that were washed days earlier.

Len preferred to live in a home of high-ceilinged rooms for effective convective circulation of air, with open living spaces and floors of bright, clean, and comfortable carpeting which did not hide stains and upon which he could lounge now and then, and with wide and airy windows to let in a lot of sunlight. He especially liked it to be rather sparsely but tastefully furnished so that one could navigate easily without fear of colliding with or stepping on bric-a-brac. In order to implement those specs in his own home, he and Magda had designed and built it from scratch. He was aware that when one bought an existing home there was not much one could do about its physical aspects; but, he thought, one could at least decide how much furniture or what kind of carpeting to put in it.

Len thought that Trish's kind of crowding and sprawl reflected a certain propensity in people who, like himself, achieved suburban middle-class status by their personal effort, rather than being born into it. A sudden acquisition of enhanced purchasing power can trigger obsessive buying, a problem that was perhaps more acute with women, Len suspected. One day, he heard two female psychologists on a TV talk show panel discuss the growing habit of impulsive buying now that society was more affluent. One of them said: "When I get depressed I go out and shop." This was during a period of economic recession in the U.S. when radio stations (National Public Radio, for instance) were urging listeners to "go out and buy something," as a way to push the economy out of its slump.

Len had encountered that "go and buy" mentality before, up-close. When he started his first job as a professor, a colleague asked him a casual question at lunch one day to make friendly conversation:

"What was your first reaction when you got your Ph.D.?"

Len said his main reaction was relief: "Yippee! I never have to do another examination in my life!"

His colleagues countered with: "In my case I went to a store at a mall and said to myself: 'I can afford to buy anything I want from this store.'"

What distinguishes one person from another, Len thought, is knowing when to apply the brakes, or learning to throw away or give away old things when new ones are purchased. Some people just take it in and accumulate it, and eventually they get crowded out of their own houses. Len found it depressing to live in a house choking with stuff. The problem was not only aesthetic or physical (in the mere sense of colliding with stuff all the time) but also sanitary; a house choking with goods was a potential breeding ground for bugs and vermin, particularly roaches and spiders, which disgusted him.

Recognizing that Magda had a rather pronounced acquisitive tendency herself, Len bargained with her early in their professional lives: Each time she bought something new and substantial she should give away something of comparable size. Soon Magda became a frequent donor to Easter Seals society and the Salvation Army and those two organizations called her weekly to see what she had to give out.

With Trish it was trickier. In the early days of their relationship, Len worried about picking up bugs from Trish's house. So he kept his bags zipped up when he visited her, but eventually he relaxed and resigned himself to the situation. He indicated to Trish the need for less hoarding and stowage and more tidiness (with pointed but gentle hints, or just by compulsively tidying the place whenever he came to visit). But he said not a word about bugs and vermin. Having been intimate with Trish these past several years now, Len realized that the matter of Spartan tidiness was one point on which he was going to have to capitulate. He would just have to stand guard over the intimate space of his own study and surrender to chaos everywhere else. He knew how hard it was for an old dog to learn new tricks. An old dog himself, he appreciated people who did not try too hard to change his ingrained habits.

While ruminating about Trish's clutter-prone lifestyle Len drifted back to sleep, ignoring the tray of breakfast which had been sitting there before Trish came. They brought lunch around noon and by that time he was up and reading a book. They took his vital signs and pricked him for a blood sugar test. Everything was normal, they told him. He ate lunch without enthusiasm. He didn't wish to have the hospital staff thinking he declined both breakfast and lunch; that might elicit a lecture from the doctors about the desirability of eating so many meals a day; maybe this time they would up the ante to seven meals a day! He waited for the doctors.

13
Reentry

Darling, go home, your husband is ill.
Is he ill? Let them give him the pill,
Come on dear friends, just one more dance
Then I'll go 'way for my poor old man
Then I'll go home to my poor old man.

AROUND 2 PM the doctors trooped in like the cast of a play, all in white lab coats, led by the consultant and followed by his retinue of residents and whatnots. "And how are we feeling today, Mr. Obi?" the consultant asked. Len said he was fine and ready to go home. Then they ignored him and huddled in a busy caucus focused on his EKG chart and vital signs and lab results. All he caught from it was "A-Fib." Mischievously, he asked them whether "a fib" meant someone was lying about him. The senior resident sniggered. The consultant said "No: A-Fib is short for 'Atrial fibrillation.' A-Fib means that the atrium, the upper chamber of your heart, is pumping with some irregularity." Len replied that in high school he had learned that the heart had two chambers, the auricle and the ventricle; did he also have a third chamber called the atrium? At that, a familiar voice chuckled at the door.

Magda had sneaked in unnoticed behind the gang of doctors, at the point when Len was asking about "a fib." Now she cut in and told the doctors her husband was always like that, wanting to know everything. She walked over and gave Len a peck on the cheek and he introduced her: "My wife and favorite nurse, Magdalene Obi." The doctors smiled at Magda and she continued:

"My husband went through high school one century ago, and he has lived in a cave ever since. That's why he does not know that the upper chamber of the heart is now called the Atrium. And he likes to distract his care givers with silly questions."

Len clapped and said: "Nice lecture, my dear!"

The team of doctors then swirled out of Len's room and Magda followed them, returning soon to report that he was being discharged to the care of his primary physician. She went out to collect his discharge papers and came back a half hour later. Len left with her after expressing gratitude and saying goodbye to every staff member present on that floor.

He and Magda headed home to Cleveland, with Magda behind the wheel of her car. Like Trish she was a confident and competent driver. In fact, when his family traveled together Magda usually drove. Her pace was peppy, and that earned her reputation, when they were in Nigeria, as "the woman who drives like a man," since ladies were supposed to be tentative if and when they drove. Len fell asleep again as Magda sped northward to Cleveland. Riding in a speeding car always had a soporific effect on him. About an hour down the road Magda cleared her throat.

She asked Len: "I hear a Nigerian lady was with you at the hospital. Vina told me. Who is she?"

Well, there it was, Len thought. The cat was out of the bag, yet he stalled. Magda continued:

"Vina said the lady joined your flight in Rome. Do I know her?"

Len said: "We met her at that birthday party Tina gave for her husband a few years ago."

Wasn't that four or five years ago? Magda asked him. Had Len been in touch with her all that time? Only occasionally, Len replied, lying for no reason, and thus losing the chance to simplify his life right then. But although it was a lie, it included enough admission and ambiguity for Magda to latch onto and leverage out the rest of the truth. But she did not; instead, she retreated into silence. Len thought she was waiting to get them home before reopening the topic: When Magda was upset she typically clammed up. She was silent for another hour, even as they stopped for gas half-way home. When she returned to the wheel she appeared to be listless and pre-occupied with some troubling thought. She opened her mouth a few times only to shut it without speaking. Len waited, ready to cut the Gordian knot right there. Then she sighed and said she had to go to the UK the following week.

This is anti-climactic, Len thought, not without some relief. He was reminded of the anecdote of the clever boy who broke a glass window in his father's study while playing baseball. His mom told him to call his dad and report what he just did. Jimmy, the boy, remem-bered his father's temper, thought about the whole thing, picked up the phone and dialed his dad's number.

"Dad. Me and Pete were playing baseball in the yard and, you know the big bay window in your study?" His father groaned, "Oh no!" and Jimmy continued: "Well, I broke the little one next to it." And his dad said, "Thank goodness!"

Magda's news was about John, the youngest of her three broth-ers still living. John was in the UK on extended business trip and used the opportunity to seek better diagnosis and treatment of a lingering problem he had grappled with in Nigeria. He had been treated for ulcers before and that problem seemed to have reappeared in recent months. Even after he started bleeding and painful stooling his doctor kept treating for ulcer. His problem got worse and so in England he sought a second opinion. The news Magda got the night before was that John had colorectal cancer, and doctors wanted to start chemotherapy right away. There was a sizeable community of her family members living in England, a few of them practicing physicians, but in any kind of crisis she was the one they relied on most for support and comfort. She had to go there now, rather than wait for her scheduled vacation time in the fall.

Len commiserated with her and agreed she must leave as soon as possible. How soon would that be? She said one week, to give the hospital where she worked a little time to alter duty rosters and cover her absence. The rest of the way home they planned her trip and feeding arrangements for Len and the boys while she was gone. Every time Magda went to Nigeria or the UK on her accustomed two-week vacation she left them much cooked food parceled and frozen in small lots, each labeled and ready for a meal. But they were lazy and when she got back she was mad because most of the parcels of cooked food were still there, untouched. This time she lectured Len on how to thaw out, warm up, and serve the food she was going to leave for them. If she was going to exert herself to cook and package it for them the least they could do was eat it, instead of calling her in England to ask what to eat, as they sometimes did. Len kept quiet, knowing he was the chief offender.

14
No Divorce

A lady told me the other day
No one can take her sweet man away
I asked her what was the mystery
She said coconut water and rice curry

MAGDA SPENT THREE weeks in England rather than the fort-night she planned for and which was the usual duration of her vaca-tion trips there. The extension to a third week became necessary because John's treatment not going well. For visa, business, and fam-ily reasons John had to return to Nigeria after three weeks of chemo-therapy, but he planned to go back to the UK in a couple of months for more tests and follow-up. Magda returned to the U.S.

Two weeks after her return, her friends came to visit her as a group. Word had gone out about her brother's illness and the women came to welcome her back and express their wishes that her brother would recover soon. But they also came because every time she went to England, Magda brought treats for her friends, mostly snacks and toiletries. Usually she came back with pound cakes, Cheshire cheeses, Digestive biscuits, toffees, and PG Tips tea. And whenever they visited her they had a good treat to English tea and took away confections.

As always, such a group visit on a Saturday or Sunday was also an occasion for camaraderie. Women like to exchange gossip and recipes at such gatherings and Len thought that women had more fun among themselves when gathered together than men had in their own caucuses. There were quite a few of them on this occasion. The sitting room could not seat a large group, so some of the ladies gathered around the coffee table, squatting on their haunches, Oriental style, on the deep-pile carpeting. Others sat on the extra-large bean bag that, six feet across, commanded the space in front of the fireplace.

Whenever they gathered like that Len served them wine as a livelier alternative or addition to the tea Magda brewed for them; then he would quietly withdraw to his study in order not to dampen their enthusiasm or get his ears burned by the raunchy jokes they sometimes shared. He only emerged every half hour or so to refill wine glasses or tea cups, and serve them cheese or crackers. The younger wives, who aspired to hosting small dinners like the ones Magda gave often, asked Len questions about the wines and cheeses. He and Magda were wine drinkers all the way to when Len was in grad school, and their home was always well stocked with wines. He was happy to oblige them: What wines went best with what dinner fares, which ones should be served chilled and which one at room temperature, whether it was safe for one to start with some vintner brand and then go on to others as the evening wore on, etc.

Today, one of the ladies described her reaction to the move "The War of The Roses," which she had just seen. Unfortunately, Len had come in to refresh the drinks when the lady opened up on that topic. He listened for a while and then commented that he had a few colleagues who divorced or got separated from their spouses but still preserved a harmonious relationship or even close friendship with the same spouse. He thought that was a more civilized way to end a marriage because it caused the least harm to all parties involved, especially children. But, he added, it seemed that such notion of friendship after divorce was alien to Nigerians; whenever their marriages broke up the fall-out was nearly as spectacular as in "The War of The Roses."

At Len's comment all hell broke loose. Some of the ladies jumped up in excitement, others slid off the couch to kneel and deliver their opinions with fists thumping the floor or the wooden edge of the coffee table. The prettiest of them, a teacher who usually displayed a robust spirit of self assurance, asserted that if ever her husband even thought of leaving her she would deal with him in such a manner as to make the scenes in that movie look tame by comparison. Her vehemence was frightening: She actually pounded her right fist into her left palm as she said "deal with him." Sensing that the lady had a problem, Len regretted his comment.

But the ladies were only restating what Len knew was the common Nigerian perspective on marriage. To Africans in general, marriage was perceived as a one-way and once-only journey. Divorce was uncommon. Once you got into matrimony, all the social and cultural pressures constrained you to stay in it. In his parents' time the men found relief by taking more wives, but it was an asymmetrical relief since the wives could not take multiple husbands. Listening to his elders as he was growing up, and to his friends in high school, Len was quite surprised to gather that in some traditional cultures it was permitted for a married woman to keep a concubine that did chores for her when her husband began to pay diminished attention to her. Indeed, a common proverb in Len's native dialect held that if you told a child to name a man it knew, the child was likely to name its mother's concubine. But such an arrangement must be difficult and furtive, Len thought, because a wife was constrained to live in the home of her husband and so had limited capacity for independence or privacy.

But times and mores were changing and wives of the present generation at least had the voice to condemn polygamy and concubinage. Therefore, when news items were about spectacular divorce cases among celebrities, or when movies like "Kramer versus Kramer" came out they were hot topics for discussion among young Nigerian wives everywhere. Of course men were not as concerned with that topic as were their wives. Len had unwittingly become a participant in that strange debate raging in his own house on an otherwise pleasant weekend afternoon. So he sat down to listen a little more as the ladies vented passionately about what to do if they faced the prospect of a divorce.

As they described their views on the sanctity of marriage, Len was reminded of an ingenious trap that villagers often employed to catch fish. A fish could get in easily to take a smaller fish set as bait inside the barrel-shaped trap, but when it turned around to get out it was deterred by nasty spikes; it was trapped. Len saw that the views of marriage held by these women was like that fish trap: Its only outlet was death. He was brought back from his fish-trap rumination when, to his astonishment, Magda piped in to say that a man should not enter into marriage if he wasn't ready to die in it. They chorused, "Yes!" but none of them said anything about a wife dying in the marriage too. As far as the ladies were concerned, divorce was always to be laid at the feet of the man, not the woman. Len thought Magda gave him a sly look with that comment of hers. Was it a message to him about Trish? He got up and walked back to his study with a little unease. Little did Len know he would have occasion to recall Magda's words on this topic — and let himself be paralyzed by their import.

15
Setbacks

The old home town looks the same
As I step down from the train
And there to meet me is my mama and my papa
Yes, they'll all come to meet me
Arms reachin', smiling sweetly
It's good to touch the green, green grass of home.

SIX WEEKS AFTER that "War of the Roses" discussion Magda got the sad news that John had passed away in Nigeria before he could return to the UK for more treatment. He was a lecturer in a School of Agriculture but liked to moonlight as a pastor, ministering to the members of a little church in his neighborhood. It was of course a Nigerian predilection: Some commentators estimated that every third building in each Nigerian town was a church or a chapel of sorts (if one included homes with shrines and altars built in for worship and rituals in small groups), and about 15 percent of the population practiced or aspired to practice as pastors or bishops or archbishops, many of them self-designated prelates. That was in the southern states of the country, of course; in the northern states, with the majority of citizens clinging fanatically to Islam, the proportion of preachers and prevalence of ramshackle churches was lower.

The commentators joked that the more corrupt and debauched the Nigerian society became, the faster the churches proliferated.

John had his own church and when he got home from the UK and told his congregation about his health problems they declared it was foolish to travel so far and spend so much money for a "white man's" esoteric cure when all John needed was round-the-clock chanting and singing by their local "Prayer Warriors." As long as you kept them fed and lubricated and motivated them with the rustle of cash in their "Offerings Basket," they guaranteed deliverance by their Good Lord, provided you were deserving of it. So John surrendered to their noisy ministrations and they went to work. It did not help that he was also fasting through their ministrations, at their behest. They were still at it two weeks later when John gave up the ghost. And since he was their pastor they prescribed for him what they called "a befitting funeral" (the euphemism in Nigeria for a lavish funeral ceremony and feast), naturally at the expense of Magda's family.

Magda traveled again, this time to her home town to assist in the funeral rites for her baby brother. It was for such emergencies and for her annual vacations that Magda accumulated the vacation times that accrued to her on her job. She had another week of earned vacation time, and she combined it with sick time to cobble together a three-week stay in Nigeria. There were family matters to attend to; and her other brothers and sisters would be there for the funeral, so it was going to be an intimate family occasion, albeit a sad one.

For Len a season of vicarious bereavement had started. When Magda was gone a week and a half, Trish was hit with the first punch of what was quickly to become a torrent of blows from an unkind fate. News came from Nigeria that her father died: His chauffeur lost control of his car on a clear stretch in broad daylight, and the old man died following the crash. As happened so often in superstitious

Nigeria, rumor spread that he was killed with magic by enemies. Len was sometimes startled by obituaries that lamented that "The Wicked Have Done Their Worst," even when the deceased just collapsed and died in public and autopsy showed he had died of heart attack. Few Nigerians believe that one could die a natural death —especially, not in this case where Trish's father's car was in a one-vehicle accident in a noonday and without hitting a tree or another vehicle. If it wasn't a result of witchcraft, they reasoned, why was the man's driver unharmed, though he was at the wheel when tragedy struck?

As the oldest child of her father, Trish had to go and arrange the funeral. Villagers advised her to stay away because whoever killed her father might be out to get her too, but she ignored them. Trish often told Len how close she and her dad were. The old man doted on his two daughters and Trish had only fond memories of him. His death would be hard on her, Len knew. One hour after hearing the news from Trish on the phone Len called a Detroit travel agent and arranged a reservation for her two-week trip to Nigeria; he knew she would be too disconsolate and disoriented to focus on logistical details. Another couple of hours later he was on the road to Columbus.

When he arrived she fell into his arms and wept softly. He stayed two days with her while she made arrangements for her trip. Because she was coming home from America, a "land flowing with milk and honey," her townsmen would milk her resources to exhaustion. As her dad had been a man of substance in his community, he was expected to get "a befitting funeral." She had to travel with ample supplies, down to paper cups and plates, napkins, plastic cutlery and a baked cake. Those items could be purchased in Nigeria, perhaps at competitive prices, but the villagers thought it was better when carted in from America at considerable effort and cost.

16
His Pink Slip

Count your blessings, take them one by one
Count all your blessings see what God has done.
Count your blessings, take them one by one
And it will surprise you what the Lord has done.

WHILE MAGDA AND Trish were both in Nigeria attending to funerals, Len had freedom from both of them, something he was not used to. It was an opportunity to take a holistic look at his life, to ponder his future and reassess his priorities. More fundamental than the question of when and how to bring about a break-up with Magda and take up with Trish were the questions of where he wanted to live and what job could take him there. In other words, what were his career plans and options?

Len always considered himself on extended leave of absence from his permanent position in his Nigerian university. There is no question but that his heart was still anchored in Nigeria while he sojourned in the U.S. Whatever contributions he could make to human progress would go much further in Nigeria (where such help was sorely needed) than in the U.S. where there was a surfeit of experts and professionals in every field. Even in terms of his personal needs rather than philanthropic contributions to human development, Nigeria made more sense than America as the place of his final abode.

The U.S. was an excellent place to get a good education and practical skills and an even better place to run a career. Jobs were more plentiful, versatile, and more lucrative, and offered the individual more scope to become an important participant, a team player rather than one who merely took orders or gave them. But when one approaches retirement, as Len would in a decade and half, the U.S. was a depressing option as a terminal abode. It was a terrible place to grow old. The "senior citizen" here was not as valued as in Len's native Nigeria. After retirement in the U.S. a man had mostly idleness, loneliness, and relative poverty to look forward to.

Even one's family, down to his grandchildren, tended to drift away from him and get caught up in the busy pursuit of their own lives. They might even (horrors!) consign grandpa or grandma to the tender mercies of the dreaded "old folks' home." In contrast, the retired grandpa in the Nigerian society was regarded as a sage, a patriarch, and as a valuable living link to the family legacy, and the ancestors. Len dreaded the possibility of growing old in the U.S. In a decade at most he must transition back to his ancestral home. The main damper was that Nigeria had become more deeply mired than ever in mediocrity, with a succession of military governments run by idiotic "generals" who conceived half-baked ideas and then ordered them to be carried out "with immediate effect and automatic alacrity" as in a Mickey-Mouse show.

Len was also unsure that either Magda or Trish would be willing to accompany him back if and when he chose to return permanently to Nigeria. With Trish, that question had never even been broached: Her children were generally one decade younger than his and would perhaps still need the U.S.; or, at least, Trish would be inclined to think so. She had already shown how strongly she felt against a move from

Columbus to any other city. Len thought that Magda would be more amenable to returning with him to Nigeria in the long run, but he remembered how eager she had been to go back home to Nigeria in 1981, and yet how she had left him just as eagerly in 1989 when she grew tired Nigeria's chaos, corruption, and rotten infrastructure. He couldn't be sure Magda would not do the same flip-flop again.

All of those considerations, though, pertained to a distant future. For now his happiness required that Trish come fully into his life. Len appeared to all who knew him as the direct antithesis of the male chauvinist. Still, he found himself starting to understand what motivated polygamy in traditional African societies. In his case it would enable him to eat his cake and have it! But he came back down to earth, and once again resolved to tell all to Magda when she returned from Nigeria.

As if the destinies agreed with his assessment, a chance suddenly appeared for him to secure more firmly his NASA job. For nearly fourteen years he had worked at NASA under the auspices of on-site contractor companies. It was one thing to work for NASA as he did, and a different thing to belong at NASA, as an employee, a civil servant with enhanced job security and better perks. And just now a rare vacancy opened up for a scientist at his level to be designated as a civil servant, which was like a tenured faculty position in a university. Len found that he met the stated requirements, and he applied for the position. He was hopeful and confident and looking forward to using the new position to leverage a separation from Magda. Since all the applicants were internal candidates, the selection process would be swift.

But Len did not get the job: Soon after Magda and Trish both returned from Nigeria he received a letter saying he had not met the requirements. Len thought that was an unfortunate way to word the letter of rejection because he knew he met and exceeded all the requirements. If they had just said they chose a "better-suited" candidate there would have been no issue. In his prior capacities as head of an academic department and dean of a school at a university, Len knew that often you were picking a "primus inter paria," or first-among-equals. But the words they used in the letter turning him down opened their decision to question. Characteristically unafraid, Len questioned them, asking to be told which specific requirement he had not met. The local NASA leaders squirmed at his question. Three times he was invited to a different Director for a chat. But they had not coordinated their excuses and so they gave conflicting assessments of Len's qualifications, even misstating the year he earned his Ph.D. (which was apparently a key determinant of seniority). So Len wrote a formal appeal, something not usually done at such a highly politicized establishment, especially not by a contract employee.

The bosses delegated a few of Len's colleagues to talk to him about not making waves. Len refused to commit himself, and so they marked him down as a troublemaker. Len soon heard through the grapevines that some big shot at NASA was miffed that he dared to question their judgment. The cause of their unease became obvious when it emerged that the candidate they selected was a young white scientist and a favorite of a NASA big boss. Rumor had it that the big boss wanted this candidate to be "fast-tracked" to executive levels for preparation to join the top administration. There was nothing unusual in that; in fact it was a common operating procedure at NASA to accelerate promising (or favored) persons to executive ranks. However, Affirmative Action was then a controversial, hot-button issue in the U.S. and a sore point for white American males who felt discriminated against. If Len's disgruntlement leaked out to the public there might be an undesirable media attention, just when the future of that particular NASA base was thought to be in deep jeopardy. The situation was delicate for all concerned.

Soon the big boss who was miffed with Len got ammunition to fire his shot. A few months earlier President Bush, Jr. had announced a sea change in NASA's mission: It was changed to play down the research function and enhance the exploration ventures. That put the research centers, like the one in Cleveland where Len worked, on the potential chopping block. Their subventions were to be pared back and rumors indicated strongly that two research centers (Huntsville and Cleveland) were going to be closed outright. The prospect of diminished funding was used to settle political scores as quite a few researchers were told there would be no funds to support them in the calendar year just starting. Len was one of those who received that notification. Being in his 50s, Len decided to retire.

To keep his mind usefully engaged while in retirement and also earn some income, albeit a pittance, Len added one more course to his adjunct teaching at engineering departments in two Cleveland-area universities. He still relished the prospect and process of imparting knowledge to the interested and gifted youngsters who would become the leaders of tomorrow. Since his arrival on the scene as an acknowledged scientist, an expert in his own little field of human endeavor, Len always kept a résumé ready and constantly updated — in fact, he had prepared two versions of his curriculum vitae. The longer version was targeted at academic institutions, which he kept an eye on for a good chance to return to academic life if a good opportunity came along; that CV included lists of his "scholarly publications" in all scientific outlets. The shorter one, a one page "executive summary" of his CV, targeted more general administrative job openings, such as the type available in government, NGOs, and UN agencies. Both of these versions opened up with Len's personal mission statement:

> When you receive a good education you become a co-custodian of human knowledge and thereby assume a corresponding duty to help disseminate and propagate that

knowledge to future generations, as your contribution to world progress.

In other words, Len liked to each. What he found off-putting, especially on U.S. campuses, was the hassle to wipe the noses of indolent students who felt they were entitled to easy grades. The most outrageous thing that happened in Len's teaching career was when the mother of an adult student in his class called Len at 10 pm one day to ask why her son had flunked his course. Len barked at her and slammed the phone, and she reported him to the dean. In his view, pop psychology was dulling intellectual drive among U.S. students, which was why they tended to be out-performed in standardized tests by students from Europe and from the developing countries. It was not unusual nowadays to find articles in U.S. magazines arguing that assigning failing grades to students damages the self-esteem of such students! And if a child misspelled "house" as "h-o-u-s," his teacher was supposed to say, "Terrific! But you omitted the 'e' at the end." What is terrific about such performance? Len wondered.

However, now that he was out of a job, Len was willing to take on more courses to teach. The rewards of teaching were sometimes quite sublime, coming from the least expected sources. Len took on a Chemistry class at a distant, rural campus of Kent State University. Actually, it was more like the class took Len on. He was recruited to it by the Dean, a friend of his, who sought someone to teach Chemistry to the nursing juniors at his campus because the assigned teacher suddenly became unavailable. One unfortunate drawback of adjunct teaching, Len knew, was that you were always dragooned at the last minute, without enough time to prepare. It could not be otherwise, however, because if the hiring department had enough advance warning it would engage a full-time teacher or instructor for the course rather than take chances with an unknown adjunct teacher.

From his college days Len was not particularly fond of chemistry, an aversion that arose from the time of day when his chemistry labs were held —right after lunch. The nauseating effluents of chemical reactions made him feel like reversing the process of eating. He balked at teaching the Chemistry class, but the Dean said to him: "If you can teach Chemical Engineering you certainly can teach Chemistry for us." He knew that Len had been chairman of a university department of chemical engineering. Len took on that Chemistry class, and he came to enjoy teaching it, but it was a side show and he cast about for something more substantial to do. He decided to invest some of his retirement savings in a business. He had been soldier, academic, and scientist; now, maybe, he should add "entrepreneur" to that list of careers.

During the Reagan's presidency it was deemed necessary for the American worker to save a nest egg for his or her own retirement. Individual Retirement Accounts and 401(k) schemes sprang up, sweetened with employer matching mandates. Deferment of taxes on that saved income helped make the scheme attractive. The individual is expected to spend the savings after retirement, when overall income was diminished and consequent taxes lower. Such savings were invested by the banks and so helped spur the economy. It was a win-win idea.

When Len returned to the U.S. on his sabbatical leave he took bold advantage of that scheme because he knew that his retirement would come sooner than for most of his colleagues as he started on the scheme late in life. While his colleagues earmarked two to four percent of their wages to save in 401(k) and IRA portfolios (because four percent was the cap on employers' matching contributions), Len put fiffteen percent of his earnings into 401(k). Magda complained strongly about his locking up such a huge portion of his income for the foreseeable future, but Len persisted. And that persistence was about to pay off now that he had decided to retire.

When he left NASA his retirement savings amounted to the equivalent of two years of his NASA wages. It was a tidy sum. He decided to invest some of it in a business venture with Magda. He considered going into a consulting business based on his professional expertise and registered a company for that purpose, but he knew he would have to hustle against the big players for an occasional contracts; that was no easy task. Happily, Magda had formulated a sound business plan already and she explained it. It involved transporting Medicare and Medicaid clients to pre-arranged schedules, at reimbursement rates set by those two giant agencies. The pool of potential clients was vast and the sky seemed to be the limit for such a business. Len agreed.

He and Magda then decided to add a sister business for selling medical equipments, another sector with extensive potential clientele. Perhaps also they could eventually expand the medical equipment sales to Nigeria, where the need for such equipment was great. Len quickly saw the merits and the potentials of both ideas. He fronted the seed capital with loans taken from his 401(k) investments and they were in business.

Magda, ever industrious and full of initiative, headed their new family business as CEO while Len functioned as COO. Len was responsible for administrative and financial matters while Magda covered clinical matters. Magda combined that role with her day job as a full-time nursing manager in a hospital, but after one year, as the family business grew, she too retired to concentrate on running that business full-time. Her retirement benefits from the hospital, paid to her in one lump sum, were also plowed into the family business, and they were able to embark on rapid expansion.

With Len engrossed in their family business, he had to put his dreams of happiness with Trish on hold. Since a good deal of all Len's accessible borrowings and distributions from his 401(k) were now tied up in the business, he was dependent on that business for a living at present and in the future. He was now bound to Magda with two chains: The legal shackle of marriage and the financial tie of their business partnership. Each time Len remembered Magda's declaration, that a man should not enter into marriage unless he was prepared to die in it, he feared what she might do if he announced an intention to decamp to Trish.

17
Earthquake

If in the dusk of the twilight,
dim be the region afar
Will not the deepening darkness
brighten a glimmering star?
Then when the night is upon us, why
should the heart sink away?
When the dark midnight is over,
watch for the breaking of day.
Whispering hope, oh, how welcome thy voice
Making my heart in its sorrow rejoice.

AFTER THE SUMMER vacation, Trish had barely started the new term when tragedy again dealt her a near-knockout blow. It was just before noon on a Thursday that the shock waves of tragedy reached Len. He had just concluded a meeting with sub-contractors who supplied motorized scooters to his company and returned to his office when, a call came through from Trish's number. What a welcome change for her to call him at an unaccustomed time. He shut his door and said, "Hello, Honey! I'm delighted to hear from you." But the Trish who spoke to him was dull and heavy.

"Honey," she moaned, "Honey, oh honey!" She moaned again and said, "He's gone. He's gone!" And she moaned again. Len asked her who was gone and why was she in distress?

Then she said, "Joshua is gone. My son is gone!"

Gone where? Len pressed. Trish moaned again and said "Josh is dead." Len did not believe he heard correctly. He asked Trish to repeat herself, and she managed to say that Joshua died that morning during physical exercise. Two soldiers from the local US Army base, who brought her the news, were taking her home. She was calling Len from their car as they drove her home.

Len gasped. "Oh God, don't let it be true. Dear God, why this? Why now? Why Trish again?" He no longer believed in God but in times of emotional crisis, ingrained habits can resurface from the deep subconscious. He was speechless, as was Trish, who just moaned over and over. It was as if their spirits, his and hers, were communicating silently to each other. Finally Len said to her, "Honey, I am on my way. Be there in two hours. Honey, hang in there, please! You know I love you very much."

Len did not think to tell anyone where he was going, or why. He wasn't even thinking, but went to his car and drove straight down to Columbus. On the way he called Magda and told her that he was heading to Youngstown. He lied to her again, but this was no time to explain things, to be held back by arguments. Right now, he simply had to be with Trish, and he would accept the consequences later. So he told Magda that he was summoned urgently to a meeting of referees participating in a Youngstown tournament starting the next day. He said he had forgotten his phone charger in his office (which was true) and so would not be reachable until he returned. Magda was so busy herself with the crush of work that she seldom missed Len anymore when he took off. It had become easy to deceive her with lies.

When he arrived, Len ran to Trish's bedroom and found people surrounding her. Trish was a basket case. An older male, her ex-husband's cousin, held her hand while two of Trish's lady friends sat on either side of her at the foot of the bed. As soon as Len entered one of the ladies quickly got up to make room. He sat down and cradled his arm around her. He did not say a word, nor did Trish. She just leaned listlessly against Len, her open eyes staring at nothing, the moans coming at intervals from deep within her chest as her head lolled rhythmically from side to side. They sat that way for a while until the ladies and the man withdrew discreetly.

Trish's daughters, Vivica and Jara, stepped in from the hallway where they had stood when Len arrived; their eyes were glazed in shock. The younger one sat down on the other side of her mother, threw her arms around her mother's neck, and broke into sobs; the older daughter sat on the floor at Trish's feet, sniffling repeatedly as though she had a head cold. All four of them sat together, a family huddled in distress and helplessness, saying nothing to each other. Trish just moaned.

After a long interlude, frozen in the shock of shared misery, Len tried to drag Trish over to lie properly on the bed and under covers so she might get some rest. But she resisted. She knew that more guests would be arriving soon to commiserate with her and she wanted to receive them. What a brave woman, my Trish, Len thought. She agreed to be led downstairs to her sitting room, to sit and receive the sympathizers she knew would pour in as people returned from work in an hour or two and heard the news.

When Trish closed her eyes, overcome with exhaustion, Len tucked a shawl around her, and then signaled to the daughters to step out with him. They went into the kitchen. Had they eaten lunch yet? They shook their heads and Len called to order pizza. He hated the stuff, as he disdained all "fat food," and would not eat it himself, but he knew how much young people liked it. Then he asked to be filled in on the details of their brother's death, but the girls had only sketchy information. Their mom called them home from school around 10 am; she had been escorted home by two military men. By the time the girls reached the house, their mother had called Len and then some of her friends and relatives. When Viv and Jara got home the two men, one of them a sergeant, took off their caps and greeted them in a solemn voice. Then they took their leave, promising to return later that day. That was all the girls knew.

Len braced them both against his sides, one in each arm, and kissed them on their temples. He took them back into the room where Trish sat numbly and mute, staring into space. The pizza arrived, Len paid for it, and the girls withdrew to eat at the table. Len broached the painful topic of notifying Trish's relatives back in Nigeria that her son, her beloved first born, her only son, was dead. Trish roused herself with the greatest effort and made the calls. Then she leaned over again against Len. He held her, rocking her from side to side to steady her so she could tell him what happened.

The soldiers came around 9.00 am, two men in sharp olive-green uniforms. Seeing their grim faces, Trish sat down heavily, knowing at once it was about Josh. The men took off their caps but remained standing akimbo, each with his hands crossed behind his back. Trish wondered whether it was a matter of liability Josh had got into; the boy was rambunctious sometimes. Some trouble with the law? Had he been in a fight? The sergeant took a deep breath and said:

"Madam, I cannot tell you how sorry I am to bring you sad news about your son. Joshua passed away this morning. On behalf of our commander and the U.S. Army we bring you our deepest condolences."

Trish screamed and passed out. When she came to, the Sergeant was still standing, leaning anxiously over her. She asked, "Was it an accident?" The man said no, that Josh had collapsed after a vigorous morning exercise on the drill ground of the military school in Richmond, where he was undergoing Advanced Individual Training, having graduated the week before from Basic Training (or Boot Camp). Medics in his unit tried their best to resuscitate him, but Josh did not respond. At the base medical center Josh was pronounced dead. The, the sergeant offered to take Trish home, as she was in no condition to drive. Hemming Trish in on both sides and each holding her by an elbow in case they needed to support her, they walked Trish out of the office and into their car. She called Len from the men's car.

They brought her home and stayed standing while she called her daughters' schools. The men took her to each school to pick up her daughters, and then took her home again. To each girl she merely whispered: "Josh is dead; he collapsed this morning after exercise." Each girl gaped at Trish in shock and disbelief. When the men ushered her into her house the sergeant asked if there was someone else they should call to be with her, but Trish did not seem to hear: She was heaving and quaking with sobs. They promised to be back and were about to leave Trish and her daughters to grieve in privacy, then the sergeant mentioned that they were going to notify Joshua's wife.

The mention of a wife gave Trish false hope. Perhaps they were talking of someone else: Her son was not married, she told the soldier. But as he hesitated, frowning, Viv, who overheard the conversation, tugged at her mom, nodded, and whispered to her mom that Josh had indeed been in a common-law co-habitation with a young woman. Viv did not know if they had married quietly, but Josh told her he now had a wife. The sergeant said goodbye and the two soldiers went away, leaving Trish to wail anew at this new revelation. She called the cousin of her ex-husband, who called some of Trish's friends, who rallied to comfort her, as they were doing when Len arrived.

So, here was Len, no wiser than the ladies about what to do next. Did Trish want to be taken to Richmond to view Joshua's body? She hesitated, and then said, "Let's get more details when the soldiers return," thinking that by then they might have the autopsy result. Right now, Josh's wife was taking center stage in the tragedy. Trish uttered "wife" with all the distaste and anger she could muster at that time. She opened up about Josh marrying without so much as hinting it to her. But it was in keeping with Joshua's new character; the boy had rebelled completely against his mother who loved him so much. Len had absolutely no sympathy with the curious American pampering of "teenage" as a period when a person is supposed to become a rebel against his or her own parents, and against all authority figures for no reason other than that it was "the thing to do." He must have been a teenager once, Len reflected, but people of his generation never let that go their heads. It was vintage America to let people go crazy between the ages of thirteen and nineteen, and then expect them to resume cold sobriety and sanity from then onward.

Len tried to croon *Whispering Hope* to the still moaning Trish he held in a tight embrace, but his voice broke into sobs. He shut up and began to reflect on Josh. Like all rebel sons he was once Mama's boy, the apple of Trish's eye, on whom she doted for so long. He was the first child, whom Trish bore while she was still a student, the baby she carried in a bassinet right into class and sometimes nursed discreetly in a corner of the room as the class went on. He was the baby boy whose proud papa, Trish's ex-husband, used to bounce on his knees in the good old days of domestic tranquility, the scampering little boy who kicked balls around with his dad; he was Mommy's little helpmate when his two sisters were born in turn and he rocked their cradles to get them to sleep in a corner of the kitchen while their happy mother pottered about to cook them meals.

Josh was the boy who, before he attained the age of reason, was drafted by the heavy hand of fate into the outsize role of "man of the house," when his restless, shiftless dad left them and fled to Nigeria a step ahead of the law —all because he was an unthinking man who disdained to soil his hands with the toil that America extracted from everyone as the price for making a living in this land of opportunity. Josh was the bright boy whose prospects of a comfortable childhood were truncated by a dad who was going to be permanently unavailable, leaving Trish to tackle alone the rigors of honest daily toil and the endless rounds of worries.

When Len came into their lives Josh was an engaging, bright child approaching his thirteenth birthday. Len saw him grow steadily in size, intelligence, and love for his capable mother who was hobbled by single parenthood. In middle school Josh was described by his teachers as a good-mannered and intelligent boy, and in high school, Josh's football coach chose him for that extra attention and close mentoring that he reserved for his most promising protégés. The keen-eyed coach had caught a glimpse of Josh's athletics potential, telling Trish that, if Josh could rein in his occasionally rough behavior while in the company of his peers, if Josh could channel all his energies and focus on academic and sporting activities, he was most likely to excel in life. When Josh won his first athletics letter (which got emblazoned on the expensive wind-cheater jacket that his mother had proudly splurged to buy for him), the coach was pleased to mention the possibility of an athletics scholarship to a good college.

Indeed, a few of those colleges and universities had begun to woo Josh with brochures and letters of cautious promise, when some dark force seemed to take a hold of his mind and propel his behavior towards a collision with his mom and then with society at large. The boy became headstrong and started hanging out with some furtive and self-centered teenagers of whom his mom did not approve. Len began to suspect that Josh was secretly drinking the beers Trish stocked in her refrigerator and garage to entertain her friends. Once, Len told Trish he could have sworn that someone was drinking the wines he kept in Trish's basement —where Trish had installed for Len a countertop refrigerator to chill his drinks.

Sometimes Trish encountered some rough characters in her house at odd hours, even late at night up in Josh's room (which shared a wall with her own bedroom) and ordered them out of her house. Josh resented that and began to challenge his mom about it. He began to show signs of having succumbed to the deplorable syndrome of the wayward teenager, a condition said to afflict young men and women, especially those over whom there was no father's firm hand to mold them into conformity with respectable society. It was a sad outcome that most African professionals in the diaspora dreaded for the children whom they were unfortunately forced to raise in the permissive cultures of Western societies.

Joshua's schoolmates who were of African parentage had begun to avoid him. He had strong leadership qualities and used to attract a following among his peers. Now Trish noticed that the college-bound ones came to her house to hang out with Joshua less and less, until none came at all. But Joshua was not fazed because other neighborhood children were filling the void and drawing Joshua into their circles: Rough, listless, shiftless youth whom Trish did not like one bit. But Trish was honest about the situation, and said to Len on some occasions that Joshua had become quite difficult to like. If he were not her son, she confided, she would not like him or want him dating her daughter, either.

A big, strapping lad, Josh went from resenting and challenging his mom to trying to intimidate her because of her petite size and sensitive nature. They began to have flaming rows. A couple of times Josh smashed Trish's bedroom door to go in there and look for things that he was not supposed to access. On one of those occasions, after Len came to visit and saw the hole and cracks in Trish's bedroom door, he took her around town to look for a solid, oaken door to replace the old, hollow one Josh broke. Josh was not able to breach the solid new door, but in his next furious attack he tore out the housing of the lock from the door jamb. Len feared what might happen if Josh had one of his maniacal fits while Trish was in her bedroom.

Josh basically behaved as he pleased, appropriating from the refrigerator, the kitchen, and the house anything he fancied, without consulting his mom or sisters. The result was a foregone conclusion: From being a star athletic prospect almost positioned for a short walk to college, Josh struggled to finish high school. And then he considered himself graduated from his mom's home as well: He moved out without telling his mom whither he was bound.

He did take his key to the house with him, and soon Trish realized he was stopping by during work and school hours when she and her daughters were out, and indications were that he was not coming alone. Trish replaced all three locks with more secure, deadbolt locks, a rather expensive undertaking for her financial circumstances. Then she discovered that someone was breaking in through the casement windows, and since nothing valuable was stolen she knew it was Josh. She told Len only a little of these dismaying capers by Joshua because she figured they were her cross to bear, and she bore them with grace and dignity.

But eventually, some restraining influence crept over Joshua. Trish consulted her daughters, who were in better contact with Joshua than she was, and was surprised to find that she owed Joshua's welcome reform to the influence of a young lady whose attention Josh had begun to cultivate. "Lady" was perhaps not the best word to describe the young woman, but Trish was grateful for whatever person or thing brought deliverance from Josh's frightful careening into roguery. The scheming young lady was smart: She wanted to sell her favors dearly and insisted that Joshua get a job to support her, so he landed a job as a delivery guy for a local furniture franchise. It was not the kind of job on which Trish thought her son should build a career, but it was the beginning of an honest, if not exactly respectable, independence.

Josh began to bring that girlfriend to Trish's house, and when Trish made discreet inquiries and found she was not an altogether savory character, she slowly and subtly tried to peel the girl away from Joshua. Above all, Trish wanted Joshua to return to college track eventually, and the sooner the better. She didn't want him to get mired in a dead-end situation as a precocious and unambitious father for some woman's children. Trish had friends whose sons ended up in that trap and ultimately became deadbeat dads, at odds with the law. So she talked to Joshua more and more about his girlfriend. Joshua was uncomfortable with that and, to get his mom off his back once more, he decided to move away from Columbus altogether.

The last time that Len and Josh had a *tet-a-tet* was just before Josh left town, and it was to be the last time Len ever saw Josh alive. Josh had approached him to sound him off about joining the military. It seemed that recruiters had targeted him and were pressing. Len intimated that he was not thrilled, and told Josh to consider the matter long and hard, since a military career could be a quick trip to the pine box, given the never-ending wars the U.S. fought in distant lands. At best it could mean the suspension of a young man's progress through college to the middle class, as happened in the case of Len himself. Josh had heard Len was an army officer in his youth, and he asked Len what it was like. Len told him that his own diversion into the army was made necessary by a civil war in Nigeria; he had had no choice. "When your country is embroiled in a civil war or a struggle for survival," Len advised Josh, "it is your bounden duty to fight, if you are able. However, you are not in that situation now."

In any case, if Josh really wanted to go into a military career he should try and do what Len did: Earn a commission into the officer rank, which wasn't easy in the U.S., especially not without a college degree or time in the Reserve Office Training Corps (ROTC). But if Josh really wanted to go in as "other ranks," he had best try the U.S. Navy or Coast Guard because they seemed to offer quicker routes for a nomination to an Officer Cadet school, where he could eventually climb towards a commission. Len also considered the Coast Guard and the Navy, especially the Coast Guards, as a truly defensive arm of the military, in contrast with the Army, Marines, and Air Force which charge off to attack other countries tens of thousands of miles from continental U.S.A. and call that "defense." Len was aware that he and Trish were in accord on that point.

Len learned later that Josh had signed up with the Army and gone to boot camp for training. Trish did not talk about it much because she knew Len was not overjoyed, nor was she; in fact, she had rather her son went to college, even if it was to play football. But she had little leverage in the matter; if Josh decided to go into the military, that was that.

And now Joshua was dead, and it wasn't even a soldier's glorious death on the battlefield, but a sad little bodily malfunction. In the coming days an autopsy was to reveal that the cause of his death was really a congenital anomaly: His heart went into runaway flutter upon vigorous excitation during his morning sprints. He did not die from anything the military did wrong or could have prevented —except by advanced screening to detect his innate susceptibility to *tachycardia* (ventricular fibrillation). In a layman's terms, and in the fatalistic world view of Nigerians, it was just his time to go.

Josh was covered by a $100,000 policy provided by the army, but since he was married, only his widow could claim that money. The Army would release some advance money to Trish so she could make quick arrangements for Josh's funeral, but the bulk of the insurance pay-off would eventually be released only to his surviving wife.

Trish was advised to choose a funeral home in Columbus and notify the local Army office as soon as possible so Josh's body would be brought home for last rites. Even in her monumental grief, Trish found strength to decry Joshua's stupid and secret marriage, which now provided handsomely for an outsider to reap where she did not sow: "As if Josh's dying is not enough tragedy we now have to rely on the goodwill of this strange woman to get money to bury him."

Mourners kept streaming into Trish's house. The magnificent African tradition of communal solidarity in the event of death kicked in at once. People brought prepared food and munchies; the men came with drinks. Some came with rugs and blankets and pillows ready to stay there and keep a vigil all night. Everybody looked grim and somber, exchanging greetings in whispers or with nods and grunts. There would be a formal memorial service on a date to be agreed between Trish and the many social organizations to which she belonged, because they all wanted to register their formal presence. However, the impromptu all-night vigil on the days following a death did not need organizing or invitation; it just happened. It takes a village to raise a child, Len reflected, and it also takes a village to bury that child and cushion a family from the razor-sharp edge of raw bereavement.

Len gave money to Trish's older daughter to cover anything that might be needed suddenly. Then he took Trish up to her bedroom to broach the matter of funeral arrangements and a place of interment. Once again Trish surprised Len with her sagacity: She revealed to him she already had purchased a plot for herself in a nearby Catholic cemetery. She would now arrange to have Joshua buried there, thinking that Joshua's "so-called wife" would not object to that choice. Trish added that she would apply for an adjoining plot to be designated for her and she would pay for it in installments, starting as soon as she could. She chose a funeral home down the road from the cemetery. Clenching her teeth, she called the cemetery and the funeral home and arranged to go over and discuss details. Trish stiffened her back and braced her shoulder to the grim tasks ahead.

It was Friday night, and Len realized he had to contact Magda. But what was he to tell her? He was not ready, or willing, to go back to Cleveland. He could not even contemplate leaving Trish alone in her present condition. Then he brightened as an idea hit him. Instead of chancing a live exchange and awkward questions if he called Magda's cell or his home landline, he called Magda's office number knowing she checked that line for messages quite often. He left her a message saying he was OK and expected to come home Sunday evening. He left it at that.

Trish's living room, sitting room, and the kitchen-cum-dining room were all crowded with men and women, some of whom talked, while other cried softly. From time to time they broke into singing hymns. Teenagers who were Joshua's peers, schoolmates, friends and so forth gathered in the sitting room and the family room also, consoling Joshua's sisters. Joshua's wife was not among them. The woman never once showed up at Trish's house throughout that season of bereavement, which caused Len to wonder. He thought she was devastated too and grieving alone quietly, but Trish grumbled that the woman knew better than to come and remind them of Joshua's folly in marrying her without the knowledge of his family. Friends and relatives were sure to wonder who the lady was, and what was she to tell them? That her only son Joshua had eloped with a strange woman without ceremony? It was good that the lady stayed away.

Len took Trish up to her bedroom, locked them both in, and then took her in his arms. They sat on the edge of her bed and he began singing the lyrical songs of mourning remembered from his youth. One that always pulled at his heartstrings was sung over and over when his mother died, in his eighth year, and the Christian community gathered as she lay in state, dressed in her wedding gown as was the custom then:

"Cheta na mbosi onwu, nke ga-adili mmadu...." (*Reflect on your dying day, a day that comes to all persons....*)

Leaning on Len, Trish began to press heavily against him. Blessed relief, he thought, she was falling asleep! He woke her gently, had her slide up to lie full-length on the bed, kissed her, and covered her up, and then he returned to singing funeral hymns. Igbos had an insightful proverb about death and mourning: "When you mourn for someone else, you also mourn for yourself," which is the very point that John Donne made in his famous elegy, "Send not to ask for whom the bell tolls; it tolls for thee." With tears creeping down his cheeks, Len softly sang to himself.

> *Whispering Hope,*
> *Dies irae, dies illa....*
> *Ave Maria O maiden, O mother....*
> *Angels of Jesus, angels of light....*

He fell silent after a while, his tears and sniffles coming thick and fast: From childhood, Len had always cried at funerals. He thought Trish was sleeping, but she slowly reached up and gently swiped his tears. They broke into sobs as he enfolded her in his arms. They fell asleep locked in embrace.

One week later Len was back in Columbus to attend the funeral ceremony for Joshua. This time he told Magda exactly where he was going and why, thinking the telling would precipitate a row that would bring matters to a head. If Magda now faced him with a choice between herself and Trish, he was ready to settle that issue once and for all. But Magda did not force the issue. Instead, she took refuge in a technical question: In what capacity was Len going to this young man's funeral? Len replied that "capacity" did not matter: He was going, period. Magda told him he was going on his own, not as a representative of the Obi family; was that OK? Len said it was, and they left it at that.

Trish had mentioned to Len the magnificent cortege of military ware that had brought Joshua's body home for burial and deposited it in the chosen funeral home. So Len arrived in Columbus in time to watch the procession as they moved Joshua's body from the funeral home to the chapel where it was to lie in state for viewing that evening. It was quite a sight! The U.S. military certainly knew how to bury their own with dignified pomp and pageantry. The procession was led by a team of military outriders on impressive motorcycles riding in tandem, two abreast. He'd never seen such muscular and shining motorcycles before, or such riders looking serene and well fed, snazzy in their sharply pressed olive green uniforms. Then came Army vehicles festooned with Old Glory, then two stretch limousines, and then other vehicles in a procession. They swept into the chapel premises looking like a band of angels swinging low in sweet chariots. Len, himself a veteran of war and a jaded observer of too many military funerals in his time, was awed. He had never seen anything quite like it.

Before he left Cleveland to attend the funeral, Len had decided that he was going to give Josh a military salute of his own, from one soldier to another. It took a lot of searching but he was able to locate a black beret in a ladies' shop in downtown Cleveland. In the tradition of Len's army, which was the Biafran Army (hence a derivative of the Nigerian Army and the British Army) a salute was a special ritual. In the first place, you did not give a salute without having a uniform hat or cap on. It perplexed Len that U.S. military personnel seemed not to mind saluting or being saluted by someone who was bare-headed! The principle of that hats-on salute was implied in the military Dress

Code, which stipulated that head dress was to be worn at all times. Saluting one's superior officer is the most common formal ritual performed by a soldier, many times each day as a way to foster discipline and acknowledge the pecking order. One could not perform any formal military duty half-dressed. Therefore: no cap, no salute. If your superior officer happened upon you at a moment when your head was bare you just stiffened your back and said, "Good Morn, Sir!" (And it was *Morn*, no matter what time of day it was.)

Len was old-fashioned that way, so he was glad to find and buy that beret. He had it in his pocket ready to don when his turn came to file past the casket of Josh, whom he looked upon as his proxy son. Another thing about the salute Len learned in Officer Cadet School: Like the British accent it was clipped short and sharp, with the boots snapped together and the torso drawn up ramrod-stiff. The first time he saw US soldiers salute their officer, in a movie, he thought it was sloppy: shoulders slouched, neck bent, feet splayed, languid arms raised to the temple while drooping like wet noodles. He thought it was either a spoof or a reluctant gesture towards an officer you didn't really respect. He did not like it one bit. In his army you would have been brought up on charges for such an insipid salute. He was going to give Josh the real deal: a proper, crashing, quivering soldier's salute. For this one last occasion in his life he was going to be Captain Lennox Obi, the war-tested, battle-scarred army officer.

Joshua's memorial service was held in a large chapel-cum-hall down the road from the funeral home to which his last rites were entrusted. The crowd was astonishingly large. Josh's peers were all there, formally dressed for the occasion, each a respectfully groomed young man or woman. Parents were a little less formal, but each person was decently attired. Viv and Jara showed up in gorgeous black dresses with white trimmings, which took Len's breath away. As soon as he saw them Len went briskly over, braced them on either side of him, and solemnly gave each a peck. "Courage," he said, and they nodded. Len and the girls were struggling to keep their eyes dry. Trish was led in, attended by a team of her female friends. She was dressed in formal Nigerian attire. She sat in the front row, directly in front of the casket, clutching the triangular-folded U.S. flag that the soldiers had formally presented to her. She stared straight ahead as mourners filed past and greeted her; she mumbled back her reply.

Her courage and dignity reminded Len again that the human spirit can be ennobled by grief and tragedy as by joy and triumph. The previous year Len's two granddaughters and their half-sister had perished in a fire at the home of Len's son and his wife. Len had felt proud and grateful that his son stood tall and strong as his two daughters lay, partly charred, on the gurney in the hospital where they were taken by Emergency Medical Service. Len's son lost composure only once when he exploded, kicking over a tray of beverages in the waiting room. He also declined to go in and view the bodies of his daughters, leaving Len to go in and perform that sad rite for the family. Otherwise, Len's son was brave and dignified in the face of his compound tragedy —proof that he had matured as a man. Len was enormously proud of his son on that occasion.

This time it was Trish who held her head up as if to defy death; she clearly wanted to be strong as she buried her son. This was the very last time Joshua would need his mom, and she was not going to let him down. She was so brave and noble in that moment of crushing grief that Len's chest swelled with pride and love for her. The lines were very long. They queued to view Josh's body and take final leave of a man everyone had liked as a youth but avoided as he lost his way in the final years of high school. His old friends and mates from elementary and junior high school had shown up in force, outnumbering the adults. None of them cried as they passed Joshua's body, laid out in an open casket, his face glazed with preserving waxes. The dignified and silent grieving with which people buried their loved ones in the U.S. contrasts markedly, Len thought, with the unabashed wailing and thrashing and nose blowing one encounters at similar circumstances in Nigeria. Trish sat there, greeting every person that filed past the bier, making a heroic effort not to break down.

As the long viewing line began to thin out Len decided it was his turn to go up and bid Josh goodbye. He stepped into the restroom, wiped the tears off his eyes, pulled out his beret, and fitted it on his head. As he stepped out of the restroom and turned left in solemn military style, he nearly keeled over, for it was forty years since he last did the goose-step slow march. What a tragic comedy that would have been, in front of that swarming crowd! He could not exhibit the aplomb of Field Marshal Viscount Bernard Law Montgomery who fainted while standing at stiff attention on parade waiting for review by Her Majesty, Queen Elizabeth II. The old boy fainted in the best tradition of the army. He did not slump or sag; the cameras showed him just falling over backwards like a stick. Old soldiers, they say, never die: They just fade away. Montgomery did his army proud that day in the hot sun. But Len would rather not fall down today!

With stiff and slow steps ("One, Toop-Three...") Captain Obi approached the casket, a big and shiny monolith of dark wood inside which Josh lay in a soldier's final pose of attention, his crisp dress uniform topped by a black beret with red trimmings. Len got to Trish, stopped, nodded to her, and she nodded back to him. Then he wheeled sharply around, being careful not to wobble again. He wasn't going to fumble this special last act for Josh —not now.

Everyone watched as he slow-marched up to Josh, bent down and gave him a peck on his shining forehead. Len fancied that he saw on Josh's calm face a proud soldier's faraway look of unbowed surrender to a superior force. He stamped back two steps and flung up the lightning salute he was accustomed to. Then, his arms held stiffly beside him at attention, Len softly said to Josh, "Goodbye, son. Rest in Peace." He did another about-turn and walked away, his lips smarting strongly. He realized the embalmer's wax had transferred to his lips when he kissed Josh, the same substance which had made Josh seem to glisten with sweat. He went into the restroom and washed his mouth over and over, but the taste and sting remained. It was the taste of bitterness, he told himself, the bitter taste of death.

When, one year later, Len and Trish discussed that funereal night, Trish said she was grateful that Joshua's childhood friends has all shown up, even though they had avoided him in the couple of years before he died. Len suggested that the reason they stayed away was not that they loved Joshua any less, but perhaps that their parents had discouraged them from further association with a boy who seemed headed into manhood in the wrong way. Trish sighed in agreement and then opened up about having recently had similar struggles with her daughters as she had with Joshua in his teenage. The daughters both struggled at the tail end of high school and eventually made do with GEDs.

"I can't seem to motivate them to seriously consider college," she reflected sadly.

To Len, that seemed like a tragedy. Trish had a Bachelor's and a Master's degree. That says she was at least a good academic role model for her children, but the model went further. Both of Trish's parents were college graduates. Her ex-husband went through college also, as did his own father. In other words, her children came from a lineage where the distinction of being a college graduate went back two generations. Were her children going to break that tradition and grind out their lives in dead-end jobs? Africans consider the raising of the next generation in one's lineage as the single most important task that each person faces in their lifetime. It is the wish of every African to raise offspring that outstrip him or her in attainments, especially in academic achievements. To that end the African makes great sacrifices to give his children the best chances.

But Trish's children appeared to regress their heritage —from college educated grandparents and parents, all the way down to the educationally moribund ranks of people who barely finished secondary education. That must be a big cross for Trish to bear, Len reflected. A person given to superstition might conclude her karma was so bad that an impatient deity was exacting retribution in her present life rather than wait for her next incarnation as expected. Vina, that friend of Magda's who surprised Len and Trish at the Cincinnati hospital, openly expressed an angry repugnance at Trish's pursuit of Len; Vina used to come to Trish's home and warn loudly about the "consequences" of her dalliance with Len. Len, who was in denial about Trish's bad reputation (and who habitually scoffed at anything "supernatural") was offended by that, and told Vina to mind her business. But in time he began to wonder whether Vina was alluding to the manifest regression of Trish's family and her constant deluge of bereavement and setbacks. Trish did seem to be getting more than one person's fair share of calamities.

The regression of her children was a sore point for Trish, more so because it was an outcome that one could avoid through one's own efforts. Nearly all of her friends had put their children through college, including one friend that was a kitchen porter at a local prison, whom Trish described as being often indigent. If they could do it, why could Trish not do it? She had fought hard to head her son away from becoming a deadbeat dad early in his life. But while Josh's premature death saved him from that dreaded outcome of unplanned parenthood, Trish was not so lucky with her daughters. The girls did not marry or go to college; the older one started making babies right after high school. Actually, rumors about her promiscuity started surfacing during her high school years, so Len was not surprised when Trish told him her daughter was pregnant soon after high school.

But Len was distressed, for several reasons. Trish was distressed, and that was enough to cause him distress. Also, as an educator by avocation he was dismayed because it had been his stated intention to nudge Trish's daughters back onto the track to college when he and Trish married and he could take the girls fully under his wings. That older daughter, especially, seemed the one to break the jinx of regression and give Trish a reason to smile. Len used to discuss careers with that daughter, and she seemed to have some will to make something of herself. Now it was all in ruins, and Trish must chalk up a batting average of "0-for-3" on her score sheet in raising children. Still, Len sought to cheer Trish up. He pointed out that "the children we are forced to raise in the USA will become Americans in temperament and will eventually manifest the social graces and disgraces of Americans."

Still, Len, whose convictions were totally pragmatic, found other reasons for regression among Trish's brood. He could not exonerate Trish from failing to discharge her burden to the best of her ability. True she had been abandoned, while still struggling with entry into adulthood, to the status of a single mom, bearing a burden meant for two. True she lived thousands of miles from home, where the care and support of her own parents might have helped in her task. But then, had she done her best? Fate had handed her a lemon, but did she try to make lemonade with it? With her days filled to the brim with juggling social activities, community involvement, professional quests, and domestic chores, did she devote enough attention to the need to push her children up the hill, instead of just telling them to climb?

Sometimes Trish's daughters made comments that suggested they resented the amount of attention Trish paid to her own needs. They teased her about her clothes and shoes taking up all the space in every closet of the bedrooms and then spilling over down to the basement. Or they observed that their mom was often on the road to this and that function even though her anxiety disorder (those panic attacks) made driving hazardous for her. They were too often expected to rely on their own resources. Like Trish they were discreet about family matters, shielding her with evasive answers when they were asked about her. But with Len they learned to ease up a little and air some modest complaints now and then. Even Len, in denial as he was over any character flaws in the woman he loved, noticed that Trish was a bit of a narcissist.

On the other hand, Len could not blame Trish too much. Coming from an unsophisticated and conservative background, she didn't have an opportunity to sow her wild oats before plunging into early marriage and the subsequent demands of premature single-parenthood. Her young adulthood was truncated as she passed from teenage straight into the cares of mid-life. It was understandable that she should revert to teenage self-awareness when she began to earn an adequate income. Who would condemn her if she now craved a little material self-indulgence? After all, she was a woman, as she pointed out to Len the night they met.

As the days came and went and the bustle of visitations by mourners began to diminish, Trish expressed a wish to bring some closure to her tormented feeling of loss by visiting the scene where her son had died, a *Via Dolorosa* sort of pilgrimage. So Len rented a car and drove Trish and her brother, the priest, from Columbus to Richmond. There she talked with officers and men of Joshua's unit —particularly those who were present at the time and scene of his death.

The long journey to Richmond and back was itself harrowing. The sculpted terrain that made necessary constant twists and turns along that route across mountainous West Virginia also made dense fog a constant hazard. Along many stretches visibility plummeted to near zero and progress, even at twenty miles per hour, was made on a wing and a prayer. Abandoned vehicles littered that route. Suddenly one of them loomed in your face within inches of collision. Only disabled trucks were marked with flares, but even then one didn't see the burning flare until one got practically on top of it. But Len got them there and back, with Trish's brother spelling him at the wheel a few times.

A few months after Josh's funeral, Len's family business faced a sudden cash crunch and he needed help in a hurry to complete payroll. He mentioned his predicament to Trish and she lent him $10,000 which, she said, was what remained from money she received from the U.S. Army when Josh died. Len was touched by that gesture and most grateful that she trusted him to repay that loan promptly. And he did repay Trish within one month, so that, between the two of them money was never an issue —until the end.

18
Dominoes

We shall gather by the river
The beautiful, the beautiful river;
Gather with the saints by the river
That flows by the throne of God.

AFTER THEIR BRIEF discussion about Trish on the day Magda picked him up from the Cincinnati hospital, Len was hoping that Magda would force him to choose. To be forced would of course make things easier for him, but the little argument before he left for Joshua's funeral proved that it was a forlorn hope. Magda had avoided — indeed evaded— a chance to bring up the affair she suspected was going on between Len and Trish. Len was amazed by that. But it was not long before he understood why. It appeared Magda had stumbled on the entire cache of Trish's letters to him, read them all, and now understood how deep it went. But her response was not to confront Len; instead, she quietly embarked on a behind-the-scenes crusade of harassing Trish. Neither woman made Len aware of the cold war between them, but one year after the death of Joshua, Len sensed that Trish was cooling on him. He puzzled over it and agonized, but by the time he realized how things stood, Trish had slipped away and was staying aloof from Len. Thereafter, she was like a shadow, present but intangible.

Not long after that season of grieving for her son, Trish was plunged into yet more sorrow by news from Nigeria about the youngest of her three brothers —Jacob, a veritable maverick. Trish and her siblings were very smart people, but business acumen was not their forte. That was evident to Len from the fact that Trish sat for a long time on the $25,000 Len sent her as seed money for a business venture. That money had languished in Trish's bank account for months until it was reduced to $20,000, a substantial chunk of which got swallowed by an unexpected exigency, after many more months. Trish really did not know what to do with that money or how to go about starting a business. Len nagged her about registering a business, but Trish dragged her feet. She was the ultimate procrastinator. Len gave up and did it for her, selecting a business name, setting up a compact work station in her basement, completing the requisite forms for her and sending her money for the prescribed registration fees. Trish's main strength was intellectual, not entrepreneurial. All her siblings were of similar dispositions, except her youngest brother Jacob.

Jake was different. A budding entrepreneur, he was starting to purchase a firm toehold on the crowded and slippery slopes of modern business when he was struck down by a cruel fate. Like most Nigerians of his generation, Jake did not specialize in one enterprise but dabbled into any venture that promised a good return —and he was good at it. His quest for business took him to the Far East, Europe, and North America. He resided in Nigeria but came to Columbus now and then to visit Trish.

When tragedy struck Jake down, Trish was devastated once again. Already numb from constant grieving, she recounted to Len the circumstances of her brother's death, in a resigned sing-song voice. The details were yet murky. Any time an upwardly mobile young man fell ill in Nigeria or was accidentally hurt or killed his business associates or his family's adversaries were blamed: People said only nefarious machinations would cut a man down in his budding prime. Trish's father —Jake's father—had died from the aftermath of a one-car accident and the rumor mill said the accident was murder by proxy, induced by juju.

With young Jake the circumstances appeared even more sinister. He had developed arrhythmia and palpitations and gone to see a physician. The criminally crazy doctor took a notion to try an experiment, anesthetizing Jake and plunging a needle directly into his heart to administer some medication he thought would regularize Jake's heartbeat. Jake went into a coma and never woke up. He left behind a young wife and a baby daughter, whom Len would meet later when they traveled to Columbus after Jake died.

Len was no stranger to that kind of horror news from Nigeria. His own father, his older brother, and his own nephew (the older brother's oldest son) had all died in one hospital in Nigeria —at different times, but from similarly clumsy doctoring that would be actionable in the U.S. When one went to a doctor or into a hospital in Nigeria, one took one's chances, due mostly to an atmosphere of carelessness and corruption breeding recklessness in medical practice because there was no accountability. After all, Nigerians point out, doctors trained in Nigeria make splendid physicians and specialists when they come to practice in the U.S., where standards are strictly enforced, but when they practice in Nigeria they were hit-or-miss doctors.

Once again Trish had to hurry down to Nigeria, to attend the funeral of her close relative. Len saw her off and provided some financial assistance, but, characteristically, Trish would not articulate her needs and Len had to guess what they were. And when she returned from that funerary trip she did not contact Len.

Jake's young wife came with her little daughter later that year to enjoy a breather from endless but customary rounds of condolence visits by her relatives and friends, and also to thank Trish for being a pillar of strength to all while herself grieving for Jake. Len found out the young lady was visiting Trish and he went to Columbus to see them and offer his condolences. Nothing evoked deeper compassion than seeing so young a woman and her baby bereaved under such needless and tragic circumstances. Trish herself was subdued. A habitual attendee at Mass and singer in the choir, she now retreated further into her faith. Her family leaned on her but she leaned on no one. She used to lean on Len, but not anymore. She no longer behaved like his Trish.

19
Her Pink Slip

You Are My Sunshine, my only sunshine.
You make me happy when skies are grey.
You'll never know, dear, how much I love you.
Please don't take my sunshine away

IN THE LAST budgetary year of Bob Taft's second term as Ohio governor, a new austerity measure was announced for the State, and part of it was trimming back government outlay, prison and library services among them. As with all policy pronouncements of big government, it took months for the details of it to take shape and filter down to the foot soldiers in the trenches.

Curtailment of library services did not come as a surprise to the discerning public. As people embraced the unlimited reach of the personal computer and the internet revolution it was initially thought that libraries were doomed, except perhaps those run by big institutions like universities —because they served specialized fares to captive consumers. It was altogether surprising, and a credit to public libraries, that they adjusted the nature of their services to take advantage of the cyber revolution and stay alive. Patronage of the public libraries blinked only momentarily, and then recovered as more and more users came to libraries on slightly different quests, mainly to use computers for browsing online information, or to look for merchandise or for jobs. Libraries also proved useful for holding meetings of small community groups that could not afford the expenses of renting meeting rooms in hotels, or as ad-hoc offices by start-up entrepreneurs, as individuals or in teams.

The fate of a prison library is tied up with that of a prison itself, and in increasingly conservative Ohio, prisons were under the gun, targeted for privatization and subjected to the knife even as their ranks were bursting with floods of new convicts created by a conservative, get-tough ideology on crime and punishment. Trish's job was on the line. Prison staff positions would be cut, especially peripheral functions like the library which the same reactionary ideology viewed as mere featherbed in a penal system that needed to be lean and mean. The retrenchment practice usually adopted in government establishments was "last-in, first-out"; individual merit was seldom taken into consideration. Being at the bottom of the seniority totem pole, Trish was aware that she was going to be retrenched, and that denouement came quickly. At the end of spring that year she received the dreaded pink slip. She took it with grace.

Teaching was always Trish's main avocation, and if she wanted another salaried job it would have to be in teaching. The time was good for seeking a teaching job: The impending long vacation was when schools got ready for the next school year. Her credentials were good and teachers of her subject, Biology, were always in demand. She had taken the trouble to keep her teaching license current through her stint as prison librarian. However, the budgetary blight that hit the prisons did not spare the school system and it soon became obvious that she would not find a teaching spot easily or quickly.

Being jobless intensified her desire to start a business of her own. She renewed her search for a suitable business even as she contacted schools in the districts for a teaching position. Trish, a thoughtful and resourceful woman, had put away a little bit of money for the rainy day, and she proceeded to draw from it enough to pay for her utilities. Len pitched in generously as well, and food was kept on the table for her children. But misfortunes, they say, never come singly.

One day soon after, Len got an unusually late evening call from Trish's older daughter, Vivica, who was in high school. It was 11:30 pm and Len had just got home from a jazz concert at the local community college. There must be trouble, Len thought. Trish's family had never called him before, though sometimes when he spoke with Trish and asked after the children, Trish would pass the phone to her daughters to say Hi to Len. And the 11:30 pm timing was ominous. With a note of concern in his voice, Len asked Viv if everything was OK. The girl said, "No. Mom is in the hospital. She broke her arm."

The word "broke" did not register in Len's mind the way it was intended to do. Americans used the verb "break" rather loosely, to mean "incapacitate" or render non-operational, especially so children. "The clock is broken" did not necessarily connote a fracture; often it just meant it is not working. So Len was not alarmed. He told her to call him back when her mom returned from hospital, no matter how late it was. Now that he used a cell phone he was able to take calls from Trish or her children any time without fear of interception, as long as he was in the privacy of his study or in his basement office.

The basement office in his home was where Len did all work that required extra privacy, such as preparing his teaching lessons or grading examination papers whenever he was engaged in adjunct teaching at area universities. He also summered in that basement office and for that reason had a futon day bed installed there. He now retired to his basement office to await the expected call from Viv with a status report on Trish. He must have dozed off on the desk chair because at 1:30 am Magda gently opened the door to the office and asked him if he was OK; she had woken up to go to the bathroom and noticed he was not in bed. He said he was fine, that he had fallen asleep while reading an incident report from the soccer game he refereed the previous day, where there had been a brawl. He must finish his own report tonight because it was due in the morning. He would come to bed when he finished. Magda went back upstairs.

Len was puzzled: still no call had come from Trish's house. He called her cell phone and was asked to leave a message. He called her house number and got the same prompt. Now he was worried. He stayed in his office all night, calling Trish every hour or so. Finally, at 7 am Trish's daughter answered the house phone. Her Mom was still not home. Len questioned her closely and realized the matter was more serious than he had thought.

It appeared that as Trish made ready to go to bed at 10 pm the previous night she noticed the lights in the living room downstairs were still blazing, though her children had retired for the night. She headed downstairs in her long and billowy night dress, not bothering to turn on the hallway light so she could see well. But as she stepped on the top step of the stairway she tripped on some object and went sliding down fast on her backside, screaming as she went so that the children all awoke. She ended up in a heap at the bottom of that staircase where she crashed into the wall. She must have spun around as she slid because when the children got to her, her left arm was under her body and her face was flattened against the wall that stopped her. She could not get up and when they tried to lift her she screamed. She also had a gash on her forehead which was bleeding profusely. One of the girls called 911 and the other ran to a bathroom and got cotton balls to stanch the bleeding. An ambulance arrived within minutes and took Trish to hospital.

"Goodness!" Len said to himself, "Someone upstairs must have it in for Trish this season." He told the girl he was on his way. For a while now he had kept a change of clothes and a bag of toiletries in Trish's bedroom as well as a few changes of underclothing in a drawer of her dresser, just in case. He dashed upstairs and told Magda he was going to a hearing and a follow-up over the soccer fight. He would be back in the evening. Before she could ask more questions Len ran out, jumped into his car and headed to Columbus. It was 7:45 am when he started, and while the traffic lanes headed into town, in the opposite direction, were already crowded with vehicles, the roads out of town were clear, thank goodness. By 10 am he was at Trish's house; he had never made it that fast before. Trish's younger daughter was home and waiting for Len. The older daughter had gone to school, leaving directions to the hospital for Len, who headed there with the younger daughter, Jara.

When they got there Trish was in surgery. Len gave the girl money to go and eat breakfast in the hospital cafeteria. He walked there with her, bought a cup of coffee for himself, and left her there to eat while he went back to the waiting room. Then he went back to his car to retrieve a book to read. At noon Jara came back from the cafeteria and sat beside Len to wait. At 12:30 pm Trish was wheeled back from surgery to the "Admitting" station where a nurse gave instructions for Trish to be taken to her room. Len and Jara followed. Trish was still asleep as they transferred her to her bed and tucked her in.

A low-back couch was against a wall in Trish's hospital room. Jara stepped over to it, curled up and went to sleep. Poor thing, Len thought, she must also have kept a vigil all last night. He took a pillow and a blanket from Trish's room and tucked Jara in, gave her a peck on the forehead, and went over to Trish, whose regular, rhythmic breathing showed she was in deep sleep. Her left arm was in traction and hanging from a pole affixed to the head of her bed. Her head was swaddled in a bandage going over a bump on her forehead. She looked like a victim from combat so Len looked for a purple paper napkin at the coffee station, found one, cut a heart-shaped patch out of it and, borrowing a safety pin from the reception desk, pinned it to the bandage on Trish's head. Then he settled to read, and to quietly recall the other times he and Trish had each kept vigil for the other in a hospital. His was on that fateful flight home from Rome when he passed out and was taken to a Cincinnati hospital where Trish fussed over him, to his great delight.

Hers was a couple of years after that, when Trish had an elective surgery. During routine annual physical check up, her gynecologist had advised her to have her uterus removed as a precaution against uterine cancer. Trish was intrigued by the idea and quite positively inclined, since she had no intention of making any more babies. She consulted Len purely as a courtesy; Len knew Trish well enough to sense when her mind was made up about an undertaking. Besides, it was her body, thus the decision was hers alone to make. He told Trish to use her own judgment. She smiled and said she would do it. It turned out to be a simple operation and she recuperated after a couple of days in hospital, during which he spent the two nights sleeping on a couch in her hospital room. As part of her discharge instructions the doctor had looked Len and Trish in the eye and told them to refrain from any sexual activity for a few weeks. Len had no difficulty with that, but when he came back to Columbus after a week, Trish tried hard to persuade him to ignore the advice; Len resisted and, instead, smothered her with affectionate kisses.

It was past 3 pm when Trish woke up with a faint moan. Her daughter sat up briskly and joined Len at Trish's bedside. Trish looked at them, puzzled, and asked, "Honey, where am I?" Len smiled and said: "At the *Frutticato*," and Trish smiled weakly. He kissed her on the mouth as Jara told her she was in hospital; she fell at home and broken her wrist. Vivica had called Len and he came. Trish tried to get up but found she couldn't. Cradling her daughter with her good, right arm, Trish looked tenderly at Len and said, "What would I do without you, Honey?" Her daughter leaned over the bed and hugged her carefully, asking if she was OK. Trish said she was, but her head hurt. They must have had her on video surveillance because right away a nurse came in with a glass of water and two pills in a cup and gave them to Trish. "Pain killers," the nurse explained.

Trish closed her eyes and threw the pills at her open mouth. She quickly grabbed the cup of water from the nurse and took a big swallow, grimacing as it went down. She did not know that one of the pills hit her face and fell on her chest, and the nurse did not notice it either, because she was looking at the IV bag at the moment Trish threw the pills at herself. But Len saw it and asked Trish whether she took both tablets, emphasizing "both"; she said, "yes of course. Didn't you see me toss them into my mouth?" Len said, no: He saw her throw them at her face, but one bounced off her chin and landed on her chest. He picked it up, showed it to Trish, and told her to open her mouth. He pushed the pill into her mouth, and she bit his finger playfully as he did so. Len took the glass from the nurse and fed Trish more water. Again she made an awful face as she swallowed the pill and the water.

Trish kept grimacing after the swallow. Len asked her if the medicine was bitter and she said she did not know; she swallowed it quickly and so the taste did not register. Why then was she grimacing? Len queried her. She looked daggers at him and said, "Honey, carry your wahala commot!" Len laughed and the nurse asked what Trish said and what language was that? Len explained that it was Pidgin English and it meant: "Take your trouble and get out of here." The nurse chuckled and walked out.

While Trish and her daughter talked, Len followed the nurse out to the corridor and asked about Trish's condition. The nurse explained that they had Trish in surgery through the night. Her wrist sustained compound fractures in the fall and they had to insert a couple of steel pins. Trish also had concussion when her head hit something, and her right ankle got sprained too. Trish was going to spend another night in the hospital before they would decide if and when to release her.

Len went out and called Magda. He told her the hearing on the fight during his last soccer game was over but he had been prevailed upon to referee another game that evening. He was tired from not having slept much the night before, but they had no one else to cover the game, so he agreed to do it. If they finished too late for him to come home tonight he would check into a hotel. Since he always carried his referee's bag in his car as well as a change of underclothes, he was OK, he assured Magda. He went back to Trish's room. Trish thanked him again for coming and he said to her, "One good turn deserves another." Which good turn? she asked, and he reminded her of their return flight from Rome and the diversion to a hospital in Cincinnati.

Trish's older daughter called; she wanted to come to the hospital. Len took the younger girl home and brought her older sister. Trish was asleep when they got back to her bedside and they sat to wait till she woke up. The daughter watched TV while Len read a bit and then worked on his laptop PC. Then he went for a walk to stretch his legs.

When he returned, Trish and her daughter were in an intense conversation about something that happened at school. Trish was displeased; her daughter was defensive. He went out again to give them some privacy; he walked some more. When he got back again the girl was stern-faced and said she wanted to go home. Len kissed Trish and took her daughter home. The girl did not say a word on the ride home, and when Len asked if everything was OK, she said her mother was old-fashioned. She did not elaborate and Len did not press her. They rode home in silence. Len told her he was going back to spend the night in the hospital with Trish.

Viv said she had dished out a meal for him when she came back from school earlier. She warmed it up for him in the microwave oven and he ate it gratefully. After he brushed his teeth and made to leave, she handed him three bottles of chilled water. They knew Len for drinking a lot of water through the night, sometimes up to half a gallon; and he wouldn't drink any water that had any hint of a taste. So they always had bottled water set aside for him in Trish's house, even though they sometimes teased him about it. Putting the bottles of water in a bag, he got a pillow and a quilt and grabbed his bag of spare toiletries from Trish's bedroom. The girl bade him good night, and locked the door as he left. When he reached the hospital Trish was asleep again. She was under continuous sedation through the IV tube that fed into the same left arm hung up from a pole. It was late and he made himself comfortable on the long couch.

When Trish was discharged from the hospital Len went back to Cleveland but called her every evening to ask how things were going. It was hard, Trish said, because doing housekeeping chores with one hand was awkward. Her daughters tried to help but they were not very good at any of it. Things were crawling along, Trish said. She sounded resigned, neither happy nor sad.

20
Deliverance

Somewhere, over the rainbow
Skies are blue
And those dreams that you dare to dream
Really do come true.

A FEW WEEKS later Trish called Len on a Friday, sounding excited. Could Len come down that day? She had some good news to announce. Len said OK, but it would be the next day; there was not enough time to make arrangements to leave on such short notice. Trish said tomorrow was fine, but wasn't Len going to ask what the news was? "Well, I'll tell you, anyway," she said. She was easily displeased if Len showed no curiosity when he should. Trish was impatient by nature: If he said to her, "I have something special to tell you when I see you tomorrow," Trish would be agog. She would ask and plead and coax him to say it now! Like a child, she could not wait for surprises. It was the same way if she had news she deemed important: She expected Len to be eager to hear it right away, but he preferred to wait to be told when the teller was ready to volunteer the information.

Trish's good news was good indeed: She received a letter from the Westerville School District of Columbus offering her a full-time position as Biology teacher for the upper classes of their high school.

She had accepted the position and would start in one month, in time to prepare for the fall term. Len congratulated her with excitement and told her he would be down to her place before noon the next day. Len was scheduled to participate in a Youth Soccer tournament in Toledo and Magda thought he was headed there, but when he got into his car the next morning he called the organizers and said he was going to miss the tournament due to an unplanned business trip out of state. He headed to Columbus.

When he got to North Columbus Len stopped at a Giant Eagle grocery store and loaded up on drinks as he always did when he went to visit Trish. It was going to be a festive weekend with her friends flocking to congratulate her and to celebrate; there would be food galore and drinks were needed. Len bought cases of Gran Spumante, Muscato, and Sangria: the sweet wines Trish and her friends liked. He also carted up beer: Becks, Heineken, and Guinness stout. Nigerians loved Heineken but Len preferred Becks. For himself, Len usually cached selections of Merlot, Shiraz, and Chardonnay stowed in Trish's basement. He liked to buy them in large lots partly because of the 10 percent discount he got for buying in cases. The cases were always waiting there in the basement for Len because nobody else drank dry wine in that house.

Trish often teased him about his wine preferences. "If I didn't know you better, honey, I would think you were a snob or a masochist." Len explained that sweet wines had their occasions, and she had seen him drink them when he munched peanuts, cheeses and crackers, or the dried meat and fish she usually served him as snacks outside of meal times. But he couldn't have sweet wine with his meals. Nigerian dishes, especially, had strong flavors from spices, dried fish and other seasonings, unlike foreign dishes that were often a bland affair of mayonnaise, butter and sugar. Any Nigerian can tell *egusi*, *ogbono*, *okro*, or *onugbu* soup apart even if blindfolded, but sweet wines blurred the distinction. He and she agreed to disagree over wines.

Len saw large crowds come and go through Trish's house that weekend, exactly as he expected. Nobody came empty-handed, either. Ladies brought cooked dishes knowing Trish was literally single-handed with her left arm still in a sling since the cast was taken off. The men came with American beers, Guinness stout and the inevitable Heineken. Trish teased them by pointing out that nobody brought soda pop, and one guy said that was because soda pop was for women and children. "Chauvinist!" Trish muttered playfully at him.

After they had all had dinner and quite a bit to drink, Len got up and proposed a toast to Trish:

"Here's to a remarkable woman," he said. "She is the hostess with the mostest, the princess of my heart. She is the most gracious woman I know, and also the smartest. How smart? Well, knowing that she was going to be writing on chalk boards with her right hand soon, she spared that hand and broke the left one!" They roared with laughter and drank to her good health and common sense.

Len was happy for Trish: Things were looking up. If only he could give her that one thing they both wanted —that wedding ring. Soon, he thought, soon. He retired first, to her bedroom to read and listen to jazz as he sipped a little chardonnay. She came up later, after the last of her guests had left in the small hours of the morning. He was still reading when she fell asleep, tired from the evening's impromptu party.

After another half hour Trish began to toss and wriggle, but she kept her back to Len. Then he realized the bright bedside lamp light by which he read was interfering with her sleep. He put his book away, went and brushed his teeth, lay down and gave her back a massage. Then he turned off the light, jack-knifed into her back, enfolded her in a bear hug, and went to sleep too. It wasn't easy any more to enfold her completely. She was plumping out a bit, and Len reflected that it had been ten years since they met; Trish was no longer a spring chicken. Still, she was comfortable to hug, and life was good when she was in his arms.

As always, the weekend just flew by. When Monday morning came around he felt like Tom Sawyer. He just sat there, silent and morose. Trish came up from the kitchen after making breakfast and noticed Len's mood. She needed no telling why; she had seen it before, and she expected it this time. She sat beside him on the bed and he mumbled "So many years now." She hugged him and said it would all come together soon. Len started crying softly and she let him cry for a while. She handed him tissue paper to dry his eyes, and then she went down and brought his breakfast up to the bedroom.

Trish started her new job in July and Len got busy over the establishment of a new branch for the family business. The first week of school Trish called him often to report how much she enjoyed her teaching job. The formality of group exposition in class was in stark contrast to the strictly one-on-one and more casual exchange she had with those she assisted in the library. She began to note the abilities and potentials of the students she taught, as well as their personalities and their propensities to disruption and mischief, and — when she talked to them individually after school— their family backgrounds and problems. Contrary to general lore propagated by the media and the movies, she noticed that most students really wanted to learn and appreciated information and advice, especially when it was given to them individually. Of course the serious ones were quieter in class and tended to be overshadowed by their louder and more showy classmates who craved attention, any kind of attention. Teaching was fun for her —at least initially.

The more frustrating experience of drudgery and irritation set in only in the next term, when some students began to voice disaffection with the grades they got, and that intensified after her first PTA meetings with parents, some of whom came with an air of entitlement, convinced that they had to pose as advocates for their children instead of collaborators with the teacher. Some parents simply chose not to heed early signs of trouble hinted by the teacher on periodic reports issued about struggling students. One mother was combative about Trish's failure to notice and reward her son's latent genius. So Trish explained with an anecdote suggesting that the mother herself was the one who needed to adjust to the true merits of her son. It was an anecdote she heard from Len but it was probably apocryphal. At the end of a school year a mother learned that her son was to be held back one year. She rushed to the principal's office and fumed, "Why are you flunking him? His report cards always said he was trying. Isn't that good enough?"

The principal called for the boy's file, studied the progress reports, looked up and said wearily to the mother:

"You don't' understand, Madam. Your son is very trying!"

That school year was good to Trish. The excitement of her first few weeks dipped only a little when the novelty wore off students and the lead trouble-makers began to assert themselves in class. It dipped a little again when Trish began to encounter some combative parents, but all that subsided when she let them know she would not be put off her game, when the segment of her students who really wanted to learn began to grow, to assert themselves and to ally themselves with Trish and relegate the troublemakers to occasional episodes of disruption.

Trish no longer gave Len daily blow-by-blow accounts of happenings in her class. She got busy with her out-of-class preparations for class, testing and evaluation, writing reports, attending meetings, and so forth. Len took it as a good sign that Trish's chit-chats with him about class happenings tailed off to once or twice a week, unless he took the initiative and called her. Len was busy as well, managing the growth of his business with its spreading area of operation, growing clientele, and burgeoning cost of operations in both time and money terms. He went down only once to spend the weekend with Trish. It was early in May, just before the school year ended. The occasion was her birthday. They took a three-day driving excursion around southern Ohio, taking in a broad sweep along the Ohio River valley.

This latest drive in southern Ohio was like revisiting some places they had seen in the past. Len used to take such drives with Trish in late summer, when students of the little colleges along the way were still on vacation and the tranquility of the southern Ohio countryside impressed itself on you, and hotel accommodations were easier to get and not too expensive because of the lack of academic activity around. On one such trip Len took Trish back to her Alma Mater, OU at Athens. They spent two days there, revisiting Trish's old haunts, which made her voice go husky with nostalgia. In the hustle and bustle of adult life everyone comes to think of their college and high school days as idyllic, care-free times. Trish was no different. That return to Athens was for her a trip down memory lane, a pilgrimage to simpler times. She thanked Len over and over for the treat.

And they had also had a summer-time drive to two small but beautiful and historic southern Ohio college campuses: Miami University at Oxford, Ohio; and Wilberforce University, near Dayton. Trish's children were in tow this time, so Len took them to the National Museum of the U.S. Air Force, an adjunct of the Wright-Patterson Air Force base in Dayton. The accessible display of vintage aircraft was exciting for the children, especially Trish's son who was then a high school freshman.

It was three or four years since their last drive in southern Ohio. The drive Len took with Trish this time was also different because it came in early May, when campuses were teeming with students, but it was for her birthday celebration. And anyway, a campus that was a beehive of activity would bring even more nostalgia to Trish and perhaps encourage her to view the students she now taught more as collaborators than adversaries in the challenging task of teaching and learning. This time they started in Marietta, which has a gorgeous truss bridge over the Ohio River and right at the border with West Virginia. From Marietta they drove to Parkersburg, and then on to Athens where they spent a night again amongst Trish's old haunts. The next day saw them through farm country to Chillicothe, and back to Columbus. Since Trish had to be back home on Sunday to get ready for Monday classes, they did not have time for a more extended trip, but they had a marvelous time of it.

All in all it had been an interesting and intellectually rewarding school year for Trish; she had had a welcome chance to put her primary qualifications to good use for a while. She looked forward to more of the same in the next academic year.

But once again fate decreed otherwise. A pleasant surprise came from the Marion Correctional Institution. Employment outlook had brightened in the Ohio public sector and a few more positions opened for prison staff. Trish was recalled and asked to head a prison unit, a position she had held before being transferred to the prison library in the first place. Her qualifications and her reputation for initiative and for excellent work was remembered when MCI had a chance to replenish its depleted ranks of employees.

This put Trish in a bit of a quandary. She and Len discussed the situation. On one hand, she had really enjoyed teaching, notwithstanding the occasionally trying antics of some reprobates and their mothers (always mothers, never the fathers). She knew that the many leaves of absence she had taken from her teaching duties in order to travel to funerals had taken a toll of the goodwill she had accumulated in her school. In as much as she didn't expect similar exigencies in the future, she knew she could not count on any more goodwill should she need time off for any reason. Beyond that, the Unit Manager position in the prison paid better than her teacher's wages, so Trish went back to MCI.

And Len's business was going very well too. Four years after its launch, the family business was grossing enough to start repaying some of the investment from Len's retirement savings. That gave Len an idea. If Magda could do it, so could Trish. He could set Trish up in a business of her choosing and she could grow it to a point where he could join her to run it, and so construct a landing jetty on the other bank of the river so to speak. He had already registered a business for Trish and set up an office for it; all that was needed was the capital.

As summer came around, Len resumed his Youth Soccer refereeing activities in central Ohio and used it as a cover to resume weekend visits to Trish. His business was well established now. Having hired some reliable staff (including, especially, a loyal and efficient office manager), Len could disengage himself from its day-to-day operations. He could spend long weekends with Trish (which included Fridays and often Mondays), during which he would keep in touch with the office by phone and by email.

Len and Trish utilized those extended weekends to plan a business venture. They scoured her neck of the woods for business ideas, looking at small business ventures in Columbus, going out and talking to business owners, searching for a viable and promising business they could buy. Twice they traveled to distant U.S. cities where Trish knew someone who ran a small business that could be replicated in Columbus. Eventually, Trish and one of her friends found a suitable business to explore. It required buying a franchise from a nation-wide chain. Participation prices started at $200,000, with the requirement of a minimum down-payment amounting to 10 percent of the purchase price. With banks not lending money to start-up businesses, twenty grand was a steep sum of money to contemplate, but Len had a place where he could get that money with relative ease: His 401(k) investments. Since it was his own money (as Magda had her own separate retirement investment), Len could get the funds by taking a distribution or a loan from the funds, which he did.

Soon Len sent a $25,000 cashier's check to Trish, intending it to be used for the franchise. He had not forgotten that Trish had loaned him $10,000 recently. That loan from Trish, and the fact that he repaid it to Trish in a matter of weeks, helped buttress the bond of trust between them which was already established by their love. Len felt he could trust Trish with his very life. Of course $25,000 was a big gamble in terms of expected return, but Len had high hopes for this joint venture with Trish. As he said to her, "Nothing ventured, nothing gained." After all, he and Magda had started their family business with exactly that much capital, and in three years it yielded an annual gross income of over a million dollars.

That bumper return had emboldened Magda and Len to pump more of their retirement savings into the business, and in three more years it had grossed annual sales of just below four million dollars. Of course it was a high-risk business with exceedingly high liability insurance rates, and it was also labor-intensive, so that workers' wages consumed 85 percent of their gross intake. But it had provided ample living for the family, more comfortable than when he and Magda brought in salaries from their respective outside employments. If Trish obtained even just half of the return rate Magda achieved, with the $25,000, she too could soon provide herself and Len a parachute for the jump they were contemplating.

Trish was on Cloud Nine, and so was Len. Not only was this a concrete aid toward actuating Trish's desire for financial independence, as well as for providing a platform for Len to step onto; it was a resounding gesture by Len to affirm his confidence in Trish and his love for her.

Soon, perhaps, their dozen-year dream of union could be realized. But it was not to be. Though Len prodded Trish from time to time to be more proactive with inquiries over her application for a franchise, Trish was laid back about it, more so after resuming her employment at MCI.

In the end, the expected franchise failed to materialize. Nebulous reasons were given. Trish was eventually told that Ohio already had too many franchises in that chain. She knew that the city of Columbus had only one other such franchise, but she was astute enough to recognize that the real reason would never be revealed to her, namely, that her franchise would be one of a kind, run by two black women neither of whom had prior experience in running a business. Private business networks had not yet developed enough confidence in black people to extend franchise participation to them, just as mortgage banks were being revealed by undercover investigations to be engaged in wholesale discrimination against lending to blacks.

When she conveyed the news to Len he was crestfallen. It was a lost opportunity both for a viable venture and for launching his independence from Magda. And, of course, idle money seems to get frittered away. Eventually, as that $25,000 sat wasting in Trish's bank account, Len had need to take back $5,000 of it to make up payroll for his own employees in another sudden cash crunch, and that left $20,000 with Trish. Ultimately that balance evaporated, used by Trish for unplanned emergencies.

Len began to imagine there was a hex upon his dreams for Trish. Maybe the fallout from Trish's bad karma was rubbing off on him too! Not counting one's chickens before they hatch was one of the sayings of sages that Len always bore in mind. Shakespeare cast it as: "There's many a slip 'twixt cup and lip," and more contemporary wits put it down as 'Murphy's Law'; that is, if anything can go wrong it will.

21
Heart Failure

"Memente, homo, quia pulvis es
Et in pulverem reverteris."
Remember, man, that dust thou art
And unto dust thou shalt return.

IT SEEMED TO come without any recognizable warning, but perhaps the warning signs had been building up for a while and neither Len nor Trish nor yet Magda (with her acuity in matters that pertained to Len's health) recognized it for what it was. Magda did mention to Len that he was developing pronounced sleep apnea; too many times Len held his breath while sleeping, and just when Magda was about to shake him to induce normal breathing, he would cough and gasp and sputter into hyperventilation. It got worse. Len himself began to notice it: He found himself jolted awake sometimes with a sudden burst of breathing, gasping and coughing. On the advice of his doctor friends Len consulted a cardiologist, who began seeing him once a month and prescribed some pills. Len's bouts of weakness and tiredness became frequent. Things were coming to a head.

On a trip to Chicago Len was overtaken by a crisis. Once again Trish was with Len when his health crisis struck. They were in Illinois for Trish to attend another TAPS memorial service: that morale-boosting

"Tragedy Assistance Program for Survivors." This episode of TAPS was being held at Evanston, to the north of Chicago. Once again Trish was determined to attend. It would be a long journey and she had lately developed a psychological condition: An uncontrollable panic attack when she drove on a highway. Commutes along familiar routes in the city were negotiable for her, but not intercity driving with speeding cars and trucks darting or muscling past her. If Trish must attend, Len had to take her, along with Jara as she desired, to Evanston. They stayed two nights in the convention hotel.

Len went not for any keen interest in TAPS but for the sake of his love and concern for Trish. He had little sympathy for casualties from America's endless imperial wars in foreign lands. He was particularly disgusted by top politicians who sent young American men and women in harms way with brave talk of "America must be strong," but did their best to keep their own families out of the fray. Whereas the Romans of old fought similarly all over the then world for conquest and spoils, at least their political leaders were often in the forefront of the fighting —but not so U.S. politicians who voted frequently for more arms and more wars, eager to use poor citizens from inner city ghettos as cannon fodder to advance their own financial and political agendas.

Nevertheless, Len came to pity the sorrows and admire the courage of many parents, spouses, and siblings he and Trish met at TAPS — people whose loved ones made the supreme sacrifice merely to enrich the pockets of oligarchs and jingoists. Trish, too, declared that she benefitted from TAPS, that she gleaned solace from talking with similarly bereaved parents at TAPS. So Len usually went. Because he was the *pater familias,* the manifest father figure for Trish's family, notifications of TAPS events came to him.

Sometimes he tried to persuade Trish to discontinue TAPS attendance. It began to seem to him like a morbid obsession, an extension of her ceaseless grieving at home and at her son's grave. She needed to slowly let it go and let healing occur, instead of often prying open the scab. Trish gave no reply to his pleading; she just persisted in the funerary activities. But Len could not really blame her since he had never experienced the throbbing horror of losing a child of one's own. He shouldn't judge her without ever having walked at all in her shoes —those shoes with soles studded with nails and broken glass. So he always gave in and took Trish to TAPS.

The acronym was no doubt chosen with care, for *Taps* also was the name of the familiar and moving dirge played by a lone bugler each time a US service man (or woman) died in service to the country. But Len discovered anew each time that TAPS was not really a dolorous convention of unmitigated grief as the name might suggest. It was often held in a positive atmosphere, with a belief in finding strength through collective grieving, and an uplifting attitude of suspending one's own grief for a moment to comfort another person whose cross seemed heavier to bear or more recently shouldered than yours. TAPS was subsidized, so room and board were paid by the organizers, but attendees were expected to get themselves to the venue of each activity. Len bore the transportation and logistical expenses for TAPS trips, as he always did when he took Trish's family on a vacation.

As had happened on three earlier occasions when Len and Trish took a trip out of state, a major health crisis broke on Len this time. In the middle of the first night a fire alarm went off around 1 am. Everybody responded briskly, scurrying down the stairwell. Trish and Jara went quickly down eight flights of stairs, followed by a struggling Len. The commotion was so intense that Trish did not notice that Len was struggling and lagging behind. And then when they hit the ground Len realized he had forgotten his wallet in the hotel room. If it got consumed in a fire they would be unable to pay their bills or drive home (without his driver's license). Trish could not drive them home, and Jara had just got her first driving permit. So Len announced he was going back upstairs for his wallet.

He set out up the stairs, gasping for breath and stopping several times to rest, with the fire alarm klaxons screaming like banshees in his ear. Like a salmon intent on swimming upstream to reach its spawning site, Len was impeded all the way up by the continuing flood of people streaming down. He got into the room, picked up his wallet, headed down again and passed out half-way down. When he came to, the stampede of spooked guests down the staircase had eased considerably, and Len was able to stagger on slowly down, holding the rails as he went, and gasping from exhaustion. By the time he rejoined Trish and Jara, Trish was in a state of near panic. So Len quietly told her about his problem with apnea and about being under regular treatment from a cardiologist who said his heart was ailing. In the semi darkness he had no idea how Trish took the news of another diseased heart in another man that was dear to her.

Len got them back to Columbus after the TAPS event, and then, all alone, headed home to Cleveland. He had had the scare of his life, not really from the threat of fire but from realization that his heart trouble was escalating. He began to think that when his end came it would be in Trish's arms. His apnea worsened. Luckily for him, that was the last trip he was to take with her.

He contacted Cleveland Clinic after recalling he had once volunteered for a sleep study being conducted by a doctor —an exercise for which Len had worn a Halter monitor and stayed in bed through two nights and the intervening day. Cleveland Clinic now had several permanent stations for studies on sleep disorder. They found a vacant attendance spot for Len, so he and Magda went there that very night, for he was by then ailing visibly and unable to sleep at all. Each time he fell asleep his body jerked awake with what felt like a kick, and so he had gone for several days without sleep. Magda was worried; Trish never knew anything about it, and she had retreated once again into aloof reticence in any case.

Only a nurse was in attendance at the sleep center, no doctor. They assured Len that a doctor would see him in the morning, but he and Magda doubted seriously if he would make it until morning. Just after midnight things got so bad that Len told Magda to call his sons so he could say his final goodbye to them and to his grandchildren. It was 1 am when Magda started to dial the first number; then she gave up, broke down, and cried. Len hugged her as she sat on the edge of his hospital bed and said to her, between his gasps and her sobs:

"I guess it's goodbye, Maggie; the end has come. You have been good to me through four decades of marriage. You are a good woman, a wonderful wife. Take care of yourself, and of our grandchildren. Tell them that with my last breath I pass on to them the blessings of our ancestors. A copy of my last will and testament is in an envelope on our headboard; the original is in the safe. Please find the strength to carry on, my dear wife."

He pulled Magda down to kiss her goodbye and she wailed and sobbed so hard that the nurse ran into the room. But at that moment the nurse in Magda kicked in. She had been a nurse for over forty years and she wasn't about to lose her head when she most needed clear thinking. She pulled out her cell phone and called 911. She described the desperate situation to them and an ambulance sped up within ten minutes. They quickly took her and Len to the Cleveland Clinic's Emergency Unit that was only minutes away. On the way they talked to Len constantly to keep him awake.

When they arrived at the hospital a doctor was waiting. He engaged Len in a rather interesting conversation about his origins in the West Indies, his travels, the Nigerians he had met and worked or interacted with, this and that, all the while evaluating Len's vital signs by palpation and with a stethoscope. It was more like a social chat than a physical examination: That doctor was such an interesting and erudite man that Len stayed lucid and had a pleasant check up. The doctor told Len his lungs were almost full with collected fluids. That was why he could hardly breathe, especially when he tried to sleep.

They punched an IV line into Len's arm and he slowed down. But he was still sentient enough to experience intense tickling as they intubated him with slender suction tubes passed down his nostrils and snaking towards his lungs. Len did not know what else they did to him: He went out like a light. But Magda filled him in when he awoke from anesthesia. They had pumped much fluid from his lungs, which meant they had reached him just in time (or rather, Len thought, he had reached the hospital just in time, thanks to Magda's professional reaction). And, of course, Cleveland Clinic was the world's premier hospital for diseases of the heart. Len knew he was in good hands with the clinic and with the ministrations of his competent wife who had several awards for nursing excellence and diligence. Score one, again, for Magda: If he had been with Trish (again) that night he would not have made it to dawn.

Len's heart now had pronounced A-Fib and needed to be stabilized. He was held in that hospital for thirty days of treatment and observation. He did not think it possible that one could stay so long in a hospital in these modern days when most patients were discharged within a day or two of admission because the daily costs of being held in hospital wards were prohibitive. It helped hugely that Len had turned 65 just one month before that catastrophic heart failure as it was called in his chart. That meant he could draw from Medicare, and he had enrolled three months before his sixty-fifth birthday. That saved him from paying ruinous hospitalization charges out of his pocket. By the time he was discharged thirty days later and given a portable defibrillator to wear constantly at home, the total cost of his hospital intervention topped three hundred thousand dollars.

After emptying his lungs of water, the rest was a matter of observation, treatment with pills, and a battery of daily tests and checks. Magda returned to work after staying with Len through the first two days; she had to go and oversee matters of the family business. After three days of extensive intervention by his doctors and nurses Len felt strong enough to call Trish and tell her where he had been. Len told her the temblors that jolted him on that flight home from Rome and during their visit to Evanston, Illinois, were warning signs that his heart was failing. And by coincidence, Trish was with him on both occasions. The big quake finally hit him three days ago and knocked him into a hospital emergency service. It was catastrophic heart failure, they told him, and his stay in that hospital was open-ended. He'd really love to see her again, to hold her and kiss her, but if that pleasure was going to be denied him now, she should never forget him: He loved her more deeply than words could tell.

Trish expressed concern for Len's health and added that she was sure he was in the best place for treatment of heart problems. She didn't ask for details and Len didn't volunteer them. They made small talk, and they hung up. Trish did not call Len that day, or the next day; so he called her on the third day. From then on Len called Trish each day, sometimes twice on a day, to fill her in on his progress. During his entire stay of 30 days in the hospital Trish called him only two or three times. It was clear to Len that Trish was losing interest in their relationship. And why not? A dozen years had gone by; she was jaded now and he was sick, to boot, maybe terminally ill, for all Trish knew.

Len was saddened by the lack of concern his grave illness evoked from Trish. If the situation were reversed he would have jumped to her side in a flash. Didn't he drop everything and rush to comfort and assist her every time she was bereaved or just had a health problem? He didn't expect Trish to come in person, though that would have really provided a positive fillip to his recovery. Trish did not drive on the highway anymore. Of course Vivica or someone else could have brought her, but all those others were busy with their own lives and errands, full of bustle as any American. Another reason Len did not expect Trish to show up in his cardiac hospital unit was because she had to be wary regarding surprises she might run into. She couldn't have forgotten the awkwardness caused by the fact that she was with Len in the Cincinnati hospital during his first episode for heart disorder —albeit a presence that was not altogether voluntary on the part of Trish, because she was simply caught up in the flow of events when Len lost consciousness practically in her arms in the airplane.

Nobody could blame Trish for not wanting a repeat of the awkwardness of Cincinnati. But how about calling him? How disappointing that Trish was distancing herself from him just when her empathy would have meant the world to him. Then it struck him one day, after Magda had been to visit him, bringing food, affection, and cheer — that he was silly to take for granted a wife to whom he owed his life and his ease, only to pine for another woman who gave every impression of lacking in empathy. Why did his heart seem to hunger only for what was out of reach? They say the grass is always greener on the other side, but why was it so? He really liked Magda as a loyal, resourceful, and attentive wife, but at the same time found Trish irresistibly lovable. Like the aristocrat who found nothing wrong with feudalism as a way of life, sometimes Len wished he were a Muslim.... But, he sighed, the head likes, while the heart loves!

But why, for that matter, was Trish indifferent to his health, after all he had done for her? It might be due to squeamishness, he reasoned; some people are that way in the presence of illness. Or it might be out fear she was going to lose Len too, so that she wished to cushion herself by staying aloof. There was the fact that her son and her brother both died of heart problems, and now Len had had a close call with heart failure. Trish had lately and repeatedly lamented to Len that, "It looks like all the men in my life are going to die early." Len had reassured her that he had no intention of dying any time soon, but her fears were perhaps understandable: Nigerians were by nature superstitious, and in Trish's case it did not help that she had bought totally into the modern version of superstition, called Christian faith.

To distract Trish from morbid fixation on supernatural causes of her bereavement, Len told her of the year he turned eight, when his mother died, and soon thereafter his extended family of uncles and aunties and cousins lost six more members within a span of six months. The family was rocked, but it hung together. But Trish was not reassured. She had a simple mind that was captive to her beliefs, and her world was a theatre of miracles and mysteries and magic and witchcraft. Everything that happened to mortal man was controlled by unseen superior forces, and each unusual event a harbinger of evil or of divine favor. To be visited so many times in such short order by sudden deaths of her closest male relatives must seem to her an omen of judgment from on high. Her ordeal of bereavement might continue till her cup ran over, or maybe the cascade of catastrophes had expiated her sins already and she was in safe harbor at last. She couldn't tell, and nobody could blame her if she was paralyzed by dread of more bereavement.

On the other hand, it was probably more than her fear of his dying. Len remembered that Trish showed similar dispassion on another occasion, one of the most harrowing times of his life. Two years earlier, both of Len's granddaughters perished in a tragic fire in the home of his son, along with their half-sister. Though his entire family was plunged into shock and grief, it was left to Len to set aside his sorrow now and then and call Trish to apprise her of developments in the final week when his youngest granddaughter lay unconscious, battling for her life, and finally losing it. It was hard to escape the conclusion that Trish did not score too highly on the scale of human compassion. But still Len loved Trish and longed for her. Love cared nothing for logic.

So, during his convalescence at home after his first discharge from the Cleveland Clinic, Len called Trish daily, if only from force of habit. Her voice still thrilled him and he still longed to touch her, to hold her, to kiss her. He called her at least once a day during the month he spent at home before returning to the Cleveland Clinic for installation of a sentinel in his heart, the Implantable Cardiac Device or ICD. The ICD functioned like the external defibrillator he had worn day and night for one month after his first discharge from the Cleveland Clinic. The only difference was that his ICD was a solid-state device the size of a small wallet, buried in his chest, rather than a radio-sized box that he strapped to his hips, with electrodes snaking up to his chest where they were held down under his shirt with sticky gel. This time, following the implant, he was discharged from hospital after four days.

But Len knew he was still deeply in love with Trish even if she had fallen out of love with him. He went home and resumed calling her daily. It was only then that Len learned that Trish was also distracted by some personal troubles of her own. Her baby sister was fighting for her life against cancer. It was as though some malevolent deity had it in for Trish and was determined to beat her down to the ground.

22
Deluge Continues

Into each heart some tears must fall
But some day the sun will shine
Into each life some rain must fall
But too much is falling in mine

TRISH'S SISTER, PAULA, was a gentle and likeable woman. Trish used to tell Len so much about her from when they grew up together and Trish spoiled her baby sister a little. Paula married very young, had a daughter and a son, and had just been widowed when Len met her in Trish's house. She had come with the rest of her family to attend the funeral of her nephew, Joshua. Paula smiled with her eyes, was eager to please, and laughed easily at the jokes Len told, even the corny ones.

But Paula carried a ticking time bomb. Even before she came for Joshua's funeral, she had been diagnosed with lipoma. Most often lipoma is a benign tumor growing in the fatty tissues, but it can turn more deadly. In her case it did. After her return to Nigeria the diagnosis was changed to liposarcoma, which is a cancer but one with a survival rate no worse than prostate cancer in men. So Paula and her relatives were fairly optimistic about the outcome. While she received treatment from a doctor, she relied more heavily on the power of prayer. It was a conditioned reflex: Trish's immediate younger brother was a priest, their father was a knight of the Church (a tradition followed upon his death by the male child just before Paula). They were a strongly religious family. And then, like everyone else in Nigeria, Paula abandoned Catholicism ("too staid!") and began to worship with emergent, hysterically charismatic denominations. When illness befell her it was not surprising that she would think her faith would see her through.

But when occasional prayers did not work the hoped-for magic, she spent a season in reclusion at a novitiate run by nuns of her first faith, the Catholic Church. That did not help, either, and Paula began to weaken, to lose vigor, along with a significant amount of weight. Her doctor recommended that she seek treatment in the U.S., and Paula agreed. The doctor did some research and came up with the name of a good medical consultant in Columbus. Paula applied for another visa, this time on medical grounds.

That was perhaps a mistake. Many Nigerians and other foreigners, who come to the U.S. to visit, end up getting treatment for one malady or another. Then they quietly go back home, leaving their doctors' and hospital bills unpaid. Because the cost of healthcare in the U.S. is prohibitive, the bills are often sky-high. But people get away with stiffing U.S. society with the bills because it is difficult to collect from them once they leave, and of course one can't just mount a debt collecting agency at the airports! Because of such delinquency, Trish said, U.S. consulates came to require that a significant chunk of the estimated cost of treatment be paid in advance to doctors and hospitals at U.S. destination, before a visa is issued. In Paula's case, Trish told Len, the U.S. consulate demanded that $15,000 be paid to the Columbus hospital in advance. Only after the hospital reported that payment had been made would the U.S. State Department instruct the consulate to issue visa to Paula.

All eyes turned to Trish. The way Nigerian relatives tend to view personal resources is: "What is mine is mine and what is yours is ours." To be fair to Nigerians, that view is but an outcrop, or perhaps the obverse side, of the well-known African adage: "It takes a village to raise a child." The unstated corollary to that saying is that when that child grows up he or she is viewed as a community resource for her entire village. She has a duty to do all she can to advance the welfare of her entire village as well as her relatives. Every African in the diaspora is expected, indeed required to exert and extend himself or herself on behalf of relatives and kin, even to the point of self-abnegation.

In that regard, Trish had excelled for the longest time as a benevolent provider for her large and growing clutch of relatives, who came and went through her house. To fill that role, she almost became a wonder woman, reproducing the gospel miracle of loaves-and-fishes on a daily basis. But even a Wonder Woman runs out of resources to sustain miracles indefinitely. Some of the demands on this African child, Trish, were just too big. The huge fee for Paula's visa was one such demand. Trish had exceptionally robust views of her responsibilities to her kin, it was true, but $15,000 was a mountain too high for her to climb. But because she was living and working in the U.S., it was assumed she had the money or could get it somehow.

Trish was in a quandary. Her recent troubles had exhausted her purse. Her friends did not have ample means, and even if they did, $15,000 was a whopping amount of money to advance her. She was stumped, and soon she became depressed, distraught. She said one of her friends who owned a Columbus home care business pitched in $1,000, and another friend gave $200; but that was all from her friends. Trish began to flounder. The financial requirement of the U.S. Consulate for Paula's visa was, to all intents and purposes, a death sentence —a peremptory condemnation of the baby sister Trish loved dearly.

Trish became so distracted that Len picked up on her cues and got to know of her need. He came to the rescue. He could not bear the thought of Trish languishing in distress if he could help it. He told her to use $15,000 from their venture capital. Trish later reported that she had deposited $15,000 with the hospital, the State Department was notified, and Paula got her visa. In a matter of days Paula arrived in Columbus with a retinue of relatives, this time including her mother (Trish's mother), her daughter, and one of her brothers. And Trish could smile again now and then.

That still left a balance of $5,000 from the $20,000 venture capital, but Trish never mentioned that residual balance again. When Len asked about it several months later Trish said it was all gone. He did not ask where it went. He considered it used up in Trish's hosting of her relatives who came with Paula to Columbus. Her escalating burdens were a concern to Len. If she had been a mooch and asked him for more money, and if he had it to give, he would gladly have given it to her in her hour of pressing need. In his worldview that was what love was all about.

But, strangely, not one person among Trish's relatives and friends ever said "Thank You" to Len or even acknowledged his gift in any way: Not even Paula herself, nor her mother, nor Paula's adult daughter, nor even her brother the priest. After Trish crept out of Len's life and he began to reflect on her behavior, the only way he could explain that baffling ingratitude was that Trish never told her family where or how she got the $15,000. Len saw that as indicative of a major character blemish. But Len never made an issue of it.

Trish also found herself harboring her niece who came with the family from Nigeria. Pregnant upon arrival on a visitor's visa, the niece let it be known she was not going back to Nigeria, and after her mother died in the Columbus hospital the niece eventually went underground to avoid deportation. Only slightly older than Trish's own daughter, Vivica, the niece was a pleasant-mannered young lady who devoted all her time to nursing her baby when he was born. But Len had no sympathy for illegal immigrants who brought no marketable skills and who can only look forward to a hide-and-seek life of dodging immigration officers and struggling to hold down illegal and exploitative jobs that paid a pittance under the table. The hassles far outweigh the benefits and the only gain is to any US-born offspring of the furtive fugitive.

For that niece's mother, Trish's only sister —gentle Paula with the smiling eyes— the doctors did their best but Paula's symptoms grew worse. The doctors kept assuring Trish and her family that Paula would rally, that her condition was stabilized, that there was hope. A drowning man, they say, will clutch at a straw. Trish's family clutched desperately at this one, willing their baby daughter to beat the odds, praying for her as hard as they knew how. Three, four, five months went by and Paula was still getting chemotherapy intermittently, and slowly falling apart from her body's reaction to the assault. Len didn't come around to Trish's home too often now for several reasons, one of them being the creeping coolness Trish displayed, another one being Len's reluctance to crowd Trish's family in their time of gloom and stress.

Nevertheless, it was Len who picked up on an unspoken indication of the depressing prognosis. Trish's family was in denial and shock, and they hung onto the assurances of recovery from Paula's doctors. But by the end of the fifth month it became clear that Paula and her retinue would overstay their six-month visas. Trish applied for extension and Immigration apparently referred the case to the State Department because it was special, and the State Department took its time. Though nobody explained it to them, Len realized that the State Department was waiting for recommendations from the hospital treating Paula. Perhaps they saw no point in extending the visas if Paula's end was near. The sixth month passed, then the seventh. Len concluded that the hospital was not encouraging the State Department to approve the visa extension. That did not bode well for Paula.

The outlook was grim the way Len saw it, and Trish agreed when Len laid out his analysis for her. In spite of human tendency to hang on to hope and persist in denial, Trish was an astute woman. She once again braced herself for the worst. But still she kept her distance from Len, having decided to shoulder this cross alone. The end came soon, but she did not inform Len, who found out almost by accident. He called her home one evening to see how she was doing but she was not at home. Viv took the call and chatted briefly with Len. Just as Len was about to hang up the girl said: "Did Mom tell you her sister passed away?"

"Gosh, no! When did this happen?" Len inquired.

The girl said it was three days earlier. Len was shocked. He called back late that night and Trish confirmed the death of her sister. Len rushed down the next day to help shore up his suffering Trish, but she could not make any time to be with him this time. The eyes of her entire resident family were on her for funeral arrangements. Trish ran around with her brother and her niece and made the arrangements. Again Trish surrendered the new cemetery plot recently assigned to her, and she was going to have to request yet another one. She and her son and her sister would lie side-by-side at that spot. Trish was a model par excellence on how to care for one's relatives at all costs.

The funeral was low key, but again a large crowd attended because of Trish. Len, coming in from Cleveland, missed the *Requiem Mass* conducted by Trish's brother, which he would have liked to attend because it was forty years since he had been to one. But at least he arrived at the cemetery before the body was interred, with only the family and a couple of intimate friends in attendance.

After the ceremonies, Len took Trish on a long, slow walk around the cemetery. Trish had class, he thought, a superb taste in choice of cemetery as in everything else. Resurrection Cemetery, as it was known, a Catholic cemetery, was a *Mare Tranquilitatis* or sea of calm. It is one of the most soothing spots Len had seen. He liked the quiet of cemeteries, and when he was a student used to ride his bike to Cleveland's Lake View Cemetery to sit and eat his lunch or read a book in the open spaces around the mausoleum of James Garfield, a U.S. president, amidst the fluttering of colorful butterflies and the twitter of birds. The quietude of a graveyard is most conducive to reading, to rumination, and to the contemplation of human mortality.

Lake View Cemetery, while dignified by age, by lush vegetation, and by the occasional scenic grotto or crypt, was old-fashioned in the crowding and helter-skelter clustering of graves. Len disliked the overcrowding in that cemetery, just as he was put off by some new cemeteries in Cleveland that were oversubscribed too, so that the tombstones stood close and behind each other like dominoes. He thought the dead deserved more dignity, just as he also thought the encroachment of residential and commercial buildings around many cathedrals of modern cities robbed those supposed temples of the dignity they used to command in the old days when a cathedral was surrounded by scores of untrammeled acres.

He admired the open spaces and wide-apart disposition of graves in this Resurrection Cemetery of Columbus. It was one of the best appointed cemeteries that Len knew. It was scrupulously clean and free of litter; the graves were manicured. Flowers and hedges graced the place, and little grottoes of saints and angels were ensconced in picturesque settings. Len had notified his family of his wish to be cremated; however, if he could be persuaded to change his mind on that point, Resurrection Cemetery was a place he could stipulate. Its efficient grandeur was its own protection: Only a hooligan might fail to think twice before marring the tidy serenity of that cemetery.

As they strolled, Len pointedly asked Trish if she was cross with him for any reason. She assured him she was not; she was just beaten down by her cascade of bereavements. Bereavements galore, yes; but Len expected Trish to have told him when Paula died. He had really gotten to like Paula and to think of her as a proxy sister-in-law. Trish knew that; and Len did not need to remind her that the last-ditch effort to save Paula, bringing her to the U.S. for treatment, was made possible only by his sacrifice of a huge chunk of his retirement savings. That, he thought, gave him some right to expect to be informed when Paula died.

Inevitably, Len wondered anew whether he was crowding Trish too much —whether it wouldn't be best for him to give her time and space to decide if she really wanted him still, if she needed him enough to nudge him, even push him out of his complacency with a situation amounting to *ménage-a-trois*. On that cemetery walk Len decided to cool off about Trish and let her take the initiative for a while. He was at a loss as to what else to do.

During the funerary repast that followed at Trish's home after Paula was buried, Len stood aloof, unacknowledged and almost ignored. Nevertheless, he gave Trish $500 in cash to give to her brother, the priest who, as the eldest son, was head of the family; the money was to help provide refreshment for the mourners, Len told Trish. Like his earlier donations, that gift of five hundred dollars was never acknowledged by anyone in Trish's family. Weeks later when Len asked Trish, she said she had given his new donation to her brother. That was an excellent opportunity for her family to say thanks to Len for all he did to ensure that Paula came here for treatment, and to provide some refreshment for guests at the funerary reception. If for any reason they could not say "thank you" publicly to Len, they could have said it in private. But none of them ever did, in all three years from the time Trish's family arrived in Columbus with Paula to the period when Trish took up with another man and began to evade Len. Apparently, Len was no longer of any consequence to her family, having served his purpose.

With the exception of one of Trish's brothers, their entire family came with Paula and lived with Trish, including Trish's mother. In those three years Len had visited them half a dozen times in Columbus. He chatted with Trish's mother on three occasions (including on that Mothers' Day trip when Trish lit into him) and three or four times with Trish's brother the priest (including during that two-day road trip to Richmond for Trish to confer with authorities in the Army unit where Josh served and died). Up to that point it hadn't occurred to Len to wonder if there was more (or less) to Trish's family than met the eye in casual conversation.

But from that point on, and especially when Trish began to behave in strange ways towards him, Len began to wonder about the sort of family values Trish grew up with. Apparently Trish's family did not care whether she borrowed or stole all that money or got it by prostitution. And yet they were a family that made a grand show of devout Catholicism, up to knighthood and priesthood. Even if Trish never told her family what kind of windfall brought her $15,000 one fine day, did they not wonder about it? Did they think that Trish won the lottery? It was a resounding mystery to Len. But, no matter: It was a case of crass ingratitude or fatuous ignorance on the part of Trish's entire family.

That reminded Len of the "morality" debates between atheists and protagonists of religion. The latter claim that religion is the sole source of morality, but that is really a hypothesis that can be put to the test. (It is what logic calls "a falsifiable proposition.") Every religion is based on the fear of a deity or expectation of reward from that deity, no matter by what name it was called. Therefore, a religious person engages in charity for one of two reasons: Either to obtain reward from a deity or to escape punishment inflicted by same entity. In other words, religious people do moral deeds only for personal gain, any way one looked at it. But if, like Len, you had no religion and still performed acts of charity, your deed must be springing from altruistic motives. Basically, an atheist's act of charity or compassion was the real act of true morality.

23
End Game

Lean on me, when you're not strong
And I'll be your friend; I'll help you carry on
For it won't be long
Till I'm gonna need somebody to lean on.

LEN DID NOT necessarily buy the religious notion that one must stay in a marriage until death. On the other hand, he did not like the growing levity with which marriage was treated by urbanized Western elites, an attitude that was spreading. He shared the conventional wisdom which said marriage is a bond that should not be sundered lightly. The only question concerned the tipping point at which a person may or should make that profound change in his or her life. Of course it was a question for each individual to decide for themselves. But Len was not sure what his own personal tipping point was, for he had never been down that road before and had no relative who had done so.

For more than a dozen years he had resisted the powerful gravitational pull of Trish, while at the same time drifting slowly out of intimacy with Magda. At what point does attraction to one surpass duty to the other? A few years earlier that question would have been a no-brainer for Len: He was coiled and ready to end his marriage for the sake of Trish. But he waited for the right moment to come along and Trish began to cool towards him, or so he thought. In ruing his missed chances, Len found a personal meaning in the aphorism that Marcus Brutus laid on Gaius Cassius in Shakespeare's Julius Caesar: "There is a tide in the affairs of men which, taken at flood leads on to fortune. (But) Omitted...."

Lately Len had begun to fear that, after so many years of indecision he had missed the flood that would have led to bliss with Trish, that he was now "bound in shallows and in miseries." By the time Magda stumbled upon Len's cache of letters from Trish, read them all, recognized the extent of their affair, and mounted a spirited counterattack, Len's feelings toward Trish had slipped into a holding pattern, a temporary doldrums. Len was in serious depression. In fact, his doctor friends said he was in "clinical depression." Len pooh-poohed the "clinical" prefix, but he needed no telling there were weighty issues forcing a decline in his mood.

First, he was making no headway in his hopes of becoming self-supporting and independent of his business partnership with Magda (which he greatly feared would be scuttled if he left her), and he had not found any alternative pursuits that were equally lucrative. His salary from the family business exceeded what he had ever made before in any other position. Those income considerations frustrated his desire to leave Magda for Trish —or so he told himself. (The truth was perhaps that he could not dig up the courage to make that wrenching break.) Then there was the niggling problem of his health, where it seemed a near-conspiracy between his cardiac problems, his diabetes, and his hypertension, united in a debilitating alliance against him.

In the two years preceding and following his heart failure he very seldom left Cleveland, not even on necessary business trips, which he left for Magda (such as out-of-town meetings and trade fairs and workshops). There was a time when he considered such business outings to be convenient cover for diverting to Trish for a day or two without needing explanations. Now he just didn't care, and the reason for that nonchalance referred back to what he sensed in Trish's own apparently changed or changing attitude towards him. She no longer showed enthusiasm over the prospect of his visit, nor did she call him: If he didn't call her they stayed out of touch. Len worried increasingly over that situation and began to think that Trish had given up on him because he had taken too long to make the desired break from his marriage.

Trish still sounded pleasant on the phone but if Len proposed an outing with her now, she came up with reasons to parry the suggestion, decline it, postpone it, or react without enthusiasm. Many of her reasons were genuine: She was entangled and getting overwhelmed with her domestic problems, caring for her sick sister and for her daughters, or providing for the large retinue of family members who came up from Nigeria along with her sister. The long term prospects for her sister's recovery were not encouraging, and her entire family braced for a protracted battle against her illness. There were material concerns as well.

Being "children of the tropics" and always cold in the frigid climes of Columbus, Trish's resident relatives ran up her heating bills to the sky in fall, winter, and spring. A uniform complaint by all Nigerians resident in the frigid latitudes was that relatives visiting from Nigeria took half-hour hot showers daily because it was a luxury that had been denied to them back in Nigeria. And it simply did not occur to them to turn off the water momentarily while scrubbing themselves: They just let it gush full-blast. Because of the heat and humidity back home, no self-respecting Nigerian would consider going through a single day without a shower or bath, even if it was just from a bucket; they brought that habit with them. Visiting relatives didn't bother to switch off lights when vacating a room, either. Plus, they made frequent and interminable phone calls back to Nigeria, sometimes just to chat.

The reason for that profligacy was that the situation in Nigeria was chaotic and not conducive to developing a habit of conservation. In Nigeria, utilities (water, electricity, and phone services) were provided and operated by city governments rather than private enterprise. And Nigerians tended to consider all government services to be freebies, so they cheated scandalously over paying bills for utility consumption. Because of prevalent, colossal corruption, serious collection efforts were not attempted. Nor would such efforts have succeeded since tracking people was impossible in a country without a structured way to follow individuals —for instance with social security numbers. Thus it was not easy for Nigerians visiting their relatives in the U.S. to keep in view that every ounce of water, every puff of gas, every moment on the phone had to be paid for. In consequence they ran up their host's utility bills to the rafters. Trish complained often about such needless waste but in the end she gave up, what with the more pressing problems of caring for her ailing sister and holding down her job.

Such was her preoccupation with family issues that Len readily accepted her reasons for a growing lack of energy or enthusiasm for togetherness with him. Still, at the back of his mind lurked the fear that she might be slowly slipping away. Once or twice before, Len had reflected long and hard on Trish's relatives. Rather selfishly, in a quite definitely un-African manner, Len thought of them as baggage. Trish had told Len that they were her responsibility, all of them who accompanied her sister when she came up from Nigeria on an open-ended journey in search of treatment. And Trish was right: In the tradition of Africans she could do nothing but accommodate them and provide for them as best she could for as long as they needed or wanted to stay. One year had already passed since they arrived, together in a group, and the prospect of their early return to Nigeria was dim. In fact Trish had started the long process of applying for U.S. residency (the "Green Card") for her mother.

Meanwhile, the occasional trickle of Trish's other Nigerian relatives continued as before and, if anything, grew in frequency and duration now that their core family members were already settled in Trish's house. The problem that gnawed at Len's mind was that he would become sucked into sharing responsibility for the growing family. According to African tradition, if he married Trish now they all would become his responsibility too. He didn't relish the thought.

It was not the prospect of financial involvement that daunted Len. He had spared no effort in the past to provide for Trish whatever she wanted or needed and which he could afford. The large amount of money he had given to her to start a business was proof of his willingness to help her financially to the extent that he could. And he could not be happy if she was unhappy because of want or family obligations. What gave him pause was that he was basically a very private man, essentially a recluse, as some of his friends and most of his relatives regarded him. He was nowhere near as much "a people person" as Trish. Unlike Trish, Len's ideal day was one spent alone with her, a glass of wine in one hand and a book in the other, with jazz playing in the background.

Len recognized that part of that gregariousness in Trish sprang from an innate propensity to show-boating. He noted that when Boko Haraam kidnapped school girls in Nigeria and the Ohio local chapter of NIDO organized a rally of solidarity with the victims, Trish was the epicenter of it all, the banner-waving poster girl for NIDO in that exercise. While show-boating ran counter to Len's disposition, he was willing to accommodate it in Trish. But if it turned her into a beacon for large numbers of her relatives who come up from Nigeria now and then, Len was averse to too much intrusion into his privacy, or too much crowding into his living space.

All the years he and Magda lived in the U.S., only a handful of his own relatives had come to visit: He preferred to help them from a distance. Magda, though, was exactly like Trish when it came to interacting with her friends and relatives. No year passed but that Magda's relatives came to visit for a week or two. But Len's relatives in Nigeria were reluctant to come to the U.S., even when Len pressed them to visit for celebratory occasions, such as major graduation ceremonies (when he got his Ph.D., for instance), birth of his children, or a landmark wedding anniversary like his Silver Jubilee with Magda. They found reasons to decline his invitation.

It was a peculiar thing about his family. Whereas U.S. media and the general public assumed that every non-American was desperate to migrate into the USA, Len's personal experience was that his relatives were not impressed with what they heard and read about the States. Len had made desultory attempts in the past to help his nephews and nieces obtain visas for a visit, since their parents were not keen to come, but nothing came of the efforts as his siblings were no more interested in sending their children than they were in coming to the U.S. themselves. Remembering how eager he himself had been to come to America years ago, Len was at a loss to understand his relatives' reluctance to come here.

Now, Len had no trouble contemplating becoming a father to Trish's children; he already had a cordial filial relationship of mutual affection with her daughters. His friends teased that, since he had no daughters of his own, Len treated all the young daughters of his friends as equally daughters of his; true, and Len was especially fond of Trish's daughters. What gave him pause was the prospect of a sudden injection into his life of the other family members living with Trish and the disruption it might cause to his withdrawn lifestyle. Len did not like to do anything with half measures. His core concept of true love for Trish was to be a pillar of strength for her in all her trials and tribulations as well as in all her material needs.

Len was also eventually put off by the slow realization that Trish's family had not shown even the slightest appreciation for his extreme financial sacrifice to save the life of their daughter whom he only barely knew. He feared they would be the proverbial ungrateful in-laws who always expect handouts as an entitlement. Or maybe they considered $20,000 something of a fitting levy for their daughter's long affair with Len. After all, whereas a prostitute may feel grateful to a john who pays extra-generously for her favors (and while she may even go so far as to express such gratitude), her pimp is not likely to do the same. Len was not a stingy man, and he had amply demonstrated that as far as Trish was concerned, he would not stint at anything she desired and that he could afford. However, it was one thing to give generously of his own volition and quite another to have to give as a tax, a duty that elicited no gratitude.

There was also the small matter of his comfort. Because of his lifelong affliction with sweating, Len took to the basement at Trish's home or his own home, as a refuge wherein to work or to sleep, when temperatures in his immediate environment rose above 70 °F. In consequence, at his own home where he had better control of the ambient, the house thermostat was always set at or below 68 °F. (One of his sons never got used to the chill and complained often about it.) In Trish's house where the central air-conditioning barely worked, sleeping in the basement was an imperative for Len during the late spring through early fall, which made Len difficult to live with. Trish joined him in the basement now and then to accommodate this eccentricity, but it was sometimes hard for her: Most Nigerians like their ambient warm and toasty at all times, and she was no exception.

To make matters worse, after her family moved up from Nigeria to take up residence in her house, the basement became unavailable to Len. It was taken over by her brother the priest, for reasons of the extra solitude that men in his vocation crave. So, whenever Len came to Columbus these days he stayed in a hotel. That only weakened their bond even further.

Len relished the remoteness of his own relatives, which accorded well with his own reclusive personality. One tribulation that Nigerians resident in the U.S. dreaded, and which was largely spared Len, was the annoying calls from Nigeria in the devil's own hours of the night. Nigeria was six or five hours ahead of the Eastern Standard Time zone of the U.S. Therefore, when it was time to wake up in Nigeria (the time traditionally preferred for broaching serious topics affecting the family and kin) it was around 2 or 3 am in the U.S. Eastern Time zone. People did not have to contend with time zones in Nigeria. Even those who knew of the time differences between themselves and their kin abroad tended to be cavalier about it. So, one routinely got the 2 am phone calls from Nigeria, which was irritating. Len seldom got such calls, but when he visited Trish she got several of those calls in the middle of the night —and she answered them cheerfully, if sleepily. That was another reason not to look forward with eagerness to inheriting Trish's relatives. Len would probably not admit it, even to himself, but the middle-of-the-night calls and the accretion of Trish's family members in the U.S. did not help propel him forward with his decision to divorce Magda and marry Trish.

24
Cold War

A song of love is a sad song
Hi-li Hi-lili Hi-lo
A song of love is a song of woe
Don't ask me how I know
A song of love is a sad song
For I have loved and it's so

WITH TRISH AND Len no longer sizzling-hot for each other, Len was surprised that Magda chose that precise moment of anti-climax to mount a vigorous counter-offensive against Trish. It was an over-kill which only exacerbated Trish's already serious problems. Magda's ploy consisted of calling Trish to razz her about her affair with Len. Instead of going after Len, Magda chose to tackle the weaker target — which she assumed was Trish, who must feel most guilty about the affair. It was unfortunate that Trish did not complain about it to Len; so he did not know the extent of the harassment until it was too late. If he had got wind of it in time he would have pointed out to Magda that the campaign was needless because he and Trish had already cooled things down. The closest he came to learning about the campaign was when Trish told him to protect the privacy of his phone messages with a pass code. He did, and so thwarted Magda's curiosity about his phone records. Len was remiss on such little technological features until someone reminded him.

It began to seem to Len that Trish was immersing herself more deeply into her social causes and the company of her friends as one way to cope with the fact that her affair with Len was nosing down or in a holding pattern. Her friends were especially determined to nag and nudge her away from Len. All the years that Len and Trish hung together, her friends never relented in that effort. Trish said she assured her friends she was loyal to Len because they loved each other deeply. What she did not add was that she had a profound distaste for match making: She wouldn't do it to anyone and didn't like to have it done to her. Still, relentless effort and pressure from one's close friends will eventually yield results.

While some of those friends had a personal angle in pressuring Trish (like pushing their own preferred candidate —such as a male relative), others were genuinely concerned that Trish was wasting her life waiting for a married man who might have lost interest in her. Her friends hinted that, as one of the most popular and eligible ladies within her circle, she could have her pick of another man in town, or from among the various professional and unattached men she encountered in her busy social life. Why was she stubbornly stuck on Len? What was so special about him, anyway? Would he ever step up and "do the right thing" by Trish? In the old days Trish often mentioned to Len the gentle nudge from her friends, which intensified to become a push. But, coincident with the seemingly mutual decline of their passion for each other, Trish no longer confided that kind of thing to Len.

Then there was Trish's increasing involvement in social causes, which sometimes caused Len to worry that she was spreading herself too thin. The latest of those community causes was the Nigerians in Diaspora Organization (with acronym NIDO, pronounced as *knee-doh*), which Trish joined about the time that Joshua died. It was also the largest organization that Trish had ever joined, having as its pretended catchment area the whole world, but in manageable terms all of the U.S. It was intended for all Nigerians who lived abroad and wished to associate themselves as a group that could leverage the potential to impact events in and about Nigeria.

Len himself had an early brush with NIDO. When Nigeria's Senator Jibril Aminu was ambassador to the U.S. he tried to press Len into service as NIDO pioneer. He and Len knew each other from the past. When Aminu was Vice Chancellor of Nigeria's Maiduguri University, they had met and fenced under strained circumstances but parted with mutual respect. Now, in Washington D.C. to attend a conference (with Trish in tow), Len contacted the embassy in advance and went to pay a courtesy call on the ambassador for old times' sake, and was invited to the ambassador's Bethesda residence. Trish decided to go back to Columbus on schedule, while Len extended his trip by two days as the ambassador's guest.

Len spent two evenings with the ambassador reminiscing over topics of mutual interest, chief among them their respective experiences of Egypt. Like many Africans, especially Muslims, the ambassador was fascinated by Cairo, the capital of Arab and Muslim world. On his extended excursions there he had picked up enough Arabic to exchange time of day. He was intrigued to learn that Len had lived in Cairo and spoke Arabic as passably as Hausa. On the second evening he broached the reason for inviting Len to his home: He wanted to recruit Len to "help" him organize NIDO, which was then a budding idea. The ambassador, who was soon to declare himself a candidate for presidential elections in Nigerian, perhaps wanted to build an electoral constituency among Nigerians in the U.S., since Nigerian was then mulling the idea of absentee ballot. However, always reluctant to head raucous social organizations or even join them, Len politely declined the invitation.

Trish, though, later joined the Ohio local chapter of NIDO. Nigerians are great society 'joiners' who form interlocking and sometimes rival networks of focused groups that share this attribute or that one: For instance, those from the same Nigerian state or ethnic group, or those who attended the same category of high schools, like "government secondary schools," those who lived in the same US city, and even those who shared a given profession. If you belonged to such a group you were expected to recruit into membership anyone you knew who qualified.

NIDO was organized on a state-by-state basis in the USA. Initially, each US state was to have one chapter. Trish, ever keen to join social and community groups, became a member of the Ohio chapter of NIDO, which had headquarters in Columbus. Right away she got on the local executive committee. Whatever ambitions NIDO had to represent Nigerians, after a decade of existence it had succeeded in providing just one service of importance. Nigeria's Consulates General in designated regions of the U.S. (New York City, San Francisco, Atlanta), were not convenient places for most Nigerians to go for their consular needs, and the processing of documents at those consular offices took forever. So a niche existed for each NIDO chapter to bring itinerant consular officials to their locale to process passport renewals, tacking on extra fees to cover travel expenses for the visiting officials. It was a useful exercise when it worked, but like all Nigerian events it was liable to spin into chaos more often than it worked.

While Nigerians are generally gregarious, they are also fractious. The primary motivation for joining an organization is to promote one's self and one's ethnic kinsmen and women. Hence there is always intense jockeying for position among members of any Nigerian organization. The Nigerian is primarily interested in obtaining personal benefits from such organizations, profiting one's self at the expense of the larger group being an ingrained trait of the Nigerian. That was one consideration in Len's refusal to play an official role in NIDO. Trish's experience with NIDO confirmed Len's aversion: When she mentioned her NIDO activities it was in the context of her growing disaffection with the leadership and her wish (always muttered but never actuated) to resign her position. But Trish being Trish, smart, charismatic, and articulate, she was in demand, and easily persuaded to continue in any official position she occupied.

25
Roadmap

Please tell me, where do we go from here?
Where do we go from here?
We had good times when our love was strong
You can't deny.
Our love broke down somewhere down the line
And I don't know why.

A YEAR AFTER Len's heart failure, he finally decided to have a talk with Trish to lay out a timeline for his move, before he lost her totally. Trish, who used to gush in every other email with "I will always love you —always," had become rather reserved with her affection. She and Len had gone through a few cycles of euphoria, followed by mutual feelings of insecurity regarding each other's intentions. One such occasion was when Len gave a big reception for Magda's birthday coincident with their Silver Jubilee. Trish was crushed, pointing out to Len, "You just renewed your marriage vows in front of over 200 people. Where does that leave us? How do I stand?" And Len spoke from the heart when he replied to her, "Till the day I breathe my last I shall have nothing in my heart but love and goodwill for you, my one and only." He understood Trish's feeling of insecurity and he hoped she fully accepted his ceaseless declarations that, though he was staying in his marriage in the mean time, his heart belonged wholly to her. Once, he told her that he viewed marriage as a practical social formality that did not reflect what was in a person's heart.

Nevertheless, sensing that Trish's resolve was wilting, he called and told her: "I have something important to say to you," to which she replied, "Me too." They arranged to meet the following Saturday at a park in the lush woods of a Columbus Metro Parks reserve, opposite Resurrection Cemetery. The location was a good choice: It afforded Len the opportunity to visit Resurrection Cemetery, stroll the grounds, and pay his respects at the graves of Josh and his aunt Paula.

It was a lovely Saturday morning in early April, and the clearings in the park were still soggy from the season's rains. Trish arrived looking full and rounded in her snug-fitting jeans. She was a lady not far past her prime, who had leveled and rounded off the usual asperities of young womanhood. She was ripe, but not overripe. That was the way Len liked to see her. Obviously she had worked out a bit since that time when she broke her arm and Len had feared she was letting herself go. They sat on the big trunk of a fallen tree, locked elbows, and looked each other over. Len gave her a peck on the temple and left it at that. This was a business session, not a romp. Len spoke and Trish listened. Although she had sounded on the phone as though she too had something to say, she must have changed her mind, for she just listened to Len.

"Honey, we are now in out twelfth year, a landmark year. I'm sure you expected, as I did, that by now we would be man and wife. It hasn't happened yet. I hope you understand why not."

Trish nodded and Len continued. "Now I am in my mid-60s and looking down the other side of the hill. It is time to sketch a plan for our future. I have run three... no, four careers: soldier, professor, scientist, and now businessman. It is time to attend to other matters of importance to us. I have got the approval of our company's Board of Directors to retire next year with a comfortable pension. Then I won't have to worry about losing my income if and when Magda reacts angrily to my request for a divorce. You know she is CEO and majority shareholder in our business; I am subordinate to her, and she would almost certainly wreck the business than see me go easily."

It was a long presentation and Len gave it haltingly, looking at Trish all the time to gauge her true reaction. Trish just smiled, and nodded here and there. When he was done talking, Len got up to stretch his legs. Trish opened her bag and brought out a repast. She had said "snacks," but what she laid out made a splendid lunch: oven-dried fish and goat meat, *akara* (all of them among her usual specialties) and some roasted peanuts, bottled water and fruit juices, paper plates and plastic forks, and napkins. Len looked it over, made a face, and teased her.

"What, no wine or even beer?"

She jabbed her elbow playfully into his side and they tucked into the meal.

After eating they strolled the park for a half hour. Len told Trish he wanted to visit Resurrection Cemetery; she nodded quietly but did not offer to come along. Trish usually picked her time to visit that cemetery, once or twice a week, taking a bouquet ("No Plastic Flowers," a wise sign posted all over the cemetery cautioned mourners), kneeling at the feet of her beloved, pulling out individual blades of weeds, bathing the graves with her tears. Len had seen her do it once: When he got to her home and her daughter said she was at the cemetery, and Len approached Trish silently from behind and watched her pour out her grief with tears and sobs. Yes, Trish preferred to visit the cemetery alone, so she did not ask to go there with Len today.

They got into their cars and left. As they neared Resurrection Cemetery, Len saw a woman selling honey from a stand at the entrance to the sub-division next door. He pulled in and Trish followed suit. As was his habit (sometimes to the exasperation of an impatient Magda) Len first engaged the woman in small talk. Why should he buy her honey instead of stepping into nearby grocery stores and buying it cheaper? The woman smiled and said hers was special; it was not commercial. The woman caught the spirit of the banter and added that the bees lived in a tree behind her house and on some evenings she played her guitar for them to mellow their honey.

"Jazz or classical would work best," Len recommended, as he picked up a jar of honey. Trish laughed, and picked up a jar too. As Trish drove off, Len whispered after her, "Mellow honey for my mellow Honey."

He drove back to Cleveland, relieved that he had finally outlined a roadmap for the final stretch of his marathon journey into a life with Trish. He did not play his accustomed jazz as he headed north; he sang song after song of satisfaction, of joy. As he always did, he called Trish along the way from time to time to report his safety and progress. Ever since he told Trish he often felt sleepy driving on highways, Trish worried whenever he took to the road, and she too called him at intervals to ask: "Honey, are you OK?"

26
So Sad

We used to have good times together
But now I feel them slip away.
It makes me cry
To see love die
So sad to watch good love go bad
Is it any wonder that I feel so blue
When I know for certain that I'm losing you?

TRISH'S HOUSE REMAINED a beehive of activity. Her frequent soirees for friends and associates were now superposed on the background of her enlarged household: her daughters, her grandson, her mother and brother, her niece and the niece's baby, and vacationing relatives who still came over periodically to add warmth and company, in the African tradition of succor to bereaved persons.

Therefore, Len still kept his distance. He visited Trish from time to time but he was not relaxed in the presence of relatives who no doubt were wondering how things stood between him and Trish. He now stayed in nearby hotels when he went to visit Trish. During one such visit he went over as usual to Trish's house and realized there was a bit of tension perhaps occasioned by his presence. He asked Trish to come over to the hotel, and Trish said OK, later. Len went back to his hotel and waited It was 3 am when Trish finally knocked at his door. She made excuses: She had relays of guests and then fell asleep on the couch waiting for her mom to retire. It sounded plausible to Len but nonetheless a far cry from the eager Trish he used to know.

On the phone, Trish began to give dark and cryptic hints that she was afraid of dying, of being murdered by people who did not want her to carry on with Len anymore. "Murdered?" Len wondered.

"Yes. In this day and age it is easy, for a little fee, to have someone followed and killed. You can find out anything about anybody through a private investigator, for instance."

She was laying it on thick and Len laughed it off to ease her mind. The only person Trish must have in mind was Magda, and he assured Trish that Magda was not a cloak-and-dagger kind of person. Indeed, he told Trish, Magda did not have one mean bone in her body. Magda's only recourse would be to nag him, or cry by herself. Of course Len had no idea then that Magda had renewed a behind-the-scenes harassment by phone against Trish.

On another occasion when he called Trish she launched into an excited account of a recent incident when she felt she was being followed. She had diverted from the highway and onto a street, only for the car behind to divert too and stay on her tail. She pulled into a gas station, sat by a pump and waited. Then she noticed that people in the gas station were pointing at her and presumably talking about her. She looked behind and noticed that the car behind was an unmarked police car. The cop sat in his car and talked into his phone, then he peeled off and went away. Trish said she was shaken.

Len reminded her that she did have a curious new habit, albeit an involuntary one, of crawling along highways at the 40 mph minimum speed, a result of her new panic disorder for which she was under treatment. It does attract attention, he pointed out, especially of Highway Patrol, in addition to the column of vehicles that forms behind her to honk their horns rudely. If those incidents were the only source of her anxiety about being assassinated, she should relax. But Len knew that fear of danger is a highly subjective feeling that reasoning alone cannot dispel. He added Trish's suspicion of being stalked as one more factor in her growing aloofness. Len began to wonder how long he and Trish could hold it together. In a matter of months he would be retired and could dedicate his entire time and life to Trish, to protecting and reassuring her; but would he be too late by then?

Spring came around once again. It was the year Len was scheduled to retire. A slight delay of his retirement was occasioned by impending accreditation exercises for his company, and that required months of preparation. He notified Trish it might be end of the calendar year before he could get his freedom. Then the accreditation visit was postponed for three months. Len told Trish about this too. In the mean time, he proposed, two of them should take a week's vacation on wheels, by train. He checked Amtrak and Canadian Railways to compile an integrated six-day itinerary for round-trip journey to Toronto. But Trish begged off, saying she was hosting a women's workshop at her workplace during the week Len proposed. Len offered to shift the rail journey by one week or two but Trish said she did not really have the time; she could not take one whole week off work. Finally, Len said they could take a two-day trip to Niagara Falls. It would be their third: On the two previous occasions, when Joshua was in is teens, they had gone with all three children of Trish. Still Trish hemmed and hawed.

In considerable perplexity now, Len proposed to pay for a real vacation for Trish: for him and her or even for her alone, just as long as she could find some relaxation. He pointed out that Trish had not had a real vacation in a long, long time. She had been to Nigeria quite a bit lately, he allowed, but that was not vacation: It was stressful work, albeit of a domestic type. Trish had a close friend who hailed from the West Indies. Len suggested that Trish tag along the next time that friend went home to the Caribbean; he would pay for her. But Trish would not commit to making the arrangements. He ran out of ideas as to what next to suggest to her. Something was seriously up with Trish. But it still did not occur to Len to suspect she was seeing someone else. He really had Trish on a high pedestal and idolized her as an honest woman. For him, love went hand-in-hand with trust. Not wanting to back her into a corner, Len shelved the whole idea of giving her a vacation.

The end of that year was the only New Year's Eve in the fifteen years they had known each other, when Len did not call Trish at midnight to wish her Happy New Year. Usually Len did it just before or right after his family popped its own champagne bottle as the countdown from New York City's Times Square announced the New Year. Three weeks before the end of the year Trish sent him an email that said, "It looks like you will never be mine." It upset Len. He thought his arrangements were on track for his retirement in only a few more months; he thought he had carried Trish along on that plan. Because he was miffed, he didn't call her on New Year's Eve, and she did not call him either.

Len decided not to notify his plans to Trish anymore, but to surprise her when he retired and had moved out of his home. He would start with a negotiated separation from Magda and later follow up with a divorce. In fact he thought that this approach was better than keeping Trish fully abreast of developments. It was better because in the past he had sometimes raised Trish hopes, only to let her down when unforeseen obstacles on his road map forced delays and detours. This way, this time, if any more delays occurred down the road she would be spared the letdown.

Late one night a week before Christmas, Tina Ojemba called and gave Len news of the death of someone from their hometown whom they had both known when they were young. They chatted, and when they hung up Len's trend of thinking recalled that it was at a party in Tina's house he had met Trish for the first time. "Goddamn it," Len thought. It was about this time of year too, actually two weeks before Christmas that he had had that accidental encounter with the woman with the braids, who came to captivate his heart and dominate his life.

Len went and reviewed his recent emails. He found the latest one from Trish and looked at the date; it was sent on December 13. Len kicked himself: That was the day after the anniversary of their meeting. He had missed their anniversary. That was the first time that landmark date had skipped his mind, but he knew Trish would not view it in such forgiving light. Ladies do not like their birthdays and important milestones forgotten. Len felt guilty, but he also saw the missing of their anniversary as yet another unfortunate indicator of how far apart they had drifted. It reminded him of an appropriate song: the Everly Brothers' "So Sad."

Len's dam burst and he sobbed in his study. Why had time alienated him from Trish? Could he even live if she left him forever? Magda was a good wife, an honorable woman; but Trish was the one who had his heart in a stranglehold, the heart-throb of his life. Magda must have heard him from the kitchen. She tried to open his study door from the outside but, thank goodness, he had bolted it from the inside. After he regained his composure he opened the door and told Magda the phone call was from Augustina. Then he went down to his basement office, where he could be out of Magda's earshot. He lay on his futon day bed and cried softly for a long time. It seemed to him that a lovely chapter of his life may have come to a close.

27
Dark Clouds

There was a time when I thought of no other
When we sang our own love refrain
Our hearts beat as one as we had our fun
But time changes everything.

SECLUDED IN HIS basement office, Len tuned the whole-house radio-cum-intercom to National Public Radio for Dan Polletta's masterful session of jazz. More than the station's news bulletins and insightful panel discussions, it was Polletta's 9 pm to 1 am jazz sessions that motivated Len to become an NPR subscriber: That, and the weekly Car Talk show of "Click" and "Clack," the hilarious Magliozzi brothers. Dan Polletta seemed to know everything about jazz songs and singers, and Len once called in to Dan's show to compliment him on his mastery of his subject. Now he listened to the NPR jazz session as he closed his eyes to and surrendered, as usual, to reminiscing about Trish.

After a while Len went back up to the kitchen and got two bottles of wine. He poured a glass of Riesling for himself and one of "Yellow Tail" merlot for Magda who was busy in the kitchen; she still drank only Merlot and Chianti since Burgundy became hard to find. He told Magda that he was reviewing grades for an adjunct Chemistry course he was teaching at Kent State University. He went back down to his basement office, bolted his door, and spent a long time reviewing recent emails from Trish.

In the last one, Trish had lamented that Len was never going to be hers; the penultimate one said "I will always love you"; and one month before that there was an unusual message from Trish. Out of the blue Trish had emailed to ask Len for a little help. Len was cut to the quick. It must have taken a lot out of her to come to the decision to seek help, even from Len. She was no mooch. It was only the second time in fifteen years that Trish actually initiated a request for help. Usually, when she was needy it showed in her mood (in person or on the phone). Len's would then pry and probe to elicit the cause from her, and dispatch help swiftly. Now Trish was actually asking for help. And no wonder: She was still servicing her team of relatives and her daughter Jara who was jobless; Vivica had grown up and moved out of the house. Trish's email said she was "struggling with mortgage payment." Could Len help? Len went to the bank that day and wired her one month's mortgage payment. Trish was relieved, and sent her thanks: "I will always love you – always!"

The only other time Trish ever initiated a request for help was the year before that. She had gone to her Alma Mater, OU at Athens, Ohio, to attend a twenty-fifth anniversary memorial service for her friend who died during their college days. Trish went in the company of one of her friends. They planned to spend one night and made their reservation; but on getting there they found the ceremony was postponed for one day and they hadn't enough money for a second night. She called Len, who talked to the hotel manager and credited enough money from his debit card to pay for their second night and also upgrade them to a comfortable suite. That was one of the few times when Trish initiated a request for help. Sometimes, Len learned of her need quite by accident.

About nine months before Trish's need for help with mortgage, Len made a trifling inquiry and discovered Trish had a pressing need. He was getting rid of some of his office equipment. His expanding business was moving out of their suite in a commercial high-rise, into a dedicated building of its own, which he and Magda had renovated at considerable expense, expecting it to house their business for another decade. Installing custom office furniture, they also decided to upgrade their office machines, and began to give all their old equipment away to their staff. When it came to discarding old PCs, some of them of recent vintage, Len remembered he had not bought Trish a new PC or printer in a couple of years. He used to do so from time to time, setting up a small home office for Trish in her basement and another in the living room for her daughters. Her other electronic gadgets were also provided by Len: TV sets, fax machines, CD players, boom boxes.

So he asked Trish if she wanted any of her equipment upgraded. She replied that PC stuff was the least of her worries then: Her car needed major service and after paying her mortgage and other bills, which were high on account of overuse, she couldn't afford to maintain her car. Len wired her money so she could come up for air once again.

But he was careful not to overindulge Trish. For one thing, if Magda found out, there would be hell to pay. For another, he didn't want Trish to think he was trying to buy her love. He thought Trish was proud and independent, and would recoil at the thought of going out with a man just for his money. That was the Trish that Len knew —or thought he knew— in their happy days. She would not reach out to Len just to ask for help. But these days, Len reflected ruefully, she would not reach out to him anymore, for anything.

28
Magdalene

Eyes, that show some disappointment
And there's been quite a lot in her life
She's the foundation I lean on
My woman, my woman, my wife

MAGDA, TOO, HAD been sullen towards Len. Perhaps in reaction to the deepening estrangement that crept into their marriage, she had become ever more aloof and quarrelsome. The slightest thing set off a verbal fight between them and it grew worse with time. There was always the specter of Trish between them, lurking as an incubus over their marriage. If Magda brought it up Len assured her he was not seeing Trish anymore, indeed had not seen or spoken to Trish for quite a while. That was true: For a couple of years, since Trish retreated into her shell and Len got peevish, he had not seen her and had seldom spoken to her. Magda did not believe him but she would let it slide then, only for it to fester and erupt again down the line. But over and beyond emotional strain induced by Trish or her absence, there were more practical irritants.

There were his growing health problems and the pharmacopeia prescribed by his doctors to stabilize his health. He was diagnosed with essential hypertension in his mid-forties, and ten years later with

Type-II (adult-onset) diabetes. Between those two afflictions came that cardiac episode on a flight home from Rome. The triple whammy of hypertension, diabetes, and heart trouble played havoc with his libido, as did the medications prescribed to correct each of the maladies. So his sexual appetite slumped, and the decline became precipitous when he suffered catastrophic heart failure eight years after his cardiac incident over the Atlantic Ocean. And his prognosis called for more medications since none of his three major afflictions could be cured; all that could be done was to manage them indefinitely.

Magda, always the compleat nurse and dutiful wife, nursed him through his maladies, bore the trials and tedium of his illnesses, and learned to come to terms with his near-impotence. As a veteran nurse she understood that decline or loss of libido, whether temporary or permanent, was an expected price to pay for his staying alive under the circumstances. But he was deflated for her sake. He was aware that a woman's sexual appetite was not suppressed as much as a man's by the onset of menopause. And here was Magda, he thought, forced to foreclose on sexual activity on account of his own bodily malfunction. His doctors all assured him it was a correctable defect; there were pills and other remedies, and his libido would return with proper treatment as his health improved. But it was now years since he last felt the urge for sex, let alone act on it. It bugged him, though Magda never complained about it. Not directly, but he wondered whether that privation fed into the overall disaffection he noticed about her. She seemed to have become a new person, detached and joyless.

To be sure, through all the decades he had known her, Magda was not a touchy-feely woman. He could not remember a time when she displayed open pleasure at his presence. She was a totally practical woman, not sentimental like Len —or Trish. If Len sat on a loveseat to watch TV, with a vacant spot next to him, Magda might sit on the couch away from him and read her Bible, or even go to her bedroom

TV set and tune her favorite programs, which ran to Christian revivals and such stuff. Eventually she became interested in news bulletins, watching the major channels for news and analyses that no longer interested Len because they had begun to sound more like propaganda than news bulletins. Magda never developed interest in the TV programs Len liked: soccer, tennis, track and field athletics, wildlife documentaries, or Nova and similar programs on the Smithsonian and National Geographic channels. Len eventually lost hope that his wife would sit beside him, slip her arms through his, and lean her head on his shoulder in the manner of other wives to their husbands. Magda was not that kind of affectionate person.

Nor could one call Magda an aficionado of literature, even though she was an intelligent and accomplished professional, as well as passionate and articulate when it came to leading group prayers or preaching sermons at church. In the 44 years of their marriage Len knew her to read only two kinds of books with avidity: textbooks when she was a student, and later the bible or religious tracts of inspiration. In contrast, Len read on average one new book per week (and he considered himself a major patron of Amazon.com). In consequence of the divergence of their literary interests, Len and Magda had little to talk about beyond family, friends, and work. So when their children grew up and left the home the two of them were cast backwards into the roles of strangers to each other.

Likewise Trish: Through their fifteen years of intimacy Len had never seen Trish read anything but Christian inspirational tracts, either. She and Magda (both of them highly intelligent women whose intellectual horizons were unfortunately foreshortened by childish belief in a sky fairy), were victims of the delusion called religion —a debilitating canon of stone-age superstitions that have absolutely no place, Len thought, in the modern world of science and technology. His two women were proof to Len that religion dulled people's curiosity and truncated their vista.

But, curiously in Magda's case the self-imposed limits on her literary horizon did not impair her quick grasp of the essence of documents. She and Len often consulted convoluted documents containing arcane government rules and regulations in mind-numbing detail. But whereas Len often found himself lost after reading a couple of such turgid pages, he found that Magda had grasped the gist of the document upon first reading. It was of course possible that Magda read non-religious books on the sly, or remembered much of what she had read earlier in her life. Sometimes when Len started a quote, from Shakespeare, for instance, Magda joined him or finished the quote for him. Some people had photographic memory like that.

Len and Magda had met at a dancing party when he was in the army. They both loved to dance. They danced at that party, they dated, and they had stayed together ever since. Following a fairly unknown young man to his apartment was about as adventurous as Magda ever got. She was unsentimental and too reserved to be romantic. Once, Len brought Magda's reserve up as a discussion topic but she closed it with the down-to-earth comment that whenever she cooked his favorite dish, sewed missing buttons back on his shirt, washed his clothes or bought him new ones (which was rather too often!) she was showing affection in her own way. True, Len thought: It was as dispassionate as tending goldfish in a tank. With Magda, he was guaranteed contentment, and she believed that was enough; excitement was not her forte. Len gave it up.

She had been brought up with some prudish ideas. She converted to the Catholic faith while attending Catholic boarding schools in teenage, but retained her family's austere Methodist mores. For instance, she enjoyed a good glass of wine and in time became knowledgeable about wines: She could tell a burgundy from a Merlot or Cabernet Sauvignon by taste, and when burgundy lost ground to merlot among wine makers she had Len looking everywhere for burgundy to stash in her basement. Yet, Magda would never raise a hand to pour herself a glass, much less pop a cork by herself. If Len or her son or a male guest of theirs did not serve her the wine she would not drink it or even ask for it. In her social outlook, certain roles were reserved for men, and that was that.

Increasingly Magda had become an overzealous church enthusiast. From being a Catholic when she met Len, she dabbled into the charismatic congregations soon after she and Len married. She it was who opened Len's eyes to the reason why many traditional Christians were leaving the main-stream denominations in droves and joining the noisy, street-corner worshippers. She said Catholic services were boring. Upon reflection Len had to agree; and Catholic Mass went from being mystic in the days of Latin service, to blasé when, as a result of Vatican II reforms the services were heard first in English and finally in everybody's native vernacular. Take out the Latin songs and the Mass became terribly dull and trite. The priest says, "The Lord be with you," and congregation replied, "And you too" —as if returning an insult.

From initial curiosity about the Pentecostal sects, Magda became a singer-and-dancer in their highly imaginative congregational arrangements. Whereas Len knew churches and cathedrals to be sedate places with well-groomed lawns and gardens, some of the new churches Magda attended met in rented rooms at strip malls, separated from a restaurant for instance by just a thin wall, the worshippers sitting on fold-away plastic chairs. And because they were almost lay assemblies, there was much politicking in those church movements of Magda's new fancy.

None of their congregations kept together longer than a few months; again and again a quarrel erupted over leadership and money, and a splinter group peeled off to start a new church in another strip mall down the street. They needed hardly any capital investment. Because of her quiet and dignified personality Magda quickly became a respected elder in whichever new congregation she joined. Eventually, she became a Deaconess.

With such ascendancy, Magda brought her singing and dancing home, and squandered money in the process. Not only did she tithe, donating one-tenth of her hard-earned wages to some indolent charlatan of a "pastor" whose idea of making a living was essentially pan-handling, but she began to donate mucho bucks to faraway tel-evangelist buzzards that sent solicitations in droves. That annoyed Len so much that he took to responding to such solicitations with pointed messages: "Buzz off, and keep away from my household." If he got really mad he shredded the letter of solicitation and sent the resulting paper chips back to the sender.

When Len barked at them forcefully some of them took the hint and stopped; however, most persisted anyway because they did not really have another easy way to make a living. But one of them cheek-ily hurled a Psalm at Len: "The fool hath said in his heart there's no God." Len admired that man's chutzpah but ended that exchange with a riposte: "Yeah, and the charlatan hath said in his heart, there' is just one god in the universe, and he is to be found only in my book." Len did not know if Magda found out he was cursing out her "minis-ters." But one day she left her laptop PC open as she went into the bathroom. Len peeped into it and found her email in-box festooned with solicitations from preachers and "healers." The whole blamed gang of mooches were now reaching Magda in cyber space. Len gave it up as a lost cause.

Magda bought various ornate versions of the bible, especially electronic ones with apps for locating specific sermons for each day, and personalized interpretations of every prophecy in the bible; and she bought ever-proliferating "miracle prayer" books and pamphlets, hackneyed counsels for "inspiration," etc. and squirreled them all over the house. She purchased electronic copies of every single epistle or gospel or their translations and interpretations issued according to the whims of each new preacher that wanted an income or renown. She got into buying weekly stacks of CDs featuring sermons by her favorite ministers, both the local pastors and the nation-wide televangelists. She went to bed listening to their drivel on a walkman clamped to her ears, her ipad open to a gospel-of-the-day, neglected on her chest as sleep stole over her.

The whole cacophonous clamor of glorified beggars, mooches, and parasites had invaded Len's house in ways that flabbergasted him, and found enthusiastic receptor in Magda. Apparently she had come to the supposition that she could spend her way to heaven. Her entire, ample earnings were slowly getting sucked into the vacuum-powered U.S. evangelist industry. And Len dared not take issue with such folly. One year at tax fling time he remonstrated with Magda because the acknowledgment of "charitable contributions" which she handed over to the family's tax accountant put her donations in the five-digit domain —and that was just to her local church. Magda shot out to Len that it was her earnings and she could spend them as she pleased. Well, he countered, what if he decided to spend a tenth of his own earnings in adult massage parlors? She shot him an angry look and he shut up. But he sometimes had the last word by wondering why people who were so eager to go to heaven were so afraid of death.

Because Magda was a private and vulnerable person, whenever a situation hurt or threatened her she retreated into her shell like a snail. The long-running, off-again-on-again saga of Len and Trish was one such situation. Magda did not confront Len with it as often as another woman might (which, most unfortunately, gave him a false sense of impunity in carrying on for so long between two women). He was to learn later that her chosen revenge was to call Trish on the phone now and then to browbeat her. Finally, Magda moved out of their marital bedroom and into the guest bedroom.

That was the beginning of hostilities. She began to come and go as she pleased, sometimes staying away from home till past midnight, ensconced in the privacy and comfort of her office suite in her business premises, visiting her friends, or seeking solace in the company of night worshippers at her church. Len was totally a homebody and mostly worked from his home office. He sometimes felt embarrassed when friends dropped in of an evening and asked him where Magda was. He told them the truth: "I have no idea," and it sounded odd at 9:30 pm. (His compatriots thought nothing of making visits that late!) To cap it all, when Len heard the garage door go up and knew Magda had finally come home, he would suspend his work, hold his breath, and hope that she would step into his study, which adjoined the garage, for a chat. Magda knew that Len was in there, but she didn't bother about him. She puttered briefly and audibly in the kitchen and then went up to her room.

If Len brought the matter up the next day Magda replied that it was for the person at home to come out and greet the one who returned. But if Len was the one that came home and Magda failed to seek him out and greet him, she would invert the rule and say it was customary for the returned person to look up those left at home! Len couldn't win. She was plainly trying to avoid him. They lived in the same house but no longer interacted. His loneliness deepened, but since they maintained the usual decorum when among their friends or at a party or at work, nobody noticed that an abyss had opened up between Magda and Len. They even stopped saying Good Morning to each other. The tension thickened. Len feared a fight was coming. He had never had a serious domestic fight before; that was never his style.

Once, when Len and Magda were still courting so many decades ago, they had nearly come to fisticuffs because of an argument over a girl in Len's old school who had a crush on him and who appeared at his army billet one day from out of nowhere. After the girl left, he and Magda got into it. She wagged a finger at Len and he smacked her hand. Magda was outraged, pulled herself to full height and told him never to take a hand to her again. He apologized and took the warning to heart. Since that incident forty odd years earlier, he had not hit her again. Now he feared the volcanoes in their respective chests would explode any time. He did not want the cops coming to his home for any reason. U.S. cops were bad news: Their coming seldom boded well for anyone. It was not unknown for the police to answer a call about domestic dispute and end up shooting a person in his or her own home.

To forestall domestic violence, Len took a firm decision. Leaving a note for Magda, "I've moved out," he gathered a few of his possessions and moved out to an Extended StayAmerica lodge and signed up for a month. Next day he started scouting for a suitable bachelor apartment. After one week he found one and got on their waiting list. But each time they called him and showed him a vacant unit he turned it down for one reason or another. He was playing for time and waiting to draw the attention of Trish to his relocation scheme and show her he had finally started the long-awaited move out of his marriage. That went on for a whole year during which Trish showed a perplexing coolness to Len's suggestions for trips and vacations to recapture the old magic.

29
Despair

Is it really over? Is this the end of the line?
Don't tell me I'm losing the love that was mine.
If you're really leaving, take some part of me
So I'll always remember how sweet love used to be.
I wonder who's stepping into my shoes. Who can he be?
I can tell by your eyes our love has died. And it's over
for me.

THOUGH LEN HAD separated himself from Magda, because she had to all intents and purposes put herself out of his life, he felt no relief. That was one half of the equation solved. It used to be the only half that presented an obstacle, but not anymore. Trish, too, seemed to have taken herself out of his life. His quandary deepened: He was falling apart. Twice he paid for groceries in a shop only to walk away and forget to pick it up. And once he withdrew cash from an ATM, only to forget his card at the machine. Luckily it was at a bank branch located inside a large grocery store where he was well known and liked; to his huge relief they called him the next day to say some Good Samaritan had turned in the card. Len's mind was a runaway train that headed pell-mell in one direction: southward to Trish. Each time he got into those situations Len called Trish's cell and left a sobbing message:

"Honey, please hear my cry. My life is falling apart. I'm stumbling around in a daze. I've become a zombie. Won't you please call me, write me? Curse me, yell at me. But please reach out to me soon or I will die. I love you, my darling. I love you forever. I love you desperately."

But Trish was mute as sculpture. He sent her an email saying he would have killed himself if he had the courage to carry it through. If she would rather see him dead, then she might as well come and dispatch him. He could not live without her. Indeed, he came close to jumping in front of a moving bus one day but something held him back. Still, Trish did not respond. So Len tried to enlist the help of her relatives and friends.

First he appealed to Trish's younger brother, the priest, who lived with her. He appealed to him in his capacity as head of the family; he bared his soul to this priest as it in a confessional, and explained that he had left his wife and was ready to march with Trish. But the man was careful to stay noncommittal. Next Len turned to Trish's daughter, Vivica, because of the filial bond he presumed between her and himself. Viv was now a grown woman in her own right and might understand the ways of love. But she took her mother's side on the matter. "Fifteen years! Come on!" she exclaimed.

To make matters worse, Viv likened Len's situation to her own experience with the father of her two children. The man had been in her life over five years and was still dragging his feet about "doing the right thing." At that, Len put his own misery aside and gave some fatherly advice to Viv: "You gain nothing and only prolong a stalemate by insisting that only the man can take the initiative. If you really love your man and think he loves you but can't bring himself to take the plunge, take charge of the situation. He is like a little boy standing at the edge of a swimming pool on a cold morning and hesitating to jump in. Well, shove him in! I don't mean you should ambush him with a pregnancy, just that you should propose to him! What does it matter who takes the initiative as long as you make progress?" But Viv clammed up then and Len got the idea that, like her mother, Viv thought a woman should only receive a marriage proposal, not make one. Len sighed and gave up, thinking that maybe bad choices ran in Trish's family.

As the days rolled by, Len became disoriented, not sleeping well and eating little. As he drove down an aisle in a Wal-Mart parking lot one afternoon, his thoughts hijacked by contemplation of Trish, Len's car nearly nudged two women crossing in front of him. Hitting his brakes, he wound down his window with a sheepish smile. He opened his mouth to apologize to them but they came around to his window and swore at him in foul language. Len shut his mouth and began to wind his window back up without an apology. That got the ladies mad. One pounded at his window and cursed him some more, spittle flying from her lips and onto his window glass.

His nerves were shot from too many sleepless nights and his dander was up. Why did these two Harpies want to lynch him? He himself was nearly run over the week before as he walked to his parked car. He did not make a federal case of it. The driver who nearly hit him was profuse with apology, so Len smiled and told her to forget it, and she drove off. That was the civilized way to react to such situations, which arose often nowadays when vehicles of all sorts swarmed along every street, road, and highway. As long as nobody was hurt, one apologized and moved on. But not these two women —they wanted a fight, and by gad he was going to give it to them.

He wound his window down again and an altercation ensued. One of them planted herself in front of his car as if to bar his way, even though Len had no intention of fleeing. She got out a notepad and a pen from her bag and scribbled down his license number. Then she gave him a finger and joined her friend at his window, heckling. A crowd gathered. One transformation that his recent tribulations had wrought in Len was the ease with which he himself burped up foul language —profanities the use of which he used to consider *infra dignitatem*. Now he gave as good as he got.

"Watch where you're going, you damn fool driver!"

"Yeah, he must be drunk, the damn son-of-a-bitch!"

"Go fuck yourselves! Or have you done that already?"

"We will call the cops and you will get your license yanked."

"Well, do that, and stop fouling the air with your breath."

Len drove away slowly, expecting a squad car to zoom up behind him. But none came. He was still shaken when he got home. He sent a text to Trish, exaggerating the incident to get her attention:

"Hit 2 women today while drivin & thinkin of u. My fault but nobody hurt. Am a basket case coz of u."

But he never got a response to that, either. Len called Trish at night time when he knew she would be home, but she did not pick up. He left a message saying he would call again same time the next day. He did, but again her message box picked up. He tried that all week, to no avail. Then he began calling Trish's daughters and friends at night. Nobody picked up; still, he left messages, over and over. They all knew his phone numbers and were obviously screening his calls. He had become a pariah.

One day Len called Trish from the fax line in his office. He never before used it for voice calls, so Trish and her friends did not know that number. Trish picked up and Len breathlessly begged her not to hang up. But Trish banged the phone immediately. So he called her friend in Florida right away and the friend too picked up. What was Trish up to, he asked. He would kill himself if Trish did not talk to him soon.

"You don't have to do that. Trish simply wants to know that you are now serious, after fifteen years. She wants proof that you have left your wife."

That, finally, was progress, he thought. He had absolutely no reservation now about getting on to the nuptial court or even the altar (or temple, or tipi or whatever) with Trish. He took down the email address of the lady friend, and promised to send proof. He accepted the next vacant suite up for rent where he was on waiting list. He signed a year's lease and immediately hired an interior decorator to furnish it for him. The work was finished a few days after his agreed time at the Extended StayAmerica lodge ran out. He was ready to tell Trish he now had a place of his own wherein to receive her.

But first he had to level with Magda, and he thought it was going to be a pained talk. How does one tell his wife of four decades that he was leaving her permanently for another woman? But he needn't have worried about it. When he got to his house he found that Magda had changed all locks, including the code to the overhead garage door, so Len could not get in. He rang the doorbell and Magda came to the door. She would not let him in until he said he had come to say goodbye. He expected her to ask him to explain himself, but she did not. Evidently she had come to the end of the road with him too. She just said: "When you move your things out of here, don't come back." Len moved most of his personal items to his new apartment.

The last time his oldest son, who lived out-of-state, came with his family to celebrate Magda's birthday, Len had talked to his sons together, told them about his unhappiness, and notified them he intended to leave their mother. Though not pleased, they did not object; they were aware of the tension in the home. So now, Len just sent them a brief email telling them he had moved out; he copied the email to Magda. Now everything depended on Trish. She could save his life with a word, or she could take it away with silence. Len took photos of himself in his new apartment and emailed them to Trish's Florida friend, along with a copy of his lease, saying he was ready to get a divorce the very moment Trish said yes.

But Trish remained silent. It was unnerving! What more could Len do? Well, "If the mountain will not come to Mohammed, then Mohammed must go to the mountain." He got into his car one morning and journeyed to Columbus, leaving at 9:30 am to arrive just as lunch break was starting at the prison where Trish worked.

On the way to Columbus Len did not play his accustomed jazz. He feared it would exacerbate his despondency. Like blues, which is eponymous for melancholy, jazz is often intended as a mirror on which to reflect one's heartbreak. True, if you have any "soul," bebop will get your body twitching to the staccato rhythms of the piano or the organ, the guitar or the bass, and then send you skyward with the saxophone wailings. Nevertheless, vocal jazz is all about pain, unrequited love, wounded hearts and teary lives. He needed to concentrate on the highway and the driving instead of brooding and crying.

But inevitably his lips found song, out of habit. This time his subconscious mind latched on to a love song that used to move him, even as a child who did not understand what love really was: The tremulous query of Miki and Griff

> *Have I stayed away too long?*
> *Have I stayed away too long?*
> *If I came home tonight*
> *Would you still be my darlin'?*
> *Or have I stayed away too long?*

Before Len knew it tears were streaming from his eyes as he sang. He pulled over, rested his head on the wheel, and let it rain down his cheeks. He collapsed into sobs and wept again for Trish, his beloved Trish. He finally composed himself and resumed his journey, tuning his radio to those AM-frequency stations that broadcast obnoxious and hate-filled commentaries aimed at polarizing U.S. society with incitement against "liberals." He had learned long ago to tune to those stations when he was in danger of dozing off during long journeys on the highway. That usually worked up so much anger to keep him. Thus distracted from his despondency, he was not crying when he reached Columbus.

Nevertheless, when he pulled up at MCI his chest was pounding with an agitation he had not felt since first he approached a girl one-on-one during high school. A lump formed in his throat. Yes, he was a proud man, but today he would grovel to Trish if that was what it took. When he arrived at the prison he was told Trish was at a panel interviewing prospective prison staff; it was going to be a long one but if he announced himself at the interview venue down the road someone would go and summon Trish for him. He did as he was told. He announced himself as Joe Thomas (two of his middle names), because did not want Trish to have a chance to refuse to see him. Trish came out, saw Len, and stopped dead in her tracks. She eyed him coolly. Then her eyes narrowed.

"What are you doing here?" she queried him.

"I have come to see you, honey."

"Why? Don't you have your dozen grandchildren to occupy you anymore?" Trish demanded.

"I do, but I'm going crazy with longing for you. Why won't you answer my messages?"

Avoiding eye contact with Len, Trish said, "I am at work right now. I can't talk to you."

"I know. That's why I came just before lunch hour. I shall wait until your interviews are over, then we can go grab some lunch and have a little talk," Len pleaded.

Trish said the interviews would go on for a long time, maybe another hour or more.

"That's OK. I will wait right here" Len promised.

Realizing she wasn't going to fob Len off lightly, she agreed to meet him at 1pm. She suggested that he go to a nearby public library to browse or do his work in the mean time. She knew him well: He was in fact about to ask her for directions to the nearest public library. Len agreed and drove off, his heart lighter. He would get his chance to try and woo Trish back, or at least get an explanation from her for what she was doing to him. He spent a relaxed hour at the library and then went back to the prison at 12:45 pm. He was eager, agitated. But when he arrived at the interview venue he was pole-axed with a bit of treachery: Trish had flown the coop.

"Oh, you're looking for Trish Adoja? She left here a half hour ago. She was in a hurry."

"Did she leave any message for me? I am Len."

"No, but Ms Adoja looked troubled. We thought it might be a family emergency."

Len's jaw dropped. He felt deeply betrayed. What a cowardly, low-down trick. Trish must have been in a panic at the prospect of explaining her conduct to Len. Otherwise she would not have abandoned an important duty to flee like a thief surprised in the act; she took her job seriously. He felt tears of chagrin about to well up in his eyes, and he quickly wheeled around to shield his disintegrating dignity. As he shuffled in defeat towards the door one of Trish's coworkers came up and whispered, "Ms Adoja said she wanted nothing more to do with you." Len mumbled that he would go and park himself at the prison gate, but the young lady cautioned that it was a bad idea. There were security officers to consider, and it was best for Len to avoid making a scene. She was sorry, but Len must leave quietly.

Len drove straight to Trish's home and rang the doorbell. He rang it many times, walking round the house and peering into windows now and then. Nobody answered. It seemed nobody was home. He parked in her driveway and waited. Just as he was wondering what to do, his cell phone rang. The caller identified herself. It was one of Trish's close friends. The lady had never before called Len and did not know Len's phone number; she must have just got it from Trish. Len realized they were inside Trish's house and refusing to answer his ringing. There was a nasty edge to the lady's voice. It sounded stiff and somber, brassy with a Darth Vader menace. She lit into Len right away, without any pleasantries: What did he mean going to harass Trish at her house and at her workplace. Len said he was not harassing Trish; he had gone there just to plead for an explanation for her recent behavior.

"Oh, she owes you an explanation?"

"I don't know about 'owe'," Len replied, "but the situation certainly calls for one. I just need to know where I stand with Trish now."

"But you are still married, aren't you?" Trish's friend demanded.

Len said that was precisely what he had come to discuss with Trish. He had left his wife and was ready to get a divorce finally, but he needed to know that Trish was ready for him too; she had been aloof lately. Did she know where he could find Trish? He was going to stay parked in the driveway until Trish came out and talked to him. The lady said if he did that the cops would be called, and she sounded like she meant business. Len did not need a scene in front of Trish's house, so he scribbled a note: "Please call me," and stuck it at Trish's door. He drove back to Cleveland, dejected. He called her three, four times on his way but all he could do was leave those ineffectual messages. He was beaten. When he got home he sent her another email:

"Trish, Love of my life! Through my negligence it seems I've let a song go out of my heart, a priceless blossom to wither in the doomed garden of my life. Won't you forgive me? Even the gate of heaven is not shut so tight against the true penitent. I am remorseful. Mea culpa, mea culpa, mea maxima culpa! Honey, save my life please. I love you more dearly than ever a man loved a woman."

It suffered the same fate as his other messages: Len was just baying at the moon. But he was not done yet. He would never give up on Trish as long as he drew breath. Two weeks later Len was back in Columbus with another plan to get Trish's attention. He had contracted an aerial messaging company to fly a pleading message over Trish's home the next day, a Saturday, and a repeat of the same message over her church the day after that, at the time when Trish and others would be emerging from Sunday Mass. The message to be flown read:

"LEN '*HEART*' TRISH 4EVER. TO 4GIVE IS DIVINE, TRISH!"

But what if Trish was not looking up at any of those times? Len decided to alert her. He drove to her home that Friday evening with a note giving information about the sky message. Into the envelope he also slipped a CD of the "Songs of Pain" he had compiled since she turned her back on him. Checking into a hotel near her home, he went to her door. Trish who was home, Len could hear her voice, but she would not come to the door. She rebuffed him through Viv, who answered the door. That proved to be checkmate for Len. He slunk home to Cleveland the next morning, tail between his legs. But Trish was not done with him. While he flailed and thrashed about wondering what to do next, he got a thunderbolt of an email from Trish:

"This is an attempt to help you. You must cease all forms of communication to me at once. You are harassing me and I ask you to cease and desist immediately. If you set foot on my porch one more time I shall call Law Enforcement."

Len wondered what had come over Trish, his lively, charming, witty, beautiful Trish. Yes, he had kept her waiting for fifteen years, but she had seemed content to wait. In the recent past he kept her apprised of his plans and time lines. He had lately expressed his remorse, and indeed had groveled to her pathetically. As an inducement to say yes, he had offered her all manner of blandishments: A world cruiser, a new Lexus SUV, rehabilitation of her family to a better home, enough capital (again!) to set her up in a business so she could retire from salaried drudgery. He had appealed to her directly by phone, text, email, letters, and aerial message. He had tried to enlist her daughters and her friends to help persuade her. What more could he do?

But one thing was certain: Len wanted nothing to do with a life from which Trish was missing. It seemed to him that his sun had set. Yet, he thought it was inhuman the way Trish had kicked him in the teeth. He had stalled for too long, but he did not deserve to be deeply insulted like a criminal, with threats of invoking law enforcement. He would fight back.

30
Counter Attack

You've already left me and broken my heart
And told me how much you don't love me
You said you are happier when we're apart
Why must you come back now to haunt me?
Must you keep showing me pictures of him
And boasting of his warm embrace?
You've already put bitter tears in my eyes
Must you throw dirt in my face?

ONE CHARACTERISTIC THAT Len and Trish had in common was stubbornness. In fact, Len found her a kindred spirit in the way she defended her views, questioned authority when it was necessary, and defended her rights when she had to. Like Len, Trish had strong opinions. Thus far they had never clashed with each other, but that was about to change in spectacular fashion.

Len had pestered Trish lately with his ceaseless importunity: Several epistles, scores of email, dozens of text messages, and uncounted voice messages. In all he estimated, he told Trish in one of those messages, that he had sent her some 110 entreaties, none of which elicited a reply from her. That did not include his three trips to her house and her workplace since his *Ides of March* turning point, or several approaches to Trish's friends to enlist their help in persuading her to come back to him. He was doing all that out of desperation. He never sent any message that carried a threat or menace. All he said to her was that he loved her deeply and needed to hear from her one way or another. He was of the "silence means consent" generation in affairs between men and women. If she hadn't said "No," directly, all was not lost. It never occurred to him that Trish might feel put upon by so much importunity. All she had to do, he figured, was just say one word or two by way of explanation and he would back off.

Trish's swift warning about calling law enforcement was a virtual declaration of hostilities, and Len was dumbfounded. What was arousing so much vitriol in Trish towards him? Did he ever show her anything but love and affection? Had he not provided for her every need, most often unbidden, including especially when she was low and discouraged by spates of bereavement? Had he ever said an unkind word to her? Had he neglected to come to her aid even once, in the midst of her avalanche of woes, of her shower of bereavements, her many other incidents of hospitalization and misfortune? Come to think of it, had Trish ever really asked him pointedly to leave his wife for her and he refused?

It seemed to him the only explanation for her declaration of war was that she now had a new boyfriend; that she did not want Len in the way of her exploring this new man, but she did not want to explain it to Len. In fact, one of the things she said to Len on that Mother's Day rebuff to his roses was, "I don't owe anybody an explanation." And that was contrary to the pledge she had made to him long ago when he suggested it was OK for her to talk to other men. She had promised to let him know if ever another man came into her life. It also struck Len that Trish's rebuff was couched in almost the same phrase her janitor friend used when she warned Len that cops would be called. Clearly, Trish and her friends had rehearsed her rebuff to Len.

To make matters worse, some of Trish's friends came to bat for her against Len. One was a man who collaborated with Trish in heading the Columbus faction of NIDO. The man emailed Len asking him to back off Trish, and Len told him to mind his business, and the man replied saying if Len wanted "a mud fight" he would get one. Len ignored him and instead sent Trish another email saying he had received her message sent via a third party, and he was taking her on in a "mud war" of words. Len said he would appeal publicly to all those who knew of their fifteen-year affair. Having already moved out of his marital home, he had nothing more to lose.

Then all hell broke loose. Trish had a few aces up her sleeve, and she played them all at once. Though Len had just pledged to her in writing that he would refrain from coming to her house anymore, she nevertheless filed a "Criminal Protection Order" against him in a Columbus court of law. She was going for the jugular. Trish's CPO complaint charged Len with "stalking" and "harassment," and the document sought to order him to keep away from and not communicate in any way with Trish until the substantive case was resolved in court. Soon, a court date was set. The swiftness and aggressiveness of her lawsuit perplexed Len. So he made enquiries and found out that Trish's new boyfriend was an attorney who practiced in the state of Maryland. Evidently, Trish's new beau wanted a showdown with Len in an arena where he, as a lawyer, had an advantage. Len recognized him as the master puppeteer behind the scenes, with Trish as his marionette.

Len was nothing if not stubborn. That man had no idea that Len never shied away from a fight. Starting from his childhood school days he had never before backed down in the face of a bully. He would not do so now, even though his ostensible adversary would be Trish, the love of his life. Len was not intimidated. He knew Trish had no "stalking" case that would withstand close scrutiny in court. For one thing, all his messages to Trish, whether written or oral, sated clearly he loved her so much he would gladly lay down his life for her. For another, when, in her very last email to Len she told him never to set foot on her porch again, Len replied with an email in which he stated, apologetically, that "A person's home is their castle. I shall respect your wish and not come to your door again." If her new boyfriend wanted to construe that as stalking or harassment then he could not be a competent lawyer.

Later events in court would prove Len right in that conjecture: The man didn't have the smarts. To begin with, he insisted on representing Trish in the "stalking" proceedings. That in itself was dumb. Even Len knew an adage that "A lawyer who represents himself has a fool for a client," by which is meant that any emotional baggage a lawyer carried into a case can only impair his objectivity and performance. The corollary is that a lawyer would be foolish to represent his own family or consort. And then it was explained to Trish's lawyer repeatedly, by the court, that he could not represent her anyway because he did not have courtroom privileges in Ohio. The rules required him to have a locally registered co-counsel. Still he did not get it: He kept trying to wriggle around that procedural technicaliy, causing the case to be postponed ("continued") on two occasions. That farce went on till the presiding magistrate patiently lectured Trish on her need to get a local lawyer to prosecute her case. But that would require Trish to involve herself in substantial expense, something Len knew she could not or would not do. It was one thing to use her boyfriend as lawyer and pay him with certain services, and quite a different matter to fork over real cash to a Columbus lawyer in good standing.

As if choosing to represent his own consort in court, contrary to conventional wisdom, was not folly enough, Trish's boyfriend-lawyer (who was now commuting frequently from Maryland to Columbus) was heard stating to court officers that his services for Trish were "pro bono." Len wondered whether that claim amounted to fraud on both their parts. On the part of the lawyer, his services to his consort can hardly fall within the denotation or even the connotation of the term "pro bono," which Merriam Webster's Collegiate Dictionary defines as "professional and especially legal work donated especially for the public good." So his services for Trish cannot be "pro bono" if she is paying him in kind with miscellaneous services.

On her part, Trish was not indigent and therefore cannot qualify for charity (which is presumed by the phrase "public good"). But from what Len was now learning about Trish's character, she just might have declared herself indigent so that her boyfriend's services could be presented as "pro bono." Either way, thought Len, Trish and her boyfriend were only soiling the tattered image of Nigerians as fraudsters. What a disreputable pair they would make, Len thought, if they carried on in this manner: He, the supposed professional, and she, his amateur sidekick —a twosome like Don Quixote de la Mancha and Sancho Panza, together fatuously clueless as bumpkins. They would only give ammunition to those who have whispered all along that Trish was a bit of a scofflaw; that she had been in criminal partnership with her ex-husband.

Of course it is one thing if a flippant man, wishing to impress, boasts about doing pro bono work, but quite a different matter if such a claim were made on a business expense statement with a view, for instance, to reaping tax benefits. In the latter case, thought Len, Trish and her lawyer would be lending credence to the widespread view of Nigerians in the U.S. as inveterate fraudsters. Like the similarly unsavory reputation of the Italians in America as members of the mafia, the image of Nigerians as habitual scammers is not monolithic; it is constructed brick by sordid brick. Were Trish and her lover adding their own brick to that edifice?

However, Len thought, Trish in all probability no longer worried about smarts or honesty or legal niceties. From revelations now wafting up about her true character, Len surmised that she was by now so deeply burrowed into the man's pocket and crotch that she cared little about what he might have above his waistline, and even less about what attributes he lacked above his neckline. Their sophomoric decision to prosecute him for stalking was proof enough that they were klutzes. Her boyfriend-cum-lawyer lacked sound judgment on several fronts, and so did Trish herself —and Len began to revise his long-held opinion regarding her perspicacity. On several issues that Len knew of, she had chosen (or was rumored or suspected to have chosen) to cut corners and operate at the murky edge of rectitude. If she would not toe the line, she just might in time put herself outside the law like her ex-husband.

But even if Trish and her boyfriend were dumb, Len knew better than to cling to his old, naïve assumption that innocence was adequate shield against accusation. He had come to realize that in litigious America the best protection against false accusation was a competent legal defense; and getting such help was a matter of being willing and able to pay. Len was able and willing. He retained a good lawyer and they went in to the Franklin County courthouse of Columbus to lock horns with the marionette and her puppeteer.

Noticing body-language intimacy between marionette and puppeteer during a court hearing, Len naturally wondered, in the words of a jazz song, "How long has this been going on?" Len had no way of knowing that, but soon got a glimpse of an answer. Information inadvertently dropped in the court stenographers' office during the interminable "discovery" process that went on for six months, revealed that their relationship was by no means a recent thing. Len learned that Trish had been seeing this new man for a considerable while, before she decided to dump Len altogether. Even as she was appropriating Len's $20,000 retirement savings, she was *in flagrante delicto* with another man. Those who believe in karma say that the gods of retribution note such facts.

No wonder Trish preferred lovers who live far away from Columbus: That way they had little chance of catching her at her admitted game of "messing around." Distant out-of-town lovers could not surprise her, for they must of necessity schedule their visits to her. It was a clever precaution, but Len already knew how clever Trish was. No wonder too that, when Len made his final move to retire, to leave Magda, and finally stake his future on Trish 100 percent, she blurted out that she had only been "messing around."

But Len could not complain. He had carried on with Trish for fifteen years, deceiving his own wife all that while. His excuse was of course that he was in love with Trish. Only Trish knew what her own excuse was for messing around with other men. Len remembered the long-ago fears of his sister and his cousin that he would come to grief over a bad girl; only, Trish was not a "girl" anymore, she was a grandmother. And her "bad girl" deception was not really of the sort that one could discern up-front or even from up-close. In Trish's case deception ran deep, like still water.

But what goes around comes around, they say. Of course her daughters watched her messing around. And, taking their cues, they regressed their family pedigree. If Trish was reaping the whirlwind in her progeny it was only because she had sown the wind with her open conduct. One cannot blame her children too much for what they become. Raising children by exhorting them to follow the straight and narrow may have its merit, but it cannot be as effective as actually showing them good example through one's own actions. A plant raised in poisoned soil cannot be healthy to eat. Len regretted that his extra-long and open affair with Trish could not have been a good example for her children. After all, they knew he had a family in Cleveland; he had discussed his family with them a few times. Come to think of it, he reflected, most of Trish's Columbus friends that he knew of had gone through failed marriages. It appeared likely they were playing the same "messing around" game that Trish spoke of; birds of the same feather flock together. And her children could not help observing her circle of friends.

In addition to suing Len for "stalking," Trish opened a second front in her offensive against him: She journeyed to Cleveland to meet Magda. Since Trish no longer drove on highways, she was taken there by her NIDO partisans. Their cover was the launching of a new NIDO chapter for Northeast Ohio, during which Magda sat at a Sponsor's Table set aside for her because she and Len had made a large donation towards the launching event on behalf of their business. Trish was chaperoned by two of her NIDO-executive colleagues, the president of her Columbus chapter and the president of the Cleveland chapter —two men generally know as low-grade hustlers perennially touting for any Nigerian cause that promised public visibility. Trish opened her well-prepared gambit. She recited her confession to Magda who, being a guileless woman, gave Trish instant absolution with only a banal comment: "I leave you to your conscience and your God."

But Trish was not done. She had not come merely to seek forgiveness from Magda. She came with the aim of doing grave damage to Len. The upshot of her visit to Magda that evening was that she turned over to Magda the trove of letters Len sent to her over the years. Trish said she was doing that to relieve her mind. Then, in a *coup de grace* Magda was told how much money Len had showered on Trish over the years: Trips to Europe and to Nigeria, expensive gifts and jewelry, and a $20,000 donation.

Trish's "mea culpa" to Magda may have had some element of remorse in it; only Trish and her conscience knew the truth of that (as Magda implied in her absolution). However, in snitching like a prison rat about Len's largesse, Trish's mean intention was to set Magda on the warpath against Len. It worked, but by then Len had left Magda and moved out of their home, so it did not really matter too much to him. And still Trish was not done ratting on Len. Some demon was pushing her to go for the jugular, and she pulled all the stops. In a quick follow-through Trish also forwarded to Magda, and to others, all of Len's recent messages.

Trish apparently no longer cared who found out what fact about her. On that Mothers' Day when Trish spurned Len's bouquet of roses, her own mother (a taciturn woman with sad eyes and a sympathetic mien), was lurking around barely a dozen feet away while Trish gave Len a tongue lashing. Not yet acculturated to American life or acclimatized to the frigid climes of northern latitudes, Trish's mother confined herself to the seclusion and sanctuary of Trish's house. She understood English: Len had chatted with her a couple of times before. She could not have failed to follow their quarrel as Trish loudly lambasted Len. In fact, the old lady passed Trish and Len twice as she pottered about in the background.

When Trish finally took a breath with heaving chest and Len asked her what happened to the love she used to declare for him, Trish looked him in the eye and said, "There was no love. We were just messing around." Trish mother had just shuffled past them and into the kitchen; she most likely heard that bit about "messing around," but she was so exercised she didn't seem to care what her mother might have overheard.

Trish's outburst knocked the breath out of Len and he looked up sharply with a gasp, his jaw lack as he pondered the meaning of it. He could not believe what he just heard. Was it true? Or did she plunge in the knife and twist it just to exacerbate the wound because of her new mood of viciousness? He looked into Trish's face to see if she was just being facetious, but what he saw was frightful. Her jaws were clenched tight, her face contorted, her eyes narrowed to a slit. She was the concentrated essence of malice. Her devastating statement was matched by the look on her face, so venomous and intense there was no doubt regarding her sincerity.

Her statement struck Len like the twin impact of a double-barreled shotgun fully discharged into his heart. The first sentence in that statement was categorical and self explanatory. The import of the second one took a moment to sink: It was intimation that Len was not the only man she had been seeing all those years. She had been spreading her favors "around." It was a callous admission of whoring, pure and simple. Len could not fathom what she gained by that admission, except to spite him.

Len himself had read much about wicked women; but, not being experienced in the ways of women, he only half-believed those stories. He thought that many of them were either entirely made up or at least exaggerated, like the boasts he heard so often in locker rooms and in the faculty clubs he visited in Nigerian universities. But here, well into the seventh decade of his life, he was finally face-to-face with one of those super-bad man-eaters about whom his sister and cousin had fretted early in his teenage. And to think that he had held this ogre in his very bosom for one decade and a half! He used to say that no experience in anyone's life was a total waste; even in the worst case one at least learned a lesson.

But this devastating practical lesson from Trish was more education than he ever wanted, one that he would never forget. It was the brutal underside of reality. Growing up, Len reflected, is really running the gauntlet of a steady trickle of disillusionment. *C'est la vie*, Len said to himself; it was a favorite lament of his, and perhaps the only loaded French expression he knew. Tears of chagrin, and creeping snot from his nose, flowed down Len's face as he looked at the woman he had loved so much for so long. Finally, he found his voice and said to Trish, sobbing: "Please pardon my tears and listen to me. I promised myself not to cry for you today because what I've come to say is too important for tears; but, here I am crying again. I'm sorry. You may have been messing with me, but I was in love with you: deeply in love. I am still in love with you."

Len cried most of the way home, his vanity wounded. European cultural chauvinists used to say that, after untold generations of arranged polygamous marriages, Africans did not understand the concept of abstract love: They married for practical reasons only, which centered on the task of procreation and pleasure of copulation. Some supremacists latched onto the medieval notion of "courtly love" in the age of chivalry, and held it as the pinnacle of human feelings: Love for its own sake was a noble emotion that went beyond anything Africans could conceive. When an African man or woman thought themselves in love, they were only parroting what they had heard, conflating lust with love (as in the "Love me tonight" lyrics of popular songs).

In his student days Len was offended by that kind of condescension when he came across it in his college literature class that was taught by a corpulent but erudite scholar who was quite enamored of Spanish writers. But now Len was confronted with evidence that vindicated that prejudicial notion. Here was Trish, Len's ideal woman (who a scant six months earlier had sent Len an email saying "I will always love you —always") openly telling Len that the love she had professed for him for fifteen years was a lie. If Len was a hopelessly incurable romantic, as his buddy Henry once called him, then Trish was a crass philistine on the arena of human emotion. It might be true, after all, that most Africans lacked the capacity for absolute, sublime love.

Now, as Len reflected on Trish's malicious statement on that day about "messing around," he rebuked himself for failing to catch a hint of her true nature all along. She had conned him big-time. Was there any difference between messing around and outright whoring?

Whoring was an accurate description of Trish's relationship to Len because all the flow of money and gifts between them went in one direction: From him to her, with just the occasional pair of socks or cooked meals coming from Trish to Len. Considering how much he lavished on her through all those years, Len thought Trish must rank as Ohio's most expensive whore, and himself as the ultimately besotted john. What kind of fool was he? Does a sane and honorable man fall in love and stay in love with a self-confessed whore and Jezebel?

Sadly, he remembered, it was not an unusual thing to happen to even the most distinguished men. There was, he recalled, the spectacular "Profumo Affair," a huge scandal that sent seismic waves around the world, especially to all countries of the British Commonwealth, among them Nigeria. The ultimate consequence of that scandal was the collapse of the British government led by Prime Minister Harold Macmillan. That tsunami crested in 1962, when Len was a high school sophomore. Lord Profumo, a Peer of the House of Lords and a minister in Her Majesty's government, had an affair with Christine Keeler, a call girl. Profumo was compromised when it emerged that Keeler had also shared her favors with a Russian spy. Ever since "The Cambridge Five" incident, an infamous spying case in which a clutch of Britain's finest young men had been recruited to spy for the Soviet Union while they were students of Cambridge University, Britain had become hypersensitive to infiltration by Soviet or Russian agents. And so the entanglement of Lord Profumo with the mistress of a Russian spy caused major panic. John Profumo was forced to resign from his ministerial position as well as from the British Parliament, and soon after the government fell.

At that time Len was a naïve high school sophomore who was brought up in the neurotic obsession of the Catholic Church with sex and other sins (which his teachers and priests and the whole Church dwelt on *ad nauseam*). So Len was disgusted by the revelation that a Lord and Minister of England had stooped so low as to fall in love with an undisguised whore. But now Len was older and wiser, and himself devastated by years of dalliance with a "messing around" paramour; his sympathies were wholly with John Profumo. He felt he was in good company as a member of the rarified club of love-compromised gentlemen.

As Len lay back on his lonely bed and pondered Trish's recent acts of malice against him his heart broke all over again. During their final phone discussion she had told Len that her friends and family were aghast that she let Len so deeply into her life and her home, that she left him with her young daughters: What if he had been a molester of young girls?

Well, what other monstrosities would Trish accuse him of next? Stealing? Physical abuse? Pederasty? Cannibalism? Had she, with lies and fabrications already tarnished his reputation with their mutual friends? Would she stop at no act of malevolence to smear him, to consign him to the gutter and clear the way to pursue her new lover? Come to think of it, did that scandalous suspicion of pedophilia come from Trish's mind? Was it from repressed memories of childhood abuse?

When Len returned to the USA in 1990 the famous case of the McMartin Preschool in California was in full swing. Rumors and allegations of wholesale pedophilia were leveled at the staff of that unhappy school, and legal battles ensued, the notoriety leading to eventual closure of the school. As if on cue, there was a sudden rash of media reports about rampant abuse of little American girls by their relatives, even by their own fathers. Len dismissed most of it as the sort of hysteria that had spawned the Salem Witch Hunts in Massachusetts so long ago.

Now he wasn't so sure, not after he read a book by a Nigerian novelist on the theme of incest. It was a fictional account to be sure, but one that focused on a vile deed that Len's people think of as the ultimate abomination (as did all people everywhere as far as Len knew). It was about a widower who out of loneliness and depravity fathered his own grandchild; the denouement was the deaths of all three of them —the man, his poor daughter, and her unborn child. That book gave Len goose bumps for a long, long time.

Trish's hint regarding thoughts of Len preying on her daughters was a boomerang any way it was cast. If it was deliberate concoction by Trish to discredit him deeply, that would dismay him even further about the deep character flaws now exposed in her: Flaws to which he had been blind through fifteen years of intimacy, euphoria, and denial. That would cast him in very bad light as well —as a gullible fool. But if Trish had not made it up, if it emanated from her mind, it raised all kinds of appalling questions about Trish's background. During the McMartin school hubbub, both serious and pop psychologists pontificated that fake accusations of child sexual abuse were often a flash-back reflecting the accuser's repressed memories of being abused as a child. So, could it be that incest and pedophilia figured in Trish's own background? Well, who knows? Anything might be lurking in the unfathomable depths of that family; religiosity was often a camouflage for those who had things to hide. The incident of unacknowledged large donations was evidence of a lack of candor in her family; and their connivance at her essential prostitution spoke volumes about their lax family attitude towards immoral sexual deviance.

His mood quickly shot up from despondent to vindictive, and quickly back. Who said "Hell hath no fury like a woman scorned"? How about a man fleeced, scorned and shunned? He would very much like to see Trish hanged, drawn, and quartered. But since the world was no longer so barbaric as medieval England, he would settle for seeing her bolted to a pillory, then tarred and feathered. Then her new lover could take her down to have and to hold till hell froze over.

So, what did he really know of Trish's background? For all he knew (which is to say all that Trish told him) she came from a balanced and progressive middle-class family. Her late father had been a well-regarded knight of the Catholic Church; the brother right after her was a Catholic priest, and the brother after that had followed their father into knighthood. Did that seemingly idyllic setting conceal an ugly secret of childhood sexual abuse? Trish never betrayed any hint of neurosis that might suggest childhood victimhood. But Len knew he was not a qualified judge of that kind of thing; he was no expert. Besides, in light of the character quirks now surfacing about the Trish he thought he knew for fifteen years, anything was possible. When you see people dressed up in their fineries and sporting their best public behavior, he reflected, you can never guess what secret horrors might be lurking in their bosoms. We are all ciphers, opaque and inscrutable. The more Len thought about it the more he concluded that all bets were off concerning who and what exactly Trish was. He never really knew her as much or as well as he had thought.

But Len could no longer deceive himself with self-righteous reasoning. He acknowledged to himself that if he did not realize Trish had a shady and unsavory past, it was because he had hoodwinked himself to overlook information that was there from the start. "There's none so blind as those who will not see." Len remembered the adage. He had willed himself to overlook rumors about Trish that reached him in his early days of euphoria, because he was in denial. After Magda impounded Trish's letters to Len he overheard her on two occasions talking with someone on the phone about Trish. Magda was giving or receiving information about Trish's reputation in Columbus. There were, it was said, two men Trish had dalliances with before or after her husband fled to Nigeria. As a result, the marriage of one of those men was shaken up.

Len discounted those rumors outright because he thought the ladies were jealous of Trish or, in Magda's case, mad enough to want to believe every gossip about Trish. But there were other, ugly rumors that Len considered for a long while before he decided to give Trish the benefit of a doubt. One such rumor really amounted to mere speculation about Trish's role in the criminal activities of her ex-husband. And there were innuendos concerning her lifestyle. Trish referred to some of them when she bought her Lexus SUV and joked to Len that people would wonder how she found the money for it. Eventually, Len too wondered whether Trish's income squared with her lifestyle, given her extended family obligations and single-mom status. And how could her family members not notice the discrepancy between her income and expenditure?

When Nigerians in the diaspora got together, especially those living in the U.S., one common complaint was the tremendous pressure they felt from relatives, including their parents, to get rich quickly. When one went home to Nigeria to visit, he or she was likely to be told obliquely about so and so from his hometown who lived abroad, had struck it rich overnight and built a mansion for his or her parents. The hapless person so pressured might point out that those who struck sudden wealth in a Western country did not always win the lottery, that in many cases they were involved in some crime or scam and got away with it. But then the relatives most often countered with, "Well, why don't you do whatever your peers are doing to get money!" It was easy for them to say because the amazing corruption in Nigeria was fertilized by the brazen connivance of the relatives of people in public office, and those relatives included ostentatious church people and prayer warriors.

Len knew about the case of two brothers, both alumni of his alma mater, who, in the 1980s came to the U.S. and became involved in drug smuggling. Their father was a "Knight of Saint Mulumba." The parents came to visit and spent a pleasant season with their prosperous sons who, curiously, did not seem to go to work regularly. After six months their father went home with a Mercedes sedan; and after another six months their mom went home too, with a Lexus SUV. Neither parent could drive, so drivers had to be hired for them. And both parents went home with enough cash to build a country mansion for the family plus two apartment blocks for rental income in their state capital. Everyone was pleased as punch, until, two years later, the brothers were caught in a dragnet and sentenced to lengthy prison terms in federal prisons. Their father dropped dead of a heart attack upon hearing of the incarceration of both of his sons, his only children. Their mother followed her husband to her grave soon after.

The unfortunate brothers were well-known, affable members of Len's Old Boys' association in the U.S., so every member was saddened as news of the imprisonment was announced at their annual meeting. But then one alumnus at the meeting wondered aloud how the parents of those boys could close their eyes to the evident fact that their sons were not making money in honest business. "Yeah!" everyone chorused. And then everyone came out with stories of their own experiences of family pressures to "get rich and come home!"

But Len was not inclined to countenance all the rumors he heard about Trish's past. Some of it might be idle speculation, probably emanating from the same people who assumed she had been involved in her ex-husband's frauds and scams. Because Nigerians had an unfortunate reputation for scam, every one of them was subject now and then to innuendoes and calumny.

On the other hand, might there have been some fire behind that smoke of rumors about Trish? Len shuddered to think that the Trish he had idolized all those years as the ideal woman might have been quite simply a whore, a promiscuous home wrecker, and a dissembler to boot. While he could not be sure that Trish had busted other marriages before, there was no doubt that she had busted his own marriage completely, and then left him in a lurch to go after yet another

Igbo man. This was no rumor. This was fact, his fact, his own tragic fact.

They say misfortunes never come singly. Len soon found himself tumbling from sadness into chagrin. On his way home from the Columbus courthouse after the second hearing of Trish's lawsuit against him for harassment and stalking, Len stopped at the large grocery shop in North Columbus where he was wont to buy provisions each time he went to visit Trish in the old days. Len would rather not have run into anyone he knew; he wasn't in a friendly mood. But his luck was not good that day. In the fruits section he ran into two ladies he knew, one of whom had a shop in Columbus that he and Trish used to patronize.

They greeted him and, with the indiscretion typical of ladies when they want to gossip, they asked him if he was coming from Trish's house. Len thought it was a facetious question. He assumed that these ladies knew of his current troubles with Trish because it was broadcast in an email that went viral. He supposed these ladies were mocking him, but he replied politely that he was coming from court —that Trish had dragged him to court. They acted genuinely sorry and concerned for him and sidled closer. The shopkeeper said, "Well, I am not really surprised." Len looked quizzically at her and she muttered that Trish used to tell them that he, Len, was only her Sugar Daddy. Len felt the blood drain from his head. Sensing that he was in denial about Trish, the second lady added that they too liked Trish; that Trish was really not a bad person, but that she kept some questionable friends.

"Sugar Daddy" was a phrase Len had not heard in the quarter of a century since he left the Nigerian university scene and went back to the U.S. In the 1980s and 1990s, Nigerian college campuses were fetid with corrupt symbiosis between some lecherous professors and indolent coeds who preferred to get their grades by sweating on their backs, a process that came to be called "Bottom Power." And from all that Len heard in the years since, the practice had become intensified and entrenched, with a certain number of "bottom power" sessions prescribed for each given course grade.

But was he, Len, a Sugar Daddy? Well, why not? A man who shells out $20,000 to a younger mistress with no questions asked is almost by definition a "Sugar Daddy." But the analogy to a Sugar Daddy relationship could not be stretched beyond that superficial point; upon closer scrutiny the analogy could not hold. For females, "Sugar Daddy" is a phenomenon of young adulthood or college age, when they might need a crutch to lean on before they found their feet, because they were unable to support themselves fully in the fierce peer rivalry of vanities. Most educated young women got out of that sordid situation when they landed jobs that paid well enough to launch them onto the middle class platform, or when they married.

It was preposterous to apply the Sugar Daddy notion in a geriatric setting. Trish and Len were both professionals, each with advanced college degrees. Both earned middle-class incomes and had done so for more than three decades. They were both grandparents, each long past his or her prime, having rolled or slid considerably down the other side of the hill. In other words, each of them was close to that grey tunnel of life known as the golden age, a time when the acquisition of baubles is expected to have long yielded to a desire for mutual support in the approaching sunset. For Trish to fancy herself still in need of a Sugar Daddy under those twilight circumstances was scandalously irresponsible. That sort of addiction to easy money was not different from the predisposition that drove her ex-husband's criminal activity and made him flee from the U.S. Would Trish never learn?

Also, that analogy would beg a major question —one that was dear to Len's jaded atheist's heart: How on earth does a supposedly religious family (with a father that was a knight of the Church, a son that was also a knight, and another son that was a Catholic priest) find it in their devout hearts to depend on a daughter who openly kept a Sugar Daddy that came often to visit the whole family brood, and who on his own initiative donated a small fortune to get their daughter medical treatment in America? How does all that square with their conscience? More to the point, did they have a conscience?

Was Trish's a religious family? Their religiosity was probably a front. Part of what drove Len to apostasy early in life from his Catholic youth as altar boy was the hypocrisy of many outwardly devout believers he knew: The pedophile/pederast priests who groped little girls and violated altar boys and insisted on hearing graphic details of sins of "immodesty" at the confessional; the mothers who looked the other way when all that molestation was happening; the Irish missionary priests of his youth who fathered half-caste children all over their parishes; and the curate, catechist, or verger who pilfered from the collection box.

On the rest of his journey home to Cleveland Len reflected on that disquieting "Sugar Daddy" tidbit. It tallied with Trish's Mothers' Day outburst when she declared scathingly to Len that she had been "messing around" all along. No wonder she was surprisingly complacent during all those years when Len only talked about leaving Magda; and then, when he actually broke out of his marriage, Trish fled from him. No wonder, too, that whenever he and Trish discussed that topic of "how long" it was usually Len that brought it up rather than Trish. She might not have been in the relationship for the duration, to seek matrimony, but only for what she could get from Len in the interim.

But Len could sometimes be brutally frank with himself. He cheered himself up a little bit with the thought that, although Trish had outsmarted and deceived him all those fifteen years, he had a good time of it and quite enjoyed the game much of the time. In terms of intellectual and emotional companionability Trish was a true geisha, giving quality time for the money she got from Len (even allowing that she had feigned emotional component involvement with him).

As he trudged home Len ran through his mind the highlights of Trish's recent acts of perfidy:

Her full disclosures to Magda and to the public of Len's communications and his largesse; her CPO lawsuit charging Len with stalking and harassment; insinuation of possible pedophilia by Len on her daughters; her apparent failure to tell her family that Len donated $20,000 for her sister's medical treatment; and new revelation that Trish had a definite preference (almost a set specification) for the particular category of men she ensnared as lovers.

31
Disillusionment

I've looked at life from both sides now,
From win and lose, and still somehow
It's life's illusions I recall.
I really don't know life at all.

FROM NOTIFICATIONS ORIGINATING from the Franklin County court at which the CPO case was being handled, Len noticed the name of Trish's new boyfriend and lover. Len checked out the man's law firm and found out he was a Nigerian, an Igbo man, with a law offices in Bethesda and in Chevy Chase —yet another Igbo man for Trish. There was nothing wrong with Trish scoring another Igbo lover, except it was too much coincidence: Counting Len and Trish's rumored prior lovers, this Bethesda lawyer was the third or fourth Igbo man Trish had hooked in succession. "Once is happenstance, twice is coincidence, thrice is...."

The trouble with suspicion and doubt is that, once implanted, it tends to germinate and grow with no further need for fertilization. When Len first met Trish, information that reached him about her conduct included rumors of her trysts. It was said that she had trysts with Igbo men, in consequence of which one of the men had his marriage compromised. But Len had paid no mind to the rumors: He was in deep denial. (Was there ever a true lover who did not wallow in denial over the alleged character flaws of his or her beloved?) So, Len was Trish's second or third Igbo lover; and now she had dumped Len for a fourth Igbo man. There was a clear pattern here: Trish was not an equal-opportunity lover; she had a definite preference for Igbo men as lovers.

That was peculiar for a few reasons. Firstly, while Trish spoke Igbo passably, she spoke Yoruba, English, and her native Igala language better; and in any case, in all her adult life she had moved in mixed circles where discourse was carried on in English. So her preference for Igbo lovers is unlikely to be related to the fact that she spoke Igbo. Len's friends commented that Trish spoke Yoruba flawlessly. Her Igala people were geographically interspersed with Yorubas, and the admixture was cemented formally when the two ethnic peoples got lumped together in one political zone, Benue State (which splintered later to spawn Kogi State). The upshot was that during her childhood, the schools in her home area were intimate melting pots of Yorubas, Igalas, and other ethnic peoples of the "Middle Belt" region situated around the Niger-Benue river confluence. Yoruba, a dominant language, was the *lingua franca*, so she learned it.

Len liked Trish's multi-lingual skills. He was a firm believer in cross-ethnic interaction among Nigerians. Having gone to grade school in Kano and later lived in Kaduna, then Yola, he learned to speak Hausa reasonably well. And when as a teenager he spent two years in a junior college in Lagos until after the Nigerian civil war had broken out, he learned to speak passable Yoruba. His Hausa and Yoruba had become rusty over the decades due to disuse, but he was glad to have learned those languages when he did. Without making deliberate effort in that direction he gravitated to multi-lingual fellow Nigerians. He thought of such Nigerians as progressives; that was one attribute that had endeared him to Trish.

Len liked to say that, just as Europe's various tribes ultimately coalesced into a few national groups with one predominant language in each country, so must Africa's many ethnic groups submerge their disparate identities into one national consciousness within each country. The language and culture that one grew up with was not genetically predisposed; it was an accident of one's circumstances in childhood and provenance in later life. Len's pan-ethnic disposition was perhaps a subconscious factor in his bonding with Magda, and later with Trish. However, in Trish's case he came to suspect, late in the day, that her preference for Igbo men as lovers was driven by a none-too-charitable force. That eerie feeling reflected what Trish intimated to Len about the dynamics of her own family.

Among her siblings (an older adoptive sister, a younger sister, and three brothers), Trish was the only one who learned to speak Igbo from peer interactions at school. Children the world over are known for linguistic plasticity in mixed environments, so she learned Igbo, but she did so in defiance of her father's wish. Her father had a visceral dislike of Igbos, Trish disclosed. He himself cultivated the friendship of an Igbo man or two for business sake; but he adamantly admonished his children to avoid Igbos. Indeed, her people, Igalas, had a deep prejudice against Igbos and referred to the latter as "Igbo-li" ("wooden hearted Igbos"). Most buying and selling in her homeland was in the hands of migratory Igbo tradesmen who were reputed to be inveterate profiteers. They were resented for that, precisely as Jews were resented all over Europe once upon a time, and for the same reason of their dominance in local businesses.

Trish's disclosure of her people's antipathy towards Igbos came one Sunday evening. She and Len were lounging at her home when a phone call came through. The caller was a close friend of Trish from her high school days, who lived in Florida with her family. Of all Trish's friend she was Len's favorite. She was quite diminutive, but so graceful and vivacious that Len liked her a lot and called her "Birdie." That phone conversation proceeded with much giggling and guffaws as Trish kept casting a surreptitious look at Len now and then. Len was curious and asked what the fun was about, and Trish said she and her friend were making fun of him and his peoples, whom Igalas called "Igbo-li." Len was not offended: He and Trish had such high regard for each other that a little teasing now and then meant absolutely nothing.

After she hung up the phone Trish explained the connotation of "Igbo-li." Len took it all in good humor because he knew that Igbos did have a reputation for sharp business practices. And the Igbos in turn had their unreasonable prejudices against other Nigerian ethnicities: they tended to regard "northern Nigerians" (including Igalas) as backward people. Prejudice is irrational and one hoped it would fade away with political maturity. Nigeria was rife with prejudice, and the tragic civil war of 1967-1970 was largely triggered by rampant prejudice that fomented a rash of military coups-d'état.

In view of the simmering undercurrent of "Igbophobia" in Trish's family and ethnic background, her preference for Igbo lovers was surprising. Either she found Igbo men particularly desirable (which was not unlikely, as she was a cerebral woman), or it was a matter of an ingrained lesson from her father's Igbo hatred manifesting itself in her adult subconscious as a stalking horse for predation on Igbo men. Perhaps it was a mixture of the two motives.

A subconscious wish to prey on Igbo men was further indicated by her explosive Mothers' Day declaration that she had never loved Len but had merely been "messing around" with him, and by the "Sugar Daddy" intimation from ladies whom Trish took into confidence. Analysis of the human psyche is baffling to all but the experts. But all the facts seemed to Len to point to an underlying dislike of Igbos in Trish's subconscious, which she had successfully camouflaged as a preference for Igbo lovers and further obscured with her general affability and gregariousness. Either she was diabolically clever or she was deeply conflicted about Igbo men. Len thought of an analogous "love" game played by adolescents. The girl that a boy liked best was the one he bothered or bullied the most. If one constructed that game in reverse one might get a picture of Trish's underlying motive in preferring Igbo lovers —and sequentially ruining or dumping them.

Such a deeply concealed hatred of Igbos would also explain the deepest mystery about Trish: The fact that she exhibited utter malice towards Len when she decided he was used up and needed to be discarded. Len had idolized Trish and never once said a cross word to her, had indulged her every whim, provided for her handsomely, would always intuit her problems and spare no effort or expense to solve them. Len had never shown Trish anything but gentle love, affection, and generosity. And yet when she dumped him it was not done softly, with some kind of explanation, as Len sought with scores of entreaties. She had simply slunk away, and when Len caught up with her on that Mothers' Day, she bared her fangs. When he persisted she sued him to court for stalking and harassment. That would be visceral hatred emerging from the depths at last.

Now, he reflected, Trish had stood the "Igbo-li" prejudice on its head. She had outfoxed him for so many years. She was truly the "high-sense" schemer, the marble-hearted *femme fatale* who pretends to love you for years, takes everything you have to give, material and emotional, gives nothing back, then abandons you when you are in trouble. The irony of it deepened when Len realized that Trish's fleecing of her new Igbo lover had already begun. The man, a lawyer in distant Maryland, was already commuting frequently to Columbus to represent Trish at her CPO lawsuit against Len. And, knowing Trish well, Len could only guess that she was not paying this man with money but in the oldest currency known to operate between woman and man.

Len shook his head: Trish really belonged on the cast of a "Nollywood" (*Nigeria's Hollywood*) movie. She was a Smooth Operator, an accomplished heart breaker, probably a serial home wrecker. There was a method to her operation, a system to her schemes and designs. It was not far fetched that Trish might harbor an atavistic version of an old attitude which held an Igbo man to be a prestigious prize for a northern girl, not just to catch and keep but to vanquish and move on. Whatever was the reason Trish targeted a succession of Igbo men to conquer, she made the conquests with a superb adroitness the contemplation of which evoked in Len an admiration of her cleverness. It was precisely Trish's intelligence and suave self-esteem, he reflected, that had endeared her to him in the first place. Len's own chickens had come home to roost: His own snobbish preference for cerebral women had boomeranged on him!

It was all too much for Len. He slid into a depression so deep that it seemed unlikely that he could emerge from it. He made plans to put himself out of his misery.

After that last visit to Trish to alert her to a sky message, Len slept poorly. A man who used to have no trouble staying asleep, for a dozen hours each night if he felt like it, suddenly found himself getting no more than two hours a night. He tossed and turned, he cried and sighed, he tried to read —and failed. Finally, he consulted his physician, who prescribed sleeping pills. Len bought them, but then decided to put them to a more conclusive use.

32
Redemption

The sun will come out tomorrow
So you gotta hang on
'til tomorrow, come what may!
Tomorrow, tomorrow, I love ya, tomorrow
You're always a day away!
Read more: Annie - Tomorrow Lyrics | MetroLyrics

FROM FOGGY DEPTHS Len heard a dim chatter that grew stronger and clearer as he listened, until the buzz resolved into conversations and he recognized the voices of members of his family. He opened his eyes, and the first thing he saw was the cherubic face of Kanayo, his penultimate grandson. Any time Kan contemplated an object with attention, the two great orbs of his eyes grew big and round —his two large, almond-shaped apertures, dominated by circular ebony disks around which shone lustrous backgrounds clear as the boiled white gelatin of an egg. The hypnotic gaze of those eyes evoked a smile from Len every time he turned on his PC; the large, high-definition screen of his PC was filled with a portrait of Kan's head taken when he was one year old. Now Kan was two, and his eyes still commanded attention whenever one looked in his face —those eyes, and big jug-ears. Kan is going to be a giant of a lad, Len thought, more so than his dad, Len's youngest —and largest— son.

Len blinked and smiled at his grandson. Kan smiled back and exclaimed: "Pah-pah!" And as if on cue, the whole clan of his family ran up to his bed, each beaming a happy smile at Len. His three sons were all there, and ten of his grandchildren, plus his youngest daughter-in-law.

"Where am I?" Len asked, looking at his oldest son, Obinna, who now leaned over Len's bed.

"In the hospital," Obi said and looked away.

"What happened?" Len pressed him.

"That's what we'd like to know, Dad. How could you?" Obi replied unhappily, fishing out a folded sheet from his pocket and thrusting it close to Len's face. It was a photocopy of the message to Trish which he clutched to his chest when he.... And then Len remembered, lowered his gaze, and let tears course down his cheeks. The sobs came as his sons said in a chorus, "We love you, Dad." And the tiny tots all piped in: "We love you, GanPa!" Len noticed that Obi's three sons were not there, only his daughter, Len's youngest granddaughter, was there with him. Obi read his thoughts and explained that he had hopped on the first flight that was available; it was so sudden he had no time to bring along the rest. His wife and sons were well in Seattle, and they sent their love and best wishes to Len.

"Is your mother here as well?" Len asked his son.

Obi looked down again. Looking down or away always signaled Obi's emotional discomfort. It was Len's oldest grandson, 15-year-old Chima who answered.

"Nan left here last night" Chima said.

She was here? Len asked. Chiemeka answered. ("Mecca," Len's second, son was Chima's dad.)

"Yes, she was here at your bed side every moment of the past three days. She only left last night when the doctors told her you were out of danger."

Mecca always knew exactly how to make his father feel guilty. He was proverbial in the family for his emotional forthrightness. Len hung his head at the reproach. Dear old faithful Magda, he mused. Dishonored and betrayed, and yet ever alert to her wifely and nursing duties. Did ever a man deserve a better wife? And what, exactly, had he done to deserve such a splendid and loving family? Tears flowed down his face once again. "I love you all, very much," he said to all of them, barely audibly. His youngest son Ejezie ("Jazz") was crying softly too, through his smile. He was a big cry-baby, just like Len.

That afternoon they discharged Len, telling him to expect a hospital counselor in the evening. His two oldest sons took him home, the rest of the family having left earlier, relieved that GrandPa was OK and released to come home. After Len settled in the front seat beside Mecca who was driving, Obinna handed him an envelope; it was addressed to Len, it was in Magda's handwriting. He opened it and read. It contained just two sentences:

"How could you try to do this to your loving grandchildren, Len? Is that wicked woman really worth it?"

"No, she is not worth it. Not anymore," Len said under his breath.

He smiled at his sons and asked how they found him. Obi answered. It was his email that saved him —that and the fact that he had confided his recent bouts of sadness to his sons. Jazz was reviewing his email messages when Len's popped up. As he read it and recollected his father's loneliness and pain of recent times, Jazz screamed, dialed 911 and gave the operator the gist of Len's letter as well as the address of Len's apartment. Then he called his older brother, Mecca, who lived with Magda. Jazz and Mecca jumped into their cars and sped to Len's apartment, which was only fifteen minutes away. Along the way they kept calling Len but got no answer. They arrived at the same time and pounded on the door of the secure, gated community in which Len lived. An attendant sensed their urgency and let them in with a quizzical look. They explained that their dad was in grave danger up in his apartment.

The attendant grabbed a bunch of keys and all three raced up the stairs, not waiting for the elevator. They had just arrived at Len's door when they heard the welcome sound of klaxons wailing up to the complex, announcing the arrival of the emergency squad. While the attendant unlocked Len's door, Mecca raced down the stairs to bring the emergency crew to Len's room. A few minutes later the EMS ambulance was racing to the nearest hospital as the medics inserted a tube down Len's throat and started a stomach pump. The boys pulled into the slip stream of the ambulance and rode it all the way to the hospital.

Now as they narrated the story to him, Len could feel a soreness in his throat and chest. Emergency medics did not worry too much about one's comfort when one's life was in jeopardy.

"But why am I sore in my butt?" Len asked.

"Well, we called Mom on the way to the hospital. She arrived at the hospital right behind us and insisted that they give you an enema too, since nobody knew what else you had eaten that day. Mom greased the enema tube and worked the pump herself."

Yes, reflected Len, Magda would do that. When it came to medical care of her own family she yielded only to doctors, and then only reluctantly. With nurses, she just pulled rank. If they demurred she informed them she was a veteran of forty-odd years of nursing in three U.S. states and on three continents. "Let me handle this, please!"

When Len and his sons got into his apartment they went into his study, a second bedroom that Len had fitted out as a well-appointed office with efficient amenities. Jazz spilled out from his PC, which was always on and tuned to "Jazz-24," an internet jazz station. His youngest son arrived right behind them after taking the grandchildren to Magda's house. The children loved "Nan's House." They loved its large, open space for back flips and cartwheels, and large leather couches for trampoline bouncing. Above all, they liked its extra-large bean bag that was six feet in diameter, around which all thirteen grand children lay on their backs one day for a panoramic group photo that Len shot from the overhanging second-floor balcony. Magda called it the most sensible piece of furniture Len ever bought. The children especially loved Nan's endless cooking and serving, and her special indulgence of their roundhouse mayhem.

As all Len's three sons had now assembled, he brought out a bottle of cognac, the last one from a cache he brought home from his last conference trip abroad. He gave it to Obinna to open and pour out three shots. They drank a toast to his health and then to the whole family. Mecca proposed a toast to their mom and they drank to her health and sagacity too. Len asked them about their lives, their careers, their children. They just talked, all of them intent on not leaving Len to brood on his thoughts again, at least until the hospital counselor came and took over the vigil. Obinna called the airlines and arranged to leave for Seattle next day with his daughter; reluctance was written all over his face, but he had done his duty as the oldest son. All Len's sons had risen magnificently to the occasion, as had Magda. His debt to Magda could never be repaid in one lifetime, and he was a jackass for wrecking their marriage just to chase a chimera — a chimera that had almost cost him his life.

It is the business of shrinks to take their patients back over and through their innermost dark thoughts, the more thoroughly to understand the demons and chimeras that foment suicidal thinking. When two hospital counselors arrived, Len's sons left to join their children at Magda's house, but first they made Len promise to call them every half hour after the counselors left. The counselors slowly teased apart the tight knot that encased the hurt in Len's psyche. Methodically they coaxed him to reveal the highlights of incidents and thoughts that got him into his deep and dark frame of mind in the last month.

After they left, Len found he could revisit the mental scenes of his recent anguish with a good deal of equanimity. He remembered vividly how the final acts of his life's drama had unfolded over the past year. He remembered the near-fatal evening of reminiscence over Trish, and the events leading to that evening. He was at peace now as he reviewed them. He now understood the meaning of the saying "You have never fully lived till you have looked death in the eyes and survived." He had survived. He would live for his family.

Well, they told him he had been unconscious for three days and three nights, not responding to any stimulus of touch, sight, or sound. But Len knew exactly where he had been —and it was not a journey of three days. It had lasted years as his mind wandered all over the meadows of his heart, revisiting the scenes of the last fifteen years of his life. It was only when that journey ended that he opened his eyes and beheld his baby grandson Kan watching him, willing him to open his eyes. Now his eyes were open, in more ways than one. It had been a fortnight since his sons brought him back from the dead, and then took him home from hospital. He woke up this morning feeling

great. The day was gorgeous, with sunshine pouring through his bedroom window.

He had something special to do today: He was driving down to
Columbus, to an interesting day in a certain Franklin County courtroom. The "stalking" CPO lawsuit of Trish against him was going to
be finally heard. After the last hearing when Trish's lawyer-boyfriend
stalled the case into yet another postponement, causing the magistrate to urge Trish to hire another lawyer, Trish had retained a local
lawyer as co-counsel to her boyfriend. The court had notified Len
accordingly by post. Len hoped soon to take the stand and denounce
Trish for fifteen years of duplicity, of "messing around" with him —
years essentially of prostitution and grand larceny. He was going to
skewer her and enjoy doing it. The first three emails he read after he
woke up this morning were from his sons. Each one said, "Go for it,
Dad. We love you!" They were acting in concert. They remembered
today was his day to slay the dragon, and they were all behind him.

Two weeks ago the two hospital counselors had urged him to exor-
cise Trish's ghost once and for all: "The truth will set you free," they
had told him. Len recalled the routine rounds of systems checks that
mission control go through before a space shuttle or rocket blasts off
on a mission. "All systems GO," was the final signal for count-down to
ignition. Len's systems were all "Go." He had spent yesterday shining
his oxfords, laying out his best suit, a new shirt and matching tie. At
each court hearing Trish had slunk away from proximity to Len, and
she had evaded eye contact with him. But today Len was going to get
Tarissa Adoja's attention, look her squarely in the eye and mouth to
her: "Fuck you, Tarissa!"

33
Finis

Yes, it's a good day for shinin' your shoes,
And it's a good day for losin' the blues;
Ev'rything to gain and nothin' to lose,
'Cause it's a good day from mornin' till night.

LEN WON. AFTER three postponements ("continuances," in the arcane jargon of courts) Trish's "stalking and harassment" complaint against him was dismissed during evidentiary hearing, for lack of merit. Poor Tarissa Adoja and her new lover-prey: They were too clever by half, Len reflected.

The nightmare was over. His final thought on Trish was that, like water, she had sought her proper level and finally found it. Therefore, she should be left to settle there with no more let or hindrance —at least not from him. He knew there was still meaning in what he and Trish used to say to each-other, that love defies logic. He was not sure his love for Trish was dead altogether. But if not dead, it surely must be on life support. He shouldn't have insurmountable difficulty suppressing it in future to reach out for a normal life. Good riddance to bad rubbish.

His healing process would now start.

About the Author

Lyn Thomas is an engineer by training who has worked as a scientist and academic. Now retired from academia, Thomas maintains www.cutthebabble.com, where he discusses the nuances of written communication in US English.

Thomas's nonscientific publications, in addition to *Rogue Lovers: The Story of Tarissa*, include *Seeing the World in Black & White* and *A Potemkin Paradise*.